Domini Highsmith lives in historic Beverley, East
Yorkshire with her partner, a university professor.
She wrote six pacey thrillers as Domini Wiles, and
under her own name two terrifying novels about
an abused little boy, *Frankie* and *Mammy's Boy*,
recently published to critical acclaim.

DOMINI HIGHSMITH

LEONORA

WARNER BOOKS

A Warner Book

First published in Great Britain in 1992 by Macdonald

This edition published by Warner in 1993

A CIP catalogue for this book
is available from the British Library

ISBN 0 7515 0150 6

Printed in England by Clays Ltd, St Ives plc

Warner
A division of
Little, Brown and Company (UK) Limited
165 Great Dover Street
London SE1 4YA

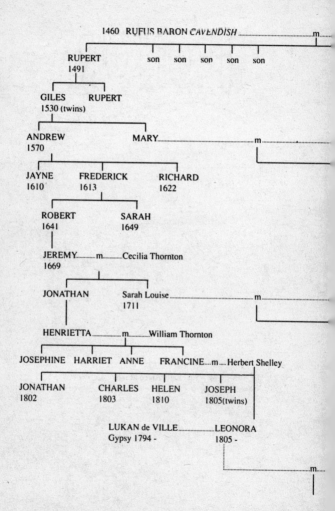

1460 RUFUS BARON *CAVENDISH* .... m ......

RUPERT   son   son   son   son   son
1491

GILES   RUPERT
1530 (twins)

ANDREW   MARY .... m ......
1570

JAYNE   FREDERICK   RICHARD
1610   1613   1622

ROBERT   SARAH
1641   1649

JEREMY .... m .... Cecilia Thornton
1669

JONATHAN   Sarah Louise .... m ......
             1711

HENRIETTA .... m .... William Thornton

JOSEPHINE HARRIET ANNE   FRANCINE .... m .... Herbert Shelley

JONATHAN   CHARLES   HELEN   JOSEPH
1802   1803   1810   1805 (twins)

LUKAN de VILLE .... LEONORA
Gypsy 1794 -   1805 -

                                                        m ......

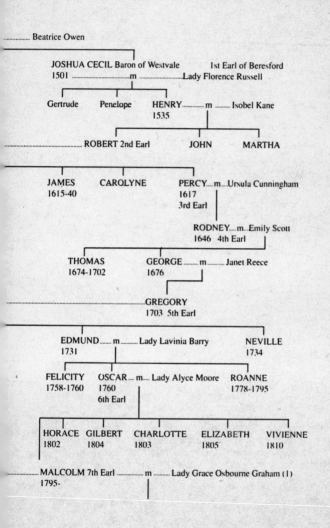

.... Beatrice Owen

JOSHUA CECIL Baron of Westvale　　1st Earl of Beresford
1501 .... m .... Lady Florence Russell

Gertrude　　Penelope　　HENRY .... m .... Isobel Kane
　　　　　　　　　　　　　　1535

.... ROBERT 2nd Earl　　JOHN　　MARTHA

JAMES　　CAROLYNE　　PERCY ..... m .... Ursula Cunningham
1615-40　　　　　　　　　　1617
　　　　　　　　　　　　　3rd Earl

RODNEY ..... m ... Emily Scott
1646　4th Earl

THOMAS　　GEORGE .... m .... Janet Reece
1674-1702　1676

GREGORY
1703　5th Earl

EDMUND ...... m .... Lady Lavinia Barry　　NEVILLE
1731　　　　　　　　　　　　　　　　　　　　1734

FELICITY　　OSCAR .... m .... Lady Alyce Moore　　ROANNE
1758-1760　1760　　　　　　　　　　　　　　1778-1795
　　　　　　6th Earl

HORACE　GILBERT　CHARLOTTE　ELIZABETH　VIVIENNE
1802　　1804　　1803　　　　　1805　　　　1810

MALCOLM 7th Earl .... m .... Lady Grace Osbourne Graham (1)
1795-

CHAPTER ONE

I

Herbert Shelley was fired with lust the moment he first set eyes on the girl. She was a trainee parlour maid who came into his presence fresh from her family's country hovel, having first been scrubbed to shiny pinkness and garbed in hand-me-down clothes. So awed was she by her new surroundings, so fearful of the eminent gentleman who was now her master, that her fingers clutched at the housekeeper's skirt and her eyes bulged with wonder at everything she saw. She was much younger than he had expected, certainly no more than twelve years of age, judging by her height. She was plump and surprisingly pretty, with a shy smile and straw-coloured hair that fell in undisciplined ringlets around her face.

'What is your name, child?'

She glanced first at Mrs Norris, then down at her feet and whispered shyly: 'Daisy, sir.'

'And how old are you, Daisy?'

'... er, twelve, sir.'

'Twelve,' Herbert repeated, licking his lips.

'Think so, sir. Maybe eleven, maybe twelve.'

'Good ... good ...'

He forced himself to make a cursory inspection of the two older servants hired that day to work in the kitchens and laundry. He little doubted that they had been selected as the best of an inferior bunch since both, in his measured opinion, left much to be desired. They were of the usual standard to be found at the hirings: scrawny-limbed girls with lank hair and blemished skins, and with a little too much of the world in their eyes to be of interest to a man of Herbert's very particular tastes. He was looking for fresher, sweeter meat with which to tantalise his palate.

When he returned his gaze to the young girl he felt the stirrings of arousal warming his blood and could scarce believe his good fortune. Here was no vulgar country servant already coarsened by hardship and ill-use, or a maid-of-all-work thrown back on the market by a bored master or a jealous mistress. This one was special. He would have wagered half his fortune that this one was still a virgin in spite of her obvious attractions. Herbert moistened his lips again. Such children had become a rare delicacy in Regency London, where the pleasures of wealthy gentlemen were of paramount concern and the flesh of poor men's daughters came cheap and often succulently tender. He was convinced that no man had touched her. She was still pure, and that purity shone like a jewel he was determined to possess. Even as he waved the housekeeper and her newly acquired charges from the room, his gaze was fixed on the younger girl and his mind was calculating how, where and when he would deflower her.

Daisy Kimble had been brought to the hirings at the May Day Fair by the only man with whom she had ever had any close contact: her father.

'There be work for ye, gel, in one of them big city places,' Harry Kimble had said as the first fingers of a new day plucked at the sombre sky above the Downs. 'Aye, an' a full belly an' a warm, dry bed, if'n ye earn it.'

There had been no goodbyes. She had simply pulled on her bonnet and her only pair of shoes, crossed her small woollen shawl over her shoulders and followed her father into the crisp morning. She left behind a simple, God-fearing family who scratched an uncertain living from a patch of land in a remote corner of the Sussex Downs. Like those others of their kind who eked out the days from dawn to dusk and counted the passing years from one hay-cut to the next, the Kimbles were obedient to that most cruel of all masters: poverty. For them a poor harvest meant a reduced share of the gathering and less bread in the crock. The smallest malady among the livestock could result in a season without meat or milk or coin enough for rents. Even a shortage of winter brushwood could mark the difference between survival and starvation. That year had been one of hardship, with late frosts nipping away the young shoots and a sickness in the house that carried off the new babe and left its mother with a crippling, feverish cough. Harry Kimble had already parted with five of his eleven children at the annual May Day Fairs. Now circumstances compelled him to trudge the fourteen miles to Moorgate on an empty stomach to sell yet another daughter into service.

Francine Shelley witnessed their arrival at the fair from a window of the carriage to which she had retreated when the stench of the cattle pens and the press of the crowds became too much for her. She sipped a cup of hot, sweet chocolate, careful that no drips should stain the mustard-toned satin of her gown. She was a beautiful woman in her early thirties, slender and golden-haired, with sad grey eyes and a pale, smooth complexion admired by men and much envied by other women. By contrast her companion, while of a similar age and height, was a very plain individual whose simple brown frock did little to improve a thin, somewhat angular figure. Beneath the rim of her bonnet her hair was a mousy, indistinct colour and her skin sallow. Indeed, her only claim to beauty was in her eyes, which were large and well shaped, and as rich a shade of brown as might be seen in freshly turned earth.

Anabel Corey was a servant who counted herself amongst the more fortunate of the lower orders. She was more than contented with her lot in life, for she enjoyed an enviable standard of living and suffered no serious abuse from either the master or any of his male companions. More importantly, she had become a truly devoted companion to her mistress, and while propriety demanded that so deep a friendship between a lady and her maidservant be cloaked in secrecy, they had nonetheless nurtured over the years an almost sisterly affection quite rare in the circumstances.

The modest compartment of the carriage was crammed with items purchased during the morning: sacks of flour guaranteed to contain no chalk, excellent lace-work by the yard and rolls of printed cotton at a fraction of the price asked in the better London shops. Francine had employed two fifteen-year-old girls, one to help with the laundry and scullery work, the other to assist old Sarah in the kitchen. There were servants a-plenty to be had in London, but often they were sly and lazy, or came from backgrounds where dishonesty and disease were a way of life. In a climate where lower servants were often little more than guttersnipes in pretty bonnets, the mop fairs still offered girls from simple country homes who were not yet wise in the more unsavoury ways of the city. So it was that fine ladies like Francine Shelley could be seen searching among the dog-pounds and cattle-pens of the crowded, muddy fairground for young girls who were sufficiently unworldly to be shaped by their mistress into decent servants. She looked at Anabel and smiled.

'Do you remember when my mother hired you from this very fair when you were only thirteen years old, Anabel?'

The woman nodded. 'Indeed I do, Miss Francine,' she replied with a warm smile. 'I was small and hungry and frightened half out of my wits by all the noise and bustle.'

'Oh, it was all so long ago,' Francine said.

'Yes, and still I give thanks to the good Lord that I was one of the lucky ones. Miss Henrietta gave me a decent life, a happy home, even an education, and for that I've always been grateful.'

'Dear Anabel,' Francine said. 'You have repaid her a thousand-fold with your devotion to us all. And are you still happy with us after all these years?'

'Indeed I am, Miss Francine. As God is my judge, I swear I wouldn't change any part of it, even if I could.'

Francine smiled her sad, wistful smile. 'No, my dear Anabel, I don't believe you would.'

From the window of the carriage she saw the big man in rough country clothes and battered hat striding through the mud, and the ragged child following at his heels, dragging behind her a long-handled broom made of hawthorn twigs. The two did not make their way directly to the area where the hirelings waited in sad little bunches, pinched and prodded as often by the merely curious as by a potential employer. Instead they went to the lace-seller, where Harry Kimble spent his last few pennies on a length of blue ribbon to adorn his daughter's grubby bonnet. Together with the broom, this would advertise her ability to carry out the simple, everyday tasks of a parlour maid. It was the first gift ever to pass between father and daughter, and the first pretty thing the child had ever owned. It was clean and bright and as blue as the summer sky against her dingy clothes. She stood in the mud, smiling, while his labourer's fingers struggled with the impossibly delicate task of knotting the ribbon to the brim of her bonnet.

'Come, hand me my cloak, Anabel. I wish to look more closely at that little girl over there by the lace-seller's stall.'

The heavily built groom handed his mistress down from the carriage and accompanied the two women across a mud-caked patch of ground where straw had been laid to make walking less hazardous. Francine was watching the child with a practised eye. She had no need of an extra parlour maid, and heavier duties would be out of the question for one so young, yet she was tempted to take her on, for all that. Here was a child who showed little outward sign of the poverty from which she so obviously came. Beneath the rags she was sturdy and strong, with a clear, unmarked skin and good teeth. There was also an air of innocence about her, a promise of purity in a world where hunger and virginity rarely shared the same bed. The farmers and country gentlemen who prowled the fairs in search of the day's profit would pay most handsomely for such a find, and would use their new property exactly as they saw fit. To Francine it seemed a pitiful shame that such a child should be sold on the open market and thereafter made available to any man who had the money or the authority to take her.

'Here, let me help you with that.'

Harry Kimble snatched the hat from his head and stepped back as if struck by a sudden blow. He hunched his big shoulders and bowed, lowering his gaze respectfully. He was horribly aware that his clothes stank and his boots were encrusted with mud, and it shamed him to see the lady's fine satin skirts and velvet cloak brush against his dirty breeches. She had spoken kindly and smiled directly into his face as she took the ribbon from his clumsy fingers and transformed it into a pretty bow with streamers. The gentleness of her manner and the richness of her clothes rendered him speechless. Hovering close to the lady were a tight-lipped maid in a handsome brown dress and a groom in blue livery who, from his secure and lofty position in the world, glowered at the lesser man. The lady turned to him with her kindly smile and asked:

'Are you the child's father?'

'Aye, ma'am,' he managed to utter, nodding vigorously.

'Is she for hire?'

'Aye, ma'am, that she is.'

'She's an extremely pretty girl. How old is she?'

Harry Kimble ground his hat in his hands and did a rapid mental calculation before stammering: '... er ... coming up ... eleven or twelve years, I reckon, ma'am.'

'And will this be her first position?'

'Aye, ma'am.' He mauled his hat in agitated fingers while stooping and bobbing his upper body in acknowledgement of his lowly status.

'Good, then I will take her,' Francine announced. 'But I will pay not one penny more than the going rate. I offer you a

6

fair hiring price, plus food, clothes, shelter and wages for the girl so long as she is in my employ. Will that suit you?'

'Aye, ma'am. Reckon it will.'

'Good,' Francine smiled, leading the girl away. 'My man Griffiths will pay you.'

'Aye, ma'am ... thank'ee ... thank'ee kindly, ma'am.'

With that brief exchange Daisy Kimble was taken away from her father to become a member of the Shelley household. Long before some lecherous farmer could tempt Harry Kimble with gold or silver, or some young show-off pay the hiring fee simply to use her and pass her around for the pleasure of his friends, Daisy was safely employed and taken away in the lady's comfortable carriage. She had fetched a fair price and Harry Kimble was not disappointed. Nor was he sorry to see her go. There were sons at home who could turn in a better day's work for the food they ate, and older daughters to do such cooking, washing and stitching as met the family's simple needs. Daisy was one less mouth to feed and one less problem to fret over when the lads from the Downs came sniffing around at harvest time. He stood for a while watching the fine carriage lurch through the mud toward the nearby road, then he replaced his shapeless headgear and strode off in search of two pennyworth of roast potatoes and hot soup to settle his growling stomach. He would be home by nightfall, and tomorrow there would be ale on the table and bread in the crock. With the lady's coins jangling in his pocket, he knew that nobody in his house would go to bed with an empty belly before the next harvest was gathered in.

For Daisy it was a long and dusty ride into London, where the din of traffic along the cobbled streets and the press of people on the pavements seemed nightmarish to a child more accustomed to the quiet isolation of the countryside. On arrival at the Shelley house she was given the first hot bath she had ever known. Steaming and scented and frothy with soap, it eased away the dirt and fatigues of the long journey. It also removed those stains of the outdoors and all the familiar country odours that had once been part and parcel of her everyday existence. Her scalp was cleaned with alcohol, her hair lathered and rinsed until it squeaked in protest when wrung out by the housekeeper in whose charge the grubby newcomer now found herself.

'Cleanliness is next to godliness,' the woman insisted, poking a fat finger into one of Daisy's ears. 'An' 'twould not be fitting to see dirty servants in a fine house the likes of this'n. Very particular the mistress be about dirt an' grime, *very* particular.'

Mrs Norris was a woman of quite awesome proportions, with fingers like fat pork sausages and thighs so huge in circumference that her feet had become strangers to each other. When she stood in an upright position with her legs planted wide apart and her arms folded across her body, it seemed that the weight of her bosom, imprisoned though it was behind the bulging bodice of her gown, depended solely for its support upon the twin props of her forearms. She supervised the purging of the new parlour maid with such meticulous attention to detail that neither stain, blemish nor common flea could have escaped her scrutiny. Little by little the old and miserable were erased to make way for the new and wholesome. Even the nails of her fingers and toes were scrubbed and clipped to suit the rules of the fine household in which she was to live and work. Her new mistress, she was informed, was a woman of taste and quality, a gentle lady who would tolerate neither slovenly habits nor a careless appearance in her household staff.

On the orders of the mistress, Daisy's ragged clothes were thrown out with the rubbish and she was dressed in a frock of plain blue linen. Draw-strings had been inserted at the neck and sleeves to ensure a reasonable fit, and the hem turned up by several inches to allow for her lack of height. She was also given an apron of crisp white cotton to fasten about her waist with broad ties, and a lace-trimmed mob-cap too soft and floppy to restrict the unruly curls of her hair. The child was delighted with her new clothes, common enough attire for the servants of a city house, yet more grand than anything this simple country girl had ever dreamed of owning. With the precious blue satin ribbon now adorning her maidservant's bonnet, its ends falling in twin streamers down her back, she stared into a looking glass and barely recognised the person she saw there.

'Oh, if onny me dear Ma could see me now,' she exclaimed. 'If onny me dear old Ma could see me now.'

She was barely able to contain her excitement when she and the two other hired girls were ushered into the suite of rooms on the ground floor to meet the master of the house. There she saw a large, stern-looking man with greying hair and whiskers, dressed in a beautiful velvet coat and a vivid red waistcoat, standing before the fireplace with his hands clasped behind his back. He sounded kindly enough when he questioned her, but his eyes glinted like polished black buttons and he stared at her in a way that struck fear into her heart. She bobbed an awkward, hastily learned curtsy and trembled a little under the piercing scrutiny of her new master.

In that instant when his gaze first fell upon the smooth curve of Daisy's shoulders and the pert breasts newly budding behind her tightly fitting bodice, Herbert Shelley felt a powerful quickening of the blood that told him he must have her, and without delay. Soon her duties would bring her to the attention of other men who would be just as swift to recognise that here was meat so fresh as to delight the most jaded of palates. The moment she was allowed beyond the confines of the house she would become potential prey to every passing male: lusty grooms and stable lads, merchants, peddlers, young bloods with insatiable appetites, wealthy local gentlemen with gold to buy what charm alone no longer attracted. And even inside the house she would not be safe, for he had friends and business acquaintances bold enough to beg of their host a favour he could not, without loss of honour, refuse. It was simply a matter of time before some hot-blooded opportunist tried to pluck this ripening blossom from under his very nose, leaving him with second pickings. If he was to claim the best of her for himself he would have to do it soon, while she was still untouched. All this passed through his thoughts as his eyes travelled over the gift his wife had inadvertently found for him at the May Day Fair. He was not by nature a patient man, and already his need to possess the girl was a matter of some urgency. He might well have resorted to more drastic measures, had he suspected then that several frustrating weeks were to pass before he could attain his ends.

Herbert Shelley had established the habit of visiting a voluptuous French woman in Harrington Court on Tuesday evening of every week. Her favours were by no means cheap, but as a vigorous gentleman now in his sexual prime, he was willing to pay for those particular pleasures usually denied by wives of delicate and genteel breeding. Madame Marie-Louise Jordan was a widow in her mid-thirties with strong carnal appetites and an under-developed sense of sexual restraint. Her voice was deep and husky, with a heavy Parisian accent that added a certain extra spice to her often bawdy conversation. She dyed her hair a fashionable bright red and painted her lips and nipples with cochineal to give them a luscious, bloodied appearance. Like most women of her time she was quite fat, with huge, big-nippled breasts and as many quivering mounds of flesh as a man might wish to pinch and knead for his gratification.

'Does your lady wife ever do *this* for you, *mon cheri*?' she asked whenever he made her kneel between his legs and work upon his genitals with her big, hungry mouth. Talking about Francine always excited her. 'Does she? Does she suck you like this?'

'She is my wife, not a common strumpet,' he often reminded her. 'She has never refused my ... ah, that's hellish good ... my attentions.'

'Ah yes, *mon cheri*, but *this*?'

'No ... ah ...' He felt the sharpness of her teeth on his tender flesh, soothed by the gentle heat of her tongue, her lips and fingers stimulating his inflamed passion. 'No ... she is a lady and ... ah ... she lacks your ... your ...'

Marie-Louise raised her head and grinned, her mouth wet

and tempting. 'My Continental expertise?' she offered.

Herbert reached out and grabbed her head with both hands, lifted his hips and at the same time pulled her down to meet the thrust. He groaned and worked himself against her, knowing that she was capable of swallowing his penis right to the hilt.

'Your *enthusiasm*, whore,' he gasped, arching his back. 'My dear lady wife lacks your whore's *enthusiasm*!'

Although he continued to visit his mistress every Tuesday, Shelley became increasingly obsessed by the little parlour maid. On the evening of June sixteenth, more than a month after Daisy's arrival, he decided that he would waste no more time in exercising his rights as man and master of the house. For weeks he had suffered the exquisite temptation of being confronted almost daily by the object of his desire, only to be denied access to her by the presence of his family and staff. In his determination to keep her exclusively for himself, he had given strict orders that she was to be supervised and chaperoned at all times, that she must never venture beyond the gates of the house or be left alone with any male member of his employ, man or boy. At those times when there were guests to be entertained, he insisted that Mrs Norris confine her young charge to the upper floor, away from curious eyes and fleshly appetites. No trainee parlour maid had ever been so well protected as was Daisy Kimble in her new employer's home. It was just unfortunate that all these precautions, while undoubtedly keeping her safe from the advances of other men, also helped keep her beyond his own reach. As time progressed and his every attempt to procure access to the girl was thwarted, what had begun as a healthy desire intensified to become a burning obsession. He began to watch her at every opportunity, spying on her from windows or partly open doors while she played with the children or went about her household duties. He made her the subject of lurid sexual fantasies in which she yielded her virginity time after time to his demands, yet still remained the luscious, exciting child of his dreams. In his imagination she became both willing

11

partner and clever tormentor, accomplice and tender victim. By this time he had all but convinced himself that she deliberately played upon his emotions, tantalising him with her innocence, dangling her virginity before him and challenging him to take the bait.

'Take it I will,' he swore, each time his loins moved with the need of her. 'Take it I will.'

When at last he knew he was to have her that very night, Herbert found himself trembling with nervous excitement and suffering hot flushes of anticipation that left him with a layer of perspiration on his forehead and upper lip. By nine o'clock on the evening of the sixteenth he was sitting with his family in the drawing room, replete after a good dinner and terribly conscious of the calm, steady ticking of the mahogany grandfather clock in the corner. At midnight he would make his move. Until then he could relax and savour the passing minutes, certain in the knowledge that this time he would have his reward after the long weeks of self-denial.

He had planned his conquest carefully. Francine was spending one of her increasingly rare evenings at a soirée with fashionable women friends. He expected her to return home about ten-thirty and go directly to her own rooms on the first floor. As part of his scheme, Mrs Norris had come across a full bottle of sherry cunningly placed behind the drapes in the main dining room. Believing it to have been left there by one of the previous evening's dinner guests she had, just as Herbert had anticipated, spirited away her find without a word to her master or mistress. He had then given her the night off and watched her huffing and puffing her great bulk up the back stairs to her room. By midnight she would no doubt be collapsed in a happy, drunken stupor. The two eldest boys, Jonathan and Charles, were away at school until late the following month, which left only the younger children for him to worry about. The nine-year-old twins, Joseph and Leonora, were sharing a small sofa in the arched alcove on the other side of the room. As always, they were reading from the same book, their heads bent close together, palest fair and

12

darkest chestnut showing two sides of the same family coin. Daisy was sitting with five-year-old Helen in a smaller chair set closer to the fire and directly in front of Herbert, so that he could observe the little maid's every move.

He glanced across at Anabel, his wife's personal maid, a thin, plain woman as lacking in interest as were the shapeless and lack-lustre clothes she chose to wear. With her hair scraped back from her face in the most severe fashion, and with neither a hint of colour nor a touch of pretty decoration to alleviate the drabness of her attire, she was as safe from her master's advances as any woman might ever contrive to be. Gradually overcome by the warmth of the room, she was now dozing on a stool beside the big fireplace, her back resting against the polished slate surround and her head lolling. She was clearly unaware that the heat of the blazing logs had raised a crimson patch on her right cheek and a similar scorch along her forearm.

While the grandfather clock marked off the seconds with sombre dignity, Herbert imagined himself creeping through the darkened house on the first stroke of midnight, stealing up the rear stairs to the servants' garrets on the second floor and coming upon Daisy while she slept in her tiny room at the end of the passage.

'I do not mean to take you with tenderness, my little temptress,' he muttered, so softly that the words barely reached his own ears. 'I'll teach you who is master here, and who knows, in time I might shape you into the finest whore in all London.'

He took up his long clay pipe, stretched his legs across the hearth and observed the subject of his desire through half-closed eyes. She was seated in a velvet-covered armchair with Helen at her side and a picture book opened across her knees. Her head was bowed over the book so that her golden curls hung in pretty coils around her face. In her blue satin sash and slippers and her Sunday frock of striped blue cotton, she was so fresh and well turned out as to more closely resemble a child of the family than a simple parlour maid. Her cotton neckerchief had loosened just sufficiently to reveal a delicate

13

wisp of hair nestling in the nape of her neck and a faint dusting of freckles warming the flesh above her tiny breasts. The sight so excited Herbert that he began to speculate as to the exact spot where he would place his first kiss. He sucked more rapidly upon his pipe and watched her through a narrow curtain of blue smoke, devouring her plump young body with his gaze.

II

In that summer of 1815 Herbert was well into his fifties, a stout man with thinning, grey-streaked hair and neatly clipped whiskers dividing his fleshy face from upper lip to temple. Although several inches shorter than he would have liked to be, his thick-set frame compensated in width and weight for what it lacked in height. Too many years of dinner-table excesses had increased his girth to quite considerable dimensions, and although this rendered him something of a martyr to digestive problems, it offered, or so he firmly believed, a distinct advantage over taller but less well-endowed gentlemen. Being also of a pompous, rather grandiose character, his physical appearance was nothing if not impressive. He was a model of good taste from his Naples yellow hose to his huge fancy waistcoats; from his buckled shoes to the high, formal collars trapped behind the folds and flounces of his neck linen.

'An extravagant wardrobe is the hallmark of the true gentleman,' he would remind his family whenever the subject of his attire arose and he felt obliged to strut before them like a portly and colourful bird of paradise. 'It is the single most obvious factor separating the tasteless common man from his betters. It is the instantly recognisable distinction between success and miserable failure. Even the jangle of gold and silver, so sweet to the ear of a well-to-do man, acquires a baser ring when the pocket in which it sits is shabby or poorly lined.'

Lacking the pedigree and status of a nobleman, he had learned

14

to recognise the value of impressive packaging. In a social climate where a man's worth might be measured by the cut of his coat and the cost of his hose, he was leaving nothing to chance.

Herbert's finances remained reasonably stable despite his growing devotion to the gaming tables. He received a yearly income from land in Sussex purchased for a fraction of its true value when its owner fell upon hard times. He had a modest fortune invested in stocks and bonds and a small but lucrative interest in Watmough's and Grant's, bankers. It was much to his credit that he had managed to elevate himself from rather humble beginnings as the son of a silk merchant to his present position. Once he had struggled to maintain himself in modest grandeur amongst the lower middle classes; now he dressed, dined, gambled and entertained according to the higher stratum into which he had so successfully projected himself. He considered himself deserving of the very best. After all, Francine was more than just a beautiful socialite whose gowns and jewellery were the envy of women all over London. She was a first cousin to Sir Oscar Cavendish, Sixth Earl of Beresford, and therefore a member of one of the country's wealthiest and most powerful families. Through her mother Henrietta she could trace her line right back to the first Baron Cavendish, whose youngest son beguiled from King Henry an earldom founded upon the ravaged lands and properties of Beresford Abbey. Her cousin Sir Oscar was the present heir of that first earl, while Francine sprang from the untitled line of the baron's eldest son, Rupert. Marriage to Francine had been Herbert's greatest achievement, marred only by the fact that he was unable to get his hands on the whole of her fortune. Much of it had been secured for the future benefit of her children by a condition of marriage which he had hastily agreed to at the time and now, nearly fourteen years later, was still unable to undo. Even so, her private income and family connections added greatly to the prestige of her husband. It still gave him a feeling of gratification to recall that precise moment when the long-coveted jewel had at last come within his reach.

15

'I will agree to marry you, Herbert Shelley,' she had told him solemnly, 'on condition that you accept only one-third of my inheritance as your own, the rest to be kept intact as security for any ... for any children we might have in the future.'

Her cheeks had flushed and her sad eyes had refused to meet his own, and Herbert, quite taken aback by her sudden change of heart, had stared at her in shocked silence. Twice he had proposed marriage to this beautiful, eminently suitable young woman and twice she had rejected him. If now she relented, but insisted upon imposing certain conditions on their union, then so be it. Wanting her as he did, he had been prepared to promise her anything. And besides, promises might be broken and contracts altered at a later date.

'Do I have your word, sir?' she had pressed.

'You have indeed, my dear.'

'Then I am ready to become your wife.'

'Oh, my dear ... you have made me a happy man ... a happy man.' He had kissed her then for the first time, and with a little more ardour than intended, for he was unable to conceal the passion she aroused in him. She had shuddered and drawn away, and he had been well pleased with her modesty. He knew that any reluctance on her part to acknowledge the physical side of their contract would soon be overcome, once they were safely wed.

The one-third of her dowry that came available to him included the house in Garden Square which was now their home. It was an enclosed property of stone and brick, recently modernised and of quite splendid proportions. It was also ideally situated now that the more fashionable quarters of the city were advancing in order to accommodate a growing number of affluent families. Just as the wealthy City and East India merchants were flocking in their thousands to areas like Stamford Hill, so the gentry and aristocracy took their fashionable stand in Westminster and St James's. So it was that the Shelley home, once isolated amid acres of common land, had been swallowed up in the gradual expansion of St James's. Indeed, it had become so well situated in recent years that on fine days the cream of London society could be viewed from the upper windows as they promenaded along the streets or gathered like colourful blossoms on the lush lawns of nearby Green Park. With much bobbing of curtsies, bowing of heads, raising of hats, and fluttering of fans, they provided as fine a spectacle as could be seen from any window in the city. Herbert considered himself an uncommonly fortunate man. He sat down to cards with nobles, dined and supped with millionaires, relaxed in the sumptuous drawing rooms of society's best. He could well afford to place his faith in Fortune, because here was a man who regularly tempted the Fates yet always managed to land squarely and firmly on his feet, however precipitous the fall. So nearly had he met with disaster in the past, and so far had he managed to lift himself above it, that he had come to believe himself virtually indestructible.

'I have been blessed with the golden touch,' was his favourite boast. 'I am by inclination a gentleman and by nature a true winner.'

There were many men, their purses and promissory notes made forfeit to his success at the gaming tables, who would not dispute the truth of his conceit.

Herbert smiled now as he counted his many blessings. The drawing room was on the first floor of the house, a warm, comfortable room that was free of draughts in spite of its more than generous dimensions. A log fire burned in the grate, and beside the hearth of grey-green slate were set Herbert's high-backed chair and embroidered footstool, and the tall, ornately carved side table on which were kept his best decanters of port and brandy. Of all the rooms in the house this drawing room, with its elegant furnishings and beautiful proportions, most reflected the refined tastes of the Shelley family. Herbert appreciated the rich velvets of gold, green, crimson and blue, the wealth of corded silk fringing, the expensive furniture and stylish ornaments. Above the massive slate fireplace hung his favourite piece, a painting in oils of Francine in her wedding gown, set in an oval gilt frame surmounted by two gilded eagles.

17

'I drink to your beauty, madam, and to your noble good taste,' he muttered, raising his glass to the woman whose devotion and personal fortune had altered his life so considerably.

She was pictured at her little Chippendale desk, a delicately lovely nineteen-year-old dressed in elaborate turn-of-the-century elegance. Her gown was of heavily beaded and embroidered pink taffeta over matching petticoats. Her hair was piled high on her head and dressed with fresh flowers, leaving a few coiled ringlets falling around her ears and neck. She was wearing the rich opal necklace sent to her as a wedding gift by Sir Oscar Cavendish; that glittering, much-envied masterpiece of gold filigree work set with no less than twenty matching opals. To Herbert the painting represented his greatest triumph: the winning of Francine and the forging of links, however tenuous and reluctant, with that noble family. The artist had certainly earned his exorbitantly high fee, for he had captured to perfection the subject's delicate beauty, the translucent fairness of her skin and that wistful, almost sad expression ever present in her eyes.

Herbert nodded drowsily, content for the moment to draw on his pipe and enjoy the lazy turning of his thoughts. His gaze returned to the plump white flesh of Daisy Kimble and a quiver of excitement passed through his body. Tonight she would be his. In a few more hours the long, frustrating delays would be at an end and little Daisy, with her budding breasts and tantalising innocence, would belong to him.

That year was certainly an improvement on the last as far as the Shelley fortunes were concerned. Christmas had found him almost on the brink of ruin, his fortune depreciated by years of heavy gambling and profitless business ventures. Only by the illegal pledging of two of Francine's more valuable properties in Pimlico and Stamford Hill had he been able to keep the more pressing of his creditors at bay. Then, at the eleventh hour, a series of fortuitous events had occurred to swing his fortunes back into the black and refill his depleted coffers. After months of accumulated losses his run of bad luck at the card tables came to an end with a win of almost a thousand pounds; enough to satisfy his tailor and a host of petty traders poised to deny him access to their products. It was also enough to stave off the day when he must confess his losses to Francine and face a cap-in-hand visit to Sir Oscar Cavendish for yet another loan.

It was at this time that he almost fell foul of his major creditor, the niggardly and acid-tempered Lord William Corby. The man had won thousands from Herbert at faro, mainly because he had craftily increased the stakes with every winning hand. Since no man gambles more recklessly than he who can least afford to lose, Herbert had found himself on a downward spiral of higher stakes and poorer cards, certain that each new hand would bring a change of luck. Added to his losses were the crippling interest rates to which he had so foolishly agreed, charges that grossly inflated the original debt. Matters came to a head at the New Year hunting party at Lord Corby's country home in Kent, to which were invited those men most heavily in the man's debt. His intention had been to tighten his financial grip on his guests by threatening them with debtors' prison unless arrangements were made for their obligations to be met in full within a set period of time. It was a common enough practice and one that could net the erstwhile benefactor handsome dividends as desperate men made ever more intemperate pledges in order to avoid incarceration. Lord Corby was a ruthless man, a scoundrel willing to ruin friend and enemy alike in his relentless pursuit of profit. He also enjoyed any confrontation that showed him to be stronger, wealthier or more powerful than his associates. It appealed to his sense of personal value to have men grovel before him.

'Now look here, Shelley,' his lordship had bellowed after pacing the floor for quite some time, listing Herbert's faults and failings. 'It's debtors' prison for you unless you pay up. What the hell, man, this debt is too long overdue ... too long overdue.'

'But I had thought ... that is ... if Your Lordship would be so generous as to allow a little more time ...?'

'Time?' Corby had yelled at the top of his voice, his face purpling with indignation. '*Time*? You dare to ask for more time? Damn it, sir, you presume too far upon my good nature. I'll see you behind bars first. You have a week in which to settle in full, and that, sir, is my final offer.'

'A *week*? But surely ... that is ... Your Lordship gave me to understand ... only a few days ago ... I mean, with all due respect, sir ...'

'A week, Shelley, and after that I ... ah ...'

At that moment Fortune stepped in to lend a helping hand. Lord Corby suddenly clutched at his chest with both hands and collapsed to the floor with a failure of the heart which dropped him like a felled oak. One moment his anger had filled the whole room, the next he lay gasping on the carpet with his limbs twitching in jerky spasms. He looked like a helpless insect flipped on to its back and unable to right itself. The incredulous Herbert neither went to the man's assistance nor made any attempt to raise the alarm. Instead he rifled through the dying man's papers in search of Francine's property deeds and his own hand-written promissory notes for sums amounting to over fifty-three thousand pounds. And that was not the limit of his new-found good fortune. In that richly furnished private room, with his would-be conqueror expiring at his feet and no living witness to the event, he suddenly found himself face to face with the opportunity of a lifetime. He had never been a man to set scruples before profit or honesty above personal advancement. With barely a moment's hesitation he lifted from his lordship's desk the promissory notes of four wealthy men of his acquaintance, all of whom were also weekend guests and seriously in debt to their host. This done, he glanced at the purple skin and bulging eyes of Lord Corby, then lowered himself to his knees to place a hand over the stricken man's chest. He could detect only the faintest heartbeat, no more than the feeble flutterings of that noble organ's death-throes. He hauled himself back to his feet and walked slowly across the room to fling the door wide upon its hinges. After clearing his throat with a delicate cough, he called out in tones of convincing distress:

'Alarm! Alarm! Someone sound the alarm! His Lordship is taken ill. We need a doctor. Alarm! Alarm!'

The rest had been extraordinarily easy. Claiming to have won the notes in a game of cards, he demanded early payment at a high rate of interest and within a month of the funeral had netted himself a clear profit of over one hundred thousand pounds. Lord Corby's timely death had not only released him from the stranglehold of debt and the risk of prison; it had also swelled his fortunes to give him a higher standing in the city and greater freedom at the gaming tables. And today, several months later, his luck still held at the tables and his more pressing accounts were settled in full. Fate had favoured him once again, and throughout the crisis his family had remained in ignorance of the black void of debt into which their futures had very nearly been plunged.

III

Herbert's lips now curved into a smile of self-satisfaction. He stretched his legs again and crossed them at the ankle, a movement that caused Daisy to lift her head and glance up at him with a shy smile. He wondered if she would smile when he took her, or if she would fight for her virginity, weeping and pleading with the master to leave his poor servant untouched. Or would she simply lie unmoving and silent beneath him, too terrified to protest as he had his long-awaited fill of her?

'What the . . .?'

A sudden feeling of unease caused him to look up with a start, his scalp prickling. His eyes met the steady, violet-tinted gaze of his nine-year-old daughter, Leonora, and for one discomforting moment it seemed that she was staring into the very heart of him, marking his faults and failings, measuring his guilt. A flush rose to his cheeks and he shifted in his seat like a man caught red-handed in some felonious act. Leonora was sitting as still as a statue beside her brother, her legs crossed at the ankles and her hands neatly folded in her lap.

Her long hair hung about her shoulders like a veil of chestnut-coloured silk. It seemed to catch the shimmering firelight and hold it, auburned and coppered, within its dark waves. That she and Joseph could be twins was still a matter of some astonishment to their father. He would never understand how two who were conceived in the same act of passion, nurtured side by side in the same womb and born only minutes apart, could be so unlike in every way.

'Well I never,' old Dr Wainwright had exclaimed at the birth. 'Twins without a doubt, yet not a similarity to share between them. I swear I never saw a pair who looked less like brother and sister.'

'Ah, but they will be close enough in spirit,' Francine had smiled, well satisfied with her babies. 'For long generations the Cavendish twins have been uncommonly close in their love for one another.'

'*Shelleys*! These two are *Shelleys*!' Herbert had felt obliged to remind her, yet the babies had grown to favour their mother's side, just like their brothers before them. And they were close, as Francine had predicted.

Joseph was very fair, with soft blond hair and pale blue eyes, while his sister was dark, with those black-lashed, oddly tinted eyes the like of which were unknown within the Shelley family. Joseph was shy and modest, with a retiring, almost nervous nature. By contrast Leonora was a stubborn individual who knew her own mind and quietly imposed her will upon everyone around her. She was vibrant and spirited, a disturbingly beautiful child who seemed to have inherited a touch too much natural arrogance from her aristocratic ancestors. Her brother would never have dared hold his father's gaze with such open defiance, but Leonora's proud nature knew nothing of compliance. Neither threat nor punishment would oblige this little madam to bow to a higher authority. While her lovely face seemed almost without expression, her eyes had a cold and knowing glint as she stared steadily back at Herbert. She was accusing him without words. She had seen him lusting after Daisy and she knew his secret. She *knew*. His daughter was not yet ten years old, yet already she was wise enough to recognise the lascivious nature of her father's private thoughts.

'Enough! Enough of this!'

With a growl of anger he slapped his palms on the wooden arms of his chair and sprang decisively to his feet. Damn it, he would not allow himself to be disturbed by one of his own children. It was not fitting that a man of his standing should feel himself reduced in dignity by a slip of a girl whose experience of the world could be measured in just one short decade. His sudden movement caused Anabel to emerge from the depths of sleep with a cry of alarm. She clutched at her scorched forearm and covered her cheek with her hand, convinced that both were freshly injured. Joseph closed his book and rose to his feet just as Helen, who had fallen asleep across Daisy's lap, awoke with a start and turned down the corners of her mouth, ready to cry at her lustiest, should it prove necessary. Leonora instinctively reached for the hand of her twin, her face placid and unconcerned as her father's sudden outburst shattered the tranquillity of the room.

'Take the children away, Anabel,' Herbert snapped in a voice that was harsh. 'Take them away at once.'

'But sir, Miss Francine gave them leave to wait ...'

Herbert rounded on her angrily. 'Do you dare to question my orders, woman?'

'No, sir, but Miss Francine ... that is ... I thought ...'

'You are not paid to *think*, woman, only to obey orders and attend to your duties. Now, take the children to their beds ... *at once.*'

'Yes, sir.'

Anabel bobbed a polite curtsy and hurried across the room to disentangle Helen from her sprawled position across Daisy's knees. The child was quite pretty and almost as fair in colouring as her mother, with soft brown eyes and a dimpled, mischievous smile. She would never be the beauty her elder sister promised to be, but she was pleasing enough in her own way and mercifully sound of mind and body. She was also the master's favourite, being the only one of his children not to bear the distinctive Cavendish stamp. Anabel ushered her

23

gently to the door, gathering the other children as she went. She paused to drop another small curtsy to the master, noticing the angry flush on his cheeks and the whiteness of his knuckles as he clenched his fists together behind his back. He was staring sullenly into the fire. Something had greatly displeased him.

'Will there be anything else, sir?'

'No.' He fluttered his fingers in a gesture of dismissal. 'That will be all. Go to bed, all of you.'

'Good night, Papa.'

'Good night, Helen, my sweet.' He stooped to kiss the cheek of his small daughter and for a moment his face relaxed and the stern features softened into a smile. Then he glanced over Joseph's fair head and caught sight of Daisy hurrying along the hall with her skirts clumsily hoisted to reveal plump calves and childishly shapely ankles. Excitement touched him with familiar fingers. He licked his lips.

'Good night, Papa!'

Herbert started. Once again his eldest daughter had taken him by surprise. As he looked down at her the smile on his face was replaced by a deep scowl. Light from a nearby lamp cast reflections in her eyes, giving them a deeper hue that was almost cobalt. Her smile was altogether too bold, too knowing. He forced himself to remember that no child of nine, however challenging her stare, could possibly represent a threat to his intentions.

'Good night, Leonora.'

He muttered the words bluntly and without affection, then turned back to the fireplace, snatched up an iron and poked at the logs until they spat and crackled with new life. His eldest daughter had a damnably unsettling manner. There was too much of the Cavendish in her. Francine was so tender and ineffectual in her dealings with the girl that she was allowing her to become self-assured in a manner quite unseemly in one so young. Because she herself was a woman of excellent pedigree who had married below the expectations of her family, Francine was guilty of filling her daughter's head with the kind of grandiose stories and lofty ideals guaranteed to

24

encourage in the child such airs and graces as were far in excess of herself. It must not continue. Leonora's attitude was a source of constant irritation to him. She was not and never would be the noble lady she imagined herself to be. He would speak to Francine first thing in the morning and forbid her to discuss the Earls of Beresford and their elegant histories in the hearing of that disquieting child.

IV

The house had been dark and totally silent for over an hour when the grandfather clock struck midnight and Herbert, wearing only his long night-shirt and carrying a single small lamp, tip-toed up the back stairs toward the servants' quarters on the second floor. When he reached the first floor landing he paused, squinting into the darkness and listening carefully for any small sound to indicate that someone might still be awake to witness his nocturnal prowlings. No light showed beneath the main door of Francine's rooms. Leonora's room, which was part of the same suite, was also in darkness. He stepped back into the enclosed staircase and continued up to the dimly lit second floor, where a metal lantern inlaid with panels of coloured glass was kept burning throughout the night. Along that passage lay the rooms of all the female staff save Anabel, who slept in a small room adjoining her mistress's bedroom on the floor below. The curtained nursery was to his right, the narrow door of Daisy's room to his left. He could hear the rhythmic snores of Mrs Norris as she slept off the effects of her stolen sherry. There was no other sound from anywhere else in the house. Still moving on tiptoe, he pushed open Daisy's door until a shaft of light from the lantern fell across the bed where she slept. Her cheeks were slightly flushed, her hair tousled. One dimpled arm was thrown in childish abandon across the pillow, the other bent over the blankets by which she was only partly covered.

'Oh, you little whore . . . at last . . . at last . . .'

Herbert stared down at the girl for a long time, savouring the moment. He felt the blood quicken in his veins to run like molten fires into his genitals. When he could bear the waiting no longer he set his lamp on a hall table and stepped inside the room, leaving the door slightly ajar to warn him of approaching footsteps. By the light of the lantern he drew back the covers and gently gathered up Daisy's cotton shift until it was bunched around her neck and shoulders, leaving her body exposed to his scrutiny. Now he could see her fleshy thighs and the faint triangle of pubic hair newly sprouting below the neat round of her belly. Her breasts were firm but under-developed, her nipples set like tiny pink rose-buds in the creamy young flesh. She slept on, unaware of the hands and eyes that explored every detail of her body. Then she whimpered softly, stretched her arms above her head and turned her face into the pillows.

That movement, so innocent and yet so sensual, had Herbert completely inflamed. He groaned out loud and felt his heartbeat race with pent-up excitement. It had to be now. He could wait not a moment longer. He lifted his own night-shirt, placed a hand over the mouth of the sleeping child and threw his bulky body down upon hers. In the same instant he had her thighs parted and, grunting and gasping, he thrust himself inside her. She awoke in terror and began to struggle, but the feeble flailing of her limbs only served to heighten his passion. The whole thing was over in moments. The long weeks of anticipation, the sexual fantasies, the frustrations, had all welled up in Herbert to create a great wave of lust that had him spent within seconds. In the very act of taking her he felt his manhood desert him and his wetness flood out in its stead.

'Damn it! Damn it! Damn it to hell!'

He cursed long and loudly. Let down, unsatisfied, he pawed and groped at her flesh in the vain hope of calling back his ebbing desire. He was furious that his pleasure had been so short-lived. She was ruined now. She would never again have so much to offer him. The prize was lost. The sweet moment of deflowering, the torn barrier of her virginity, was gone forever.

'Stop snivelling, you stupid girl.'

Seeing Daisy as the sole reason for his disappointment, he spoke in an angry whisper as he flung himself away from her and snatched at his crumpled night-shirt. 'Cover your nakedness, girl, and say nothing of this ... *nothing*. You are not to speak of it to *anyone*. Do you understand?'

Daisy clutched at the covers and nodded her head. She was hurt and bewildered. Tears streamed from her terrified blue eyes and her lower lip trembled. She was shivering from head to toe.

'Not a word, girl. Be sure and hold your tongue or your mistress will throw you out into the streets where you belong. There'll be no more wages and easy living for you, my girl, if the mistress ever hears of this.'

Daisy nodded again, still silent save for her quiet sobbing.

'Damn you, Daisy Kimble,' he snarled into her frightened face. 'Damn your tricks and temptations.'

He left the room as quietly as he had entered, this time closing the door very carefully behind him before retrieving his lamp and tiptoeing away. He did not notice the swift little shadow that darted ahead of him along the corridor, the agile shape that slipped silently down the back stairs and into the darkness shrouding the first floor. Unaware that he had been observed, he continued down to his own rooms on the ground floor. Once inside he threw a velvet robe around his shoulders, gulped down a large brandy and dragged his high-backed chair very close to the fireplace. Muttering and cursing under his breath, he hunched forward in his seat to stab at the dying embers of the fire with a long poker. He could scarcely believe that the lengthy build-up of desire had petered out so cruelly, that his long-awaited pleasure had been so short-lived. Damn the girl. She had no right to lead him on, only to prove such a galling disappointment when he finally managed to get between her legs.

CHAPTER TWO

I

It was early August, a little over a week before the twins' tenth birthday, and Francine was resting in her room overlooking the spacious garden. The children had spent a good deal of their time recently at the Russell house in Kenton Street, where Squire Russell's bitch had produced a litter of five pups. Bess was a big russet and white setter bred from Irish stock and noted for her obedience and gentle temperament. Her pups should prove to be excellent gun-dogs and were expected to fetch around fifteen guineas apiece. Joseph, always the soft-hearted lover of things small and helpless, had singled out the last-born pup with the reddest coat and was set on rearing it as a pet. Leonora had generously offered to forego her own anticipated gift so that Joseph might get his dearest wish, but Herbert would hear none of it. His response to the suggestion had been most emphatic.

'A dog? Here in the house? Certainly not. I would as soon bring a horse or a dairy cow into the parlour.'

'Oh, *please*, Papa,' Leonora had pleaded. 'A pup would be no trouble to anyone, and perhaps we could train it to guard our property as the Squire's animals guard his.'

'The Squire's animals stink,' Herbert reminded her. 'They are also noisy, slavering and hairy. They stain the carpets and foul the pathways and gardens. Dogs are for outdoors, Leonora, for the hunt and the shoot, not to be fondled and fussed over like playthings. Besides, they harbour fleas and intestinal worms. I shudder even to sit in the same room as such a dirty animal.'

'But Papa, if the pup is healthy ...'

'I have made my objections quite clear, Leonora. There is nothing more to be said on the subject.'

'Then Joseph is to be disappointed?'

Father and daughter had stared at each other; he impatient to turn his attention to other matters, she quietly persistent in her request.

'The subject is now closed,' Herbert had said at last, his voice cold. 'You may tell your brother to forget his foolish notion of bringing a dog into this house.'

Although his decision made the twins very unhappy, on this occasion Francine was reluctant to intervene on their behalf She had already succeeded in persuading Herbert, much against his better judgement, to allow Joseph to be educated at home instead of going away to school with his elder brothers. Her arguments had rested upon the fact that he was doing so well under the tutorial supervision of Mr Bartholomew, a retired schoolmaster with an excellent reputation, but in her heart of hearts she knew that she could not bear to see her twins parted from each other. Nor would she have the least stalwart of her sons exposed to the rigours and conflicts of life at public school. It had not been an easy task, but eventually she had won him a reprieve. The boy must be satisfied with that, and would have to put aside his longings for a pup.

Francine sighed deeply and rested her hands in the rich folds of her skirt.

'Are you comfortable, Francine?'

29

Anabel's hand came to rest on the slender shoulder of her mistress. In the privacy of those private rooms she was free to speak to her mistress as friend and confidante rather than mere employee. It was a privilege not to be expressed in the presence of the master. Should such familiarity ever be brought to his attention he would consider it proper to put an end to their long friendship.

Smiling warmly, Francine reached up to cover Anabel's hand with her own.

'I'm quite comfortable, thank you, my dear.'

Anabel reached out to adjust one of the tortoise-shell combs decorating Francine's hair, then seated herself in a low, armless chair close to the window. She pulled a beaded silk ball gown across her knees and examined its sleeve-trims of gold Vandyke lace, one of which had been badly snagged on the door handle of a carriage.

'Will it mend?'

'I'll do my best,' Anabel promised. 'The thread is a good match, so I think I'll manage well enough.'

'Bless you, I am rather fond of that gown.'

'Yes, I know. I often recall the night of the Beresford Ball, when you wore this gown for the very first time, long before it was altered to suit today's fashions.'

'Oh, yes, and I have kept the overskirts and extra petticoats safely stored away in the hope that one day it will be remade to its original design.'

'I can almost see you now,' Anabel said, dreamily. 'You were dancing with Sir Oscar, and you looked as lovely as an angel in all this shimmering gold silk and gorgeous beading ... gold satin shoes ... amber earrings and choker ...' She set down her work with a sigh. 'Oh, yes, I can see it now ... all those sparkling chandeliers and stained glass windows, and his Lordship so tall and handsome, whirling you around the Great Hall as if ... as if ...'

'Hush, Anabel. The ball was a long time ago.'

'Oh, I'm so sorry. It was thoughtless of me even to mention it.' Her shoulders rose and fell in a heavy sigh. 'It's just that sometimes ...'

'I do understand, dear Anabel, but the sweeter the memory the less often it should be disturbed.'

The two women fell silent, each with her own thoughts, her own private recollections. Francine's chair had been set well into the window recess so that she could see almost the whole of the main garden where her family were enjoying the bright summer evening. Her hairbrush lay idle in her lap, its silver top-side glinting in a shaft of sunlight that also lit her embroidered robe with a splash of brilliant colour. Beneath the robe her body was still slender and girlish in a low-cut dress of cool gauze. A fire was burning in the big fireplace despite the warmth of the evening, its dancing, flickering flames more welcoming than an empty grate. The ticking of the grandfather clock in the corner was like the steady heartbeat of the house, rhythmic and dependable. A muslin curtain billowed lazily in the evening breeze, and from the open side window came the sounds of bird song, the drone of busy insects and the lilt of familiar, beloved voices.

Francine smiled contentedly as she looked down from her favourite position before the long, south-facing window. Everything she held most dear in life was down there in the garden. She could see the man who had cherished her for fourteen years without once suspecting that his name and affection had been taken as hasty second best. She had never loved him. She knew that real love was an all-consuming, once-in-a-lifetime experience, and her heart had been claimed by another long before Herbert Shelley had first set his covetous gaze upon her. She had never loved him, yet she had borne him five beautiful children and trained herself to suffer his repugnant sexual advances without complaint. No woman could have proved a more dutiful and loyal partner to her husband and master, but it was guilt, not love, that made her so. It burned like an unquenchable fire in her breast, and the long years had taught her that guilt could be as painfully enduring as love itself.

Her sigh was a soft whisper in the quiet room as she gazed down at the five children who were her compensation for lost dreams, her hopes for the future.

31

'I am reimbursed five-fold,' she said softly.

'Indeed you are. Each one is a blessing, Francine.'

'Yes, I am five times blessed, and yet ...'

'... and yet you cling to a dream,' Anabel said gently. 'You love him still, after all these years ...'

'Hush, now,' Francine said sharply. 'You are pledged never to speak of such things ... not even in private ... *never.*'

Down in the garden the two eldest boys, freed from the disciplines of school life for the duration of the summer, were in boisterous spirits and restless for adventure. Thirteen-year-old Jonathan had grown tremendously in the last half-year. He was tall for his age and bore a striking resemblance to Francine's side of the family, and to her cousin Oscar Cavendish, Sixth Earl of Beresford, in particular. He had the same shock of fair hair, the frank gaze and piercing, dark-lashed blue eyes. In his recently acquired maturity could be seen the broad shoulders, long limbs and proud, almost arrogant bearing that were the hallmark of the Cavendish line. Francine watched him with a proud heart. By far the most handsome of her three sons, he bore the stamp of the aristocrat in his even features and quiet self-assurance. He stood now with his hands clasped behind his back and his legs placed firmly apart, a stance completely natural to the boy and achingly familiar to Francine. In profile he could well be taken for the Earl's own son.

Just then Francine caught sight of Daisy Kimble sitting alone among the rockery plants at the far end of the garden, her head lowered and her fingers idly plucking at a tuft of grass. She was wearing a dark dress that was a little too tight across the bodice and a few inches too short at the hem. Her shoulders and neck were covered by a triangle of light woollen cloth. She looked sad and withdrawn.

'Anabel, is Daisy still working as she should?'

'Oh yes. Mrs Norris says she's one of the best girls she ever had. She's hard-working, obedient and very clean.'

'But she is not happy, Anabel. When she first came to us she was a bright, cheerful little thing who took pleasure in her surroundings. But then she seemed to lose interest, to withdraw from us all as if something had wounded her deeply. Look at her now, sitting alone with her head bowed, staring at nothing.'

'Perhaps she's homesick for the country,' Anabel offered cautiously.

Francine shook her head. 'I fear it goes deeper than that, but she refuses to be drawn on the matter. Anabel, do you think it possible that ...'

'Yes?'

'Well, that one of the manservants ... a footman, perhaps ... even though she's only a child ...?'

Anabel shook her head. 'I doubt if any man has harmed her. The master is very strict on those matters, especially with Daisy, since she is so young and pretty.'

'All the same, I'm worried about her. She looks so unhappy, so alone.'

'I'll speak to Mrs Norris again,' Anabel said.

'Yes, I think perhaps you should. Oh, Anabel, the garden is so beautiful this year. It saddens me that all this must fade and fall to nothing.'

'A temporary loss,' Anabel reminded her, bowing low over the intricate lace-work on Francine's gown. 'Everything will blossom again next year, regular as clockwork and twice as pretty.'

'But changed, Anabel. Nothing is ever quite the same, is it? Everything changes.'

Anabel offered no reply. She saw that a shadow had crossed the pale face of her mistress, leaving that bleak, almost stricken expression in her eyes as silent proof that her heart, broken all those years ago when love was snatched away, had never truly mended. There was nothing she could do for Francine except share her secret tragedy and love her for the quiet strength that had brought her this far.

She set down her work for a moment and gazed down from the big window. The gardens were indeed splendid that year. She could see almost the whole of the main lawn, with its clipped hedges and stately row of Lombardy poplar. Beyond the rockery, in the farthest and most secluded corner of the garden, the branches of an ancient oak formed a canopy against the glare of the sun, bathing the bench below in softly dappled shade. Fuschias and cosmos and dainty ground blossoms competed to produce the most appealing displays in the flower beds, while cascades of rich ivy transformed the dull brick walls into a backdrop of living green. Another of that season's successes was the profusion of colourful gaillardia growing between the poplars, their bright, distinctive hues declaring to all that the Shelley gardens were among the first in London to produce these delightful newcomers to English soil.

'Just look at those two,' Francine exclaimed, her sudden melancholy forgotten. 'My sons spar and box like common prize-fighters. Where *do* they find all their energy?'

On the grass below the windows, Charles had tossed aside his grey velvet coat and vest and rolled up the sleeves of his shirt to reveal sun-browned forearms. He was a robust and very good-looking boy, though somewhat less striking in appearance than his elder brother. Like many children who found themselves the middle one of three, he had learned to grow in the shadow of the first-born whilst constantly giving way to the needs of his youngest brother. Even so, Charles was a likeable boy with a generous nature to off-set his often unpredictable temper. He and Jonathan now grappled each other in earnest, each struggling to throw his brother to the ground. Their antics caused Helen to clap her hands together with enjoyment, laughing and calling out her encouragement as the brothers tumbled and wrestled on the grass.

A ripple of laughter drew Francine's attention to the two figures sharing a bench set at an angle on the lawn. Joseph and Leonora were playing cat's cradle, passing a length of corded silk from hand to hand in a series of clever and very attractive shapes. The boy was slight of build and pale in colouring. He was small-boned like his mother, and suffered the same anxieties of health whenever the damp, cold days of winter came around. His features were neat and finely drawn, less rugged than those of his brothers but noticeably handsome in their own way. He was a talented boy, clever and diligent in his studies, though increasingly reluctant to join the rough and tumble of the real world beyond his home. His father believed him delicate, but what Herbert saw as faults Francine recognised as those qualities most conspicuous in herself: refinement and sensitivity.

'You always smile in a particular way when you look at the twins,' Anabel remarked.

'And mothers are not supposed to show favouritism,' Francine smiled. 'You are right, Anabel. My own dear mother would not have approved, I fear.'

'Perhaps not, but twins are special in themselves, and also ... well, perhaps a woman is more tightly bound to her first-born daughter than to any other of her children. There is a bond between them, is there not?'

'Oh yes,' Francine agreed. 'Little Helen is her father's darling because she's the only one of his children to favour the Shelley line. But Leonora is different. Leonora is a true Cavendish and she is *mine*. She is *all mine.*'

As usual the twins were dressed as much alike as their different sexes would allow; Joseph in a white frilled shirt and blue linen trousers, Leonora in a high-waisted frock of white gauze over a petticoat of blue silk. The mustard tones of his waistcoat were matched by her cashmere shawl, while the richer blue of his coat found its echo in her wide satin sash. As he passed the intricately shaped thread into his sister's waiting fingers their eyes met in a glance that spoke volumes. Between them was a special closeness rarely encountered in non-identical twins. These two had never been parted save for those four minutes which lay between her birth and his, that brief span of time which determined who was to lead and who was to follow for the rest of their lives. It was as if the boy, born on the heels of his more forceful sister, had settled for a lesser destiny, a smaller share of those attributes Leonora had claimed in abundance. It would have pleased their father better if their positions had been reversed.

Leonora had always possessed an uncanny knack of sensing

when the eyes of others were upon her, an almost sinister talent that never failed to take Francine by surprise. This occasion proved to be no exception. One moment she seemed fully absorbed in her childish game, the next she was meeting her mother's gaze with those beautiful eyes whose exact shade of blue was impossible to define. They were the colour of the ocean, of sapphire or turquoise with hints of green dependent on the light, yet they could just as readily glow with the deeper shades of wild cornflower or primula. Few women were fortunate enough to have been blessed with such captivating eyes and such long, naturally black lashes. With her lovely face and coppery chestnut hair, Leonora Shelley, just days away from her tenth birthday, was already blessed with everything she would need to guarantee her future happiness.

'Oh, yes,' Francine said. 'That one is all mine. How I wish poor Mama might have lived long enough to see her grown.'

As she returned her daughter's brilliant smile Francine was modest enough to acknowledge that no direct gift of hers had endowed the child with such beauty. Leonora was the sum total of all that was desirable in the Cavendish bloodline. She was beautiful, intelligent, ambitious and strong-willed. No man would ever better her nor any master bridle her free spirit. She was destined for greatness, of that her mother was certain. In Leonora were embodied the last of Francine's hopes and dreams. In time she hoped to see her married to one of the wealthier Cavendish cousins. She might even live to see her lovely daughter become that most envied of women, Countess of Beresford and mistress of the magnificent Beresford Hall.

She sighed deeply and closed her eyes as a host of memories, bitter-sweet and sharp in their sting, stirred in her heart. Mistress of Beresford! Would it ever be so? Would Destiny be kinder to Leonora than to her mother before her? If only it *could* be so, then Francine's prayers would surely be answered. The hurts and disappointments of a lifetime might be forgiven, laid to rest, if only her beloved Leonora could snatch for herself those treasures that had so nearly been hers.

II

The following day saw a deterioration in the weather that kept the family indoors and rendered the gardens virtually inaccessible. Storms during the night had saturated the lawns, and the sheer force of the rain had snapped off many flower heads and left them half buried in the muddy ground. By mid-morning the storms had eased to become a series of fitful showers relieved by periods of brilliant sunshine. The rumble of thunder could be heard in the distance, and occasionally the sky would darken ominously before sunlight burst through to bathe everything in a golden, newly rinsed glow.

'Come here and sit with me, Helen, so that we can watch the colours of the storm together.'

Leonora hoisted Helen on to the window-seat in the nursery to show her the rainbow arcing across the sky. The younger girl was drowsy and unresponsive. She emitted a noisy yawn and, knuckling her eyes with her fists, snuggled sleepily against her sister. Leonora pulled her across her lap and leaned against the window frame with a restive sigh. She could see a phantom-like image of herself in the glass, a small girl in a satin bonnet and soft muslin gown, with huge dark eyes and glossy ringlets falling over bare shoulders. The storms had made her restless. This was the quiet time of day following lunch, when Francine rested in her bedroom and even the activities of the servants fell into a brief lull. The boys had decided to risk the capricious nature of the weather in order to visit their friends at Squire Russell's house in Kenton Street, where Jonathan and Charles would no doubt enjoy a few hands of cards while Joseph romped with the pups. They had left the house like three young gentlemen of quality, all elegantly dressed in top hats and impeccably tailored walking clothes. Their father had taken lunch at his club and was not expected home until early evening.

Tonight there would be guests for dinner, among them the amusingly flirtatious Sir Reginald Lennard, and that caricature of out-dated elegance, the elderly Lady Mildred

Thettersly. Leonora looked forward to helping her mother dress for the occasion, knowing in advance that Francine would be the loveliest lady at the dinner table. Helen would be allowed into the drawing room for only a few minutes, but Leonora, escorted by her shy twin, would be free to show off her newest gown and take a pre-dinner glass of sherry with the guests. It promised to be an exciting evening, but until then Leonora must find some way of keeping herself amused now that her plans for the afternoon had been washed away by the rain. A whispered voice drew her from her reverie just as Helen began to snore softly in her arms.

'Let me take the little one to her cot now, Miss Leonora. Oh, she's fast asleep, bless her. Your arms must be quite cramped.'

'Thank you, Anabel.' Leonora smiled, then dropped her hands into her lap with another heavy sigh.

'The Devil finds work for idle hands and makes mischief in empty heads,' Anabel scolded gently. 'There's stitching to be done, Miss Leonora, and book-learning, too.'

'Yes, I know, Anabel. Perhaps later ...'

'The storms have made you restless, as they always do.'

'Yes, I suppose they have.'

Anabel shifted the weight of the sleeping child in her arms. 'If you will not occupy yourself, why not go to your room and rest while the house is still quiet?'

'No, I believe I would rather stay here for a while,' Leonora replied, sighing again as she turned back to the window. 'Everything looks so fresh and clean after the rain.'

She felt Anabel's hand rest lightly and briefly on her hair, then listened to the rustle of silk and the tinkle of silver nursery toys as Helen was lowered into her cot in the alcove. Leonora was very fond of Anabel. The thin, sallow-skinned woman had a loving nature that seemed to shine out from her dark brown eyes to add a certain prettiness to a face of otherwise comely proportions. She was now in her early thirties and had been with Francine's family since childhood, moving to the house in Garden Square when her young mistress married Herbert Shelley. Unlike the nurse and the housekeeper, whose moods would fluctuate according to the time of day and the duties required of them, Anabel was one of those rare women blessed with a temperament that was constant and reliable. Her loyalty to Francine had long ago exceeded that which was normally expected of a servant for her mistress. Indeed, the two women had grown so close that Herbert would surely have felt compelled to intervene, had he guessed the true depths of their friendship. Fully aware of this, they were careful to moderate their behaviour in his presence. It was sufficient for him to be aware of Anabel's capabilities and to value her honesty and discretion. Over the years he had been content to watch her assume far more than her intended measure of responsibilities. Decent servants were neither easy to find, cheap to train, nor simple to keep. Whether by accident or design, Anabel had allowed the Shelley family and their needs to become her whole life, and in return had made herself indispensable.

'Leonora, shall we go downstairs to see how the arrangements for dinner are progressing?'

Leonora shook her head. 'You go, Anabel. I'd rather stay here with Helen in case it thunders again and she wakes in a fright.'

'Very well, but you should remember what I said about the Devil and idle hands.'

'I will, Anabel. I will.'

As the door closed quietly behind Anabel, Leonora used her handkerchief to rub a layer of condensation from the glass. The rainbow was fading. Another brief shower of rain had left a glistening sheen on the roof of the coach house, so that reflected sunlight sparkled here and there like diamonds dropped upon the tiles. Just then a movement at the far end of the kitchen garden drew her attention in time for her to see a fat man in a dark tailed coat slip through the rear gate and stride across the vegetable patch. He paused at the lower corner of the coach house, glancing this way and that as if reluctant to be spotted by anyone working in the grounds. Then he hurried across the herb garden and entered the house by way of the scullery door. The man was Herbert

Shelley and he was entering his own home as furtively as any criminal. From the scullery area he could, with care, reach his rooms without meeting any other members of the household. Once there he might remain undisturbed until the evening, since nobody would be aware of his return. While Francine believed him to be spending the whole day in important business at his club, he had slipped back to the house with no intention of making his presence known. Leonora was probably the only person who realised that her father was in the house. And she knew *why* he was here. She knew his secret. For weeks she had watched at windows and listened at doors and wondered what to do with the knowledge, with the sense of outrage growing inside her.

III

'Hell and damnation! Hell and damnation!'

It was late afternoon and rain was once again lashing at the windows when Herbert flopped across the bed with a loud groan. It had happened again. No sooner had he pushed himself into her than his passion was spent. A couple of thrusts and it was over, leaving his lust unsatisfied and his self-esteem severely bruised. It was incredible that he, an experienced man of the world, should suddenly see his performance reduced to that of a fumbling novice. Daisy Kimble was young, available and tremendously exciting, yet he found himself incapable of making anything but the most mediocre sex with her. Twice every week for two months he had mounted her with the strength of a stallion, only to suffer the humiliation of premature ejaculation.

For her part Daisy did precisely nothing. She neither welcomed nor resisted him, neither aided nor hindered him. She simply came when summoned, stripped off her clothes and lay on the bed with her legs wide apart, staring at the ceiling. Afterwards she dressed and left the room as if the service was part of her normal household duties. That she took no enjoyment from him was patently obvious, yet at the same time he saw no hostility in her eyes, no glimmer of complaint. He would have welcomed a look of pure hatred in place of that bland expression, and even a shudder of honest revulsion might be preferable to the dull obedience with which she endured his demands. Her indifference had become almost as painful as his impotence.

'Will that be all, Mr Shelley, sir?'

He rolled on to his side and propped himself up on one elbow. She had pulled on her plain white frock and tucked her hair into her bonnet. He could see red patches on her face and neck where the stubble on his chin had inflamed her skin, and another just above her breast where his mouth had worried the tender flesh. Not since that first night when she awoke to find him already upon her had she offered him a response of any kind. She remained silent throughout and totally, infuriatingly passive. On impulse he reached for his coat and pulled a draw-string purse from one of the pockets.

'A guinea,' he said, tipping the purse so that its contents fell in a small pile on the bed. He selected a coin and held it out to her, searching her face for some flicker of response. 'For you, Daisy. A whole guinea to spend as you wish. Here, take it. Take it.'

'For me, sir?' She gave a brief shrug of her shoulders but made no move to accept the gift.

'Take it,' he urged, reaching out to grab her by the wrist so that he could press the coin into her hand.

Daisy stared at the golden guinea lying in her palm, then extended her arm for him to take it back. Her untidy curls danced about her face as she shook her head.

'Begging your pardon, sir, Mrs Norris will think I stole it, and then the mistress will punish me.'

'Well, then, you must keep it hidden.'

'No, sir.' Daisy shook her head again. 'Can't, sir. Mrs Norris'll see.'

'Don't you *want* the guinea?' Herbert asked, becoming exasperated by her stubbornness.

41

'No, sir.'

'Good God, child,' he suddenly exploded. 'Will nothing I do ever satisfy you?'

Daisy flinched and bowed her head, fixing her gaze on the carpet close to her feet. She cleared her throat and, in a voice lacking any emotion, asked again:

'Will there be anything else, sir?'

At that moment Herbert caught sight of himself in the huge oval mirror dominating that side of the room. His legs were hanging over the edge of the mattress, pale and deeply veined in the unflattering lamplight. Flesh hung around his middle in such quantity that his navel had become embedded in a deep, fist-sized hole. His neck was flabby and his cheeks heavy-jowled, robbing his face of any handsome appeal it might once have boasted. In the dark glass the bed and its ageing occupant were captured as if on canvas, in cruel detail. He did not like what he saw, the crumpled covers and stained sheets, the indifferent girl holding a golden guinea as compensation for his latest failure. Below his belly hung his flacid genitals, small now in their redundancy, their almost comic appearance adding insult to the twice-weekly injury. Only slowly did he become aware that there was another face trapped in the glass, a small, familiar face almost concealed amongst the hangings on the other side of the room. A pair of dark eyes were looking back at him, witness not only to his adultery but to his self-disgust.

'Leonora! Oh my God! Leonora!'

While Herbert sat as if rooted to the spot, staring wide-eyed into the mirror, poor Daisy burst into tears and rushed across the room.

'Don't tell,' she wailed. 'Oh please, Miss Leonora, don't tell. The mistress'll have me thrown out on the streets and there'll be no work for me in any other house. Oh please, Miss Leonora, say you won't tell. Say you won't tell.'

Leonora recoiled in distaste as the sobbing Daisy clutched at her hands. She had crept into her father's rooms by way of the main door in the lower hall, then tip-toed through into the bedroom and climbed on to the big chair in the corner. She had been sitting there among the shadowed drapes, quiet and watchful, for a long time. Now she tried to escape but felt something cold and hard pressed into her hand and Daisy's fingers closing around her own.

'It's yours,' the girl said, her face stained with tears and contorted with weeping. 'The master gave it to me. Take it for your silence, Miss Leonora. Don't tell the mistress. Please, oh, *please* don't tell the mistress.'

Herbert's abrupt roar startled them both. 'Out of my way, you stupid girl!'

A heavy blow sent Daisy staggering across the room with a wail of pain and alarm. She ran back the way she had come, past the bed and the mirror, and disappeared through the small door leading to the scullery area. Now Herbert towered above Leonora, his face white with rage. To cover his nakedness he had pulled on a long robe that fastened with a tasselled belt around his middle. Its vivid greens did little to improve the present tincture of his complexion as he grabbed his small daughter by the shoulders and shook her violently.

'How long have you been here?' he demanded. 'And by what right do you spy on your own father in his private rooms? How dare you? How *dare* you?' His fingers bit into her flesh. 'What did you see? Tell me the truth, you little witch. Tell me what you saw.'

Leonora shrank before the shouted words, yet continued to meet his gaze with mutinous eyes. In her mind was a confusion of lurid imagery, in her heart a tumult of sorrow and revulsion. Her silence and her unflinching stare seemed to increase her father's fury two-fold.

'You saw nothing,' he bellowed, his face so close to hers that she could smell the brandy on his breath and feel his words ringing and echoing in her ears. 'Do you hear me, child? You saw *nothing*.'

Undaunted, Leonora lifted her chin with a small but stubborn toss of her head. It was a gesture of open defiance.

'I *saw*,' she retorted in a hissing whisper, 'I was right here and I *saw*.'

'Liar!' her father snarled. 'Liar! You saw *nothing*.'

Without warning he shoved her away from him with such force that she lurched against the door frame and struck her shoulder on the hard wood. In a sudden release of pent-up emotions she rounded on her father with her fists clenched and her violet-coloured eyes blazing.

'I saw what you did to Daisy,' she cried. 'I was here all the time and I saw. I saw.' Then she gathered up her skirts, turned on her heels and rushed from the room.

Herbert dashed after her, only to stop when he reached the lower hall and was confronted by a servant girl in the process of polishing the rich pine panelling. As Leonora skidded round the curve of the staircase followed by the master wearing nothing but a loosely fastened night-robe, the girl set down her polishing cloth and stared from one to the other with open curiosity. Herbert adjusted the belt of his robe and glowered after his hastily departing daughter. Then he returned to his rooms, slamming the door behind him.

Anabel was on her way downstairs when she encountered Leonora rushing headlong along the first floor passage, her hair dishevelled and tears coursing down her cheeks. She caught the distraught child in her arms and held her tightly, feeling the sobs that shook her small body. Very gently, she led the girl to her room and sat with her in an armchair until she was able to regain her composure. After several minutes had passed she brought a glass of water and phial of smelling salts, then bathed Leonora's tear-stained cheeks with a handkerchief dampened with rose water.

'I must speak to Mama at once,' the child said, her lower lip trembling and her voice unsteady. She was obviously very distressed, but she was angry, too, more angry than Anabel had ever seen her.

'Why, child? What happened?'

'I mustn't speak of it,' Leonora said. 'Except to Mama.'

Anabel stroked Leonora's dark brown hair. 'Miss Francine is still sleeping. She needs to rest in preparation for her dinner party this evening. Why don't you tell me all about it, then we can decide together what is to be done.'

Leonora lowered her head. She felt choked, stifled by

emotions so unfamiliar that she scarcely knew how to describe them, even to herself. All the pain and anxiety of the last few weeks, worsened by the strain of concealing her ugly secret, rose up in her now as if to overwhelm her. She had been betrayed, of that she was certain. Somehow, in her father's nakedness and in Daisy's shame, Leonora herself had been betrayed.

'Leonora?' Anabel continued to stroke the child's hair. 'What is it, my dear? You are normally so calm and cheerful. What on earth could have happened to upset you like this? And what is this in your hand? A guinea? Now I wonder where that came from?'

'A guinea for my silence,' Leonora said. 'Daisy gave it to me.'

'Daisy? And how would she, a poor parlour maid, come to own a golden guinea?'

'It was given to her by my father,' Leonora blurted, tears welling again in her eyes. And suddenly it all came out in a flood of words over which she had no control. 'I saw them just now. The two of them. In Papa's bedroom. Daisy took off her dress and then ... then they were both naked. I saw them, Anabel. I was watching and I saw them ... what they ... what he did ... it was horrible ... horrible.' She broke off, her small fists beating at her skirts in impotent rage.

Anabel pulled her into her arms and rocked her to and fro, making soft, soothing sounds with her tongue. It was a long time before she judged the child capable of continuing.

'Are you sure, my dear? As God will be your judge, are you absolutely certain of what you saw?'

'Oh, yes, I'm sure,' Leonora nodded, dabbing at her eyes with the handkerchief. 'And this is not the only time. It happened on the night you fell asleep by the fire and burned your cheek, the night Papa sent us all to bed before Mama came home.'

'And since?'

'Many times. Perhaps twice or more every week. Sometimes he creeps into Daisy's room when everyone else is asleep, just to ... just to ...'

'Hush, child. Hush, now.'

'I hate them, Anabel. I hate them both.'

Anabel took Leonora's face in her hands and looked steadily into her eyes. 'Now you listen to me, child,' she said firmly. 'Your Mama must never hear of this. You must never tell her what you have seen or what you know.'

'Oh, but I *must* tell her, I *must*.'

'And who do you think will benefit from the confession? Think what it will mean, Leonora. Your Mama will suffer a terrible shock and Daisy will lose her home. The story will then become common gossip, the talk of every servant and shopkeeper in the city. The shame of it will break poor Francine's heart. Oh no, my dear, for her dear sake you must say nothing.'

Leonora squared her shoulders and sniffed back the last of her tears. Her eyes were large and bright, their colour deepened to a glossy midnight blue.

'Then who is to be punished?' she demanded.

'Nobody.'

'But I don't understand, Anabel.'

'Trust me, and one day you will be glad of my advice. Daisy is only a servant, Leonora, a good girl who must obey her master even when he makes her do something she knows is wicked. I feared from the start that she was too pretty for her own good. To be rich and beautiful is to be doubly blessed, but to be poor and pretty is to bear two burdens. I have often given thanks to the good Lord for making me so plain of face and figure that no master would ever make such demands upon me.'

'Then Papa is wicked indeed for forcing Daisy to do wrong things.'

'Nothing in life is quite so simple,' Anabel said with a gentle smile. 'Your Papa is just a man like any other, and every man suffers from periodic fires of the blood that must be cooled if he is to remain in good health and humour. We must remember that he is also a gentleman of some standing, and as such he is entitled to take his pleasures where, and from whom, he chooses. Remember that all men are masters in their own home, Leonora.'

46

'And the mistress of the house?'

'She must obey her husband and keep herself only unto him.'

'While he is free to do as he pleases ... *anything* he pleases?'

'Yes, my dear.'

'But that is so unfair, Anabel.'

The woman shrugged. 'The good Lord never promised us that life would be fair. It is a difficult world, with many rules that must be obeyed without question.'

'Unless one is fortunate enough to have been born a *man*,' Leonora retorted. 'It seems to me that men are conveniently exempt from the rules they impose upon others.'

'Yes, Leonora. This is indeed a man's world, and you would be well advised to learn that lesson now, while you are still young.'

'I think I hate my father, Anabel.'

'But you love your Mama, and for her sake love must be the stronger emotion.'

Leonora continued to look at Anabel for long moments. Only gradually did she come to accept that bringing the incident out into the open would subject her beloved mother to unnecessary pain while resolving nothing. The fires of the blood from which her father suffered would no doubt continue to plague him, and Daisy's humble birth would ensure that she was always some man's chattel. It was Mama who mattered, Mama who must be protected. She leaned against Anabel's bosom, drawing comfort from the woman's closeness and her clean, fresh smell. She realised she could never divulge what she had seen. She must swallow her own feelings of outrage and pretend the incident had not taken place. As she turned the golden guinea over in her fingers, she knew that her silence was to protect her mother's peace of mind, not to preserve her father's dignity. She would pretend it had never happened, but she could not forget and she would never, ever forgive.

IV

That evening Leonora was allowed to wear her new dress for the first time. It was of the popular classic design in soft Indian muslin over white satin. The slender skirts were gathered into a tiny bodice and weighted around the hem with a wide border worked in silver and scarlet silks. The same pretty motif decorated her slippers and trimmed the scarlet satin sash encircling her waist. Anabel had dressed her hair with ribbons and beads after first pinning it high on her head and teasing the ends into long ringlets to hang over one shoulder. A single ruby drop nestled at her throat, its deep, fiery colour finding an echo in her red-toned hair.

'You look beautiful, Miss Leonora.'

'Thank you, Anabel.'

Leonora watched her reflection in the mirror. Her face was solemn, her eyes dark and troubled. The day had changed her. She was still struggling to come to terms with what she had seen, to gather her terrible secret into a burden of more manageable proportions.

'It's for the best,' Anabel whispered, reading her thoughts.

'I know that,' Leonora replied with a tight smile. 'Mama must not be hurt. Have no fear. I will keep my promise.'

Anabel watched sadly as Leonora glided from the room with all the natural elegance of a young princess. The child was still deeply distressed by her experience, and this particular pain would not be halved by sharing it with her brother. Knowing that the children kept no secrets from each other, Anabel had made her promise not to speak of the incident to Joseph. It was doubly hard on Leonora to have to carry the burden of her knowledge alone.

By five-thirty the huge table in the dining room was laden with a magnificent array of food. Francine had ordered lark's tongues from Dunstable to impress Sir Reginald Lennard, whose wife Christina was particularly fond of the delicacy. For Lord and Lady Mornington there were pork pies delivered only that afternoon from Melton Mowbray, and to please Lady Mildred Thettersly, a small case of fresh red mullet had been brought by special delivery from Weymouth. The guests were also to be offered a selection of boiled and roast meats, poultry, bacon, game, salmon, oysters and cod. There were tarts, pies, ices and sweet puddings, a variety of sugared biscuits, several fine cheeses, butter, fruit, nuts and salad. Ranked along the sideboard with the silver plate and side-dishes were over a dozen bottles of sherry, madeira, champagne, claret and burgundy, with port and brandy for those who preferred them. She had provided for her distinguished friends in the lavish manner for which she was now renowned. No guest had ever left Francine's table with anything less than complete satisfaction.

Sherry was served in the drawing room as the guests arrived, though most of the men preferred to take a glass of brandy to crisp the stomach before dinner. Sir Reginald and Lady Lennard were the first to arrive, accompanied by their eldest daughter, Winifred. Francine was both proud and delighted with the way Leonora greeted their eminent visitors with a charm and self-assurance far in excess of her years. It was almost as if she had suddenly matured, as if tonight marked the end of childhood for an already accomplished young hostess now ready to take her first grown-up steps in society. Joseph watched her too, with adoring but troubled eyes. He seemed to sense that she was changed, that some subtle and insidious thing had slipped between them. Yet he was proud of his lovely sister and more than a little envious of her natural ease among other people. By the time all the guests were gathered in the splendid room with their pre-dinner glasses, it was clear that as a hostess Leonora was a great success.

'And what special gift might you be expecting for your birthday next week, my dear?'

The question was heard by everyone since it was asked by Lady Mildred Thettersly, who was hard of hearing and seemed to believe that everyone else suffered from the same

49

affliction. She dominated the room in her wide, old-fashioned petticoats and beaded gold brocade, with her hair piled precariously high on her head and her body stooped beneath the combined weight of gown and heavy jewellery. 'Something pretty, I'll wager. A new gown, perhaps, or a necklace of sapphires to match those devilishly pretty eyes?'

Leonora glanced at her parents. Francine was indeed the loveliest woman in the room. Elegantly dressed in beaded silver satin, she looked younger and more beautiful than ever. A hint of rouge reddened her lips and a tiny smear of saffron edged with charcoal emphasised her pale, well-shaped eyes. Beside her stood Herbert, glass in one hand, pipe in the other, his brow furrowed as he looked back at his daughter with a glower intended to put her firmly in her place.

Leonora shuddered, chilled by the unspoken anger trapped inside her. When she looked at her father she saw not his fine blue saxony coat and yellow waistcoat but his naked, bloated belly bearing down on Daisy Kimble; not his stylishly cut trousers and polished shoes but his distended genitals and sweating buttocks. Beneath the splendid garb the gentleman of quality was no more than a brute, ugly in his nakedness.

'Leonora?' Francine spoke gently, disturbed by the brooding expression on her daughter's face and acutely aware that a hush had descended upon the room while this silent dispute passed between father and daughter. 'Leonora, my dear, did you hear Lady Mildred speaking to you? She will think you very ungracious if you decline to answer so simple a question.'

Something shifted inside Leonora. She lifted her chin in that way she had of showing her defiance, of giving quiet rein to her anger. 'A puppy,' she announced in a loud, clear voice, her eyes holding those of her father with a look that challenged him, boldly and quite fearlessly, to contradict her. 'Papa has finally agreed to Joseph having one of Squire Russell's puppies. Is that not so, Papa?'

Herbert stared at her, his mouth agape and his fingers gripping his wineglass so tightly that the knuckles were turning white and bloodless.

'Herbert, can this be true?' Francine laid her hand on her husband's arm. She was amazed by his sudden change of heart, especially on a matter about which he had already expressed such strong feelings. 'So Joseph is to be allowed the dog, after all?'

'It is perfectly true,' Leonora announced. She held aloft a single golden guinea and turned prettily on tip-toe until every eye in the room was upon her. A flush had risen to her cheeks and her eyes were shining with excitement. 'Papa and I had a private wager this afternoon and I was the winner.' Once again she fixed her gaze on Herbert's ashen face as, still with the coin raised high above her head, she added bitterly:

'Here is the guinea that says my brother Joseph *shall* have his pup.'

Herbert cleared his throat noisily into the silence that followed her words. He knew he was trapped. The scheming minx had caught him in a public snare from which he had no other means of extricating himself with dignity. He wanted to stride across the room, take hold of that impudent girl and shake her until her teeth rattled. Caution alone trimmed his fury. So far she had said nothing of the afternoon's unpleasant episode. If this was to be the price of her silence then so be it. To be forced to tolerate an animal in the house, however distasteful the prospect, was a small enough exchange for his peace of mind.

'What my daughter says is quite true,' he said at last, growling the words through clenched teeth. 'I have indeed agreed to my son taking one of Squire Russell's pups.'

'Oh, well played, Miss Leonora,' Lord Mornington bellowed with a guffaw of amusement.

Lady Mildred tapped her fan against the portly chest of her host and laughed in his face. 'My compliments, Herbert. The child is as cunning as she is beautiful. She not only won her wager and her guinea, she has also tricked you into making your promise public.'

'And, by George, we'll see the promise kept,' Sir Reginald roared. 'By my boots, sir, you are pledged indeed ... pledged indeed.'

While Joseph beamed with pleasure and Herbert struggled to contain his rage behind a smile, Leonora sipped her sherry and moved about the sophisticated company with an air of quiet triumph. This day had taught her much about herself and a great deal about those who shared her world. She had seen how the force of a man's lust could make him humble himself before a common servant, and how the power of ownership could bend a girl, without effort or protest, to her master's will. She had seen the fear of exposure stopper her father's rage and force him to accommodate her demands, and so had learned that a little knowledge, skilfully played, may outweigh the greater authority. And more than this: she had tasted power for the first time and found it much to her liking.

CHAPTER THREE

I

After much argument and deliberation, Joseph finally settled upon the name Lancer for his adored new pet. He was encouraged in this by his two elder brothers, whose term-master at Harrow bore the same surname along with other quite noticeable similarities.

'An honourable name for an animal of such distinct characteristics,' Charles quipped, much amused by the pup's inability to remain upright for longer than a few precarious seconds.

'And as close a likeness to his wobbly old namesake as nature could ever be expected to provide,' Jonathan agreed, roaring with laughter as the pup's saliva dribbled over his brother's fingers.

The human object of their discussion, one Roland Algernon Lancer, was a tall, gangly individual with ginger hair and a long, sharp nose from which droplets of moisture had to be wiped or sniffed away from time to time. Over the years the contents of his mind had become pickled with alcohol, the sharp edges of his intellect fogged and softened by an over-use of opiates. He developed an impediment of speech in the vain hope of concealing his drunkard's slur, and a lurching, staggering gait designed to keep his body in the perpendicular. His pupils had become known as Lancers from their habit of mimicking their tutor's afflictions; swaying from side to side when standing, walking with a lurch and pronouncing with a distinct lisp what little Latin they had managed to assimilate. During the last Harrow term, these young Lancers had so excelled themselves on the sports field that their affectations had become a matter of high fashion to be copied in earnest by the more impressionable younger boys. For a term at least, a tutor too addled to be of any real benefit to his pupils might have been flattered to know that his physical imperfections had become vogue.

When the five-week-old red and white setter was sold to Herbert Shelley for his son's birthday, it was found to be still unsteady on its feet, a furry bundle supported upon elongated and very undisciplined legs. Despite every effort to keep itself upright, its movements were constantly thrown into disarray by an unwieldy tail; a heaving, pitching appendage over which the poor creature appeared to have no control. So they had thought to call him Lancer, and his cold, wet nose and dribbling mouth had eventually settled the matter.

Before parting with his money Herbert had insisted on having the pup examined by an expert, Mr Freddie Brocklehurst of Notting Hill, who promptly pronounced it cow-hocked, with splayed feet, and too heavy-headed for its breed. Knowing that the rest of the litter had been sold for upwards of twenty-five guineas a brace, but that a faulted dog was as good as useless to its master, Herbert refused to pay the full gun-dog price for what he called the Squire's runt, and eventually closed the deal at only six guineas. Outside in the street, the expert congratulated his client on a deal well made.

'You'll find it be a fair enough animal for a house-dog,'

Freddie Brocklehurst said, touching the rim of his hat respectfully as he pocketed the fee of one guinea agreed for his services. 'An' it'll make a fine-looking animal when it's full grown, you mark my works, Mr Shelley.'

Herbert grunted a curt reply and quickly took his leave of the man. There was a smell about Freddie Brocklehurst that was offensive to his nostrils; the fusty scent of unwashed flesh and rarely laundered clothes. The proximity of the pup was no less distasteful to him, especially since he so heartily begrudged the gift. He resented to the point of fury Leonora's clever blackmail, yet he was unable to put the matter to rights by confronting her. It was a damnable situation, and one he was powerless to resolve in any positive way. However pressing the circumstances, no man could be expected to discuss his carnal practices with his own ten-year-old daughter. Instead he had begun to watch her as he might a stranger, his temper bristling at the barely veiled contempt in her eyes whenever she looked back at him. No matter how he glowered and postured, he could not induce her to turn her gaze from his until he had first looked away. He had never cared very much for Leonora; she was too much a Cavendish for his tastes. Now he determined to guard his privacy more closely and keep her at a cautious distance, like an enemy in his own camp.

On his return from Kenton Street with the pup, an ecstatic Joseph found his sister waiting for him in the school room on the second floor.

'We must share him, Lia, just as we have always shared everything,' he declared, dumping the ungainly animal into Leonora's lap without regard for her pretty muslin gown. It wriggled and squirmed until its front paws gained purchase on her lacy bodice and its wet, sticky tongue came within reach of her face. With a shudder of displeasure she rose to her feet, gripping the writhing animal at arm's length as she offered it back to her brother. Its clumsy claws had damaged her frock and its tongue left sticky patches of saliva on her skin.

'Not now, Joseph,' she said, managing only a tight little

55

smile. 'I think I prefer very old, very sensible dogs who keep their feet on the ground and their tongues firmly under control.'

Joseph was crestfallen. 'Does that mean you don't like our birthday gift?'

'*Your* gift, Joseph.'

'But Lia, you were the one who persuaded Papa. I thought ...'

'I persuaded Papa on your behalf, not my own. And yes, of course I like him, but I will enjoy his company much more when he is trained into obedience and well past the age of drooling over us all with such frenzied abandon.'

Joseph narrowed his short-sighted blue eyes and smiled an apology. 'I'm afraid his claws have accidentally damaged your frock.'

'Yes, Joseph, and I hope you learn from this small mishap that dogs and delicate fabrics are best kept apart.'

Her brother grinned and blew a small kiss at her through pursed lips. 'Are we forgiven, Lia?' he asked.

'Yes, of course. Now, will you *please* take Lancer outdoors so that we can all have a little peace?'

She watched him walk away, his arms laden with the wriggling mass of russet and cream fur, his eyes screwed tightly shut against the frantically lapping tongue. She smiled and shook her head. The little dog's antics were so comic, his brown eyes so soft and appealing that he had endeared himself to everyone in the house within minutes of his arrival. Only Herbert remained totally immune to the lively, infectious personality that brought disruption to the Shelley household. He behaved with such hostility toward the animal that the desirability of keeping a safe distance between them was the only lesson Lancer was ever to learn of his own accord.

During the afternoon of the day of the pup's arrival, hasty arrangements were made for Daisy Kimble's employment in the home of an elderly widower in Whitechapel. At the same time a bewildered stable lad, only recently employed and loudly protesting his innocence of any crime, was soundly thrashed by his master and discharged on the spot. A grim-faced Herbert Shelley, seemingly scandalised by behaviour too unseemly to describe, allowed his silence to imply that some gross impropriety between the two had led to their dismissal.

'And I thought she was such a *good* girl,' Mrs Norris said, sniffing back a tear and dabbing at her eyes with her apron.

'But did you suspect nothing?' Francine asked, distressed by the situation.

The fat woman shook her head, then blew her nose into her apron and said: 'Nothing at all, ma'am. Never saw 'em together nor 'eard Daisy mention 'is name. Not an inklin' did she give, not so much as an inklin' that such wicked things was goin' on right under our own roof. An 'er so young ... no more'n a little child.'

Francine turned to Anabel: 'How could we have allowed this to happen?' she asked. 'Oh, I knew Daisy was unhappy. Indeed, some weeks ago I even had reason to suspect that some man ...'

'I recall your concern,' Anabel told her.

'But that young boy came to us only a few days ago, and surely he is not yet old enough to ... I just do not understand all this, Anabel.'

'The master knows best, Miss Francine,' Anabel reminded her, careful to address her mistress correctly while others were within hearing.

'Yes, I'm sure he does, and yet ...'

As Francine turned her troubled gaze from the weeping Daisy to the glowering and strutting master of the house, Anabel suspected that she had guessed the truth. A moment later the fancy was gone, dispelled by the knowledge that Francine would never place a vulnerable child within reach of a man she believed capable of such behaviour. She cast a warning glance at Leonora, saw the rebellious expression in her eyes and willed her to remain silent. Then she added, still staring pointedly at Leonora:

'We must none of us question the master's judgement ... *or* his authority.'

Daisy left in floods of tears, wearing only a plain working

dress and bonnet, and with her shoulders huddled into a thin cotton shawl. In future she would be forced to buy whatever she could afford from one of the many rag fairs where cast-off clothes, often ragged and flea-infested, could be had for a few pennies. The fastidious Francine was prepared to dress her servants out of her own pocket rather than allow such dubious garments into the house, though few but the wealthiest of mistresses followed her example. Those items of clothing recently bought or altered for Daisy were now forfeit, and would be passed on to the girl who took her place. The weeping parlour maid was only too well aware of the privileges she was losing and the duress that awaited her in Whitechapel. Her new master was a gouty old penny-pincher who chose to live in near squalor rather than pay out good money for decent servants. He had only agreed to take Daisy at reduced rates due to her age and the circumstances of her dismissal, and Herbert Shelley had left her in no doubt as to the extra duties she would be expected to perform in her new position. She was now damaged goods, little better than a common whore, and would receive such treatment as was appropriate to her station. As she followed the pock-marked groom hired to take her by foot to Whitechapel, she hung her head and wrung her hands in distress, muttering all the while:

"'Tisn't fair ... 'tisn't fair ... 'tisn't fair ...'

Leonora witnessed her departure with mixed feelings. Daisy was being punished for betraying the trust of her mistress by bedding with the master, yet she was surely innocent of any *deliberate* crime. Circumstances had simply borne her along like a helpless piece of flotsam to be deposited wherever the tides dictated. She was firstly the victim of her own inferiority, then of her master's lusts, and finally of Leonora's guilty knowledge. It seemed to Leonora that the two most critical extremes in life were poverty and power, and where poverty fell upon the female, there rested the greater affliction. No matter how low in life a man might descend, no matter how crushed by privation, there would always be some woman lower than himself: wife, whore, daughter or maidservant judged to be of lesser standing and therefore subservient to

him. Even through her child's eyes she could see the injustice
of it all. And for want of voice or status a blameless stable lad
had become Herbert's decoy, tossed into the furore on a point
of expediency. With the culpable parties so clearly identified,
who would dare cast suspicious glances at the master of the
house?

'That was very clever of you, Papa.'

'Eh? What? What's that you say?' A deep crimson flush
sprang to Herbert's cheeks and spread rapidly down to his
neck. His black stock and white linen were suddenly uncomfortably tight across his throat. Francine placed her small
hand between his shoulder blades, ready to pat his back while
he blustered and spluttered into a handkerchief.

'Do you not agree, Mama?' Leonora persisted when
Herbert's choking fit had subsided. 'Was it not *terribly* clever of
dear Papa to discover the guilty parties and punish them,
promptly and fairly, for their sins?'

Herbert squared his shoulders and scowled down at his
daughter. 'You would do well to remember this day, my girl. I
am a man who believes in dispensing justice with a firm
hand.'

'Oh, you need have no fear on that score, Papa,' she
replied. 'I will most certainly remember this day. In fact, you
may wager a whole guinea on it.'

Herbert's face purpled with rage. 'Go to your room at
once,' he hissed through his teeth. 'Anabel, see to it that she
keeps to her room, alone, for the rest of the day. And as for
you, Joseph, you may take that stinking, slavering animal out
of my sight *at once*.'

Upstairs in her room, Leonora took up her needlework and
carefully studied the design of leaves and flowers representing
the four seasons. Her lips were curved in a small, secret smile
that bore just a hint of malice.

'You must not provoke your father in that way, Leonora,'
Anabel said after a lengthy silence. 'Let it be enough that
Daisy is gone and Joseph has his puppy. Do not torment the
master with your spiteful remarks and silent confrontations.

Such games are very dangerous. I thought he would strike you just now. He was furious, yet you faced him as if ... as if ...'

'I do not fear him, Anabel, no matter if you, or he, believe I should.'

'Then you are a fool,' the woman told her. 'Oh, Leonora, will you never understand? You *should* fear him. You *must*. As master of the house he has power over us all ... even you.'

'Then perhaps one day I will have the pleasure of showing him what *real* power can do.'

Anabel became exasperated. 'Oh, yes, you have your fine dreams for the future, my little madam, but what of your life until then? You are but ten years old, Leonora, and he is your father. If it so pleases him to be rid of you, he could send you away tomorrow and neither I nor your Mama nor your brothers could do anything to prevent it.'

Leonora's eyes widened and the smile faded from her face. 'What? Be rid of me? Send me away?'

'To a school, to some private establishment so far from here that regular visits would be impossible. He might even send you abroad, to some foreign place.'

'He wouldn't ...' The child looked horrified. 'He *couldn't*.'

'Oh but he could,' Anabel said. 'It is his right.'

'*His* right? Why must you always speak of *his* right? What of *my* rights, Anabel?'

'Oh, child ... child, will you never learn that *you* have no rights? If you cannot think of yourself in this matter, then at least consider Joseph and your Mama. Do not push your father too far. Do not force him to punish you.'

'It is he who should be punished, not I.'

'And not Daisy, and certainly not that innocent stable lad, yet still it is so, they *are* punished,' Anabel concluded.

Leonora fell silent, her hands resting in her lap and her eyes downcast. When at last she spoke again her voice was calm and her eyes glistened with unshed tears. Knowing her as she did, Anabel guessed that it cost her dearly to yield when pride and instinct told her she was in the right.

'Very well, Anabel, from now on I shall have a care for my father's anger,' she promised.

*

During this time of emotional upheaval Leonora developed a thirst for knowledge of her Cavendish cousins and their mutual ancestors. She had an excellent memory, and there were times when she astounded Francine by recounting some past event in such detail as to bring history alive with her words, or by describing the particulars of a gown worn by some splendid matriarch at a function held centuries before she was born. Her knowledge of Beresford Hall was both substantial and quite extraordinary when it was remembered that everything she knew had been pieced together over the years from the stories her mother told her. She spoke of the beautifully preserved cathedral hall as if she had seen it for herself; of the stained glass windows and hanging chandeliers, the branched staircase of Italian marble, curved galleries and lofty Gothic arches; of the magnificent, vaulted Long Gallery where hung the painted ghosts of arrogant, ambitious and wonderfully colourful men and women of a dozen generations.

'All this is part of your heritage, Leonora,' Francine constantly reminded her. 'The Cavendish blood is in your veins.'

'I know that, Mama. I can *feel* it. And one day Beresford Hall will be my home. I feel that, too.'

Although Herbert had forbidden all such conversations, mother and daughter came to treasure those times when they could sit together and speak in lowered voices of the Cavendish family, past and present. For Francine these meetings were a welcome respite after the years of silence in which Beresford Hall and its occupants had become like shadows, precious, fragile things stored away in the darkest corners of her mind.

As Leonora listened and learned she began to develop a tremendous sense of her own identity. That first illustrious Cavendish, Joshua Cecil, Baron of Westlake and First Earl of Beresford, had begun life as the mere seventh son of a baron. He was without title or inheritance, yet he coerced a king in order to win himself a place in history, then claimed a ruined

61

abbey on which to found himself a dynasty. He too had discovered how to play upon the weaknesses and vanities of others in order to achieve his own ends. He too had possessed a will to succeed that would not submit to mere circumstances of birth.

'This shall be mine,' the virtually penniless Joshua had sworn when first he saw the magnificence of Beresford Abbey and its thousands of forested acres. 'By the Devil I swear all this shall one day belong to *me*.'

And so it had, and three hundred years later a ten-year-old girl nurtured a strange affinity for the ancestor who had beguiled and manipulated a king in order to further his own ambitions. Her own genealogy sprang from his elder brother, Rupert, thereby excluding her from Joshua's line of inheritance, yet she believed herself to be as much his legatee as were the children of the present Earl. When Sir Robert Cavendish married his cousin Mary in 1614, and when Sir Gregory married *his* cousin Sarah in 1729, the two family lines were inextricably linked. And now, in this summer of 1815, Leonora Shelley took to herself the knowledge that the blood of Beresford's earls ran in her veins, and with this discovery came the first real awareness of her own destiny.

II

By the end of November Herbert had seen a considerable reduction in his fortunes. Certain of his investments had proved ill-advised, and now he was gambling more heavily than ever in an effort to make up his losses. His luck had peaked in mid-August and dried up completely by the end of the month. Then a run of bad cards had forced him to leave the gaming tables at White's for want of ready cash to meet his immediate obligations. Now he felt obliged to withdraw from Boodle's while his credit was still good. On Wednesday evening he made his excuses and prepared to leave early with the intention of doing his gambling in a less public place until his fortunes altered. At all costs he must avoid any hint of rumour, any whispered speculation as to the state of his finances. Neither friendship nor loyalty existed in any depth around the gaming tables, where even a man of substance might be plunged into ruin if rumour branded him a bad risk and his credit was discontinued during a run of bad luck. He had explained as much to Madame Marie-Louise Jordan the previous afternoon while she bent over a chair in her bedroom with her skirts thrown over her head and her huge, quivering buttocks swallowing up his genitals with every thrust of his hips.

'Watmough's and Grant's are refusing to extend my credit. Lean forward just a little, my dear ... ah ... yes ... es. I am badly in need of a loan. Nothing substantial ... ah ... perhaps a thousand or two ... ah ... mere petty cash, as it were. What's that you say, my dear?'

A series of groans had issued from the seat of the chair, where the face of Madame Marie-Louise was buried among the cushions and covered by the folds of her gown and petticoats. From this mound of frills and satin flounces her fleshy buttocks protruded in all their milk-white magnificence. Herbert grabbed at them with both hands and began to thrust with increased urgency. Although his calf muscles ached from standing so long in that awkward position, he managed to bring some extra effort into the situation and a minute later ejaculated with a loud roar of satisfaction. He quickly withdrew himself, moved away from the chair and reached for the port, leaving Marie-Louise to pull down her skirts and emerge, red-faced and tousle-haired, from the pile of cushions.

'I believe you have a relative,' he said. 'A rather dashing young man connected in some way with Mortimer's in the Strand.'

'Oh, *mon cheri*, that would be Jean-Paul, my ... er ... *brother-in-law*,' she told him, smoothing her hair. Her lip rouge was smudged and her bodice remained unlaced, exposing one large, udder-like breast with its rough pink nipple. 'Would you like me to speak to him on your behalf?'

63

'Perhaps an introduction?' he suggested. 'And, of course, a firm recommendation from yourself?'

'Ah, but Jean-Paul will require security if he is to use his influence to obtain a loan for you.'

'And he shall have it,' Herbert promised. 'Let me assure you, my dear, that I am not without the means to secure such a loan. My present problem is merely a shortage of cash, no doubt a temporary shortage but damned inconvenient for all that.'

Madame Marie-Louise leaned close to the mirror to examine the ruby earrings he had brought for her that afternoon. They must have been worth at least eight hundred pounds, and they were certainly not the first gift she had received from him. Herbert Shelley was a very generous man when it came to buying the kind of pleasures he enjoyed. Perhaps she and Jean-Paul were about to discover yet another way of turning that generosity to their mutual advantage.

'I will gladly speak to Jean-Paul on your behalf, *mon cheri*,' she agreed, stroking her exposed breast with both hands.

'Thank you, my dear, I should be much obliged.'

Herbert was turning that brief conversation over in his mind as he left the gaming room on Wednesday night. If Jean-Paul Jordan could get him a loan from Mortimer's, he would use every penny of the money at the tables. By doing so he would convince the gambling world that he was still on top and keep his creditors at bay while winning back the money he had already lost; and his own bank would be none the wiser.

The biggest single drain on his resources was his financial commitment to a new shipping project in Scotland. Three years after the first successful steam boat, the *Comet*, was put into service on the Clyde, investors were clamouring to part with their money in the hope of making a quick killing. For some the profits were enormous, but for many an inexperienced entrepreneur the problems of design, engineering and building proved insurmountable. Herbert Shelley's pet enterprise had got off to a promising start, only to be dogged for the last three months by every possible disaster from toppled cranes to typhus among the work force. On the very day the Scottish banks began to express concern over late schedules and soaring costs, the senior engineer and major investor, Mr Isaac Phelps, was shot to death at his club by a jealous mistress. Work ceased completely as lawyers became bogged down by the complexities of the dead man's will, and long delays left his business associates struggling to avoid bankruptcy. Herbert had already been called upon to make further investments which he could ill afford, and with the cost of steel now touching fifty-two pounds a ton, little or no progress was being made. Each investor knew that to pull out at this stage would be to seal the yard's fate *and* accrue tremendous personal losses. Even now there was hope, if enough cash were found to safeguard existing contracts, but like all games of chance the stakes were high, and the danger lay in throwing good money after bad to the point of personal ruin. Herbert was caught between the lion and the wolf. He could pull out now and lose everything, or he could re-invest in the hope of future profits. This was the worst possible time for him to be faced with such decisions, when all his commitments were either running at a loss or tied up beyond his reach, and when gambling debts were once again beginning to overtake him. It was altogether a damnable state of affairs.

In the foyer of the club he allowed one of the stewards to help him on with his overcoat.

'Thank you, William.'

'You're leaving early tonight, Mr Shelley.'

'An appointment at Almack's,' he lied. 'Tiresome but necessary, I fear.'

'Indeed, sir. Here are your gloves and hat, sir.'

He was pulling on his gloves when he witnessed the arrival at the club of Sir Oscar Cavendish and his sons Malcolm and Horace. He cursed softly under his breath. The last thing he wanted was to find himself trapped in a situation where he might be required to give account of himself to the Earl. The insufferable Horace could be heard boasting in loud tones of his latest invitation to one of the Prince Regent's levees. At thirteen the boy was pompous in the extreme and too full of his own importance to care whether he was liked or hated. Very handsome and well built, at first glance he bore a striking resemblance to Jonathan, but beyond the strong family likeness the boys had absolutely nothing in common. His own son was more the gentleman than that particular Cavendish could ever be.

By complete contrast the Earl's heir, Malcolm, was a sober young gentleman with thick brown hair and a solemn gaze. His clothes were cut on less flamboyant lines, his choice of colours was more conservative and his manners altogether more proper than those of his younger brother. He was also as quietly well-spoken as the Earl himself, with none of Horace's belligerent demands for attention.

Unable to avoid a meeting without giving offence, Herbert waited near the door of the cloak room, scowling thoughtfully as he dusted the rim of his topper. He had hoped that marriage to Francine would eventually afford him access to the privileged inner circle of Cavendish associates, but to his great disappointment no such invitation had ever been forthcoming. For years Sir Oscar had financed the education of Jonathan and Charles, sending them to be educated along with his own sons and giving them a small allowance for their personal use. He had also, on perhaps a half dozen separate occasions, shown great generosity toward his cousin-in-law while steadfastly refusing to add the Shelley name to his personal guest list. And yet, even after fourteen years, Herbert entertained the hope that this situation might be rectified. Sir Oscar had a particular fondness for Francine, who in turn had a very beautiful daughter who would soon be of marriageable age. While Herbert could never seriously anticipate an alliance between his daughter and the young heir, he allowed himself to hope that Sir Oscar might be persuaded to settle upon her such property or income as might raise her to the level of his younger sons. There were also a trio of Cavendish daughters to be considered as wives for his own sons, although two of the girls were reputed to be as ill-natured as their brother Horace, while the third was said to be a saint, but only because she lacked the wits to be otherwise.

'Good evening to you, Shelley.' The Earl looked down at him from his great height but neither smiled nor offered his hand. 'I trust I find you in good mettle?'

'Passably well,' Herbert bowed with a click of his heels. 'And you, Sir Oscar?'

'The same. The same. And what of Mrs Shelley? How is my dear cousin?'

'As beautiful as ever,' Herbert replied in ingratiating tones, 'though troubled by the same small cough which afflicts her every year around this time.'

Sir Oscar stooped over his pipe, his brow furrowed. He was a man of enviable good looks, broad-shouldered and youthful at fifty-five, still agile and muscular despite his great wealth and the reputed splendour of his table. His strong grey-blond hair showed no signs of thinning, his face remained ruggedly handsome, his teeth reasonably well preserved. He was garbed in his usual princely manner: mulberry tailed coat with high velvet collar and crested buttons; crisp white shirt and stock, light grey trousers and topper. Here was elegance that could neither be bought over the counter nor cut into shape by a tailor. Oscar Cavendish was one of those enviable individuals whose breeding would show itself even if his body were clothed in rags. He dipped two fingers into the pocket of his waistcoat, withdrew a small white card and began to write upon its plain underside. Then he handed the card to Herbert with a flourish.

'Tell her to see this man, Sir Marcus Shaw. He is a physician of quite remarkable talents. I use him myself from time to time, and Lady Alyce has absolute confidence in him.'

Sir Oscar tapped his cane against the palm of his hand and wondered if this was a suitable time and place in which to speak to Shelley about his finances. It had come to his ears that the man was once again gambling like a fool and putting his name, and his money, into too many poor investments. Sir Oscar could not be expected to subsidise him indefinitely, especially when the quarterly bills from his tailor were hardly less than those of a nobleman. Something must be done to curtail his extravagances, and soon, before he plunged Francine and her children into poverty. He must indeed be brought to heel, but perhaps the busy foyer of a gambling club was not the ideal place for such a serious discussion.

Herbert bowed again as he pocketed the physician's name and address. He hated to be in the Earl's debt, even in so small a matter. He had always sensed that Sir Oscar held him in contempt as the man without breeding who had married, however distantly, into his illustrious family. And how Herbert needed to be a part of that family. He hungered for great wealth and prestige, for a large country house and a life-style more compatible with his self-esteem. He wanted so much more than the Earl's tolerance and the occasional recourse to Cavendish charity. What really galled him was the ease with which these things were being withheld from him. Both his credit rating and his position in society would be permanently established if only he could gain this man's stamp of approval.

'You must visit Beresford Hall,' Sir Oscar was saying, his deep blue gaze already seeking other interests beyond the panelled foyer of the club.

'And you must visit us in Garden Square,' Herbert replied with measured insincerity.

'I'll bid you good evening, then.'

'Good evening, Sir Oscar.'

'Be sure and give my message to Mrs Shelley.'

'Indeed I will,' Herbert promised with another stiff bow.

At the door of the club he paused to adjust his hat and button his overcoat against the chilly evening air. Beyond the foyer he could see the Earl in earnest conversation with Sir John Douglas, the honourable member for Studley West. The vociferous tones of young Horace reached his ears even across that distance, and once again he considered the possibility of wedding his interests more closely into that esteemed family. It would suit his ambitions and his sense of irony to see the imperious Leonora given in marriage to that monstrously arrogant young man.

By now Herbert knew without doubt that his affairs had

reached the point of crisis. An interview with Jean-Paul Jordan had left him simmering with indignation and no closer to obtaining the cash loan he so desperately needed. With the impudence of the devil and obviously hoping to take fullest advantage of Herbert's circumstances, Jordan had offered an unsecured, short-term personal loan of fifteen hundred pounds at precisely *double* the bank's normal rate of interest. Herbert told him to go to hell.

So far he had managed to avoid any interview with Sir Oscar that might reveal the full extent of his losses, but with the final collapse of the Clyde shipping concern he knew he could maintain his silence no longer. Something had to be done without delay. He had already waited too long for the turn-around, the winning hand that would herald the start of another lucky streak. He needed cash to tide him over until the cards were back in his favour, and before the doors of nervous creditors slammed in his face.

III

Leonora had not seen her father so agitated since the day he found her in his bedroom, spying on him and Daisy Kimble. He arrived home in the middle of the afternoon while Francine was still resting, and from the hallway Leonora could hear him muttering to himself as he paced his private sitting room. Some time later she was forced to duck into a shadowed alcove when he suddenly burst from the room and, slamming the door behind him, strode to the main staircase. A scullery maid took one look at his thunderous expression and scuttled back the way she had come, scattering ash across the tiles as she went. His footsteps rang out with every tread, marking his progress up the stairs to the first floor. Fearing that her mother was to become the victim of his black mood, Leonora, though uncertain of her objective, lifted her skirts and hurried after him. As she reached the top of the stairs she heard him slam the door of the drawing room and resume his steady, heavy-footed pacing.

She tip-toed across the landing as if heading for her room, but paused at the start of the passage and peered cautiously around the angle of the wall. From here she could see the door of her mother's small sitting room and, almost directly opposite that, the double doors of the drawing room. Even as she wondered what her next move was to be, the double doors were flung back on their hinges and Herbert appeared, looking no less agitated than when she had seen him last. He strode across the lobby and raised his fist to rap at Francine's door, only to draw back abruptly, as if some gloomy, last-minute thought had arisen to alter his intentions. With a sigh he started back across the lobby, stopped in mid-stride to scowl thoughtfully at his boots, then turned decisively and returned to Francine's door. Once there he merely re-enacted the same small performance. He raised his hand to knock, faltered at the last moment and, after first lowering his head so that his forehead rested momentarily upon his fist, returned dejectedly to the drawing room. Minutes later he emerged again, this time to hurry from the house like a man pursued, leaving a trail of slammed doors and jittery servants in his wake.

'What is it?' Anabel asked in a whisper. She had hurried downstairs to find Leonora standing in the hall. 'Leonora! Have you and the master crossed swords again?'

'No, Anabel, but something is very wrong. Papa was in a terrible mood just now, stamping and glowering and slamming doors.'

'And was it none of your doing?'

Leonora shook her head. 'None, I promise you. He came home very upset, went first to his study, then to the drawing room, and now, as you see, has left the house again in a great hurry. Is Mama awake?'

'No, she's still sleeping, and perhaps it would be wise to say nothing to her of this.'

That evening, news of a dreadful tragedy was brought to

Francine by her friend and neighbour, Caroline Rainer. She came in a flurry of rustling pink taffeta and bouncing ringlets, a frivolous woman of adolescent affectations who ravaged her face with harsh cosmetics rather than acquiesce to a long-departed youth. She was a practised gossip who dedicated much time and energy to her art. Her stock-in-trade was the whispered word, the lie, the subtle innuendo; all those tasty scraps of other people's lives upon which society fed with such relish. No sooner had that day's news reached her ears than she was dressing and ordering her coach, and well within the hour she was on her way. She wanted Francine to have this particular snippet from a reliable source rather than hear it as common tittle-tattle, flavoured and embellished to suit the teller's taste.

She swept into Francine's private sitting room and sank into the most dominantly placed chair with the light from the big windows at her back. There she fidgeted the air with her fan and begged a whiff of smelling salts and a glass of port before commencing her story. These preparations were essential in that they prepared both Caroline and her audience for what was to come. The correct balance between enthusiasm and reluctance must be scrupulously maintained lest the bearer of an ill intelligence become a party to the smear.

'Such a *dreadful* thing to have happened,' she said at last, shaking her head until the twin streamers on her bonnet danced this way and that. 'And you, Francine, must feel it more deeply than most, since you are so closely acquainted with the Wallace family. I fear the news is bad, my dear, so you must prepare yourself well to receive it.'

Francine sighed. 'While I appreciate your regard for my feelings, Caroline, I find the delay not at all helpful. Do please continue.'

'It is a tragedy, my dear. A tragedy of so shocking a nature that I can scarce speak of it without weeping afresh. It concerns Mr Jeffrey Wallace, who recently involved himself in several of your husband's business ventures ... or so I am led to believe.'

She allowed the statement to hang in the air while

scrutinising Francine's expression for a sign of confirmation or denial. When no such indication was forthcoming, she sighed and continued:

'It all took place at Boodle's this morning, not an hour before His Grace was due to sit down at that very table. There were eight players in all, including Jeffrey Wallace and his friend, that nice Mr Hallam-Spencer from Cheltenham. The others had thought it politic to withdraw from the game when the stakes began to rocket, leaving Jeffrey to play against Sir Humphrey Allsop. Jeffrey was losing heavily, though he seemed not to give a fig for his losses.'

Here she paused to close her eyes and pass a hand delicately across her forehead as if the effort of relating the story had exhausted her.

'Please go on, Caroline,' Francine prompted. 'Another glass of sherry, perhaps? More smelling salts? Anabel, fetch Mrs Rainer a foot-stool and a cushion for her head.'

After a few moments Caroline declared herself quite recovered and able to continue her story, only pausing here and there in order to create the maximum dramatic effect.

'The last card to be turned was the Knave of Diamonds,' she said. 'And they do say that poor Jeffrey had ten thousand pounds riding on a black Queen, though, of course, not a soul would have guessed it from the way he behaved. So calm, he was, and such a *gentleman*. He shrugged off his losses as if they were of no consequence, and agreed without hesitation to Sir Humphrey's suggestion that another card be drawn with the stakes now set at double or nothing.'

'And he lost,' Francine said in a flat tone.

Caroline nodded dramatically. 'He most certainly did, my dear. Twenty thousand pounds to top his previous losses.'

'Then he is ruined? Is that what you have to tell me, Caroline? Has my husband's closest business associate brought himself to ruin at the gaming tables?'

'Oh, much worse than that, my dear,' Caroline said, leaning toward Francine with flushed cheeks and the satisfied glint of the true gossip in her eyes. 'He excused himself from the table, went upstairs to one of those pretty little withdrawing rooms where patrons are invited to rest between games, and he ... he ...'

'Yes?' Francine prompted, her voice hoarse with dread.

'He ... he ... *blew his brains out.*'

In the silence that followed, all colour drained from Francine's face and her eyes widened to horrified orbs. She stared at her visitor and saw neither the smile of pleasure on her lips nor the glitter of triumph in her eyes.

'Oh, good Lord ... oh, that poor, poor man.'

A heavy sense of dread began to descend upon her. Later she would sorrow for the tragic young man and the family struck down by his foolishness, but for the moment her thoughts refused to be pushed beyond the fear that her own husband might be dragged low by these events. Even she, with her minimal grasp of the complexities of commerce, was aware that one man's fall from prosperity might well precipitate another's ruin.

'Excuse me, Caroline,' she said at last. 'I suddenly feel rather unwell. Please forgive me ... Anabel, will you be kind enough to see Mrs Rainer to her coach?'

She rose from her chair and left the room by way of the inner door leading to her bedroom. A few minutes later Caroline Rainer stepped into her carriage after pausing only long enough to pull on her soft kid gloves and adjust the ties on her bonnet. She was elated. Her news had been imparted with such dramatic effect that she carried away with her an excellent addendum to her story. The transparently honest Francine had revealed a concern more immediate and much more personal than the death of an acquaintance. It was obvious that Herbert Shelley *was* financially involved with the dead man.

At twenty-seven Harrington Court, Herbert dined in some style with his mistress. The first course was a hot and spicy turtle soup, followed by roast beef, saddle of mutton, venison, lamb and pork, with cod, cold salmon and Whitstable oysters. A selection of sauces and stuffings accompanied each dish, and the centre of the table boasted a dozen small dishes containing fruit, nuts, preserves, cheese, jellies, tarts and pies.

With every course came a different wine, from a light sherry to champagne to burgundy. By the end of the meal he found it necessary to unfasten his trousers so that his stomach might expand to accommodate the huge amount of food he had eaten.

He was in much better spirits since hearing of the tragedy at Boodle's, and he blessed the stroke of cowardice that had rendered him unable to face Francine with news of his financial difficulties. Now, instead of making that humiliating confession and begging for funds to meet his debts, he could simply sit back and allow Francine to assume that the suicide had left him on the brink of ruin. Not even Sir Oscar Cavendish could hold him responsible for debts incurred by a dishonest associate who blew out his own brains rather than face those people whose trust he had betrayed. The letter would help, of course. When a tearful Francine threw herself upon the generosity of her cousin with that well-worded letter as evidence, who but a man of stone could resist her pleas?

'So, you will take no money from my brother-in-law, *mon cheri*?'

Madame Marie-Louise had slumped back in her chair with her stays undone for comfort and her cheeks reddened with wine and brandy. She burped noisily and giggled, but there was a hardness in her eyes when she surveyed her guest over the unsightly debris of their meal.

'Not a penny,' Herbert declared, without noticing that his speech had become slurred. 'The man is either a fool or a thief to offer loans at such high interest.'

'But if the banks will not extend your credit ...?'

'To hell with the banks. And to hell with your brother-in-law if he thinks to make his dishonest profit out of a man of my standing and experience.'

Marie-Louise shrugged and pouted her lips. 'Then perhaps you were not, after all, so desperate for this money as you pretended to be, *mon cheri.*'

'Not so desperate as to fall into *that* kind of snare, and not at all, I'll wager, once my dear wife hears of recent events.'

'Ah, that is too bad ... but perhaps next time ...?'

'What? What's that you say?'

'Nothing, *mon cheri*, I merely drink a toast to your continued success.'

Leonora had sensed the undercurrents and unspoken anxieties long before dinner, when an envelope was delivered bearing the tight, spidery scrawl and elaborate seal of Herbert Shelley. Francine took the letter to her room, leaving Helen and the twins to finish dinner under the supervision of Mrs Norris. It was some time before she joined them for coffee in the drawing room and explained that their father would be staying in town for a few days until pressing business matters could be settled. For Leonora she had special news, which she saved until Helen had been taken to bed. The playful setter pawed at her skirts and whined until she stooped to fondle its ears.

'Circumstances dictate that I speak to Sir Oscar without delay,' she said. 'Because Jonathan and Charles are still at school, and knowing how Joseph hates to travel, I have decided that you, Leonora, will accompany me on the journey.'

Leonora's eyes widened and her heart began to pound beneath the soft muslin bodice of her dress. She stared from her mother to Joseph and back again, at first unable to grasp the enormity of what she had been told.

'Mama, is it true? Is it? Can I believe this? Am I really, *really* to come with you to ... to ...?'

'Yes, my dear,' Francine said, smiling in spite of herself when she saw the delight on her daughter's face. 'At last you are to have your dearest wish. We leave first thing tomorrow morning for Beresford Hall.'

CHAPTER FOUR

I

They were to take the fast early morning mail coach to Oxford, and from there a second coach to Cirencester, where they hoped to spend the night at the colourful but respectable Green Man Inn. The landlord there was a huge, hairy mountain of a man who wrestled and lifted weights for appropriate sums of money at the local fairs. Big Jack McCallister, as red and as turbulent as ever was a true Scot, took the fullest advantage of both his infamous reputation and his noble patronage. He made sure that nobody ever forgot the Kingswood Fair of 1808, when the Prince of Wales and his glittering retinue arrived *en masse* from Beresford Hall to throw the local populace into complete disarray with their antics. The highlight of the day had occurred following a wager between the Prince and his host, Sir Oscar Cavendish: a five thousand guinea purse if a man could be found to equal the royal champion's feat of lifting a fully grown horse across his shoulders. Big Jack McCallister stepped from the crowd and, with his lordship still mounted, positioned himself beneath the tall brown hunter, flexed his massive shoulder muscles and lifted master, saddle and beast an estimated seven inches off the ground. So the Prince of Wales had lost his wager and the Earl had won the day. Big Jack had been handsomely rewarded, in cash and prestige, for his tremendous accomplishment, and from then on the surly Scot had been proud to call himself the Earl's man. It was whispered in the district that he was still spending the money handed to him that day by a very congenial Sir Oscar.

After a night at the Green Man, Francine and Leonora would hire a small carriage to carry them to where Beresford Hall, flanked by dense forests and held in the fork of two great rivers, dominated the landscape in sombre gothic splendour. Finding herself caught up in a flurry of excitement and hasty arrangements, Leonora went to her bed that night with little hope of falling asleep. Indeed, it seemed that she had no sooner closed her eyes when Griffiths arrived, resplendent in maroon and green livery, to pile their luggage into the waiting chaise. Anabel was there to see them off and to issue a long verbal list of last-minute instructions. She was not at all happy to be left behind while her mistress travelled in the care of a single manservant. She drew Griffiths aside while Francine settled herself in the chaise.

'Heaven help you, Griffiths, if any harm comes to them,' she hissed.

'No harm'll come to 'em while I live an' breathe,' he replied grimly, pushing out his barrel chest and drawing back the lapels of his overcoat. 'See? Safe as in their own beds, they are.'

'Good, very good,' Anabel nodded. She could see the menacing black head of a night-stick protruding from his inside pocket. A large, bone-handled dagger hung in its leather case from his belt, and she knew that he would also keep a pair of loaded pistols on hand throughout the journey.

Also waiting to see them away was Joseph, accompanied as ever by the noisy, disorderly Lancer. Leonora hugged her brother warmly, certain that he envied her neither the arduous journey nor the time she would spend among strangers. It was still very dark, with a damp, unpleasant mist swirling about them as they clattered away through the cobbled and ill-lit streets of St James's.

Soon the progress of the coach was slowed by the inevitable daily congestion in the streets; by slow moving tinkers' carts and giant, lurching drays, by street hawkers offering radishes at forty for a penny or suspect 'drinking' water drawn directly from the Thames, and by plodding, lumbering livestock driven into the city to feed an ever growing population. With the curtains tightly closed against the noise and stink of London, they inched their way through cobbled streets that rang with the sing-song invitation of pedlars:

'Chestnuts! Luverly chestnuts!' A child's high-pitched voice rang clear and sweet to the ear. 'Roasted chestnuts, round and sound! Luverly 'ot chestnuts, round and sou ... ound.'

'Nice young watercress!' The stronger voice of a woman, raucous above the street's din. 'Nice young watercress!'

'Fresh coffee,' bellowed a rich baritone. 'Get it good and hot! Fresh coffee, good and hot!'

The Bull and Mouth in Aldersgate Street was one of the largest coaching inns in London, a bustling, crowded bedlam of a place even in the night hours. Travellers were shown into a huge, square yard with galleries three storeys high and housing several shops and coffee-houses. Their coach was to be the *Royal Flyer*, drawn by four dark horses and smartly finished in chocolate brown with black and red trim and gold lettering. Four other passengers made up the full complement of six occupying the more expensive inner seats. The rest, including Griffiths, would endure the long journey on the outside of the coach, sharing their much cheaper seats with an assortment of bags and bundles and subject to every lurch of the vehicle and whim of the weather. They were away before dawn, their bodies jarred and jolted until they were off the stones at Kingsland Turnpike and the unmade country roads made travelling more pleasant.

They covered the first leg of their journey in a little over six hours, moving toward their destination at an average speed of ten miles per hour, including stops. At the Nine Bells Inn on the Oxford Road they rested only briefly before boarding a fresh coach for Cirencester. From then on they travelled at seemingly breakneck speed through weather that fluctuated between bouts of misty drizzle and periods of torrential rain, both of which were buffeted every which way by fitful winds. In such conditions every turn of the wheels became a potential danger to life and limb, yet the four horses, blinded by rain and often stumbling over mud-holes and other hidden obstacles, were whipped onward with unrelenting urgency.

They reached the Green Man shortly after nightfall, by which time Francine was aching in every limb and in a state of some considerable discomfort. The landlord's wife, a stout, friendly woman smelling of freshly baked bread, was brought from the inn to offer her assistance. They were given one of the best rooms on the second floor, a large, grandly furnished bedroom dominated by a blazing log fire and a massive four-poster bed. After a hot, herb-scented hip bath and a supper of turtle soup, roast ducklings, cheesecakes, fruit pie and sillabub, Francine slipped between the clean, warmed sheets and did not stir again until sunlight flooded the room at dawn. Leonora slept equally well and, having enjoyed a huge supper, awoke prepared to do justice to a hearty breakfast.

'Mama and I are disappointed that your husband is not at home,' she told Nellie McCallister as they were preparing to leave after breakfast. 'We had hoped to meet our cousin's famous champion.'

'Bless you, child,' the woman roared, with a laugh as robust as that of any man. 'Big Jack McCallister's as big as a grizzly bear and twice as nasty, but I reckon he'll be touched by them few kind words.'

They set out in brilliant sunshine and travelled at a less arduous pace that gave them an opportunity to admire the beautiful countryside. A brief shower of rain left a rainbow hanging low over the wolds, its arch of colours reflected in the shimmering waters of a small lake. When at last the coach drew to a halt and Griffiths handed them down at the picturesque village of Kingswood on the easterly edge of the estates, the rain had vanished and the few remaining dark clouds were gilded with sunlight. As she stepped from the coach Leonora caught her breath and stared about her with wide, puzzled eyes. There was something about the place that touched her deeply; something almost familiar in the hunched cottages of pale stone, the glittering curve of the river and the steep-sided valley rising into woodland on every side. A brief shiver passed along her spine.

'Mama ... this place ... have I ever been here before?'

'Never, my dear,' Francine answered with a weary smile. 'But I have described it to you many times in the past.'

'It's more than that,' Leonora said, looking out across the river. 'I *know* this village. I feel I must have been here at some other time ... in the past ... Mama, I *remember* it.'

'That is impossible, Leonora. You are simply being fanciful in your excitement. Come now, let us go inside and see what refreshment is available. It has been a long and tiring journey and I think we are both in need of a wash, a meal and at least an hour's rest before we continue.'

Inside the Royal Oak they enjoyed a late lunch of hot tea, bread and butter, cold ham, eggs, cheese and a delicious apple pie with a sprinkling of sugar and cinnamon baked into its crust. After lunch they rested for an hour in an upstairs room, then changed out of their travelling clothes and prepared themselves for their arrival at Beresford Hall. Leonora's mauve dress and indigo velvet cloak had travelled well in her mother's sturdy trunk. Her favourite bonnet had been trimmed with silk pansies and violets and, framed by its wide rim, her heart-shaped face and black-fringed eyes were set off to very best advantage. Francine kissed her daughter's cheek and smiled proudly.

'I think we will do,' she smiled.

'You look lovely, Mama, really lovely.'

'Do I?' Francine asked, looking back at the mirror and frowning slightly as if that image of herself were not quite what she had expected to see. 'Do I?'

By the time they were dressed, Griffiths had managed to hire a small, covered chaise with comfortable upholstery and weighted curtains to stop the draughts at the windows. The rain clouds had completely dispersed, leaving the sky a clear, deep blue, and the recent showers had given the honey-coloured stone of the squat country cottages a warm, freshly rinsed appearance. The chaise passed through huge, wrought-iron gates bearing the distinctive Cavendish insignia with its ambiguous family motto: *In truth, avarice in all men lies.* From there the road wound its way like a narrow ribbon through wood and parkland, meadow and pasture from Kingswood to Beresford Hall. Near the end of its journey it crossed the river Wye by the bridge at Beres Ford, that deadly stretch of water containing submerged rocks, hidden caves and fierce cross-currents where once a half-starved, half-drowned Cistercian monk was plucked from certain death by divine intervention. Jerome de Beres survived his ordeal and recovered from his injuries to found, in recognition of the miracle, the great abbey that bore his name. And now, hundreds of years after that legendary event, the spot was still feared and respected by local people as the deep and treacherous Monk's Crossing.

This final leg of their journey offered a spectacular taste of the countryside at its most dramatic. The hills had an auburn tinge and the trees were dressed in their finest October foliage, with tints and shades ranging from creamy yellow to fiery furnace red. A wealth of colour met the eye in every direction as the land unfolded in a rich patchwork of field and meadow, with here and there a cluster of honey-toned dwellings or a single lonely cottage tucked among the folds. In the distance the border hills loomed, sombre-clad and brooding, against a clear sky, while into every dip and hollow autumn poured itself in pools of glistening colour. Leonora was enchanted by it all.

'Oh, Mama,' she exclaimed. 'Did you ever see anything quite so beautiful? Look there, how the river glints between the trees like a rush of quicksilver, and how the leaves drift down from the trees to make a carpet on the ground. And look, over there I can see two squirrels rummaging about in ... oh! Oh, Mama!'

The breath caught in Leonora's throat with a gasp, for a

bend in the road had brought them to the great Drive of Oaks, and there in the shallow valley stood Beresford Hall, set amid the autumn golds like a timeless and brooding sentinel. Its Gothic structure seemed to loom out of the shadows of that other time, that tranquil age before the abbey fell, first to a Tudor king, then to a would-be earl. Once again that cold, sharp shiver crept along her spine, only this time it was accompanied by a tightening of the scalp and a shudder that passed right through her body.

'But it is the same,' she exclaimed in a breathless whisper. 'Every detail is *exactly* as I imagined it. It's almost as if ... oh, Mama, I *must* have been here before ... I *must*!'

Francine shook her head. 'No, Leonora, you are seeing Beresford Hall for the very first time.'

'But how ...?' She blinked her eyes, still staring. 'I remember ... I *remember* ...'

The little coach made the long approach past orchards and lawns and formal gardens laid out in designs of perfect symmetry. At the main gate-house they were joined by a small boy in gold-trimmed livery who scrambled up beside Griffiths for the last several yards of the journey. At the far end of the cobbled courtyard stood the Hall's main entrance with its massive steps, ornate pillars and arched mahogany doors. Here the boy jumped down and hurried into a side door while Francine adjusted her hair and smoothed the creases from her cloak and gown. She seemed nervous. Her hands were trembling when Griffiths handed her down, but as she mounted the steps she lifted her head and moved with the calm grace of one to the manner born. Just then a man wearing a grey coat and high leather boots over white breeches hurried down the steps to greet his unexpected guest. This was Oscar Cavendish, recognisable at a glance by his athletic build, piercing blue eyes and familiar shock of fair hair, now liberally sprinkled with grey. He took Francine's hands and kissed them tenderly, then drew her toward the door with no more than a brief glance in Leonora's direction.

Leonora paused to stare up at the magnificent stained glass windows lovingly preserved for centuries, at the brilliant figures of blind Tobit and the Angel, of Bel and the Dragon, of brave Judith brandishing the severed head of Holofernes, of the innocent Susanna accused of adultery, of Adam and Moses, Solomon, Baruch and Esther. She gazed at the soaring, ill-fated tower of the west wing, abandoned for two centuries by all but cawing crows and jackdaws. She removed her bonnet and shook out her long hair, then turned slowly on the spot, her eyes wide and round. Once again she was aware of an odd but persistent sense of having been here before.

By the time she reached the aptly named Cathedral Hall, Francine and the Earl were passing through a door into one of the lower rooms, too deeply engrossed in their conversation to notice her. As she stepped inside she gasped in delight. Bright sunlight was slanting through the ancient stained glass windows to lay a colourful replica of each design on the polished stone floor. All the splendour of the original abbey was preserved around the massive staircase of blue and white marble. The nave was now the great Cathedral Hall where hundreds of glittering guests might dine and dance in comfort, its curving arches now housing the famous crystal chandeliers shipped all the way from Italy as a wedding gift from Sir Percy to Lady Ursula a hundred and fifty years ago. Here were pillars of carved stone, linenfold and burled oak panelling, archways with doors of oak and walnut worked by a master carver.

'Oh, it is beautiful, so *beautiful*,' Leonora breathed.

In that first encounter she was irrevocably touched by the opulent splendour of Beresford Hall and the ruined abbey upon which it was grafted. As if spellbound she crossed the Great Hall, mounted the wide marble staircase and walked the balustraded galleries, moving in and out of sun-kissed shadows and feeling the unique atmosphere of Beresford seep into her lungs with every breath she took. Her eyes shone and her cheeks became flushed with an unfamiliar excitement. Her small fingers trembled as they caressed the cool surfaces of carved stone and marble, smooth alabaster and ornately worked oak. It was like nothing she had ever experienced before. She felt herself ensnared within those massive walls, as if the great house was trying to close itself around her and somehow claim her as its own. She stood at the top of the stairs where the steps branched to left and right in elegant curves, looking down into the hall where so much of the old abbey still remained.

'Mine,' she whispered into the silence, 'Mine.'

The single word sprang from her lips unbidden, and with an intensity that startled her. She reached out a hand to steady herself and her fingers closed around the stem of a bronze urn standing at the curve of the banister. She gripped the cool metal, suddenly overwhelmed by a sense of having known and loved this magnificent place since the first monks had shuffled through its cloisters and along its arched passages. At that moment she had no doubt whatsoever that Beresford Hall was part of her destiny. She *belonged* here.

'And who the hell might *you* be?'

She was suddenly snatched from her preoccupations by the sound of a voice close at hand. It was a loud voice but of uncertain timbre, its youthful pitch only just beginning to give way to the rich, masculine tones of maturity. It belonged to a heavily built youth whose thick fair hair, deep blue eyes and aristocratic features bore a remarkable similarity to those of her brother Jonathan. He wore a beautifully cut white shirt with wide sleeves and lace cuffs, and dark velvet trousers fastened with a wide belt. From her mother's description she recognised Horace, the Earl's second son, a swaggering, ill-mannered youth of thirteen who drank and gambled like a man yet often behaved like a spoilt child. He was jealous of his siblings, cruel to servants, overbearing with guests and fickle in his friendships. As Leonora slowly descended the stairs towards him, he surveyed her from beneath hooded lids, his blue eyes cold and unfriendly.

'Well?' he demanded, and his voice, unnecessarily loud in the quiet of the Great Hall, echoed and rang in her ears.

'Well?' she asked.

'Your answer,' Horace thundered, standing with his feet wide apart and his fists resting on his hips, a pompous young man bent on intimidating the younger child. 'What is your answer, girl?'

Leonora smiled sweetly. She had taken an instant dislike to Horace and she had no intention of allowing him to bait her. 'But I have not yet heard the question, cousin Horace,' she said with a small curtsy.

'Cousin? How dare you call me cousin? How *dare* you claim kinship with me?'

'I am Leonora Shelley,' she said, lifting her chin proudly and looking directly into his narrowed blue eyes. 'And there is no need for you to shout, since my hearing is perfectly sound. For your information, *Sir* Horace, my grandmother was Henrietta Cavendish, a direct descendant of Rupert Cavendish, older brother of Beresford's first earl.'

'Oh, how very, *very* interesting.' His reply was delivered with a small bow and an exaggerated show of disdain. 'And through this Henrietta you think to claim a blood-link with the Cavendish clan of Beresford, I suppose? No doubt it was these misguided pretensions that prompted you to go prancing about the Great Hall and the stairs like a lunatic, Miss Leonora Shelley?'

Leonora maintained her steady gaze as she replied: 'Must I remind you of your own manners, *sir*? Your father is my mother's cousin, and we are guests in his home.'

'Poppycock!'

Without warning Horace suddenly lunged forward and grabbed several strands of fine hair at the tender nape of her neck. Before she could make a move to defend herself he yanked them out by the root and held them up like a trophy that shone with a coppery glow in the sunlit hall. Her gasp of pain and the tears that sprang to her eyes were obviously much to his satisfaction. He twisted the hairs around one of his fingers and curved his mouth in a cruel smile, then he threw back his handsome head and laughed in her face.

'*Cousin*, indeed,' he bellowed. 'Not only must I suffer the company of your brothers at school, but now it seems I am expected to acknowledge *you* as my *cousin*. I will do no such thing. You are but a poor relation.'

He roared with laughter once again, then turned and strode into the sunny patches of colour splashed across the floor of the hall, flinging his last comments over his shoulder as he marched away from her. '... just the snivelling brat of yet another poor relation come to beg my father's favours.'

Something welled up in Leonora, a powerful surge of emotion to which she had no alternative but to give full rein. It was as if she had suddenly become someone else, someone bigger and much stronger than her own small self. Her eyes flashed as cold fury drained her face of colour and added a steely edge to her voice.

'More than that, you ill-mannered fool,' she upbraided him, her words reverberating through the Great Hall and stopping him in his tracks as she met his effrontery with a rage she had not known she possessed. 'By my oath, Horace Cavendish, I intend to take more from this family than an old man's petty favours.'

He rounded on her, his face a mask of indignation. 'What? *What* did you say? Why, you impertinent little ...'

'And when this house is mine its doors will be closed against you, Horace Cavendish.'

Leonora made her promise with an icy, threatening calmness. Her attacker was so taken aback by her outburst that his superiority evaporated as he stared down at the pretty young girl whose fury turned her eyes to violet and seemed so much larger than herself.

'Yours ... *yours*?'

'Oh yes, it *will* be mine,' she hissed in a voice that carried right across the hall. 'As God is my judge, this house and these estates will be mine.'

Horace could scarcely believe what he was hearing. 'How dare you?' he demanded in a small, shocked voice. 'How *dare* you say such things to me ... to *me*?'

Borne on the tide of her own anger, Leonora flung her vow into the cathedral-like stillness of the Great Hall, and as she did so she was aware that she repeated the oath once made by the grasping Joshua Cavendish.

'It will be *mine*,' she cried. 'I too am a Cavendish, and one day every acre of Beresford will belong to *me*!'

II

Mother and daughter made scant conversation on the journey back to the Royal Oak at Kingswood. They were both preoccupied in the privacy of their own thoughts, and perhaps each might have been shocked to learn the true nature of the other's contemplations. Their visit had been brief but eventful. For Francine it had been a day of stirred memories, each one too bitter-sweet to be lightly set aside. For Leonora it had been a memorable experience that would, she knew, alter the whole pattern of her life.

As they left a lowering sun was beginning to smear the sky with sunset hues that ignited the trees and turned the glittering river from a dull silver to gleaming gold. It touched upon the Hall's ancient stones with a honey-toned wash and gave the great windows a fiery glow. Only the sinister tower of the west wing remained unaffected, standing dark-clad against a reddening sky, its company of black birds making lazy circles at its summit. A group of fallow deer, grazing quietly among the trees, raised their tawny heads in alarm before darting away as the sound of the horses' hooves rang on the still air.

They had travelled less than a mile along the Drive of Oaks when their carriage was overtaken and brought to a halt by a four-in-hand coach that came clattering along the narrow road at full gallop. A short, thick-set man in a long overcoat jumped down, snatched off his tall hat and approached a startled and apprehensive Francine.

'Beg pardon, ma'am, didn't mean to frighten ye. Name's Tom Tyler, ma'am. His Lordship says we're to take ye home, ma'am.'

'Home? All the way to London?'

'Them be His Lordship's orders, ma'am. Sent five of us, he did. Two men to drive, turn and turn about, two riding escort and Frank Binns to take this 'ere carriage back to Kingswood village. Your man Griffiths is to ride inside with ye and the little 'un.'

Peering up at the larger conveyance, Francine recognised the Earl's livery and coat of arms, and at least two of his employees among the four still boarded. They were all armed with pistols and well clothed against the coming night. Sir Oscar had clearly brooded upon the lengthy journey, most of which would be taking place during the hours of darkness when footpads and highwaymen were abroad. Rather than leave them in the care of a single footman, he had taken it upon himself to provide them with an armed escort. She closed her eyes briefly, her smile small and wistful. Such care was typical of the man.

'Very well,' she agreed, not without some measure of relief. 'If you will kindly help Griffiths with our bags?'

They were soon settled into the Earl's beautifully sprung coach, with its heavy velvet drapes, foot cushions and deep, comfortable upholstery. Blankets and cushions had been provided, and in a basket they found fruit, bread, cheese and wine for their refreshment. Under Sir Oscar's generous protection, Francine and Leonora would reach their destination in comfort and complete safety.

They spent another comfortable night in the best room of the Green Man, then set out for London immediately after breakfast the next day. Tom Tyler insisted that they make two lengthy stops, one at Burford and another at a small village beyond Oxford.

'His Lordship's orders, ma'am,' he insisted, cap-in-hand but with a determined glint in his brown eyes and a stubborn set to his peasant features.

So it was that they arrived at Garden Square in the early hours of the morning, several hours before they were expected home. It was left to Griffiths to see them into the house. The solemnly polite Tom Tyler declined an offer to sup, preferring instead to take the coach and men directly to the Earl's town house in Westminster. As the home-comers passed into the gravelled drive via the main gate, they were greeted by a delirious Lancer, who came at them fresh from the sodden flower beds where he had been rummaging in the moonlight. He was now five months old and heavy with muscle, a long-legged animal still blessed with an excess of lively exuberance and a deficit of self control. He raced across the lawn and leaped at Francine, his whole weight and momentum behind the muddy front paws that struck her slender body just below the ribs. With a cry she fell backwards, clutching at Griffiths for support. He in turn dropped the trunk he was carrying and staggered sideways, struggling to catch his mistress and maintain his own balance at the same time. He succeeded in doing neither. They fell to the ground in an untidy heap, the dog bounding and barking around them.

'Mama! Mama! Come away, Lancer! Come away, you stupid animal! Quickly, Griffiths, look to your mistress! I think she's hurt!'

Leonora tried to pull the excited dog away as Griffiths struggled to regain his feet. A blow from his clenched fist sent Lancer scuttling for cover with his tail between his legs, and his shouts brought other servants running from the house. Within moments Anabel, barefoot and wearing only a thin robe over her shift, had taken charge of the situation. She ordered the dog to be caught and chained, and her swooning mistress to be carried to her room.

'I'm sure it's nothing more serious than a faint brought on by the sudden fright,' she reassured Leonora. 'Thank heaven she landed on the grass, which is soft and wet. If she had fallen on the path . . . Leonora? What is it, dear? Are you all right?'

Leonora was looking down at the grass where their trunk had fallen when Griffiths lost his balance. It had burst open in the fall, and her gown and shawl were lying in the mud. Someone had lit the light in the porch so that it illuminated the scene in detail. She could see that money had been hidden in the trunk: bank notes, sovereigns, silver, golden guineas; a small fortune in cash that had obviously travelled with them all the way from Beresford Hall. Anabel hastily pushed the spilled clothes back into the trunk, secured the lid, then took Leonora by the shoulders.

'Why is it, child, that you always manage to see what you shouldn't see?'

'Are we poor, Anabel?

'No, child,' the woman answered with a kindly smile. 'You are far from poor.'

'Then why this?'

Anabel sighed heavily. 'That money is for your Papa,' she explained with reluctance. 'Some of his large investments were gambled away by a business associate who has since taken his own life. Through no fault of his own, your Papa was faced with huge debts he was unable to meet. Sir Oscar has simply come to his rescue, as any businessman might do for another. I must ask you to say nothing of this.'

Leonora nodded and allowed Anabel to steer her toward the house. On the panelled stairway she turned to watch the trunk being carried indoors. She was thinking of Horace Cavendish, recalling his arrogance and her own unexpected anger. She could still feel, though to a much lesser degree, those powerful emotions that seemed to have been drawn into her heart and soul from the very walls of Beresford Hall.

'It was wonderful,' she said, her eyes lighting up as she caught sight of her brother coming sleepy-eyed from his room to see what all the fuss and commotion was about. 'Oh, Joseph, I must tell you all about it . . . it was *wonderful.*'

Herbert Shelley returned home later that same day, remained an hour in his rooms, then left for the city carrying a stout case and accompanied by a groom. On that occasion he did not disturb his wife, who was sleeping late after the stresses and strains of the long journey. When he arrived home in time for dinner late that afternoon, he found a smart black chaise waiting outside the gate and a black-clad footman pacing to and fro along the pavement. As he entered by the front door he was met by a thin, white-haired man who introduced himself as Sir Marcus Shaw, physician to Sir Oscar Cavendish. The two men shook hands and eyed each other closely. Shelley resented the intrusion, wondering what tales this man might carry back to his friend and patron, the Earl of Beresford. In turn Sir Marcus sensed his host's hostility and, knowing Shelley only by reputation and caring little for what he had heard, made no attempt to explain his presence until asked to do so.

'Well, sir?' Herbert asked at last, bristling at the man's silence. 'Am I to *guess* the purpose of your visit?'

Sir Marcus cleared his throat. 'I was summoned here on behalf of your wife, Mr Shelley.'

'*Summoned*, sir? For what purpose?'

'Mrs Shelley is unwell.'

'Nonsense,' Herbert interjected. 'She has but a trifling cough, a seasonal thing ...'

Sir Marcus sighed and shook his head but remained silent, so that Herbert was forced to ask: 'Is it more serious than that? Is Mrs Shelley ill?'

Irritated by the man's manner, Sir Marcus opened his mouth to speak, only to close it again with a resigned sigh. It was not for him to furnish Herbert Shelley with information he had, for the present at least, chosen to keep from the sick woman herself.

'Your wife has suffered a distressing fall,' he said instead. 'I found her badly shaken and unusually fatigued, but you will no doubt be gratified to learn that she is otherwise unharmed. I have prescribed a strong tonic and plenty of rest.'

Herbert scowled at the maid who waited to hand the visitor his dark cloak and very expensive top hat. He deeply resented the physician's superior attitude.

'We have our own family physician ... Mr Soames of St James's.'

'And you would wish him to offer a second opinion?'

Herbert shrugged. 'Soames is a good man. He has served us for years with no cause for complaint. He knows Francine well, her small ailments, her little peculiarities of health ...'

'Then no doubt he will make the same recommendations as myself,' Sir Marcus muttered, shrugging his thin shoulders into the voluminous woollen cloak and taking up his hat. His eyes were narrow and almost colourless in a pink face. His hands were pale and wrinkled, as if they had been too long submerged in water. 'In the meantime, I will make myself available should Mrs Shelley wish to send for me again. Good day to you, sir.'

'Quite, quite,' Shelley said, aware that he had touched

upon the man's professional pride. 'Perhaps you will be good enough to extend my regards to Sir Oscar Cavendish when next you meet.'

Sir Marcus turned at the door and stared coldly at his host. 'May I remind you, Mr Shelley, that as a physician I am *not* in the business of carrying messages. I bid you good day.'

Although peeved by the minor altercation, Herbert felt that he had scored highly in the exchange. He had disliked the man on sight and had no wish to entertain a servant of Sir Oscar in his own home. He rang the small bell in the hall and a girl appeared from the scullery, smoothing her skirts and hurriedly swallowing the food in her mouth. She bobbed a neat curtsy that caused her ill-fitting bodice to gape, revealing rather more of her breasts than might be considered modest. Her waist was small and her hips wide, and although her teeth were poor her face was passably pretty.

'What's your name, girl?'

'June, sir. June Mellor. I'm Sarah's sister.'

'Sarah? Ah, yes, the kitchen maid. And how old are you, June?'

'Near on seventeen, sir.' She bobbed another curtsy.

Herbert chewed thoughtfully on his lower lip. The girl interested him, but she was no Daisy Kimble. The other maids never quite fired his loins the way Daisy had done.

'Tell me, girl,' he said, rather more sharply than intended. 'Was Sir Marcus Shaw offered refreshment?'

'No, sir. I was about to offer when he left. Mrs Norris said to wait until he was finished with Miss Francine.'

'Quite so, quite so. You may tell the mistress that she need not come down for dinner. I will dine with her tonight. Inform Mrs Norris, will you? That will be all.'

'Yes, sir. Thank you, sir.'

Herbert returned to his rooms a happy man. Everything had gone according to his carefully engineered plans, with no complications of which he was aware. The investments providing his main source of income had been made secure, his debts were paid, his obligations met. He had been neither slow nor shy to capitalise on the suicide of Jeffrey Wallace.

Nor did he harbour any sense of guilt along with the knowledge that his own recent departure from certain joint ventures had been a major contribution to the dead man's problems. Such were the vagaries of finance, in which no man was morally required to put the affairs of a friend above his own. Herbert had simply withdrawn his investments to cover heavy losses in other areas, and circumstances had shown that he made his move not a moment too soon. The death of Wallace could well have ruined him, but instead it provided him with the perfect answer to many of his problems. As far as Francine was concerned, he was still financially involved in Jeffrey's affairs and ran the risk of being caught in the backlash of his suicide. Better men than he were set to fall as a result of that young man's folly. Not even Sir Oscar Cavendish could fault him for being one of them.

His letter to Francine had been short and very skilfully worded so as to achieve his ends without committing anything to paper that might embarrass him at a later date. Shocked by news of the suicide, her prime concern would be for Herbert's own state of mind, yet when the letter was shown to Sir Oscar it would reveal nothing more than a businessman's concern following events over which he had no control.

'Clever,' he said with a chuckle as he recalled the wording of the letter. He poured himself a stiff brandy before crossing the room to admire his reflection in the big oval mirror in the corner. 'Damn clever, Shelley, my boy. *Damn* clever.'

He had neither asked for help nor admitted to any involvement with Jeffrey Wallace. He knew he could rely on Francine to do all that. Loyal and totally predictable, she would do everything she could to protect his reputation while seeking a way to compensate him for his assumed losses. And Sir Oscar Cavendish, already showing concern over Shelley's affairs, would be persuaded to lay the blame elsewhere and dip into his private purse once again on his behalf. So it was that Herbert had triumphed over impending disaster without so much as a stain on his good character. Under the circumstances he could hardly regret the very timely death of Jeffrey Wallace.

It was only later, when he was able to view the situation more objectively, that he began to recognise his own vulnerability. Once again he had seen how successfully a man might trade upon another's misfortune. Twice within the year he had teetered on the brink of ruin, only to find an eleventh-hour reprieve in the sudden death of a close associate. Perhaps it was time for him to make a tactical withdrawal, to quit the more dangerous games while he was still ahead. He was horrified by the thought that he too might be pushed and manipulated by others into a position of such blind desperation that he should leave the gaming tables only to blow out his brains in a locked room.

III

At Beresford Hall Sir Horace Cavendish took lunch with his mother, the Countess, in her private rooms. The day did not find him in good humour. He had slept badly and risen late with a hangover. The previous afternoon's confrontation with Leonora Shelley had unsettled him. For him, Horace Cavendish, at thirteen the undisputed leader of the Harrow Pack, to be bested by an insolent little girl of ten, was utterly unthinkable; yet it had happened. She had silenced him with her audacious words, defeated him with her contempt. Such fire, such *madness* had glittered in her violet-coloured eyes that for a moment he had almost believed himself confronted by something evil.

'What is it, dear boy? I can see that something is troubling you. Are you unwell? Do you miss your friends at school? Come, tell Mama all about it.' Horace helped himself to liver and bacon, veal, potatoes and roast beef from the hot chafing dishes. His fancy blue and green waistcoat hung open and his stock, though as scrupulously clean as his white shirt, was haphazardly tied. He rummaged among the dishes until he found the mushrooms in brandy sauce, ladled a portion on to his plate and scowled as a small oily stain appeared on the leg of his buckskin breeches.

'Horace?'

'I'm tired, Mother. I slept rather badly last night.'

'And drank too much port?' She smiled indulgently. 'I see your appetite remains unaffected, as always. That's a good sign. Come, my dear. Sit down beside me and tell me what troubles you.'

Lady Alyce patted the seat beside her. She was reclining on a roll-backed sofa of dark golden plush hung with crimson fringes. Her gown and matching morning-robe lay in waves of delicate black lace all around her, and a small bonnet trimmed with black silk flowers added to the dramatic effect of her appearance. Her skin was very pale and her grey eyes shadowed, though a touch of rouge coloured her lips and a recently applied tint had returned most of the golden highlights to her hair. More handsome than beautiful, she had the fine skin and clear, classic features much approved of in Regency England, where good breeding still mattered more than mere wealth to those of more refined tastes. As Countess of Beresford she cared a great deal for the fads and fashions of the day although she, unlike the majority of her contemporaries, refused to allow her tall, slender figure to run to fat.

By now she was much recovered from the sudden affliction that had kept her to her rooms for almost a month and given Horace an excuse to take a short break from Harrow in order to comfort her. When he sat down beside her she ruffled his hair and frowned at his solemn expression. The deep lace flounces at her wrist brushed gently across his face, filling his nostrils with perfume.

'What is it, dear boy?'

Horace stared down at the plate in his lap. He could feel the heat of the food penetrating to his skin. After a while he looked at his mother and said: 'Is the Shelley family closely related to ours?'

'What? Why do you ask such a thing?' Taken off guard by the question, she had stiffened and allowed her feelings to show briefly in her face. A moment later she recovered her composure and added, in a calmer tone: 'I was not aware that you had ever met any of those people.'

'Oh yes, Jonathan Shelley and his brother Charles are with me at Harrow, have been for three or four years now.'

'Oh? I was not aware of that.'

'But you do know the family?'

'I know *of* them,' Lady Alyce corrected, somewhat icily.

'Then you didn't see the girl, Leonora, and her mother when they were here yesterday?' He saw the Countess's face blanch and her hand fly to her throat as it did whenever she was distressed or ill. Her rouged mouth tightened itself into a hard, unattractive line.

'She was here? Francine Shelley was here, in this house?'

'Yes, Mama, with her daughter ... a thoroughly unpleasant child of about ten or eleven. I took against her on the instant ... insolent whelp. The mother I did not meet. I believe she spent some time with Father in his study, then took tea in the green room and left immediately after.'

'And what was the purpose of their visit?'

Horace chewed a piece of meat liberally smeared with rich brandy sauce. 'Come to borrow money, I'll wager. It's common knowledge that Herbert Shelley ... he's the father ... is much given to failed business ventures and high gambling stakes ... and with two sons at Harrow ...' He shrugged and stuffed his mouth with more meat.

Lady Alyce reached for her ivory fan, opened it with a loud snap and began to agitate the air close to her face. 'In answer to your original question, Horace,' she said at last. 'No, they are certainly *not* closely related to us. Like so many others from the lower stations they prey upon your father's generosity from time to time, but they have no claim on us. No claim on *him*. He and this Francine woman were ... are ... *cousins*. That is all. The Shelleys have no claim ... *no claim*!'

'I do believe the brat, Leonora, has been taught otherwise.'

'Then the brat is wrongly instructed,' Lady Alyce said in scathing tones. A moment later she sighed, closed her fan and placed a hand lightly on her son's arm. 'Forgive my sharpness,

Horace. It's just that I do so hate to see your dear, generous father made use of by those who perceive their slender blood-tie as a means of gaining access to his purse.'

Horace nodded and swallowed a mouthful of food. He did not consider the blood-tie such a slender one if the girl's story could be trusted. Even *she* might be taken for a Cavendish, and then there was her elder brother, that arrogant thorn in Horace's tender flesh. Jonathan Shelley, so like himself but slightly taller, his eyes a little more blue and his hair a finer blond, his smile and manner more likeable, his company more sought after. Damn his hide. He hated Jonathan for his accomplishments and his popularity at Harrow, but most of all he hated him for his infuriating likeness to himself.

'Mother, have you ever met the eldest son, Jonathan?'

'No, I have not!' Lady Alyce exclaimed. 'Nor have I any desire to do so. I count myself fortunate in not having met any of those ... those *beggars*.' She smiled and took his hand in hers. 'Are those people the reason for your dark mood, Horace?'

'It was the girl. She made me so ... so *angry*. I don't want to see her here again.'

'I'm sure you won't, my dear,' Lady Alyce smiled. 'And you can certainly rest assured that she will never be *invited*.'

'Good ... good.' He returned his attention to his plate, but after a while looked up with a sheepish grin on his handsome face. '... er ... Mother?'

'Yes, my dear?'

'It's about my allowance. You know, living to any kind of decent standard these days is so expensive ...'

'And you are finding it more and more difficult to maintain your position in society on the money I send you each month? Oh, Horace, you are such an incurable spendthrift.'

'But Mama, I have a reputation to protect, a certain standing in society to maintain.'

'Well, then, we will have to make more suitable arrangements, won't we, dear boy?'

Horace beamed with triumph. 'Oh, Mother, you are so good to me, so understanding. I shudder to contemplate how I would survive without your love and support. I know I could never be Father's favourite, but so long as I have you, my dear, dear Mama.'

He pushed aside his plate and embraced his mother warmly. The show of affection was quite genuine on his part. This woman was the most important person in his life and he loved her dearly. He also needed her. As the Earl's second son he stood to inherit nothing of his father's wealth, but as the Countess's favourite child his future was assured. The lands and properties already purchased on his behalf would guarantee him a reasonable income for the rest of his life, while the fortune already accumulated in his name would one day set him up as a man of substance. While his position in the family left much to be desired and his relationship with his father was not of the best, he had learned to appreciate the true value of his mother's love.

'Are you feeling better now, my dear?'

He kissed her cheek and grinned. 'Much better. You know, Mother, when I get back to Harrow I will tweak those Shelley brothers by the nose, and if ever I see their ill-bred sister on our property again, I will take her by the collar and throw her in the fish-pond.'

He roared so loudly with laughter that he barely noticed his mother's reluctance to share his mirth. He sprawled across the sofa with his head in her lap and his boots resting on a curve of deeply carved woodwork. From there he studied her pale, lined face with its coldly aloof expression.

'They have no right,' she muttered, as if thinking out loud. 'They have no right to be here in my home ... *my* home.'

'Why Mother, I do believe you dislike the Shelleys as much as I do.'

'Possibly ... possibly,' she said, stroking his hair with her dry fingers. 'Horace, it would make me very happy to know that they will never, under any circumstances, gain my son's acceptance ... not as cousins, friends, neighbours, guests ... can I rely upon you for that?'

'But of course you can.'

'Do I have your promise?'

'You have indeed, and an easy promise it will be to keep. I have yet to meet a member of that family who does not irritate me beyond bearing.'

'Thank you, my dear. You are *such* a comfort to me,' Lady Alyce smiled. 'And now let us discuss this small matter of your monthly allowance.'

CHAPTER FIVE

I

Five years were to pass before fate decreed that Horace and Leonora should meet again. By then she was a tall, curvaceous young woman of almost sixteen, alluring, fiery, ambitious, and with an unshakeable sense of her own worth. Her moods were like quicksilver, bright and unpredictable, but whether wickedly flirtatious or frostily aloof, she drew men to her side almost without benefit of conscious effort. They came to her as moths to a flame, and Leonora, while accepting their admiration as both her pleasure and her right, kept herself well beyond their reach. Not for her the wet and hasty kisses or the fumbled gropings that men in their unfathomable conceit attempted to inflict as a measure of their masculine admiration. She would not be handled like a ripened fruit in the market-place, nor would she squander her self-respect for the dubious pleasure of raising a bulge in the trousers of some callow youth seeking a quick thrill. Those who fell victim to her very potent magnetism soon learned to their cost that the fascinating Leonora had her heart set upon a richer and loftier destiny.

'What is to be done, Reece? My son is totally besotted by the Shelley girl. He's forty years old, damn it! He's too long in the tooth to turn love-sick over a fancy bit of skirt and a well-rounded bosom.'

The speaker was Nigel Fairfax, very senior partner in the business of Fairfax, Reece & Tilbury, bankers. He was a small, thin, birdlike man in his late sixties, almost bald beneath his unfashionable wig and plagued with rheumatic pains and swelling of the joints. The stiffened collars of his shirts rose to the lobes of his ears so that his head, with its freckled dome, angular nose and tiny black eyes, seemed to turn upon his narrow shoulders rather than on his neck. In his black woollen coat and waistcoat, purple trousers and white shirt, he resembled an ageing magpie whose head was permanently hunched into its feathers.

'So, what's to be done, eh? What's to be done?'

By contrast his companion was a round, pink-faced man with a mound of chins and a halo of wispy white hair. The room in which the two men were sitting was heavily panelled, with a low ceiling and inadequate windows; a dark, sombre room so crammed with furniture that each piece crowded upon its neighbour and every surface was cluttered. Their chairs were set on opposite sides of the fire, and between them stood a tall table holding port and brandy and a small salver of Turkish delight liberally dusted with powdered sugar. With the backs of his fat fingers Reece dusted a few particles of sugar from his cut-away coat, then studied his pink, blunted fingernails and asked:

'Did you speak to Shelley?'

'I did, as you advised, but to no avail. The girl is not yet sixteen. He will hear no talk of marriage for another year, at least. The man is a pompous ass too fond of his noble connections. I fancy he's looking to make a more favourable match.'

Reece lifted a greying brow into the wrinkles across his forehead. 'Indeed? That would surprise me, since she has no dowry to speak of.'

'No dowry? But I was given to understand that on marriage she would inherit some pretty extensive properties from her mother. Somewhere in Pimlico, was it not? Hampstead, perhaps?'

'Very heavily mortgaged,' Reece smiled. 'As you have already observed, Shelley has all the pretensions of a nobleman, but let me assure you that he lacks the wherewithal to support them. It will take a substantial amount of hard cash to settle those mortgages if he were pressed to return the properties to their rightful owner.'

'And is he not in a position to settle his affairs?'

Reece shook his head. 'At present, no. I would not go so far as to say he is *perilously* in debt although, like the majority of our clients, he lives increasingly beyond his means. However, so long as his gambling losses are kept to a minimum he remains solvent while making little or no forward progress. Let us say that he is at risk, and that his daughter's dowry is a long way from being redeemed.'

Fairfax leaned forward in his seat. Loss of teeth and flesh over the years had caused the lower half of his face to collapse inward, giving his smile a grotesque quality and making his nose appear even more prominent. He chuckled maliciously.

'So, the comely young thing is as good as penniless, is she? And what about the mother, the Cavendish woman? Is she aware of the situation?'

Reece pursed his lips and shook his head. 'She has no idea. The new arrangements were made in the very strictest confidence when Shelley's affairs had reached crisis point.' He paused to lick a layer of sweetness from his lips, eyed the plate of sweets and continued: 'At the time of the marriage, Mrs Shelley had insisted upon withholding two-thirds of her dowry for the benefit of any children that might be born to them. Even though Shelley agreed to this at the time, the lady was not without professional advice, and as each child was born, the legalities involved became more complex.'

'But not irreversible, eh?' Fairfax prompted.

'Indeed no, although it took our own lawyers the better part of seven months to work out the finer details.'

With a flourish Reece pulled a copious red and white handkerchief from his pocket and touched it to each nostril in turn, sniffing delicately as he did so.

'And now Fairfax, Reece & Tilbury, as his major creditors, has absolute claim on the properties should Shelley be unable to meet his obligations. And, of course, we are free to extend or withdraw his credit, whichever may prove expedient to ourselves.'

'Or to encourage him to overreach himself so that the properties become forfeit.'

Reece smiled in a wobble of fleshy chins. 'I'm sure that can be arranged. Further cash can always be made available, and who can possibly know in advance what unforeseen problems might compel a bank to call in its loans unexpectedly ...'

'... and very reluctantly, of course.'

'But of course. And once we have the properties, Shelley is without security and Christopher is free to step into the breach with an offer of marriage Shelley can not possibly refuse.'

'Reece, you are a genius,' the old man exclaimed gleefully.

'No genius, my dear Fairfax,' Reece denied with a flush of modesty. 'I am merely a banker in the business of making money. Now, let me advise you to wait another six to twelve months, Nigel. Even now our lawyers are looking into the possibility of securing similar properties in the north, belonging to his eldest sons, against a cash loan to pay off a cluster of lesser debts. If the legal complexities can be unravelled and re-contracted in the bank's favour, then ...'

'Then Shelley will be safely in our pocket!'

'Exactly, and Christopher can dictate his own terms ... *if* he still wants the girl a year from now.'

Nigel Fairfax chuckled. It was a dry, rattling sound that caught in his stringy throat to set up a spasm of coughing. Then he sat back in his seat and wiped the saliva from his lips with a handkerchief. He heartily approved of the match. The girl was a relative of Sir Oscar Cavendish, whose feckless ancestor had provided, in a fit of sheer malice, the land upon which now stood Fairfax Manor. A union between the two families might settle that ancient feud and put an end to the present Earl's hostility toward his untitled neighbours. The appearance of a brood of Fairfax progeny bred upon a Cavendish cousin would improve the blood *and* the social standing of the Fairfax family.

Nigel accepted another glass of port but waved aside the offer of a piece of Turkish delight. He was thinking about his grandfather, the tough, self-taught clerk who made a fortune buying and selling the privileged information of his clients, then played upon a family rift in order to snatch four hundred acres of the Cavendish estates. His family remained unforgiven, unaccepted in the highest circles despite their wealth, so the old man would have been well satisfied by these latest proposals. Leonora Shelley was young and healthy enough to bear her husband ten, perhaps even a dozen children, and every one related to the Earls of Beresford.

'I offer a toast to progress and progeny,' he announced, raising his glass and opening his empty mouth in an unsightly grin.

'And to the closing of the trap,' Reece smiled.

'Indeed so. Within the year we must have this Herbert Shelley so tightly bound by debts that he'll be willing to sell his daughter at *any* price.'

II

Apart from the usual round of balls, banquets and stylish gatherings, there were two truly memorable society occasions that year. One was the coronation of George IV in early January, an event of such tremendous popularity that the celebrations and firework displays continued well into the following month. From the Vauxhall gardens in London to his summer residence at Brighton, the Prince of Wales, now King George IV, was feted and toasted in an orgy of merrymaking. The country's most fashionable set had lost its posturing, pleasure-loving leader, the Great Star around which revolved a thousand lesser stars of polished brilliance. But the nation as a whole had gained a King, and at fifty-eight the incorrigible, obese 'Prinny' had at last come into his own.

The second memorable event was the wedding of Sir Malcolm Cavendish, eldest son of the Sixth Earl of Beresford, to Lady Grace Osbourne Graham, only daughter of the widowed Sir Anthony Osbourne Graham and granddaughter of the late Lord Connerston of Goole.

The ceremony took place on the fourteenth of August at the little church dedicated to St Michael And All Angels which stood on a quiet hillside above Kingswood village. Only close relatives were invited to attend the service itself, but the Shelleys had conspired to be among those who waited in the grounds of the church to see the bride and groom as they emerged as man and wife.

'Oh, Mama, I'm so excited,' Leonora whispered, gripping Francine's hand as they stood their ground among the jostling press of fellow guests. 'How did you do it? However did you manage to get us an invitation?'

'Sir Oscar made a promise, a long time ago,' Francine smiled. 'And my only regret is that Jonathan and Charles had already left on their European tour when the announcement was made.' She suddenly squeezed her daughter's hand. 'But *you* are the one who matters, my dear. *You* are the one Sir Oscar promised to invite.'

Leonora's smile was brilliant. 'And was it not unbelievably generous of Papa to make so much money available for the trip? I just *know* I am the envy of *all* my friends. That beautiful new coach and four, with our very own insignia and new crimson livery, all the extra gowns and bonnets, the lovely jewels ...' She touched the row of pearls and amethysts at her throat. 'Oh, he has helped to make this such a special occasion.'

As she looked toward the low stone porch of the church, eager to see the happy couple emerge, Leonora did not notice that her words had caused Francine's face to lose its bright expression. She was too excited to pay heed to subtle undercurrents or concern herself with the reasons behind Herbert Shelley's sudden affluence.

For the wedding of her cousin's eldest son Francine wore a high-necked blue bodice with slashed inlets of pink over soft white skirts. At thirty-eight she was still very lovely, though perhaps a little too pale and slender. She had never been blessed with the same robust health enjoyed by all her children except Joseph, and the serious fall of last year had kept her to her rooms for several weeks. Her physician was certain that some slight internal bleeding had completely healed, yet in recent months her reserves of energy had reached a disturbingly low ebb. Pale and fragile though she appeared, in her beautiful gown and plumed hat she was still capable of turning the heads of countless admiring gentlemen.

Leonora was wearing a white muslin dress over-printed with tiny lilac flowers and trimmed at the neck and sleeves with lavender lace. Her bonnet was wide-rimmed and bedecked with crape flowers from palest lavender to deepest purple, with long ribbons to match the satin sash at her waist. To protect her shoulders from hot sun or cool breeze she wore a fashionable cream silk shawl with pretty woven borders and rich purple fringing. That she was looking her most alluring was confirmed by the smiles and appreciative glances of those around her.

'Here come the bride and groom!' someone shouted, and Leonora was caught in a sudden forward surge that carried her to the edge of the pathway, where she regained her balance in time to see the couple emerge from the church and step arm in arm into the sunlit morning.

'Oh, isn't she just *beautiful*?' a woman sighed.

'And did you ever see such a gown?' cried another. 'All rainbow gauze and silver lace ... oh and just *look* at all those flowers.'

'It's wonderful ... *wonderful*,' sighed a young girl with large teeth and spotty cheeks. 'Oh dear, I do believe I shall weep.'

Leonora paid little attention to the comments of the women around her. She was staring at the groom, whom she had never seen before. Malcolm Cavendish was much fairer than herself, with a hint of red in his hair but with the same long black lashes fringing his eyes. He was tall and muscular, with

106

that easy, natural elegance already so familiar to her. His attire was simple but beautifully cut: light grey trousers and top hat, a plum-coloured cut-away coat with wide revers, beaded black waistcoat and crisp white neck-linen. He walked slowly along the pathway, smiling and bowing at the hundreds of cheering well-wishers, and for one unwelcome instant Leonora felt the barbs of envy pricking at her heart. This extremely attractive man was the heir of Beresford, and the woman at his side would one day be his Countess, the Mistress of Beresford Hall. But for the whims of fate, Leonora might have been the one to wear rainbow gauze and shimmering silver lace, with Sir Malcolm in attendance and a newly won earldom nestling in the palm of her hand. It was almost as if she had suddenly and cruelly been made aware that the prize to which her own soul had secretly aspired had just been handed over to someone else.

As the couple drew nearly level with her, Malcolm turned his head and their eyes met and held for what could have been no more than a fraction of a second. Brief though the contact was, it allowed something to pass between them, an almost intangible thing of little impact, perhaps no more than an acknowledgement of recognition between two people of the same blood. She noted his strong jaw and the penetrating blue of his eyes; he saw her full mouth and gaze of deepest violet. It was an exchange as fleeting as the space between one heartbeat and the next, yet it left a deep impression on them both.

After the ceremony there was a great rush to be among the first to partake of the special wedding breakfast laid out in the grounds of Beresford Hall. A long procession of conveyances followed the couple's brightly decorated chaise through the massive iron gates and along the Drive of Oaks, pouring in a colourful and noisy stream from the village, with every passenger eager to begin the festivities. Several of the less boisterous guests chose to hang back until the main crush of vehicles had filed on to the narrow road. The Shelleys were among them. While Herbert and Joseph wandered off to investigate the horses and dogs offered for sale at the far end of the village, Francine and Leonora sipped ice-cold lemonade in the quiet gardens at the rear of the Royal Oak.

'A penny for your thoughts, my dear.'

'They are of little consequence, Mama,' Leonora sighed. 'As a matter of fact, I was just wondering if ...' She glanced up as the garden gate opened and closed with a loud click. A big man in a mustard-coloured coat was waddling across the grass toward them. 'Oh, good heavens! Must I forever be pursued by this loathsome individual.'

'Leonora! Remember your manners,' Francine whispered, then added in more normal tones: 'Good day to you, Mr Fairfax.'

'G-g-good day t-t-to you, Mrs Sh-Shelley ... and t-t-to you Miss L-L-Leonora.'

Christopher Fairfax swept off his hat and bowed stiffly. He was a bull-necked man of medium height whose figure had expanded steadily outwards over the years. He perspired a lot, which meant that his face had a permanent sheen and his podgy pink palms were always damp to the touch. He was in his early forties, with thinning dark hair, deep-set brown eyes and a somewhat pendulous lower lip that glistened with saliva and provided a cushion on which to rest his tongue. He was a clever man whose ready wit was bridled by a stutter and whose would-be eloquence was hamstrung by a tongue and palate constantly at odds with each other. He was shy and uncertain around women in general but horribly, embarrassingly awkward in the company of Leonora Shelley, whom he adored to the point of distraction. To find himself middle-aged and hopelessly in love with a girl almost thirty years his junior was having a devastating effect on his sensibilities.

'I ... er ... I t-t-took the l-l-liberty of ordering t-t-tea and r-r-refreshment ...' he stammered, staring down at the ribbons and crape flowers concealing Leonora's face from his view.

'That's very kind of you, Mr Fairfax,' Francine said, 'but as you can see, we have just taken lemonade. We are invited to Beresford Hall for the wedding breakfast, so we must not allow ourselves to eat in advance.'

'Oh ... quite ... well ... er ... my c-compliments on your gown, M-Miss L-Leonora. You l-l-look ... you l-look s-so ...'

Leonora wickedly chose that moment to lift her head and turn the full impact of her brilliant smile upon him. He stepped back, blustering and stuttering, his face turning from pink to red and glistening beneath a fresh layer of perspiration.

'Ah, here is my husband, now,' Francine announced with some relief. 'I do believe our carriage is ready at last. If you will excuse us, Mr Fairfax? Come, Leonora, we must not keep your father waiting.' She took Leonora's arm and led her away before adding in a whisper: 'Really, my dear, it is quite heartless of you to tease him so.'

'All I did was *smile* at him, Mama.'

'You are cruel, Leonora. Why, the poor man ...'

'That *poor man*, as you call him, is old, fat and ugly,' Leonora reminded her. 'He has no right to press his attentions upon me. Why must I suffer to be seen in his company when I would as soon offer my friendship to an overweight pig?'

Francine smiled in spite of herself. 'But I feel so sorry for him,' she said. 'Could you not be a little kinder?'

'What? And have th-that st-st-stuttering idiot b-believe I actually l-l-like him?'

'Oh, Leonora, how c-c-could you?'

At that point mother and daughter clung to each other in fits of helpless laughter, their amusement barely concealed beneath the wide rims of their bonnets. They were still laughing as Herbert handed them into the carriage and Joseph made a place for his sister in the seat beside him.

Fairfax watched the fine carriage bear the light of his life into the distance. He had not, of course, received an invitation to the wedding, but he had travelled to Kingswood knowing that Leonora would be there and hoping for an opportunity to speak to her. He had seen the way other men looked at her, noted their admiring glances and despised the shyness that kept him from declaring his own feelings. His father had told him to be patient, to give the situation time to develop, but the love-sick Christopher was suffering more acutely with every passing day. His disposition seemed to fluctuate between the heights of anticipation and excitement and the very depths of despair.

'Here's your tray, sir. Oh, have the ladies gone and left already, then?'

The stout, rather elderly serving wench hovered, uncertain.

'Set it down on the table,' Fairfax said, sulkily.

She lowered the tray with a clatter. It was laden with hot tea and chocolate, fresh bread and butter, cheese, honey, plum tart, and a plate of tiny fancy cakes of every shape and colour. He watched her walk back toward the inn, her wide hips swaying with every stride, then he stared into the distance where Leonora's carriage was no longer to be seen. With a sigh he returned his attention to the tray and, by way of compensation for his latest disappointment, began to eat.

III

'Well, Joseph, I told you in great detail what to expect. Did I exaggerate?' Leonora's voice was breathless, her eyes wide and bright. 'Is all this any less beautiful than I described?'

'Not at all,' Joseph breathed, staring out at the surrounding countryside with his eyes narrowed in concentration and a look of wonder on his face. 'I am *most* impressed. Thirty thousand breathtaking acres, and all owned by one man. It devils the mind to contemplate such wealth. Look, I can just make out the border hills in the distance. They look almost purple in this light. I do agree with you, Lia, the earldom is quite ... *quite* magnificent.'

They were seeing the countryside on a brilliant summer day when the fields were gilded with ripening corn and the hedgerows were aglow with golden tansy and lady-glove, ragwort and tumbling nasturtiums. As the carriage approached along the Drive of Oaks and Beresford Hall loomed in the distance, Leonora was touched afresh by its special magic. The closer she came to the place, the more she was aware of that powerful sense of belonging she had first experienced five years ago.

Some time later they were handed down in the grounds at the front of the Hall, where swarms of titled, wealthy and influential guests had invaded the lawns and terraces. Their gowns, bonnets, jackets and parasols echoed both the vivid colours of the flower beds and the elegant lines of garden sculptures. Set at intervals along the pathways were long trestle tables draped with cloths of bright white cotton and bearing a wonderful selection of boiled and roast meats, game, poultry, pies, and pasties. There were breads, sweets, cakes and tarts of every description baked in the Earl's own kitchens, fruits from his extensive orchards, butter and cheese from his private dairy, ale from his brew-house, wines of every kind from his cellars: enough to satisfy the appetites of hundreds of hungry guests.

'Oh, how I love this place,' Leonora breathed, her eyes dancing with happiness. 'How I *love* this enchanting place.'

The terraces all around her were ablaze with blossoms: beds of roses and pots of flowering shrubs, sculpted islands of rhododendrons and leafy barriers of azaleas and magnolias. Above them all the magnificent Hall with its windows of colourful stained glass stood like a massive work of art against the blue sky. She could hear the hiss of a small fountain and feel the whisper of a scented breeze on her cheeks, and for a moment her heart was so full she felt it would burst. For five long years she had been haunted by a dream of returning to Beresford Hall. Now she knew that its special magic still had her firmly in its grip. Coming back was like returning home after a long and reluctant absence.

'My dear Francine, what a pleasure it is to see you, it has been altogether too long ... too long. And you, Shelley. I trust you are not fatigued by the long journey?'

Sir Oscar received Francine with warmth and Herbert with a noticeable coolness. He seemed taller and more elegant than ever, and when introduced to Leonora he seemed quite taken aback by her appearance. He stooped politely over her hand

and observed her in a way she found difficult to interpret, though she sensed no personal interest in his stare. It pleased her to imagine that he recognised her likeness to several past members of his illustrious family.

As she watched Sir Oscar leading Francine off in the direction of a particularly fine display of summer blossoms, Leonora suddenly realised that there was a very singular affection between them. She saw the big, handsome man slide his arm about the tiny waist of his guest, saw his fair head bend toward Francine's upturned face, and suddenly she knew that what they felt for each other was much more than just a cousin's regard. It was something she had never witnessed between Francine and Herbert, a thing so natural, so tender, that it could only be described as love. Francine and her handsome cousin might have been alone in that crowded place, for in the short time they were together their eyes and their hearts were clearly bound one to the other.

Feeling that she had stumbled upon a terrible secret, Leonora turned away to accept the glass of spiced wine offered by her brother. She was amazed to find that none of the other guests were giving the couple a second glance, for it seemed to her that their closeness was too conspicuous to be ignored.

Joseph grinned boyishly. He looked very dashing but awkward, a shy young man ill-at-ease in company. He always feared that guests would find him a dull companion to his vivacious sister, or that some important person, reduced to a mere blur in his visual distance, might take his lack of recognition for a snub.

'Father has spotted a friend and gone off with him to sample the Earl's brandy,' he said. 'I suggest you and I remain together, at least until we get our bearings.'

'Until *you* get your bearings,' she replied, and he grinned again, envious of his sister's self-assurance.

'I do find it all rather awe-inspiring,' he admitted. 'But fascinating, too. There is something morbidly compelling in standing on the fringes of such a gathering and simply watching the way people interact with each other. And the jewellery is dazzling, even though most of the ladies are wearing their lesser pieces and saving the best for the banquet this evening.'

Leonora nodded in agreement and lifted her glass to her lips. Over its rim she caught sight of a stiff, thin, elderly woman with grey hair and very pale skin, standing with a group of very grand-looking individuals on the lower lawn. She presented an imposing figure in a high-necked gown of white shot-silk, with a turban of figured gauze trimmed with large plumes adding to her already considerable height. Grim-faced, the woman was watching the Earl as he lifted Francine's hand to his lips in a lingering kiss, and the look of hatred in her eyes was as potent as a spoken curse.

'Joseph!' Leonora hissed, 'Who on earth is that woman?'

She touched her brother's arm as much for support as to regain his attention. She was quite shaken by the scene she had just witnessed. It was as if a tableau had been set up to tell a story at a glance: the illicit lovers betrayed by their unspoken affection; the jealous enemy and villain of the piece looking on from the wings and bent on destroying them both.

'What was that, Leonora?'

'The elderly women standing over there in the beaded white dress. Who is she?'

'Why, Lia, you surprise me. I thought you knew *every* member of our cousin's family.'

'She's a relative?'

'Indeed she is,' Joseph nodded. 'That imperious lady is none other than Alyce, Lady Cavendish, Countess of Beresford.'

'Sir Oscar's *wife*?'

'The same.'

'Oh, I see ... I see ...'

And Leonora *did* see. She saw now why the Shelleys had never before been invited to a function at Beresford Hall in spite of the Earl's fondness for his cousin. Lady Cavendish was consumed with jealousy. She hated Francine Shelley as only a wife could who knew that another woman had claim on her husband's heart.

'And that dashing young blood can only be Sir Horace,'

Joseph exclaimed, watching a tall, blond young man join the group after kissing the Countess's cheek. 'It seems our brother does not exaggerate the likeness between himself and Horace. Why, at a glance they might be taken for ...'

'... brothers?' Leonora offered.

The word was out before Leonora could harness her thoughts. Not even her love and loyalty for Francine could prevent the idea springing into her mind or the word from shaping itself on her tongue. That striking resemblance between the boys might exist not simply because they shared the same ancestors, but because they shared the same *father*.

Now Horace was watching her from across the stretch of lawn that lay like a rich green carpet between them. He raised his glass and bowed briefly, his grin both approving and challenging as his gaze swept over her with practised scrutiny. Seeing her son's interest, the Countess drew him quickly away, but not before her eyes had met Leonora's with that same look of hatred she had so recently bestowed upon Francine.

'Have no fear, old lady,' Leonora hissed after her. 'I would not set my cap at your precious son were he the last man on earth.'

'I beg your pardon, Lia, were you saying something?'

'No ... er ... well ... I was just wondering if Jonathan will marry Lady Fenwick's daughter. She's over there with Estelle Lacey and her parents. I like her very much, though I wonder if her mother will agree to the match.'

Joseph inclined his head in the direction of a slender, very attractive young woman in a high-waisted gown of russet and green. Louisa Fenwick was a true redhead, with copper-gold hair and a dusting of freckles across her nose and forearms. She was eighteen and very pretty, and Jonathan adored her.

'I think he hopes to marry her next year, when he comes into his inheritance,' Joseph told his sister. 'And why should Lady Fenwick refuse him? After all, she has a title but little money, while Jonathan's prospects are excellent, thanks to Mama's care and foresight.'

'And perhaps Sir Oscar will intercede on his behalf,'

Leonora said, recalling her recent discovery that the Earl had always accepted financial responsibility for Jonathan's education. 'Come, Joseph, I care little for standing still in the hot sun. Shall we circulate?'

Brother and sister moved off to exchange social niceties and introductions with the other guests, but while she sparkled in company and charmed others with her gentle wit, Leonora's mind was elsewhere. She could feel the eyes of Horace Cavendish following her from group to group, and she was careful to avoid a confrontation with him. The last few years had turned him from an awkward youth to a man of impressive stature and suave good looks, but there was a suggestion of coarseness about him that she found distasteful. She was not unaware of his reputation. She followed with interest the lives of all those who lived at the Hall, and of her childhood antagonist in particular. Through her brothers and their friends she knew of his school life at Harrow and his flamboyant social activities in London and Brighton, and from common gossip she had learned of his dependence upon his mother's devoted generosity. She also knew of his less than discreet love affairs, his extravagant gambling and his odd fascination with the more unsavoury individuals of society. For five years she had hoarded every scrap of information she could find, so that now she felt she had the full measure of his strengths and, more importantly, his weaknesses.

'But my dear lady, you are without doubt the loveliest flower ever to grace the humble gardens of Beresford.'

Horace's loud voice and bellowing laughter reached her ears above the hum of more genteel conversations. He was showing off, posturing and gesticulating before a small audience which now included the pretty and very impressionable Estelle Lacey. Leonora had known Estelle for many years and was rather fond of her. She made a mental note to take her aside at the first opportunity to warn her against indulging in even the mildest flirtation with Horace Cavendish.

By two-thirty the guests had begun to disperse, some to

private bedrooms, others to drawing rooms and morning rooms where extra chairs and sofas had been placed for their convenience. Still others preferred to sit or lie on the lawns, idling away the time between the breakfast and the evening's activities. The banquet would begin at six o'clock in the Great Hall, followed by dancing on the upper terrace and a firework display after dark. While Joseph escorted Francine to her room, Leonora remained outdoors, reluctant to put an end to her conversation with Elizabeth Cavendish, Sir Oscar's second daughter. The two had met at one of the punch-bowls and instantly warmed to each other. There was an easy, natural rapport between them.

They were sharing a secluded bench on the middle terrace, where sunlight filtered through the trees to lay lace-like patterns on the grass and the scent of flowers was heavy on the warm air. Elizabeth was a plump young woman of twenty, a little ungainly in her mannerisms and with an odd, far-away expression in her soft grey eyes. Her thick brown hair had been elaborately dressed, but her habit of constantly removing and replacing her bonnet had made an untidy mess of it.

'I've been up there *hundreds* of times,' she was saying, in a childishly conspiratorial whisper. She pointed to the very top of the west wing, which soared to almost twice the height of its neighbour on the eastern side of the Hall. 'Mama forbids it, of course, but there is no danger so long as you know exactly where to tread.'

'But how do you get inside?' Leonora asked. 'Not by the little arched door at the side of the building, for I know it's always locked and bolted from the inside. And certainly not from the gate-house. That entrance has been sealed for centuries.'

Elizabeth smiled her sad, mysterious little smile. 'There is a way over the main part of the house from the roof of the east wing. And I do believe the monk's stair, which is concealed in the walls of the tower, can be reached via an opening in the inner courtyard, though I have never found it. Did you know that from the very top you can see across four counties and account for every acre of my father's estates?'

Leonora nodded. 'The view must be quite spectacular,' she sighed. 'Oh, there is so much history, so much tragedy in those old stones. Mama told me how the abbey fell to King Henry's soldiers, how the walls were breached after a thirteen-day siege and the poor monks, with the nuns they had sought to protect, butchered and raped in an orgy of drunken violence.'

Once again that far-away look came into Elizabeth's eyes. 'They came for plunder,' she said. 'They were after the altar gold, the abbey's treasure and the caskets of gold and precious gems brought here by the nuns. It was never found, of course. Some say it was dispatched to Rome long before the soldiers came. Others suspect that it was buried with the victims when Sir Joshua ordered the crypt and all the subterranean chambers to be filled in with rubble from the walls.'

'And so the tower was eventually built over the sealed graves of the victims,' Leonora sighed. 'It is a fascinating story. Tell me, Elizabeth, wasn't it Joshua's grandson, the Second Earl, who made the upper rooms his home so that every day he could see his earldom in its entirety?'

'Ah yes, that was Sir Robert. He loved the tower, but he made a terrible mistake when he had the spiral staircase panelled with wood and lit with lamps instead of improving the windows to provide more light. One night a lamp was overturned by one of the dogs in the gate-house, and the fire was sucked up the stairwell to trap them all in their rooms. The Earl was carried to safety by his son James, who then perished in a vain attempt to save the rest of his family ... his wife and baby son, his mother and sister ...'

'And then?' Leonora prompted.

Elizabeth shrugged sadly. 'Poor Sir Robert never recovered. Grief and pain drove him quite insane, so they say. A year after the fire he climbed to the top of the ruined tower and threw himself off, leaving Percy, his horrid younger son, to inherit the lands and his titles. Look, you can still see the charred timbers and blackened stones, even after two hundred years.'

Leonora gazed at the high tower with its ever-present

company of circling, cawing birds. A rash of gooseflesh prickled her forearms and she shivered. She could almost visualise herself as Countess, standing at the summit and looking out, the way Sir Robert had looked out, over thousands of acres of Beresford property.

'It's so exciting,' she breathed. 'Everything here is so tremendously exciting. Why, I could almost ...' She broke off abruptly as Elizabeth's light shawl slipped from her shoulders. A dark scar showed itself above the collar of her gown, drawing attention to a criss-cross of finer scars now faded into her pale skin.

'Elizabeth?' She reached out to touch her fingertips to the damaged skin. 'Did you have an accident?'

The girl started as if stung by Leonora's touch. She pulled her shawl around her shoulders, shuddered and shook her head until her hair danced about her face in untidy strands.

'Don't go to the chapel,' she said urgently. 'Not the chapel. Never go inside the chapel.'

'But why? Does it frighten you? Did you hurt yourself in the chapel?'

'Never go there,' Elizabeth repeated in anxious tones. 'Never. Never. Never!'

And just as suddenly her agitation was gone and she turned in her seat to search Leonora's face with her soft grey gaze. She possessed a strange, tragic quality that touched Leonora deeply.

'Are we cousins, you and I?'

'Almost,' Leonora said. 'Your father and my mother are first cousins.'

'Then we shall be friends, *real* friends!'

'I would like that very much.' Leonora said with genuine warmth. 'And perhaps one day you will trust me with your secret and take me up there, to the very top of the west wing?'

'Oh, I will, I will. But will you *always* be my friend ... always and forever?'

'Yes, Elizabeth, I will always be your friend.'

Elizabeth continued to search Leonora's face. 'Truly? Cross your heart and hope to die?'

On impulse Leonora leaned forward to kiss Elizabeth's cheek. Then with her forefinger she made a sign over her own heart.

'Cross my heart and hope to die,' she vowed.

A moment later the curious young woman was gone, running toward the orchards with her skirts hoisted above her calves, her head lowered, her shoulders slightly hunched and her bonnet hanging precariously by its ribbons. Her clumsy figure vanished beyond the orchard wall, leaving Leonora to wonder just how close to madness Sir Oscar's daughter had been born.

With a contented sigh she closed her eyes and listened to the murmur of distant voices and the hum of busy insects in the flower beds. She intended to enjoy that quiet, shaded place for only a few mintes more before joining her mother in the room they were to share during their brief stay at Beresfor Hall. Filtered sunlight was warm on her bare arms and shoulders, and a hint of breeze stirred the gathered bodice of her gown so that it brushed her breasts with a silky caress.

'Well, well, well. So we meet again, Miss Leonora Shelley.'

She started up, alarmed by the loud and unexpected greeting. She must have dozed in the heat, for she had not heard him approach. Now Horace Cavendish towered above her, resplendent in green riding breeches and high leather boots, his shirt thrown open at the neck and cuffs to reveal sun-bronzed skin and muscular forearms. His voice was now mature and deep, though he had not learned to lower it to more agreeable tones. His grin was full of mockery when he said:

'I fear you are here to have us all disinherited and turned out like beggars into the streets.'

'I am here for your brother's wedding,' she said coldly.

'Ah, yes, my brother the aspiring Earl and his prim and proper future Countess. How disappointing for you, my dear cousin. I believe you had hoped to marry Malcolm yourself?'

'That, Horace Cavendish, is a ridiculous thing to say,' she retorted.

'Ah, but how else would you attain such authority as to

close the doors of Beresford Hall against me? Or are you now prepared to retract that childish threat?'

Realising that Horace was the same spoilt child determined to provoke her, Leonora rose to her feet with the intention of walking away. Horace stepped forward to bar her path. Their combined movements brought them very close together. He stared at her with impudent admiration, letting his gaze travel from her eyes to her mouth, then down to the pale swell of her breasts. Instinctively she lifted her shawl to cover her bare neck and shoulders, aware that her cheeks had grown hot beneath his lecherous scrutiny.

'Be so kind as to step aside,' she said.

'Not yet, my dear cousin. I have in my possession a lock of your lovely hair which has faded with the years. I think today I must claim another.'

She shrank back as he raised his hand towards her hair. 'You will do no such thing,' she informed him sharply. 'Don't you *dare* put your hands on me, Horace Cavendish.'

'Oh, such a proud one,' he grinned, allowing his fingers to brush her cheek. 'And such a beauty ... such a beauty.'

'Let me pass.'

'I will be happy to let you pass ... for the price of a kiss from those luscious red lips.'

'Never!' Leonora retorted. 'I would as soon give my kisses to a rattlesnake.'

'Or to the lusty old overseer of some stinking poorhouse, perhaps?'

'What? How dare you say such a thing to me?'

'Simple mathematics, my dear cousin,' Horace leered. 'Take one spendthrift gambler, namely Herbert Shelley, add an insufficient flow of ready cash, and the result is a future in the poorhouse. I do believe the outcome is inevitable.'

Leonora's eyes flashed with anger. 'I'll thank you to keep your insults to yourself, Horace Cavendish. Now step aside and let me pass.'

'Not until I have tasted your soft mouth, little mistress of Beresford.'

'Damn you, Horace Cavendish,' she spat angrily. 'Let me pass at once.'

Instead he stepped forward and caught her around the waist, pulled her roughly against him and fastened his mouth on hers. In spite of her anger a thrill of something like excitement went through her. The kiss was gentle at first, but just as she began to pull away from him he tightened his grip on her and kissed her with renewed passion. For a moment she responded, her body warming to the hardness of him, her lips parting against his hot, demanding mouth. Then his arousal suddenly became violent and his hands began to paw roughly at her flesh. He grunted and forced his tongue into her mouth, then his harsh fingers dipped into her bodice as if to scoop her breasts free of her gown. She was horrified to feel herself propelled backwards until she was pinned by his body against the rough surface of the terrace wall. She could scarcely breathe. His lips and hands seemed to be everywhere at once and his own breathing had become hoarse and animal-like. She struggled fiercely, convinced that this strong, sexually excited young man had but one objective. He meant to rape her.

'Let me go ... let me go ...'

'Don't fight me, wench,' he said hoarsely. 'I'm in no mood to play coy games.'

'No ... let go of me ... let me *go*!'

Leonora fought to free herself as he kissed her again. Now his hands were clawing at her gown, attempting to lift the skirts in his search for bare flesh. When she tried to scream for help his mouth smothered her cries and his tongue forced its way between her teeth. To her horror she found herself helplessly pinned against the orchard wall by the weight of his body and the press of his bent knee between her legs.

'No ... no ... no ...'

Suddenly his cruel fingers closed around her upper thigh and Leonora's fear turned to cold rage. She bit down sharply on his lower lip, and as he released his grip on her she jerked her head forward to catch him a glancing blow across the bridge of his nose. Then she snatched up her skirts and raced away across the lawn, leaving her attacker seething with pain and indignation.

'I'll have you,' he yelled after her. 'I'll have you, wench, and when I do . . .'

His threat ended in a furious growl as he dabbed a spot of blood from his lip with a handkerchief and probed with careful fingers the aristocratic bone of his bruised nose. The vixen had left him smarting and bloodied and with a heat in his loins that swelled against the tight stuff of his trousers. He had found her extraordinarily exciting. There was something in those eyes of hers, a fire that promised sexual pleasures beyond his wildest dreams. Her body had been firm and well-rounded in this arms, her mouth soft and hot and anything but unyielding against his own. Miss Leonora Shelley had an awful lot to learn about her own limitations. Her family would never have the money to make her a rich man's wife, but she was certainly seductive enough to become a rich man's darling. Horace wanted her. He wanted to pay her back for the pain in his nose and the taste of blood on his tongue, to pin that high-spirited beauty to his mattress and savagely, brutally, prick the bubble of her arrogance.

He recovered his composure with a start as a group of people strolled across the lawn some distance away to his right. Leonora's sudden flight had been hidden from their view by a thick hedging of holly bushes, but that section of terrace on which he stood was clearly visible. He saw Estelle Lacey smile coyly from beneath the fringe of her parasol and lift her delicate gloved hand in his direction. He returned her smile while executing an exaggerated bow for her benefit.

'You'll serve well enough in the meantime, Miss Lacey,' he growled through clenched teeth. 'Better an empty head than an empty bed, and I don't intend sleeping alone tonight.'

IV

The fashion that year was for pretty ball gowns in tender shades, muslin, gauze and tulle falling in Grecian style from high waistlines and tiny bodices, some with bouffant drapery of silk netting to give an illusion of substance to small bosoms, others with skirts cut to the shorter length with padded *rouleaux* around the hem for the popular weighted appearance. The favourite colours were lavender grey, mignonette green, pale yellow, white and rose. Every woman seemed to be aiming for the same look: youthful, demure, pretty and soft beside the strong colours and textures worn by their menfolk.

Leonora surveyed her reflection in the mirror and was far from satisfied with what she saw. She knew she looked beautiful in her gown of ivory crêpe with lace trims. Against its paleness her skin was translucent and her eyes and hair strikingly dark. She was dissatisfied only by its passivity, by the fact that her gown, lovely and expensive though it was, said absolutely nothing about *her*. She wanted to be a leader, not a follower of other people's ideas, and to make her mark because of her *individuality* rather than just her beauty. On that very special occasion she should have been wearing a gown of much bolder cut and more spirited colour, something that freed itself from the fashion of the day to make a statement about *herself*. She wanted to sweep down to the banqueting hall with her tiny waist pinched into a boned bodice and emphasised by wide, trailing skirts of emerald green taffeta, lush purple silk or vivid crimson satin.

'Such a deep sigh, Leonora. Why so pensive? Are you no longer happy with the gown?' Francine was wearing white gauze over pink, the whole decorated here and there with hand embroidered rose-buds.

'It's beautiful, Mama,' Leonora smiled. 'And you look wonderful ... and so *young*. I'm sure everyone will take us for sisters instead of mother and daughter.'

A clock in the room was chiming six when the adjoining door opened and Herbert entered wearing a dull red coat over fawn breeches and a waistcoat stitched with gold and silver thread. He took Leonora by the shoulders and kissed her warmly on the forehead, and when he crushed her breasts against his body she was reminded of his intimacy with Daisy Kimble and, more recently, her own encounter with Horace

Cavendish. She pulled roughly away from him, her eyes flashing.

'Tell Joseph he will find me in the Great Gallery when he is ready to go down to dinner,' she said. 'Excuse me, Mama, if I choose not to wait with you until then.'

She left the room and walked away from the east wing to the wide passage crossing the width of the house. She passed bedrooms and drawing rooms, dining rooms, libraries and studies, and where doors stood open she stepped inside to admire furnishings and decorations more grand than any she had seen before.

The Great Gallery was a room of tremendous proportions and a hushed, church-like atmosphere. Its floor was of polished walnut and its walls, no more than ten or eleven feet in height, supported a huge vaulted ceiling of decorative plaster. Set in rows along the walls were the family paintings, many larger than life-size and all housed in elaborately gilded frames. They were hung in such a way that each subject sat or stood on the same level as the visitor, giving the impression that anyone entering the room stepped into the presence of gathered nobility.

Leonora stared into every magnificent frame and was able to identify the powerful Earls and beautiful Countesses whose names, titles and histories were so familiar to her. Here were the men and women who had coloured the exclusive world of Beresford for hundreds of years: the cobalt-eyed Joshua and the pale and delicate Stephanie; the raven-haired Matilda, daughter of a Welsh baron and mother of the first Cavendish twins. Here was the handsome but tragic Sir Robert, who leaped to his death from the fire-ravaged tower, his son Sir Percy, the obese lecher, and those other twins, Hazel and Hilary, who loved and lost the same man and eventually died together as inseparable spinsters in their ninety-ninth year.

'Oh, I know you all,' Leonora breathed. 'You are a part of me, just as this house is a part of me.'

She followed a criss-cross path down the gallery, her satin shoes making no more than a whisper of sound as she wandered from one side of the room to the other with wide, fascinated eyes. She paused only briefly beside a portrait of the present Countess, noting that Lady Alyce was the only woman not depicted wearing the massive, purple-toned Cavendish Sapphire at her throat.

Toward the rear wall she found an oil painting of Sir Arthur Cavendish, the military genius destined to end his days not on the battlefield but riddled with gangrene and stripped of all his hard-won honours. And here was that other dark-haired, cobalt-eyed beauty, Lady Ursula, who had willingly sacrificed her own young life rather than risk bringing the Black Death to her family at Beresford Hall. There was even a rare miniature of the beautiful Lady Roanne, Sir Oscar's beloved younger sister, rumoured to have died in childbirth after being abducted from her home by wandering vagabonds. Every picture told its own story of love and loyalty, courage and tragedy, passion and betrayal. Leonora gazed long and hard at the painted aristocratic faces lining the walls like captured ghosts ever-watchful of the legacies they left behind. And at the farthest end of the gallery, set high upon the taller wall, she found an empty frame, flamboyantly carved and gilded, in which she imagined her own portrait would one day hang.

'All this will be mine,' she whispered passionately. 'One day ... one day ... one day ...'

'Miss Shelley? Leonora?'

Sir Oscar appeared at her side and touched his fingers lightly to her elbow. He had entered the Great Gallery to find her standing alone at its farthest end, staring up at an empty picture frame. From that angle her face was in profile, the features and colouring unmistakably Cavendish. When at last she turned her head to look at him her eyes were huge and brilliant, her face lit with a strange radiance. She tilted her chin in a haughty manner, and for a moment he fancied he saw something challenging, even threatening in her violet-tinted eyes.

'Your brother is waiting for you at the head of the stairs,' he told her.

'And what of Mama?'

'I believe she has gone down with your father.'

Leonora held his gaze for seconds more, then smiled slowly and said: 'Yes, Sir Oscar, I do believe she has.'

The sudden tightening of his features told her he had caught the double meaning in her words. He could see himself reflected in the dark centres of her eyes, a tiny, grey-clad figure trapped within her shrewd stare. She smiled knowingly into his eyes, then turned from him and, with a toss of her lovely head, swept regally from the room.

Sir Oscar followed at a slower pace and with his brow puckered into a troubled frown. His scalp had prickled and tightened as if suddenly grown too small for his head in that instant when she first looked into his eyes. He had just experienced an oddly chilling sensation that sent a shudder right through him. Had he been a superstitious man he might have believed that someone, somewhere, had stepped upon his grave.

CHAPTER SIX

I

Estelle Lacey was unexpectedly frosty in her manner when Leonora was at last able to draw her into a quiet alcove some distance away from the other guests in the room.

'I need no instructions from you on how to conduct myself, in public or in private,' she hissed, careful not to be overheard as her cheeks flushed hotly in response to her friend's whispered words.

'I am simply trying to warn you of the dangers,' Leonora persisted.

'You may keep your warnings to yourself, Leonora Shelley. I am quite capable of taking care of myself.'

'Are you?' Leonora pressed. Looking more closely, she noticed a redness around Estelle's mouth and a hint of bruising on her lips. They were the kind of marks left behind when a man forces his attentions upon a woman with little regard for the tenderness of her flesh. Leonora sighed. 'He's toying with you, Estelle.'

'That's a lie. Horace cares for me. He ...'

'He's playing games.'

'I tell you he *cares* for me.'

'Nonsense. He merely seeks to *use* you.'

'How dare you?' Estelle demanded, stamping her foot. 'Oh, how *dare* you say such a hateful thing?'

Leonora gripped her friend's hands and whispered urgently: 'You must not allow yourself to be alone with him, Estelle. He is not to be trusted. When his passions are fully aroused he ...'

'Oh, *now* I understand,' Estelle cried, pulling her hands free and glaring at Leonora as if she were an enemy instead of a trusted friend. 'You're jealous. You want him for yourself. You have failed to arouse his passions yourself and now you seek to deny me the privilege of winning his favours.'

'*Privilege? Favours?* My dear Estelle, you have absolutely no idea what you are talking about.'

'Oh, yes I have,' Estelle insisted. 'Horace really cares for me. He considers me the most attractive and intelligent girl in the whole county and I will hear no more of your wicked, jealous lies.'

'Oh, for heaven's sake, Estelle ...'

But Estelle had gathered up her skirts and turned proudly on her heels. Leonora watched her hurry away in a flounce of indignation, then sighed softly and stepped out into the garden to rejoin Joseph on his shady bench by the fountain. She could only hope that beneath the anger Estelle had sufficient common sense to heed her warning.

The wedding banquet was excellent. Only the very finest food was served, with many of the dishes so elaborately dressed that they were viewed and remarked upon like so many works of art before the more serious business of tasting could begin. Huge ice sculptures formed centrepieces for the tables, some in the shape of swans, eagles and peacocks, others forming badger and deer, still others depicting the heraldic insignia of both families. On enormous silver platters were served whole sides of beef and venison, glazed whole lamb and suckling pig, salmon and trout in aspic trimmed with crushed and coloured ice. Each place setting had its own individual flower arrangement and every guest was handed a souvenir napkin bearing the newly-weds' initials in gold and silver thread.

'Magnificent!' exclaimed one of the guests in a loud voice. 'A spread fit for royalty.'

'And therefore suitable for the Cavendish heir,' said another, with a knowing wink of his eye.

Above the tables the forty Italian crystal chandeliers twinkled and turned beneath soaring gothic arches, their lights reflected in fancy glasswear, ice sculptures and glittering jewellery. With extravagance the order of the day, and with an army of servants dancing attendance on the guests, those three and a half hours of wining and dining succeeded in their objective of producing a truly unforgettable experience.

It was dark when the dancing began. To splendid effect, the paved upper terrace had been hung with lamps and coloured lanterns and decorated with a profusion of fresh flowers. Bowls of punch and fruit salad, sweet ices and sillabub were set between sofas and chairs placed around the dancing area. At least a score of musicians, all dressed alike in plumed hats, crimson coats and white trousers, occupied a specially constructed rostrum bedecked with tinted lights. It was a warm night, heavy and sweet with summer scents.

Leonora danced with several dashing young men and one or two hopeful older ones before Joseph led her off the dance floor and handed her a glass of lemonade cooled with crushed ice. Her eyes sparkled and a pretty flush coloured her cheeks. She had rested for only a few minutes when Horace Cavendish, handsome in lavender grey and deep blue, invaded their brief respite. He was less than sober and would have taken Leonora's hand and pulled her into the dance without so much as a 'by your leave', had she not placed herself beyond his reach. There was a dark bruise across the bridge of his nose and a wound on his lower lip where her teeth had split the skin. He leered at her, undressing her with his eyes as he offered a mocking, rather unsteady bow.

'I believe this is our dance, Miss Shelley,' he slurred.

'Oh, but that can not possibly be so, *Mr* Cavendish,' she replied, bobbing a small curtsy but fixing him with a frosty stare. 'You see, I have promised this dance to my brother and the next to old Mr Seddon of Bath. After that I am pledged to dance with Estelle's cousin, Richard, and after him that dear old gentleman from …'

'Please do not bother to continue,' Horace said coldly, glancing at Joseph, then back at Leonora. 'You are clearly inundated with admirers.' His eyes narrowed into blue slits and he clicked his heels in a stiff bow. 'Another time, perhaps?'

'Over my dead body,' Leonora hissed under her breath as he walked away.

Joseph shook his head. 'He's drunk, and I do believe you have offended him, Lia. And by the look of his nose and mouth, I'd say he is not having a particularly good time of it this evening.'

'He's nothing but an overbearing bully,' Leonora retorted. 'I extend my compliments to anyone who has had the courage to give him a little of what he deserves. And now, my dear Joseph, I think it is time you danced with me again.'

With a grin Joseph set down their glasses and swept his sister back into the dance. They made a very attractive couple, he taller now by several inches, very blond and slender, she dark, curvy and vivacious. They gave themselves wholeheartedly to the merriment of the music, unaware of the brooding, peevish scowl of Horace Cavendish, who watched Leonora with a dangerous combination of hostility and desire. As other couples joined them on the dance floor, he plucked Estelle from the company of her friends and roughly, peevishly, claimed her as his partner in a lively reel.

At midnight the dancing ended and the lights were dimmed in readiness for the fireworks. Soon the sky above Beresford was bright with flares and rockets, Catherine wheels and brilliant, winking stars. Each display was met with cheers and gasps of delight, and followed by a round of enthusiastic applause.

'Our cousins certainly know how to impress their guests,' Joseph shouted above the din of appreciation. They were standing with Francine on the terrace steps, and had just watched a wonderful set-piece recalling the recent coronation of King George IV.

'Sir Oscar is a man of great style,' Francine responded.

'And great wealth,' Leonora smiled. 'One can hardly have one without the other.'

Joseph gave a mock wince and said: 'I think Father would disagree with you on that point, Lia.'

Leonora glanced at her mother and saw the smile fade from her face. She recalled the first time she had come to Beresford Hall, the sneering remarks of Horace Cavendish and the money hidden away among Francine's clothes. She wondered if Herbert Shelley was once again living so far beyond his means that Francine had been reduced to begging money from her cousin. The thought provoked a shudder, touching upon her deep-rooted horror of poverty. She knew her own future to be secured by a substantial dowry, but she feared for her dear mother, who might yet become the victim of her husband's periodic and seemingly uncontrollable bouts of extravagance.

'Oh, bravo! Bravo indeed!'

A few seconds of darkness were suddenly illuminated by the final set-piece, a dazzling portrayal of the bride and groom entwined within their combined family crests. This was the highlight of the display, the grand finale of the wedding celebrations, and the appreciation of the guests was long and boisterous. Now many of the lamps were re-lit to show tables laid with light supper dishes, cheeses and desserts, wine and hot chocolate. For those not yet prepared for their beds, there would be whist and faro in the lower rooms, music and dancing in the small inner courtyard and gossip a-plenty amongst those who stayed behind with the food and drink in the Great Hall.

'Will you be staying awake with the night-owls, Lia?'

Leonora shook her head. She could see by a darkness around his eyes that Joseph was tired, though she knew he

131

would happily forego his bed on her account, should she insist upon it.

'This has been the most wonderful day of my life,' she sighed. 'But all good things must come to an end, and I admit to being *very* tired. Are you ready too, Mama?'

'Oh, yes,' Francine said. 'We have a long journey home in the morning, and it is now almost one o'clock. We should all take a good night's rest after the day's excitement.'

'But first some hot chocolate,' Leonora suggested. 'Joseph, dear, would you mind?'

She took her mother's arm and led her to one of the long tables close to the main staircase. She was eager to distract her mother's attention away from a group of rowdy guests gathered on the far side of the Great Hall. Among them she had spotted Herbert, laughing and ruddy-faced with drink, his arms around a fat woman in blue whose breasts seemed to be bursting like over-blown balloons from her gown. He had obviously found himself a companion for the night, and as the two vanished through one of the other doors Leonora glared after them. She doubted that her father would make his way back to his own room before morning.

That night Leonora slept beside her mother in a heavily carved four-poster bed hung with red and gold brocade drapes. The room was small but adequate, with dark pine panelling and two casement windows opening on to the gardens on the eastern side of the house. An adjoining door led to a very comfortable dressing room complete with hip-bath and private closet. Beyond that was the room shared by Joseph and his father.

It was almost four o'clock, with a small, bright moon hanging high in the sky, when Leonora crept through the dressing room, drew back the heavy drapes of that other bed and stood for a moment looking down at Joseph. By the light of the lamp he looked paler and more blond than ever, with short, yellow-tinged eyelashes and a mouth so soft and full that it might have belonged to a girl. On impulse she stooped to kiss his cheek. She wondered how he would react in the morning, when he discovered that he had spent the night alone in the big bed because his father had chosen to sleep elsewhere.

Back in her own room she seated herself close to one of the windows and looked out at the night sky. There was a chill in the air that penetrated her thin cotton shift, so she pulled her shawl around her shoulders before opening the window wide to breathe in the fresh night air. Her stay at Beresford Hall was almost over. Tomorrow she would be back in London, and already she could feel a touch of sadness, a sense of loss. She doubted if the bland but well-bred Lady Grace Osbourne Graham, lying beside her handsome new husband in their marriage bed and destined to become Countess of Beresford, would ever experience the powerful affinity that she, Leonora, felt for this place. It was a strange and cruel twist of fate that had brought her so close to her dream while holding it still so far beyond her reach.

'Father was away the whole night,' Joseph whispered to her at breakfast. 'I believe he was at one of the Earl's gaming tables, and if his dark mood is any indication, I fear he must have lost more hands than he won. He and cousin Oscar were quarrelling in the library this morning, and some reference was made to money and assets squandered on the turn of a card.'

Leonora glanced around to make sure that Francine was not close enough to overhear their conversation. She urged Joseph to the far end of the buffet table where bowls of fruit salad and baskets of warm bread were placed.

'What on earth were they quarrelling about? Did you hear any more of their conversation?'

'Well ... no ... not really ... only snatches.'

'Oh *do* tell, Joseph.'

'I can't, Lia. It was a private conversation. And besides, the door was closed, so it was impossible for me to hear more than the odd word or two.'

Leonora sighed in exasperation as Joseph moved away to sample the pastries. She was joined by Francine, who picked delicately at the small portions of fruit and cheese on her plate. Sometimes her slightness took Leonora by surprise, and on this occasion she was tempted to pile her mother's plate high with food and beg her to eat every scrap. She resisted the temptation and was grateful when a talkative woman friend claimed Francine's attention.

Joseph placed a large, plump pastry dusted with cinnamon and sugar on his sister's plate. Then he studied her face very closely before saying: 'This place makes you different, Lia. A change came over you the moment you stepped down from the carriage yesterday. You seem to glow here, to come alive in a very special way. You even *feel* different, somehow. It's as if ... as if you no longer belong to me ... to *us* ... as if you belong *here*.'

'And you feel nothing of this in yourself?'

'No, but I think I understand how deeply it touches *you*.'

Leonora smiled sadly and set down her plate, the pastry unsampled. 'Coming here was like coming home and leaving is painful,' she said quietly, placing a hand over her heart. 'It actually *hurts*, right here.'

'Oh, Lia, is it that important to you?'

'Yes,' she nodded, without hesitation. 'I would rather be here than anywhere else in the world.'

'Then you would be happy to live here?'

'*Live* here? Oh, Joseph, if only I could ... if only ...'

'Even as the wife of Horace Cavendish?'

She stared up at him, her eyes suddenly huge and dark. 'What? *What* did you say?'

'I could be mistaken in what I heard, Lia, but I think you should give careful consideration to the idea. You must be certain in your own heart what you *really* want and how far you will go to achieve it.'

'So they were quarrelling about myself and Horace? But did Father make no mention of Gilbert, the younger son? Surely he would not see his daughter married to such a monster as Horace Cavendish?'

'I don't know, my dear. I overheard so little and perhaps it's irresponsible of me to repeat it. All I'm asking you to do is consider the possibility so that Father's plans for the future do not take you entirely by surprise.'

'But why *Horace*? The very idea that I should ever consent to become the wife of that man is quite ludicrous.'

'Is it, Lia? Even though such a marriage would bring you the Cavendish name, make you a lady and give you a part of all this? Are you *sure* you would not jump at the chance to marry him in order to gain a secure place for yourself at Beresford Hall?'

Just then a laughing young woman pushed between them to reach into one of the many bread baskets set upon the table. As they drew apart Joseph held her gaze, his eyes searching hers for an answer to his question. She could offer him none, for at that moment she was unable to weigh the prospect of becoming Lady Cavendish of Beresford against that of being Horace's wife.

Several other buffet breakfasts had been laid out in those sumptuous ground floor rooms whose huge windows were thrown open to the scented breezes of the inner courtyard. From here the great buttresses of the west wing, set against a blue sky hung with shreds of cloud, could be seen reflected on the surface of a rectangular pond sunk into the very centre of the courtyard. Surrounding the pond were ancient stone walkways long ago worn to marble-like smoothness by the sandalled feet of Beresford's original occupants. The pillared arches, sheltered and shady, were mute reminders that the old abbey cloisters had been preserved right there at the very heart of the great house.

'Our carriage is ready, Leonora. You will need your cloak if you are not to catch a chill. I think the breeze is a little cooler today.'

'Yes, Mama. I'll be out directly. Did you speak to the Countess?'

'No, dear. The opportunity did not arise.'

'But should we not . . .?'

Francine smiled a little sadly. 'No, my dear. Lady Alyce is busy with her friends and I don't believe we should encroach upon their time together. Ah, here comes your father, at last. Our departure will be delayed if he is yet to break his fast.'

Leonora turned to the window as her mother moved away.

From there she could see Lady Alyce on the far side of the courtyard. Dressed in a narrow, high-necked gown of dark green satin, she looked very much the regal and gentle semi-invalid society painted her. Only her cold grey eyes gave the lie to that kindly image. They were shrewd and watchful, not the eyes of a mild-mannered invalid but those of a bitter and formidable woman. She received her guests with all the dignity of her station and yet, while offering nothing that might be construed as a social snub, had skilfully avoided even the briefest exchange with any member of the Shelley family. She seemed to look upon her less wealthy relatives with contempt, and each time her gaze fell upon Francine the hatred in her heart was laid bare.

Horace Cavendish, seemingly none the worse for his heavy drinking of the night before, was a changed man in the company of the Countess. Here he was relaxed and softly spoken, charming and lovingly attentive toward the mother he adored. As she observed them together Leonora recognised the flaw in the armour of that overbearing young man. She knew he relied upon Lady Alyce for the money in his pocket, but now she saw that his dependence went much deeper than mere avarice. It was clear that he fed upon her pride in his scholastic achievements and basked, with almost childish pleasure, in his position as her favourite son. Watching him, marking his unexpected vulnerability, Leonora allowed herself to wonder what it would take to rob him of both.

'Do you deny, then, that you would marry Horace to gain a secure place for yourself at Beresford Hall?'

Joseph's words came back to her with such force that he might have spoken them afresh. She started, then turned to find her mother standing beside her. It was time for them to go down to the carriage to begin the long journey back to London. As they crossed the Great Hall Sir Oscar appeared to take Francine's arm, and while outwardly his manner was merely that of a concerned host for one of his guests, Leonora sensed once again the secret yet very potent bond of love between them.

An anxious-looking Lady Elizabeth stepped from one of the

alcoves and hurried forward to grasp Leonora's hands in her own. She was wearing a beautiful muslin gown in soft rose pink, but her long hair hung in untidy strands over her shoulders and her red satin shoes were stained with dried mud.

'Will you remember me, Leonora?' she asked, using an urgent stage whisper that carried to every ear in the Hall.

'Dear Elizabeth, of *course* I will. We might even write to each other. Would you like that?'

'Oh yes ... but ... but ...'

'But?' Leonora prompted, reaching out to harness a tendril of unruly hair. Elizabeth's features puckered in a frown, then brightened as an idea occurred to her.

'It could be our secret,' she said, brightly.

'Indeed it could, if you prefer it.' Leonora took a pencil and a scrap of paper from her purse, scribbled down her address and handed it to Elizabeth. 'Here is my address in London. I do hope you will write to me very soon.'

'Oh, I will, I will.'

Elizabeth kissed her warmly on both cheeks, then rushed away with the precious scrap of paper clutched in her fingers. Leonora watched until she was out of sight before continuing on to where Joseph waited for her at the main door. Together they walked out into the sunshine slanting across the paved terrace, then down the steps to the lower main driveway, where their smart new carriage was among those waiting to depart. She paused to raise her eyes to the tower of the west wing, and her hand came up to touch that area between her breasts where an ache, a hunger, had settled on that first visit to Beresford Hall five years ago.

Leonora was amazed to find Horace at her elbow as she was waiting to be handed aboard. Once again he was wearing an open-necked shirt with unbuttoned cuffs, fawn breeches and high leather riding boots. His hair shone with golden lights in the bright morning sunshine.

'I hope you have enjoyed your stay with us,' he said, stooping to kiss her hand.

His smile was sheepish, almost endearing, and he looked so

like Jonathan that she found herself responding with warmth to his unexpected pleasantries. Then a glint of mischief in his blue eyes reminded her of his uncouth attempts to ravish her right there on the terrace. She snatched her hand free and tossed her head proudly. The grinning Horace was undaunted by her show of indignation. He touched her elbow very gently and leaned so close that she could detect the gingery scent of an indigestion remedy on his breath.

'Please forgive me,' he whispered, softly and with a disconcerting sincerity. 'I was rude and boorish in my behaviour toward you and now I heartily beg your pardon.'

Leonora was astonished. She stared into his deep blue eyes, looking for the mockery, the veiled contempt. She found neither.

'You ... you were quite insulting,' she reminded him.

'And you punished me soundly for it,' he said, touching his lip and nose, where the marks of her anger were still visible. 'So, will you not tell me now that I am forgiven?'

Leonora hesitated, suspecting some trick. 'Well ...?'

'Please, Leonora. *Please*?'

She found herself weakening before his smile and his heartfelt pleas. Her own smile came slowly.

'Very well, you are forgiven, sir,' she told him with a small curtsy.

'Then I am once again a happy man, and I look forward to seeing you again, my dear Leonora ... and very soon.' He lifted her hand to his lips and pressed a lingering kiss upon it, then helped her into the carriage. As he did so he surreptitiously pressed something into the palm of her hand.

'A small token of my respect and admiration,' he whispered, with a warm and vivid grin. 'May it serve to remind you of the value I place upon your kisses.'

Leonora felt her cheeks flush hotly as she muttered her thanks. Only later, when she and her family were comfortably seated and all their goodbyes had been said, did she open her hand and stare down at the gift. As she did so the colour drained from her cheeks and her brief pleasure turned to humiliation. He had tricked her after all and she, turned to vanity by his clever flattery, had allowed herself to become a silly, gullible plaything in his hands. As his parting gift Horace Cavendish had given her a farthing, the coin of lowest value, the beggars' coin.

'What is it, my dear? Are you feeling unwell?'

'It is nothing, Mama.'

'But are you sure, Leonora? You are suddenly very pale.'

She managed a tight smile and was grateful when the carriage lurched forward and the others turned to wave from the open windows. Horace was standing on the steps with his hands on his hips and his head at an arrogant tilt. She knew without raising her eyes that he was grinning with malicious amusement. Tears of embarrassment pricked her eyes as she looked again at the beggars' coin lying in her palm, its surface stained and distorted by years of passing from hand to grubby hand. At that moment not even she, wounded as she was by the insult, could begin to image what that cruel gift would one day cost the giver. It lay in her palm like an ugly brand, prompting her to mutter a vow into the noisy clatter of hooves and the creak of carriage leathers.

'As God is my judge, you will pay for this, Horace Cavendish. You will pay most dearly for this.'

II

Throughout the following year Herbert Shelley fell deeper and deeper into debt. Always in the forefront of his mind was the conviction that the next game, the next hand, the next card would mark the turning point when his luck would change for the better. While every failure left him depressed and filled with remorse, the emotional pendulum of the compulsive gambler soon carried him to yet another peak of zealous expectation. He sold the first of Francine's expensive gowns at Christmas after an unsuccessful run at the tables, and the first piece of her heirloom jewellery in March, when a particularly unpleasant moneylender had the effrontery to present himself at the house. After that he became more cautious, taking a little here and a little there to help finance his losses and keep the creditors from the door. By appearances he was as he had always been: a man of impeccable, if somewhat extravagant, tastes. In private he was a very troubled individual reduced to robbing his own family in order to stay the tidal wave of debts threatening to overwhelm him.

Francine had been ill throughout the previous winter, had barely recovered her strength during the humid summer, and was now bed-ridden yet again for the duration of the colder, wetter seasons. Much to his annoyance and inconvenience, Herbert's visits to her bedroom to exercise his rights as husband and master had, as a consequence of her ill-health, become increasingly infrequent. Sir Marcus Shaw had been most specific and quite unnecessarily blunt regarding the matter.

'Your wife is far too ill to be expected to suffer your attentions, Shelley,' he had announced in the most pompous tones, as if addressing a much lesser man. 'She must be left alone, *strictly* alone.'

'But what of my rights,' Shelley had blustered. 'What of my marital rights, sir?'

'If your wife's health is of even the smallest concern to you, sir, you will forego your rights until such time as she is recovered sufficiently to receive them.'

'And just when, may I venture to enquire, might that time be anticipated?'

'Some months, I fear. Until then, I trust you will accept my superior knowledge on the matter and take steps to ensure her comfort and, let us dare to hope, her speedy return to health.'

Herbert had smouldered with anger for days following that conversation, yet there was precious little he could do to rectify the situation when any default from duty on his part might so easily reach the attention of Sir Oscar Cavendish. So the seasons had progressed, with scant improvement in either Francine's health or his own finances. Money was short and any trinkets he could acquire had to be turned into ready cash to spend at the tables in pursuit of the big win. This meant that Herbert, finding himself the unhappy victim of one adverse circumstance after another, was eventually pressed into buying cheap sexual satisfaction on the streets. In this very personal and sensitive area of his life he had also encountered certain misfortunes. When the 'widow' Marie-Louise Jordan returned to Paris in the winter of 1821 she took with her a small fortune in expensive gifts and the husband who had been posing as her brother-in-law. She left behind a host of outstanding accounts and a string of lovers infected with the French Pox. For six weeks Herbert had been suffering the pain and indignity of submitting himself to various doctors for treatment. One insisted that a series of hot, evil-smelling poultices be applied to his genitals twice daily to heal the chancre, another attempted to dry up the pustules with a powder made from hemlock and camphor, while yet another prescribed frequent and severe leeching to remove the toxins from the blood. The combined ministrations of these learned men eventually removed all outward signs of infection but left him feeling weak and listless. For a further three months he had been in too much discomfort to enjoy anything but the occasional street whore. Now that his health was fully recovered he had to be content, for a while at least, with hiring a back bedroom at the Stag and Hounds and having girls procured for him by one of the less savoury customers. Thus he spent part of every Tuesday evening, convinced that a man of his fastidious personal habits would not be visited by the French Pox a second time.

'Calls 'erself Joan, Mr Shelley, an' she's young and cheap, just like you said.'

Herbert looked with some distaste at the short, thin-faced man standing before him. This was Clegg, a one-eyed ex-convict who caught rats in the sewers of Newgate and White-chapel to sell as dog-bait in the ever popular rat-killing matches. He had brought with him into the room a smell of unwashed clothes, stale sweat, and some underlying stench that might have been from excrement clinging to his shoes. It was unlikely that any part of his body had ever known the benefit of soap and water. He fingered his cap respectfully in the presence of a better man, though his leering grin and general demeanour were less than deferential.

'How much?' Shelley demanded, touching a handkerchief to his offended nostrils.

'Two guineas, sir.'

'What? Two guineas? Two guineas for this ragged little street urchin?'

The man stood his ground. 'She's a young 'n,' he grinned. 'You asked for a young 'n, Mr Shelley, an' I brung it, an it'll cost you two guineas.'

'Then you may take her away, I'm not interested.'

'But you didn't even *look* at 'er, sir.' Clegg's smile faltered as he saw his profits slipping away. It was a cold, wet night and he was eager to get to the chop house for a good supper and a few rounds of best stout. He twisted his cap and tried again.

'She's worth at least a guinea, Mr Shelley.'

Herbert pursed his lips and was careful not to show an interest in the girl. For the occasion he was wearing only a heavy outdoor coat over a loose shirt. The rest of his clothes were laid neatly across a chair and his boots were standing to attention by the fireplace. Time and preparation were important to him if he was to enjoy any other entertainment on Tuesday evenings. Cheap sex was not to be savoured or lingered over like the real thing. He preferred to make these encounters as brief as possible.

'Five shillings,' he said at last.

'Five shillings? Nay, she's worth double that.'

'Not to me, Mr Clegg.'

Herbert looked at the small girl standing in a corner by the door. She was wearing a shapeless woollen dress that was stained in places and tied around the middle with a length of string. Around her shoulders was a grubby triangle of rough wool, on her feet odd shoes that were unlaced and several sizes too big. There were scabs on the backs of her hands and between her fingers, where the skin was split to reveal the raw flesh beneath. While the two men haggled over her price, she looked at the floor as if the squalid world in which she existed

142

no longer held any fears or surprises. The smell of poverty emanating from her was no less objectionable than that coming from her companion.

'She's filthy. And she stinks to high heaven.'

'Ah, now that's because she's been a mudlark, Mr Shelley. I took her from one of the hovels around Woolwich only a couple of weeks ago. Spent her whole life in the Thames mud, she has, grubbing about for coal and iron and old bones left behind by the tide. There's lots to be sold for a bite of bread or a drop of gin. Half a stone of coal is fetching a ha'penny these days, an' I 'eard as how a young 'n can raise a whole penny or more on just six pounds of bones.'

'How old is she?'

Clegg shrugged his broad shoulders. 'Who knows? Some of 'em start on the game at eleven or twelve, soon as they realise there's an easier way to put food in their bellies than standing up to their middles in mud and slime every low tide.'

'And how many others have had her?'

The man shrugged again. 'Dunno, Mr Shelley. Book-keeping don't count fer much in this business. Let me see, now ... two weeks out of the mud ... that's maybe ...' He paused to scratch at his face with filthy fingernails, rolling his eyes as he struggled with the calculation. '... oh, no more'n twenty-five or thirty, I reckon.'

'Hardly a virgin, then, to be fetching high prices,' Herbert said flatly. He pursed his lips and stared at the girl. She was tiny and thin, with stick-like legs and a belly distended by hunger. She was all dirty rags and bones, but her face was pretty enough beneath the grime and she was young, *very* young. He licked his lips and said: 'I'll give you seven and sixpence, and that's my final offer.'

''t ain't much, Mr Shelley,' Clegg grumbled.

'Take it or leave it.'

The man puckered his brow in a fierce frown, then nodded his head grudingly.

'All right, but that don't include a few extra coppers for the girl. Fair's fair, Mr Shelley. She'll be needing something to eat afore I put her back to work.'

'Very well, seven and six for yourself and a copper or two for her.'

Herbert tipped coins from a small draw-string purse and counted out seven shillings and six pennies into the man's palm, careful not to touch the filthy skin as he did so.

'Now get out and don't bother to come back,' he told him. 'I'll leave her outside the door when I'm finished with her.'

'Right you are, Mr Shelley.'

Clegg pocketed his fee, replaced his shapeless hat and moved to the door, where he gripped the girl by the shoulders and held her against his coat as if bringing a dog to heel. She barely reached as high as his waist. He smiled knowingly and touched the length of his forefinger to the side of his nose.

'Any rough stuff'll be extra, Mr Shelley. All damages got to be paid for in hard cash, beggin' yer pardon sir.'

'Yes, yes, now get out and leave us alone.'

With a grin Clegg gave the girl a shove and left the room, closing the door very quietly behind him and waiting on the landing until he heard the key turn in the lock.

Inside the room Herbert pulled off the girl's clothes and hoisted her on to the bed. She was even smaller and younger than he had at first thought, with not a trace of pubic hair and no signs of womanly growth on her ribbed chest. He pinched the tiny nipples lying flat and useless against her skin. Even before he opened her legs his nostrils told him that other men had emptied themselves there, and suddenly his passions were inflamed and his mind alive with fantasies. He flung her over on to her face, lifted her buttocks and rammed himself into her with tremendous force. She made no protest, but had she whimpered or cried out the sounds would have been drowned by the grunts and yells of the man so brutally using her. Minutes later Herbert ejaculated with a roar and collapsed across the bed, pinning her beneath his considerable bulk.

He must have fallen into a doze, for some time elapsed before he became aware of sounds beyond the door of the room and small movements between his body and the mattress. He rolled over and shoved her away to rummage around for the rags she had been wearing. He did not look at her. It would have sickened him to watch the miserable creature dress.

From the seat of a chair close to the bed he took a small bottle of Hungary water made from rosemary, cedar and turpentine in an alcohol base. Then, using a wad of cotton wool specially cut for the purpose, he very carefully applied the perfumed substance to his genitals. His motives in doing this were two-fold. He had no wish to proceed to his club reeking of poverty and stale sex, nor would he risk catching any disease the girl might have brought with her from the stinking mud of the Thames. When he had cleaned himself to his own satisfaction he dressed and reached for his purse.

'Here you are, child.'

She reached out her hand, turning her face upward in such a way that he was reminded of the prettiness beneath the grime. For one uncomfortable moment he felt a pang of sympathy for the dirty, ragged child standing before him. She had been plucked from one abominable existence only to be plunged into another. His beloved Helen was the same age, perhaps even a year or two older, yet already this child had experienced first-hand much more of the world than Helen, God willing, would ever need to be aware of. He reached into his purse to fish out a few more coins.

'Here are some pennies for you. Take them to the chop-house in Meadow Street for a four-penny dish of bread and cheese or a tuppenny hot potato and a bowl of soup.' He scowled, irritated by her silence and her dull-witted stare. 'And here's a little extra to buy yourself a pint of stout or something. Go along then, girl. Get out ... get out.'

He re-locked the door behind her and poured the remains of a half-bottle of port into a glass. He felt better for relieving himself in sex, and tonight he was feeling more confident than he had for many months. Perhaps at last his luck was about to change for the better. He desperately needed a long run of wins at the tables. His affairs were already hovering around that critical point at which a man might find himself, through no real fault of his own, completely swamped by his financial commitments. His debts were increasing at a frightening pace.

Jonathan had already announced his intention to ask for the hand of Lady Louisa Fenwick later in the year, and for this he needed his inheritance. Charles was determined to sink his personal entitlement into an engineering project to market his own inventions the moment he came of age. Both were growing impatient of Herbert's continued refusal to discuss either their future plans or the condition of their legacies.

'But my dear, you are withholding their rights,' Francine had pressed only a few days ago. 'Indeed, our sons would have been helping to manage their own affairs for several years, had you not insisted upon shouldering the entire responsibility yourself.' Then her face had become over-shadowed, the way it always did when troubled thoughts shaped themselves in her mind. 'Oh Herbert, do assure me that the children's properties are safe. If I thought for one moment that . . .'

'That *what*, exactly?' Herbert had demanded with all the heartfelt indignation of a guilty man too close to exposure for his peace of mind. 'That I have stooped so low as to cheat my own children out of their inheritances? And would you care to explain, madam, how these properties could be anything *but* safe when you yourself, my own dear and loving wife, have thought fit to fetter them with such legalities as would take a team of lawyers years to unravel?'

Francine had fallen silent before his outburst, and so he had successfully transferred the guilt and deflected, albeit on a merely temporary basis, a confrontation regarding the family's very precarious financial affairs.

Herbert blamed Sir Oscar Cavendish for many of the problems leading to his present predicament. The man stubbornly held himself aloof when his acknowledged support would improve the Shelley fortunes overnight. At the wedding the previous year Herbert had drawn the Earl aside and proposed, on Francine's behalf, a union between the children of both families. He had seriously suggested that, for a price to be agreed upon, any one of his three sons would provide a finer husband for the witless Elizabeth than was likely to be found elsewhere. When this failed he offered Leonora, beautiful, healthy and also with aristocratic blood in her veins, as the tastier bait. He would give her in marriage to Horace or Gilbert on condition that Sir Oscar settle upon her a dowry compatible with the match. All settlements agreed upon would, of course, include a large sum for Herbert's personal use. The proposals had been made in earnest, but Sir Oscar had all but laughed in his face.

'Not one penny,' he had hissed. 'And you can abandon any foolish scheme you might have to ingratiate your children into my family.'

'*Francine's* children,' Herbert had reminded him with a sly smile. 'Your own flesh and blood, Sir Oscar. Your own *cousin's* children.'

'Sir, you presume too much upon a slender blood-tie.'

'Then let me presume upon your good taste, both as a father and a man,' Herbert had smiled, attempting a more personal approach. 'My daughter Leonora, though as yet barely of marriageable age, is a beauty by any standards; the kind of woman who can fill a man's dreams by moving his loins. Any one of your sons would thank you for such a wife, and your grandsons will be strong and sturdy. At least give the matter your consideration, Sir Oscar.'

The Earl had been deeply affronted by the suggestion that he might wish to barter his way into someone's family like any common man looking for advancement. He had never cared for Herbert Shelley. Now he began to despise him.

'Enough of this,' he bellowed. 'I will have no offspring of yours to sire my grandchildren, Herbert Shelley. By heaven, sir, you test my charity too far. This subject is now closed. I will not hear of it again.'

So Herbert had quarrelled with the very man he had sought to make use of, and from there his progress had been all downhill. The bank had been generous, of course, perhaps *too* generous. The lawyers employed by Fairfax, Reece & Tilbury had spent many weeks untangling the complexities of Francine's bequests to her children, and at last the bank had agreed to make use of them on Herbert's account. Fresh documents had been drawn up to provide them with irrevocable claim on properties, incomes and profits relating to the legacies. All Herbert had to do was obtain Francine's signature on each new contract without alerting her to its contents, a relatively simple task for a cunning man in possession of a trusting wife. Thirty-seven thousand pounds had so far been advanced against the mortgages, but the cash was all gone, leaving the last four repayments overdue and Herbert floundering beneath a mountain of unpaid bills. Tonight at the tables his luck must change; or perhaps tomorrow he would improve his stakes by approaching the bank for another loan against the mortgages. One thing alone was certain: if any of his children tried to claim their inheritance within the next few months, their demands would expose him to consequences of a quite disastrous nature.

Herbert tossed the empty bottle on to the bed and glanced around the shabby room before leaving. The little mudlark was crouched on the gloomy landing outside the room. She did not look up as he stepped around her and he gave her no more than a second glance. If he had her again he would pay Clegg only five shillings for the privilege, because with every passing day she would become more prone to disease and therefore less desirable.

III

It was a cold, windy afternoon in March. The weather had been grey and depressing for weeks, with too few of those sunny, hopeful days that lifted the heart with promises of spring. Leonora welcomed a rare opportunity to neglect her studies.

'Leonora, I do wish you would reconsider. You know your Mama disapproves of the Laceys, and that Estelle ...' Anabel made tut-tutting noises with her tongue and shook her head gravely. 'Such whispers I've heard about that young woman recently.'

'Shame on you, Anabel,' Leonora smiled. 'You really

should learn not to give credence to common gossip.'

'Oh, Leonora! You should be the last person on earth to lecture anyone on the subject of listening to tittle-tattle,' Anabel exclaimed. 'Oh, you little madam, and you with your ear to every door and your eye to every keyhole, and never a morsel of news reaching the house but what you've heard it ahead of us all.'

'Don't exaggerate, Anabel!'

'And that's the only reason you are going over there to see Estelle Lacey this afternoon. You're frightened of missing some juicy little tit-bit she might have picked up in some man's bed.'

'Now, Anabel, that's quite enough of that,' Leonora gently reproved. 'Estelle's unhappy and in need of company. Her note says she's confined to her bed with some kind of stomach upset.'

'Aye, and that's likely to be something she's picked up in some man's bed, if you ask me.'

Leonora smiled again as she placed her hands on her hips and turned elegantly this way and that, staring at her reflection in the mirror. She was wearing stays originally made for her mother and now altered to fit her own more rounded figure. Made of cotton and trimmed with pretty lace, they were stitched and boned to hug her tiny waist and lift her breasts until they bulged like firm, pale fruits from their shapely cups.

Anabel shook her head. 'I really can't imagine why you want to bother with such uncomfortable things when the good Lord gave you a figure most women would die for.'

'Stays are coming back into fashion,' Leonora informed her. 'And besides, I intend to make the most of what I was born with. There's no crime in that, is there?'

'Not if it's put to honest use,' Anabel muttered, fussing at the lace trim newly stitched to the lower edges of the stays.

'And so it will be.'

'Not by the likes of Estelle Lacey, it won't. And that cousin of hers is no better since his father sent him up to the Naval Academy. He struts around Brighton like a common sailor, with his hair dyed as black as coal and his arms tattooed from wrist to shoulder. Hold still while I fix this bone. There, it's done, and may the Devil tweak your nose for your shameless vanity.'

Leonora turned away and, still with her hands on her hips, peered over her shoulder to view herself from the back. Not even she, with her critical eye for detail and her constant striving for improvement, could find fault in what she saw.

'I'll wear it tonight,' she said. 'I want to discover if it pinches anywhere, so you can fix it for me before Lady Kershaw's dinner party. My new mulberry gown must look *perfect* on the night.'

Anabel clicked her tongue again, but she was smiling when she asked: 'And for whose benefit will *that* be, I wonder? You are becoming a wicked flirt, Leonora Shelley. You take liberties and feel safe enough to flutter your eyelashes at every eligible young man in London since your father won't let you marry for at least another year. And that poor doting Mr Fairfax doesn't get so much as a kind word.'

'Don't tease, Anabel. Oh, the absolute *nerve* of that man. It makes me cross to think that he actually came here to ask Father for my hand. Can you imagine that? Can you see me wedded to an old, overweight, stuttering buffoon who goes to pieces each time I so much as *look* at him?'

'The very idea is ludicrous,' Anabel reassured her with a grin. 'But how would madam feel if the proposal had come from Horace Cavendish, I wonder?'

Leonora held a blue satin gown against herself and twirled about the room as if dancing with an invisible partner.

'You're teasing me again, Anabel,' she said. 'Oh, just look at the time. Estelle is expecting me at her bedside and here I am, standing in my stays when I should be on my way to Portland Square. Come, stop trying to provoke me and help me to dress.'

Leonora was now seventeen, a young woman of many accomplishments and quite extraordinary beauty. More than a year and a half had passed since the wedding of Malcolm Cavendish, yet still she felt, keenly and deeply, the insult placed upon her at the close of those glittering celebrations. Each time she looked at the beggars' coin she recalled the loathsome way in which Horace had fingered her body, kneaded and pinched at her breasts and filled her mouth with his hungry tongue. He would have taken her right there and then, standing against the orchard wall in broad daylight, with scores of other guests lounging about the nearby lawns and terraces. The man was an animal. To him she had represented nothing more than the relief of an urgent bodily function. He had seen her as a mere vessel for his sexual gratification, and for that she would always despise him. Whenever the beggars' coin served to remind her of that degrading incident, she was convinced that she would die a spinster rather than submit herself in marriage to such a man.

'There,' Anabel proudly announced. 'Ready at last. And you take care to speak to her mother before you go rushing into her sick-room. We don't want you bringing any nasty infections back to the house.'

'Oh, do stop *fussing*, Anabel.'

'Here's Sawyer to take you safely there and back. Stay close to him and don't go flashing that saucy smile of yours to all and sundry along the high street.' She plucked at the folds of Leonora's gown and adjusted the lining of her cloak yet again before allowing her to leave the house. 'And you, Gordon Sawyer, don't you *dare* let madam out of your sight to go wandering off on her own.'

'No ma'am,' the big man said, touching his cap and drawing himself up to his full height as he fell into step exactly three measured paces behind his lovely young mistress.

Anabel sighed deeply as she watched them leave. Leonora was so sure of herself as she swept along the pavement with her head held high and her trusted servant marching like a military escort at her heels.

'Proud, high-minded little madam,' she muttered, with a smile of affection. Then she stepped inside and closed the door, and a short time later she was sitting beside Francine's bed, patiently coaxing the dear lady to eat a little bread and butter and hot beef soup.

Leonora arrived at the Lacey home in Portland Place just as afternoon tea was being served. Mrs Amelia Lacey received her guest with her usual brand of airy, absent-minded hospitality. She had been attractive once, but the use of cosmetics made from white lead and vinegar had destroyed both her hair and complexion while she was still in her early twenties. Now she wore expensive wigs, high ruffles at her neck and make-up of a kinder composition. Her face, lips and eyelids were badly scarred beneath the layers of herbal powders and rouge she applied each morning in the privacy of her room. She resembled a tall, stiff doll with painted plaster features, crimped hair and a tiny, crimson rose-bud of a mouth that had lost the power to smile.

'Estelle will be *so* pleased to see you, my dear,' she enthused. 'Poor girl isn't at all well, you know. A woman's complaint ... pains in the belly ... that sort of thing. Ah, here comes tea. I'll have it carried up for you. No, I won't come up, my dear. Must get on, you know. Things to do.'

Leonora was startled by Estelle's condition. The poor girl was obviously very ill. Her cheeks were flushed, the skin pasty and beaded with perspiration. She was bright-eyed and feverish, with a wild, almost desperate look about her. Some weeks earlier her hair had been dyed that gleaming, reddish blonde much favoured by young society ladies, but now the roots showed dark against her scalp and her long tresses had the neglected appearance of tarnished brass. In the pretty, cluttered room she reclined against high pillows amid drapes and flounces of lace and embroidered silk. She might have been a cherished but damaged ornament, displayed amongst a host of finer treasures.

'Bless you for coming, Leonora,' she whispered. 'I have been at my wit's end these past weeks.' She grasped her visitor's hand with fingers that were dry and hot. 'I need your help. There is no-one else I can trust. You must promise to help me ...'

'I can promise nothing until I know the problem,' Leonora cautiously replied.

'Oh, if only I had listened to you all those months ago. If

152

only I had heeded your sound advice. I've been a fool ... such a fool ...'

'You look so ill, Estelle. How long have you been like this? Have you been seen by a doctor?'

Estelle closed her eyes and winced as if in great pain. 'Yes, yes,' she said, wearily. 'Dr Steadman, our family physician, came to see me yesterday, but the old fool could only tell me what I already know. I am three and a half months pregnant.'

'Oh, no. Oh, my poor, foolish friend. Do your parents know?'

'No, and they must not.' She clutched at her visitor's hands again. 'You must bring me some tansy and pennyroyal to procure an abortion, Leonora ... and chives, bring me fresh chives for the poison ...'

'Poison? What poison? I don't understand ...'

'Just do it, Leonora. I have the recipes if you will help me make them up ... and I need something to ease this terrible pain ... oh ...' She fell back across the pillows, exhausted and perspiring heavily.

'But what is causing the pain? And why are you running such a fever? Surely it's not the baby?'

Estelle shook her head. Her lips were dry and cracked. 'An infection ... oh, please help me. I must be rid of this child. I must be rid of it.'

'But you will kill yourself in the process,' Leonora protested. 'You are far too ill to suffer the remedies you suggest without inflicting further damage upon yourself.'

At Leonora's words Estelle began to weep, quietly at first, then with great, deep sobs that seemed to rack her whole body.

Leonora patted the feverish hand and made what reassuring comments she could until the sobs subsided. She knew that for the last year and a half Estelle had been entangled in a distressing, supposedly secret affair with Horace Cavendish. The silly, impressionable girl had been so flattered, so overwhelmed by his attentions that she had foolishly allowed him to seduce her on the night of the wedding banquet at Beresford Hall. Since then he had treated

153

her abominably, slipping in and out of her life, and her bed, as his quicksilver moods dictated. He had acquired the habbit of shunning her most cruelly for long periods of time, returning periodically to slake his lusts and re-establish his dominance over her. And now she had come to this, pregnant and sick with anxiety.

Several minutes elapsed before Estelle relaxed sufficiently to dab at her eyes with a square of lace-edged silk. Every movement of her arms caused her to wince or whimper with pain.

'Does Horace know he is to be a father?' Leonora asked.

'He knows.'

'And he offers no solution, no support?'

'Support?' Estelle attempted a bitter laugh, but the sound came out as a harsh rasp that ended on a sob. 'Why, he has even made threats against me. I became desperate when he ignored my messages, so I sent urgent word to him at the home of Lady Georgette Mortimer, his latest conquest. My pleas and entreaties only served to enrage him. He's a powerful man, Leonora. I fear he will do me harm if I try to pursue the matter.'

Leonora's brows puckered in a thoughtful frown. 'So, he's engaged in a clandestine affair with Lady Georgette Mortimer? Surely he is aware that her husband is Sir Oscar's keenest political opponent?'

'Oh, yes, and would the Earl not feel himself cruelly betrayed if he knew of it? Horace does these things for the risk, you know, for the excitement! Nothing seems to satisfy him unless it is sinful, dangerous or disgusting.'

'And a man like Sir Henry Mortimer would not hesitate to whip rumour into scandal if news of the affair leaked out,' Leonora said, as if thinking out loud. 'Even if doing so would mean airing his own wife's dirty linen in public. I suspect he would do almost anything to discredit Sir Oscar.'

'What are you thinking? That Horace will protect me if I threaten to expose him to his family?' Estelle shook her head. 'He despises me. He even took bets amongst his friends that I was so besotted with him as to do anything he suggested ...

anything ... oh God, *anything*, and now ... and now ...'

'What do you mean, Estelle?'

'He said it excited him. He said all the top society ladies are having it done ... *please*, Leonora, there is something you must do for me. You must take them out ... take them out before they *kill* me.'

Leonora shivered, touched with sudden dread. 'Take them out? What on earth are you talking about?'

Tears began to stream down Estelle's cheeks and her features became contorted with weeping. 'oh, Leonora, I know it was foolish of me, but he said ... he promised ... oh, God, I really thought ...'

'What is it? Tell me. What have you *done*?'

Sobbing, Estelle eased back the sheet to expose the upper part of her body. Leonora uttered an involuntary cry and shrank back, her hands coming to her mouth as she stared with horror at Estelle's horribly mutilated breasts. The flesh was swollen and discoloured, the darker skin around the nipples split and oozing pus. Circles of blackened wire could be seen protruding from the source of the inflammation, and the ominous stains of infection had spread over the entire breast area to distress the skin almost as far as her throat.

'Take them out,' Estelle begged. 'Take the wires out.'

'I can't ... I ...' Retching, Leonora turned away and groped for a handkerchief.

'Please ... they are poisoning me ... you must take them out.'

Leonora coughed into her handkerchief and struggled to compose herself. After several deep breaths she steeled herself and took a closer look at the sickening mass of infection invading her friend's bosom.

'Horace *asked* you to do this? He actually *wanted* this?'

'Oh, yes, though he told me afterwards that it had been only a cruel wager. He called me a stupid little idiot and laughed at my pain. It really wasn't his fault, Leonora. I took little persuading.'

'But how could you? How could you even *think* of having your nipples pierced. It's barbaric, it's ...'

'... so painful. Please, Leonora, you must help me. I cannot bear this pain ... it throbs ... it burns like fire ...'

At that moment Estelle's mother entered the room with a huge vase of flowers and a conversation already in progress. She set the vase close to one of the windows and fussed over the blossoms, prattling contentedly as she patted and coaxed them into a pleasing arrangement. She was too preoccupied with the million and one trivialities adrift in her head to recognise that her daughter had become dangerously ill.

Leonora rose to her feet. 'I must go.'

'So soon, my dear?' The doll-faced lady flitted about the room in a rustle of skirts. 'Such a pity. All that tea gone to waste, and all those lovely scones and cinnamon cakes ...'

'You will help me, Leonora?' Estelle whispered, and there was such anguish in her eyes that Leonora was almost moved to tears.

'I'll do what I can,' she promised.

'And there's a scent of oranges in this room,' Mrs Lacey announced, sniffing the air noisily. 'I can smell oranges ... or peaches, perhaps?'

'Swear it,' Estelle insisted, grasping Leonora's skirts and leaning so far forward that her poor, inflamed breasts became visible again. 'Swear you will help me.'

Leonora eased her back against the pillows and covered her very gently with the sheet. She touched the fevered brow, knowing that Estelle was beyond her assistance.

'You have my word,' she said. 'Rest now, Estelle. Try to sleep for a while. I swear I will do everything in my power to help you.'

She was pulling on her gloves at the front door when Gordon Sawyer hurried from the kitchens, sweating and red-faced from the heat of the fire. There were bits of fruit tart clinging to his whiskers and a dollop of rum sauce staining the front of his shirt.

'Do you know of a Dr Steadman in this area?' she enquired of him.

'Yes'm. Elderly gent, he is, with one leg shorter than t'other. Lives in Boxmire Street with 'is wife and 'er crippled sister. Take you over there, shall I?'

Leonora nodded. She felt like a traitor, yet she knew that professional care was all she could offer that poor, foolish young woman upstairs.

Later that afternoon she allowed Anabel to cradle her in her arms and rock her to and fro the way she had done when Leonora was a small child.

'Did I do the right thing, Anabel? Have I helped Estelle or merely betrayed her confidence?'

'You did all that could reasonably be expected of you, my dear,' Anabel told her. 'Only a fool would have tried to do more under the circumstances you describe.'

'She wanted me to remove the wires but I couldn't touch the ... the pus ... oh, it was horrible ... and she was in such pain, such terrible pain. How could she *do* that to herself?'

'Hush now. You must not dwell on it, child. The doctor you sent for will take good care of her.'

'And the baby? What of the child she is expecting?'

'You can do nothing about that, Leonora. Others must decide what is to become of it.'

'And who will decide what is to become of the beast responsible for all this misery?'

Leonora asked the question in a voice made harsh by the hostility of her thoughts. She lifted her head and touched her damp cheeks with the tips of her fingers. Tears were glistening in her eyes and on her lashes when she asked: 'Is there *always* a man to be found behind a woman's suffering?'

Her words met with silence, then Anabel took out a handkerchief, held it against her nostrils and sniffed gently. 'I believe there is,' she whispered, glancing toward the door of Francine's room. 'God help us all, my dear, I believe there is.'

CHAPTER SEVEN

I

Estelle died three days later. On the morning of her death a carriage arrived with a message requesting that Leonora visit the Lacey home immediately on a matter of great urgency. She arrived, well wrapped against a late frost, to find the family in mourning and the doctor still in attendance. She declined an invitation to go upstairs to view the body, and instead found herself sitting in Amelia Lacey's cluttered and heavily perfumed drawing room. An enormous fire burned in the gate, its crackling heat and occasional billows of dark smoke forcing her to choose a chair near the draught from a partially open window.

Across from her sat the dead girl's mother, dry-eyed and solemn in a dull red dress with lace trims and a crimson velvet sash. Her head was fixed in a proud position by the stiff white ruffles at her throat. Her grief was concealed behind a neat cosmetic mask and her tiny mouth, for once stilled of its incessant chattering, was pinched shut.

158

Mr Frank Lacey was a balding, rather nondescript man who paced the room on restless feet, often pausing to dab at his eyes with a huge white handkerchief. From time to time he blew his nose with such energy that the quiet room seemed to quake at the sound. He was dressed in smart purple trousers and a dark velvet jacket, but his shirt was soiled at the cuffs and his neck-linen so badly creased that he might have been wearing it, unfastened and unlaundered, for several days. Unlike his doll-featured wife, he was unable to keep the grief from his face or prevent it spilling down his cheeks in the occasional small flood of tears.

Also present in the room was Dr Maurice Steadman, a tall, angular man dressed from head to toe in black except for a sliver of white collar trapped between his jaw-bone and stiff black stock. He had a naturally sad expression on his long face and an apologetic, overly subservient manner. Leonora had taken very little account of him when she visited his gloomy house three days earlier. Now she looked from his clumsy surgical boot to his large, limpid brown eyes and wondered how he was capable of sitting so comfortably in an over-heated room while wearing woollen gloves and a heavy outdoor coat. She was still scrutinising his swarthy features when Mr Lacey cleared his throat and said, somewhat shakily: 'Good of you to come, Miss Shelley, very good of you to come, I'm sure.'

She nodded, dreading the questions she was certain would follow. 'Thank you, Mr Lacey, and please let me assure you that I did everything possible to help your daughter.' She glanced at Amelia. 'I went to see Dr Steadman as soon as I knew ... the moment I saw what she ...'

'Quite. Quite. We are much obliged to you. But now, my dear, I think ... that is ... I should inform you that Dr Steadman will ... er ... certify that Estelle died of an acute failure of the kidneys. That's right ... and anything else she might have said before she ... anything you might mistakenly believe to the contrary ...'

'I know what I saw, Mr Lacey, and I also know the name of the man responsible for ...'

'Enough! Be silent! I will not hear it!' Amelia Lacey

suddenly leapt to her feet, her fingers tearing at a handkerchief and her face deadpan behind the impassioned words. Her husband took her hands and led her back to her chair, then rubbed his eyes vigorously before saying to Leonora: 'Nothing you can say will bring Estelle back to us.'

'Sir, I am well aware of that, but if the guilty can be brought to justice ...?'

Mr Lacey shook his head so vigorously that tears splashed from his eyes. 'A noble thought, my dear, but so naive, so naive. What you so innocently call "the truth" would bring shame on my daughter's memory, and Lord knows she has already paid a high enough price for her foolishness. We must look to the living ... to our continued good name. Scandal can be so damaging, so destructive, Miss Shelley. Would Estelle rest in peace, I wonder, if she knew that those she loved were to inherit her shame in full?'

Leonora sighed and looked down at her hands, which were elegantly folded and resting on the rose-pink satin folds of her skirt. She was being told that Estelle's secrets must die with her, and that Horace Cavendish would not be held accountable for his part in this tragic affair. The injustice of it sliced into her like a knife. She shuddered at the memory of Estelle's disfigured breasts, and she could still see the torment in her eyes as she pleaded for help.

Out of the hubbub of sound in the street beyond the open window came the clear, high-pitched cries of street-hawkers plying their trades, ragged individuals blowing their songs like puffs of dragon's-breath into the frosty air.

'Nice fresh mackerel ... eight-a-shilling mackerel.'

'Four-a-penny oranges ... sweet oranges ... get your four-a-penny oranges.'

'Get yer fresh green peas, only a ha'penny a pint.'

Their sing-song voices seemed to echo through the quiet room, filling Leonora's head with a sudden tumult of sound.

'Miss Shelley? Are you unwell? May I get you something?'

She passed a hand across her forehead and took several deep breaths. 'Thank you, Dr Steadman. Perhaps a glass of water? I find this room extremely hot.'

The water was brought from the kitchen and Leonora sipped it slowly. Only when she had set down the glass did her hostess, who had been hovering behind her chair for some minutes, step forward to place a small tortoise-shell box in her lap.

'This is for you,' the woman said through her tightly puckered lips. 'I know Estelle would have wanted you to have it.'

'A small gift to mark our ... appreciation,' Mr Lacey added, sniffing loudly.

Inside the box was a brooch of fine filigree gold set with a huge ruby that twinkled with rich colour in the light from the window. This was the price of her silence, the tax to be levied on a dead girl's reputation. It occurred to her that the good doctor would also have his fee, his pound of flesh in exchange for the grieving couple's peace of mind. Whether a guinea or a farthing, a ruby brooch or a purse of coins, everything had its price, its current market value.

Leonora cleared her throat and looked up at the respectable elderly couple who were so desperately anxious to salvage a little dignity from the ugly death of their daughter. She had seen Amelia Lacey wearing the ruby brooch at several fancy functions. It was a much admired piece of jewellery and obviously very expensive; not a thing to be given away lightly.

'A failure of the kidneys, you say?'

'Yes, yes, that is correct.'

'And that is Dr Steadman's only conclusion?'

'Oh, it is ... indeed it is.' Mr Lacey wiped his tear-stained handkerchief across his eyes and glanced at the doctor, who nodded his confirmation. At that point Leonora rose to her feet.

'Well, now that I have paid my respects I will leave you in peace,' she said, adjusting her pink lace gloves. 'You have my deepest sympathy.'

At the front door she paused to press the tortoise-shell box into the trembling hands of Amelia Lacey.

'Keep your lovely brooch, Mrs Lacey, and rest assured that I will say nothing to harm Estelle's good name or to bring disrepute upon your family. I know only what you have told me today, that Estelle died of kidney failure. You have my solemn word on that.'

'Oh, bless you, child ... bless you.'

'I'm very sorry.'

'Thank you, my dear. Are you sure ... about the brooch, I mean?'

'Quite sure. Goodbye.'

Leonora turned abruptly and allowed the Laceys' groom to hand her into the waiting carriage. She wanted to put as much distance between herself and the Laceys as possible. She glanced up at the heavily curtained window of the room where Estelle's body lay, then sat back in her seat and closed her eyes, shivering despite her hooded, warmly lined cloak. Her mind was troubled by a single persistent thought: on the afternoon of the wedding Horace Cavendish had tried to force his sexual attentions on her in the grounds of Beresford Hall. Had he succeeded and spent his passions in that encounter, Estelle would not have fallen victim to his appetites and Leonora herself might have known the fear and disgrace of an unwanted pregnancy. His gift of a farthing was indeed an accurate measure of his respect, and it did not lessen the insult to know that he held other women in the same low esteem.

At Costerman Row the carriage was halted by a complicated and very noisy jam of vehicles, animals and pedestrians. In the already congested thoroughfare a herd of cows had met a flock of sheep moving in the other direction, and the result was chaos. Carriages, carts, hand-drawn barrows and fruit stalls all vied for right of way against a confusion of bleating animals and yelling men and women. There was a mad scramble for booty when a fish-cart overturned, scattering its contents of fish and oysters and chopped ice. In the mêlée a donkey lost its footing and fell, dragging its cart-load of cabbages to the ground to be stolen or trampled underfoot. A startled horse reared in its traces, sending a wave of panic through the snarl of confused livestock and jabbering pedestrians. Now women were screaming and fights were breaking out amongst the men, while pick-pockets

162

appeared from nowhere to extract their wicked profit from the pandemonium.

A small trap-door was lifted in the roof of the carriage and the groom's ruddy, whiskered face appeared in the aperture.

'Hold on to your seat, miss,' he bellowed above the din. 'There's a hold-up in Costerman Row, so we're trying for Ludgate Circus. Want me to come down there and ride with you?'

'That will not be necessary,' Leonora coldly informed him, recalling the way he had leered at her earlier. She had no wish to spend the remainder of the journey enclosed in a small carriage with such a man.

She felt the carriage lurch as the driver attempted to steer the horses left into Greater Middleton Street. She pulled back the curtain and stared through the window into a sea of yelling faces. Even here the crowds were thickening fast as news of easy pickings in Costerman Row spread through the streets like a flash fire. Despite the crush, the carriage made slow but certain progress away from the main surge. A particular stench rose from the streets to assail Leonora's nostrils and touch like icy fingers upon her deepest fears. It was the stink of poverty; the foul, unacceptable smell of humanity at its lowest. Dismayed by it, she was about to lower the curtain when her gaze fell upon a familiar face. A poorly dressed young woman of about nineteen or twenty was pushing her way along the crowded pavement, spitting and cursing at those who would have jostled her aside. Her clothes and hair were filthy, but beneath the grime was a country prettiness that was unmistakable.

'Daisy! Daisy Kimble!'

Leonora opened the curtain to its fullest and stared with wide eyes over the heads of the crowd. The young woman was certainly Daisy Kimble, and holding on to her skirts was a child of six or seven, a thin, filthy little girl with lank brown hair and a docile expression, wearing clothes that might once have been found among the garbage. Leonora looked back at Daisy and their eyes met in a stare of chilly recognition; the well-to-do young lady in her fine gown and carriage, the ragged street-seller waging her own personal battle against destitution.

The carriage lurched forward violently, almost throwing Leonora from her seat. She was forced to drop the window curtain in order to maintain her balance, and when she raised it again Daisy Kimble and the child were gone, lost in an ocean of jostling bodies and dirty faces. Moments later the door of her carriage was flung open and a hostile young woman scrambled inside, bringing the stains and smells of the streets into the once-pleasant interior. A vicious kick from her boot checked the progress of the man who was attempting to follow her, then the carriage door slammed shut and Leonora found herself staring into the hate-filled eyes of Daisy Kimble.

'You told on me,' Daisy snarled, and even though she had seated herself on the opposite side of the carriage, the stench of her breath was offensive. 'Took me money and told on me, you did.'

'That is not true,' Leonora declared. 'I kept your sordid secret, not for your sake or even the master's but to spare your mistress the pain of learning the truth. Whatever your problems, Daisy, your dismissal from Garden Place was none of my doing.'

'It weren't fair. That stable lad never touched me.'

'I know that.'

'It were him. It were the master's doing.'

'I know that too, Daisy.'

'Sent me to Whitechapel, your fine father did. Had his way wi' me and then sold me to that old stinker in Whitechapel what lived like a pig in spite of having money to live better. And that one turned me out to fend fer meself when me belly got so big he didn't want me for sex no more.' She paused, scratching her scalp with both hands as she eyed Leonora's gown and fashionable shoes. 'And that's where I stayed these last seven years ... on the streets. Want to come home with me, do yer? Want to share yer bed with fleas and vermin and any man what offers a coin or a 'ot pie or a tot of gin?'

'Daisy, I am so sorry ...'

'Sorry?' she sneered. 'Sorry? Tell that to my little 'un. Tell it

164

to 'er when she's so hungry her belly swells or so cold her bones creak. Tell it to her when she's trying to keep herself from some lecher what'll punch her in the face or kick her around afore he has her.'

'Look, I have a little money here,' Leonora offered, reaching into her embroidered draw-string pocket. 'If it will help you with the child ...'

Daisy made a grab for the pocket as the carriage door flew open and the uniformed groom climbed inside, his face ablaze with indignation.

'Why, you filthy little ...' He reached for Daisy with both hands, snatching at her hair and her ragged clothes. 'Out, you stinking gutter snipe. Out!'

'No ... don't harm her,' Leonora cried, but before the words were fully out, Daisy Kimble was hurled bodily through the open doorway to sprawl headlong in the gutter with her skirts awry. The carriage lurched forward and gathered momentum as the crowds thinned, and the skinny child who had been running alongside released her grip on the livery and fell back, staring after the beautiful lady who looked out as her conveyance sped away.

'Best come inside, miss,' the groom advised. 'And best hold tight, miss.'

Leonora lowered the window curtain and braced herself in the well-upholstered corner of her seat. Without acknowledging the presence of the groom, she clung to a loop of leather above her seat as the horses, now whipped into a trot by their angry driver, ploughed a free passage through the remaining chaos. Although the carriage was still hampered by an assortment of other vehicles, laden hand-carts, herds of animals and yelling groups of human scavengers, it made rough but steady progress for the remainder of the journey. When at last the groom handed her down outside the house in Garden Square, Leonora was all but exhausted.

'I *hate* London,' she exclaimed as she entered the house and removed her cloak and bonnet. 'How I hate the squalor and the stench of it. And the *noise*. My head is ringing fit to burst from the clamour out there.'

'Ah, but you like it well enough when you can dance with a handsome young man or sit down to dine at a fine table, do you not?'

Twelve-year-old Helen had come from her father's study with a book in one hand and a plate of sugared nuts in the other. She had on a white muslin dress with a green sash and a tiny, gathered bodice that revealed rather too much of her youthful breasts. She was bare-shouldered, with her fair, curly hair pushed haphazardly into a pretty straw bonnet. Once again her doting father had brought a gift to indulge her taste for sweetness, a habit that even now showed signs of spreading her figure and spoiling her complexion. There was something flippant, almost brazen about Helen that her elder sister found unpleasant. There were times when she displayed the looks and manners of a serving wench.

'I enjoy the good and dislike the bad,' Leonora said sharply, peeling off her gloves. 'Which, I suppose, makes me no different from anyone else. How is Mama?'

Helen shrugged and pouted, then popped another sweet into her mouth and sucked noisily on its sugar coating.

'Does that mean you have not bothered to look in on her today?' Leonora asked. 'Not even to enquire after her health?'

'Oh, Leonora, don't *nag* so. You know how I loathe and detest sick-rooms. They make me ill, and sometimes Mama has such a terrible cough that it pains me to sit with her.'

'What a selfish little wretch you are, Helen. Why, when Papa was ill with the gout you sat with him by the hour.'

Helen shrugged again. 'Mama has Anabel.'

'Anabel is a *servant*,' Leonora reminded her.

'And she has *you*,' Helen pouted. 'Let us not forget that Mama has her precious Leonora constantly to hand. You were always her favourite. She cares about nobody, so long as she has *you*.'

'Helen, that is simply not true. Mama has always loved us all equally. You have absolutely no cause to play the poor, neglected Cinderella. Why must you always make a silly drama of everything?'

'It is true. It is. And I don't care ... I tell you I *don't care*.'

'Now, Helen, please keep your voice down. The hall is no place for one of your infantile tantrums.'

Helen suddenly flung the plate of sweets from her, scattering shattered crockery and nuts in every direction.

'I don't *care*,' she screamed. 'Papa loves me best, and when you're married off to Horace Cavendish *I'll* be mistress of this house. Then I'll get rid of Anabel Corey and that hateful Mrs Norris and I won't ever have to ...'

'What was that you said? What do you know about Horace Cavendish?' She grabbed the younger girl by the arms and shook her roughly. 'Tell me the truth. What has father been saying to you about me and Horace Cavendish?'

'Oh, you're hurting,' Helen wailed. 'Let go ... you're hurting ... let me go!'

'Not until you tell me what you know.'

'No, I won't. I won't. Oh, Papa, Papa ... she's hurting, she's hurting me!'

'Helen! Leonora! What on earth is going on here?'

Herbert Shelley strode into the hall from his study, careful to avoid stepping on the scattered sweets. Helen immediately ran to him and flung herself into his embrace. His hand came up to stroke her bare shoulder affectionately. He glared at Leonora, who met his stare without concern.

'Oh Papa, she was horrid to me,' Helen wailed. 'She's *always* horrid to me. She pinched my arms and called me nasty names. I hate my sister. I *hate* her.'

'There, there, my sweet, don't cry. Leonora, explain yourself.'

As she looked at her father and sister, Leonora suddenly felt herself stricken by the backlash of the day's events. Poor Estelle Lacey was dead, and yet Horace Cavendish would bear no blame for his part in her ruin. Then the journey home had fatigued her, and the obvious wretchedness of Daisy Kimble's existence left her shocked and angered. Perhaps out there, grovelling for a living in the filthy London streets, was her own half-sister, a seven-year-old girl sired by Herbert Shelley. And now here was Helen, so much like the plump young Daisy of seven years ago, snuggling sensuously against Herbert's fat body and savouring the caress of his hand upon her bare flesh. A small, vaguely familiar prickle of suspicion rose to the surface of her mind, causing her to recoil in distaste. The way Herbert was fawning over his young daughter was quite sickening.

'There, there, my pretty one, hush now, hush.'

For Leonora, his coo-cooing was akin to a red rag wafted in the face of a quick-tempered bull. She lifted her chin and flashed her violet-coloured eyes in anger.

'Why not pay her a guinea, father?'

'Eh? What? What was that?'

'A guinea,' Leonora retorted scornfully. 'Pay the girl a golden guinea, father. I'm sure *that* will quieten her.'

Herbert's face purpled and his eyes bulged. 'How ... how dare you?' he blustered. 'What do you mean by that, eh? Just what the hell are you implying?'

Still holding his gaze, Leonora rang the small silver bell on the hall table. Almost immediately an anxious-looking maid appeared from the scullery and bobbed a series of curtsies as she approached.

'Ah, Sarah,' Leonora said without looking away from her father's furious face. 'See that this mess is cleared up at once, and you may inform Mrs Norris that we will take lunch in half an hour.'

'Yes, miss. Will that be all, miss?'

'That will be all, thank you, Sarah.'

As the maid hurried away the master of the house, his composure regained, puffed out his ample chest and spoke harshly to his eldest daughter.

'I will not tolerate such insolence.'

'Oh?'

'You will explain yourself, madam.'

'I think not, Mr Shelley,' Leonora replied with a knowing glance at Helen. 'It seems to me we understand each other perfectly.'

With a toss of her head she gathered up her skirts and marched upstairs, leaving Herbert staring after her, his anger once again frustrated by the sheer strength of his daughter's will.

II

The unexpected presence of Francine at the lunch table deflected any further hostility between Herbert and his eldest daughter. She appeared in a gold brocade dressing gown over an embroidered muslin shift, her hair loosely dressed beneath a pretty cotton bonnet. She presided over the small gathering like a pale and beautiful spectre, seemingly unaware of the tense, charged atmosphere in the room. She had been unwell since Christmas. That persistent cough which dogged her every winter had last year confined her to bed for many long weeks, and all the cures and remedies applied since then had done little to ease the pain or clear the mucus from her chest. Now she was very frail, with dark circles beneath her eyes and a husky, breathless quality to her voice.

'Sir Marcus recommends that I winter abroad this year,' she announced, moving the food around on her plate without tasting any of it. 'Perhaps in Spain or the southern part of France, where the air is said to be warmer and cleaner.'

Leonora and Joseph exchanged glances while Herbert made loud huffing sounds of disapproval over his huge portion of veal and ham pie. Beneath the table, Lancer nuzzled each knee in turn in his constant search for tit-bits of food.

'And it is my wish that Leonora be allowed to travel with me,' Francine added.

'Impossible,' Herbert spluttered through a mouthful of meat and pastry. 'And a damned impractical suggestion, if you ask me. She's needed here. It's all very well for Sir Marcus Shaw to make these recommendations willy-nilly, but did he give a thought to who would run this house and look to the needs of your family while you languish like idle royalty in a kinder climate?'

'We have a perfectly adequate housekeeper and a small army of servants,' Francine reminded him. 'They have managed well enough during the last few months while I have

169

been too ill to attend to domestic duties ...'

'Or any other *wifely* matters, madam,' Herbert reminded her in petulant tones.

Francine glanced at the children. 'Herbert, *please*!'

He leaned across the table, wagging his fork in the air.

'This is your cousin's doing,' he said angrily. 'I should have known there'd be trouble when he sent his own physician to attend you ... that pompous, high-minded charlatan. What does he know about anything, eh? And just who is expected to finance this extravagance, eh? Tell me that, madam. Tell me that.'

'I shall pay for it out of my own purse, and with a little help from Charles and Jonathan, who each have substantial private incomes that you have steadfastly refused to release to them.'

'What? *What*?'

Leonora watched her father's face turn from red to purple so rapidly that he might have been choking to death before her very eyes. He gaped at Francine, his food forgotten. Only after a lengthy pause did he clear his throat and stammer: 'No, madam ... *no*! It won't do ... won't do at all. Those legacies are not to be touched.'

'Those legacies are long overdue,' Francine countered.

He shook his head, still gaping. 'No, madam, *no*! This plan is outrageous. I shall not allow it ... I ...'

'I'm afraid you are to have no further say in the matter,' Francine told him coldly. 'You see, Herbert, I intend to instruct my lawyers, Jarvis and Steele, to free the properties at the end of the year. By then Jonathan will be almost twenty-one and Charles nineteen ... no longer children but proud and sensible young men. They need their independence, Herbert. I am happy to learn that Jonathan's properties in the north have realised tremendous profits over the last few years, and my city investments on Charles's behalf have done almost as well. You have kept them in ignorance for too long, and now *I* have decided to put an end to this unhappy situation. So, it is as good as settled. My sons will have their legacies, *in full*, by October.'

Herbert was speechless. He poured himself a large measure

of port and drank it in one gulp, spilling it from the corners of his mouth so that it ran down his plump jowls to stain his napkin and clean white neck-linen. Then he set down his glass, shoved back his chair and, without another word, strode from the room, slamming the door behind him.

Helen made as if to leave her seat but hesitated. Loyalty to her father urged her to follow him and offer what comfort she could in his moment of distress, but there on the table was a heavy, sweet pudding smothered in brandy sauce, plus a steaming blackberry tart and a whole pie crammed with apples, pears, plums and raisins. A small but significant inner battle was fought and lost in a matter of seconds. Her childish loyalties were not yet sufficiently developed to override the demands of a hearty appetite.

Watching Helen gorge herself at the table, Leonora was reminded of the dirty, ill-fed child she had seen clinging to the skirts of Daisy Kimble in that seedy London street, the ragged little urchin running barefoot alongside the lurching carriage. That little girl might well be a half-sister to herself and Helen, a bastard of the same blood condemned to a life of disease and hunger while Herbert's other children lived in comfort and looked to a safe, secure future. She found herself wondering what the child might look like after a hot bath, with her hair brushed and styled and her skinny body clothed in muslin and satin. She shuddered at the thought. The ease with which prosperity and privation might be exchanged was something that had always unnerved her. Sometimes it seemed that poverty kept pace with them all and would, but for the grace of a fickle God, overwhelm them with its presence.

During the remainder of the meal they were entertained by a letter from Jonathan and Charles, who had returned from Europe to their expensive Naval Academy in Brighton. Like their years at Harrow, this final part of their education was also financed by Sir Oscar Cavendish, who had always taken a very generous interest in the boys' future. The academy relied heavily upon subscriptions from wealthy gentlemen making provision for younger sons and nephews not destined to inherit family fortunes. Here they were trained as officers and gentlemen in the shadow of the Prince Regent's magnificent summer residence, where the cream of society rubbed elegant shoulders with nobility and lesser royalty.

'A college for strutting peacocks,' was how one satirist described it.

'A hen-house bulging with young cocks of fine plumage and little brain,' quipped another. 'All pampered by families of fine fortune and little sense.'

Despite the criticisms, however, the Brighton Naval Academy was enormously popular. Indeed, it had become fashionable for a man of substance to finance at least one young gentleman through his time at that exclusive seaside establishment.

The four long pages from Charles and Jonathan were full of news and interesting anecdotes about their daily lives; a long, amusing letter designed to lift their mother's drooping spirits and satisfy Leonora's insatiable hunger for society gossip. She was still much preoccupied with their words when she went to her room to rest after lunch. There she sat before her mirror, unfastened her waist-length hair from its pins and combs and brushed it carefully with a silver-backed hairbrush. She was thinking of Horace Cavendish, who had made himself the shining star of the Naval Academy, and of Estelle, whose value as a friend had depended solely upon her social connections and her willingness to impart to Leonora the secrets of other people's private lives. Estelle's cousin, Richard, also attended the academy, and it was thanks to him, and to his cousin's indiscriminate tongue, that Leonora had learned so much about the Earl's second son.

She set down her brush and dipped her hands into the fluted bowl on her dressing table, stirring the contents with her fingers. The bowl contained a mixture of aromatic herbs, dried blossoms and flower petals; a dozen summer perfumes preserved and enriched with oil of amber musk. The petals fell in a fragrant cascade to lie upon the polished wood in rich, earthy colours. Leonora gazed at them while a thoughtful smile plucked at the corners of her mouth.

'I could do it,' she said aloud. 'I have enough information to make a success of such a mischievous plan. It would be a simple matter, and so gratifying, to plant the seeds of suspicion and mistrust and watch them grow until his smug existence is plagued with uncertainty.'

With a practised toss of her head she swept back her mane of glossy hair, her heavy-lashed eyes glittering with malice. Using her forefinger, she nudged the fallen flower petals into a pattern against the dark wood. These few scented fragments might represent all those would-be scandals nipped in the bud by wealthy and influential parents. These others might show those senior pupils recently expelled for obtaining advance information on examination papers, and these the nameless accomplices they refused to expose.

'And here are dried marigold heads,' she whispered with a smile, warming to her theme. 'These will speak for poor, dead Andrew Trent.'

She was referring to the tragic suicide of the son of the Bishop of Dean, a death cunningly presented as a bizarre accident for the benefit of the public. The boy's friends and fellow students had immediately closed ranks against the curiosity of outsiders, but some details had inevitably reached Leonora's ears via the talkative Estelle. Andrew had been a homosexual, a pathetic seventeen-year-old helplessly attached to a sadistic man who used him for every perverted practice imaginable. He had also shared his lodgings, for a short time during his second term, with none other than Horace Cavendish.

And here, last but not least, was a dark red rose-bud to represent Lady Georgette Mortimer, wife of the Earl's life-long enemy and the subject of Horace's latest indiscretion.

'And what a pretty pattern of events we have here,' Leonora breathed. 'A scrap of truth, a fragment of innuendo, a lie, a hint, a minor coincidence, a small suspicious circumstance, and then ...'

With just a gentle touch of her finger she was able to alter the pattern of petals and flower heads to contrive first one shape and then another from precisely the same essentials.

'... and then ...'

She looked down at her creation with a smile and a wicked glint in her eye.

'... and then this subtle device can be made to tell a *very* different story.'

III

Some time later, while the house was quiet in those empty hours following lunch, Leonora seated herself at her small desk, took out a quill and several sheets of paper, and began to write:

'*To the Right Honourable The Earl of Beresford,*
My Lord,
We, the undersigned, respectfully desire to bring certain facts to your attention ...'

From time to time she trimmed her quill with a tiny pen-knife set with slivers of mother-of-pearl. She covered three pages before going back to the start to correct and modify, to pare and prune until the whole was reduced to a single page of tersely presented information. Only when she was satisfied with every word and phrase did she take out another sheet of paper and painstakingly reproduce the finished letter in a large, bold script bearing no resemblance to her own hand. The result, she believed, was clear and distinctly masculine. She signed it with a flourish, sprinkled it with fine sand and blew off the surplus. Then she folded it carefully and fastened it with a seal of plain wax that bore no impress. On its back she wrote the name of Sir Oscar Cavendish and the address of his London house, where she knew him to be staying until the end of the month. Contained in the document were sufficient truths to damage a man's reputation and enough falsehoods to place his family in fear of a very public and searching inquiry.

'A fine piece of writing,' she told herself, pouring a small

174

sherry which she sipped with her usual restraint.

Thus fortified, she set about compiling a similar letter which she addressed to Her Ladyship, the Countess of Beresford, at Beresford Hall. Now that she knew exactly what she intended to do, she planned her actions down to the very last detail. She had waited a long time for this moment, and despite what had happened to Estelle, she could not pretend that she was doing it for anyone but herself. She wanted to hurt Horace Cavendish for what he had done to *her*. She wanted to collect, with interest, the debt incurred when he pressed that humiliating beggars' coin into her hand.

'Say nothing of my absence to anyone in the house,' she told the maid who watched her leave by the scullery door.

'But if Miss Anabel asks for you . . .?'

'You will hold your tongue, or I will know the reason why.'

'Yes, miss. Anything you say, miss.'

Poor daylight was worsened by a heavy drizzle as Leonora slipped through the rear gate and hurried to a busy corner three streets away and took a cab to St James's Palace. She was wearing her mother's black travelling coat with the hood raised and the front tightly buttoned. She also carried a large black umbrella to protect her head and shoulders from the rain. Fixed to the rim of her neat silk bonnet, and barely discernible beneath the hood of her coat, hung a short veil of dark net that wholly obscured her features. To complete her anonymity she spoke to the driver of the cab with a heavy French accent. At St James's Palace she paid off the cab and hired another to drive her the short distance to Westminster, and from there she walked to Curzon Street, the quiet, elegant cul-de-sac just off Great Peter Street where Sir Oscar Cavendish had his town house.

As she had anticipated, her presence soon attracted the attention of one of the many urchins who haunted the area in search of a penny to earn or steal, a bag to carry or a pocket to pick.

'You, boy,' she said, beckoning. 'A small task, if you please.'

He approached from the overhang of a house where he had

found shelter from the rain, stepping lightly around puddles that shone with oily colours in the lamp-light.

'A small task, ye say? How small? It'll still cost ye, ma'am. Work's work, an' it don't never come cheap, 'specially in this weather.'

The boy was incongruously dressed in a filthy but well-cut tailed coat with velvet collars, a ragged waistcoat and a huge, very fine top hat. But for his youth he might have been a middle-class gent fallen on hard times and gone to rags and patches. He touched the rim of his sodden hat, then peered at her with suspicion before spotting the two sixpenny pieces lying in the palm of her gloved hand. He whistled softly through the gap in his front teeth.

'Two tanners, eh? An' what's to be done for 'em?'

'I want you to deliver this letter to the house across the street with the coaching lamp above the door.'

'Ah, it's for 'is Lordship then?'

'Yes, for Sir Oscar Cavendish,' Leonora confirmed, accenting the words. 'And you are not to reveal that it was given to you by a lady. Will you deliver it?'

'For two tanners?'

Leonora nodded her head. 'You may take one coin now, the other when I see the job done.'

'My pleasure, ma'am,' the youngster said, with a deep bow that sent rainwater cascading from his hat to his untidy boots. He tested the coin between his teeth, tucked the letter inside his coat and strode across the street to ring the bell of his lordship's house.

Leonora stepped back and tilted her umbrella to conceal her face as the door of the house opened and the letter was presented to an elderly woman in a dark dress and bonnet and a small white apron. As the door closed again she moved away, beckoning the boy to follow. She handed him the second coin, and the bedraggled ragamuffin in gent's apparel insisted upon escorting her to the nearest cab. Her next stop was the White Horse Yard, Piccadilly, from where the Oxford mail would soon be leaving on one of its swift round trips. Although the carrier's fee would be collected at its destination, she handed him a whole guinea to ensure that her letter reached Beresford Hall the following day. She then retraced her complicated route to Garden Square, where she removed her makeshift veil and entered the house by the scullery door, safe in the knowledge that she did so unobserved.

IV

'Beg pardon, Your Lordship. Here's a letter just come for you. Delivered by hand, it was.'

'Thank you, Agatha. Leave it on the table.'

The housekeeper placed the silver tray containing the letter on the table close to where Sir Oscar was sitting. She was a plain, middle-aged woman attired from head to toe in dark green taffeta that had seen better days. Her gaze travelled over the room, noting the full glasses and the barely touched tray of fruit and nuts, the well-stoked fire, the tightly drawn curtains. Thus assured that his lordship wanted nothing for his comfort, she left the room as quietly as she had entered.

Both Sir Oscar and his guest had been dozing in their comfortable chairs before the fire, one weary after a difficult day in Parliament, the other exhausted by a lengthy coach journey, both replete after a fine dinner and several glasses of the very best brandy. The guest was Sir Giles Powell, a thick-set individual with bushy white whiskers and a face as rosy as a summer apple. He was a ruthless businessman who had made a large fortune in shipping and an even larger one in clever investments during the war years. He was also Sir Oscar's most trusted friend.

Sir Oscar listened to the rustle of the housekeeper's skirts and the soft click as the door closed behind her, then stretched his arms above his head and opened his mouth in a lusty yawn. For dinner he had enjoyed an excellent saddle of mutton with a sweet walnut-flavoured sauce of the cook's own devising, followed by the most delicious apricot pie. Now the heat of the fire and the warmth of the brandy had lulled him into a mood of mellow comfort he was loath to have disturbed. In the quiet, darkly panelled room a clock ticked off the seconds with lazy monotony and light rain made a soft, musical tattoo against the windows. He lifted the letter from the silver tray and turned it over in his fingers, recognising neither the plain seal nor the strong hand of the writer. He broke the seal, unfolded the single sheet of paper and began to read. As he did so his features grew grim and his mouth set itself into a tight, hard line.

'Oh, my God!' he exclaimed. 'This is monstrous ... *monstrous.*'

Sir Giles straightened up in his chair. 'What is it, Oscar?'

'This letter, it's ...' He suddenly strode to the door and flung it open, yelling at the top of his voice. 'Agatha! Agatha!'

The housekeeper came running along the corridor.

'Yes, Your Lordship?'

'This letter, when did it arrive and who delivered it?'

'It came just now, Your Lordship. About ten minutes ago, I reckon. A boy brought it.'

'A boy? What kind of boy?'

'A ruffian, if you ask me, sir, though nice enough in his manners. Not one I ever saw before.'

'Did he give the sender's name?'

'No, Your Lordship, just handed me the letter, tipped his hat and went away.'

'Thank you, Agatha. That will be all.' Sir Oscar closed the door and stepped back into the room, where he stood with his head bowed, staring at the letter.

A worried Sir Giles had pulled on his jacket and replenished the two brandy glasses. He handed one to his friend and urged him to drink.

'May I?'

Sir Oscar nodded grimly and allowed him to take the letter. Then he lowered himself into his chair and rubbed his face with both hands. He looked on, deeply troubled, while his friend began to read:

'*We, the undersigned, respectfully desire to bring certain facts to your attention, namely that your son, Horace, did ...*' He paused, his mouth sagging open in amazement. 'Good heavens, Oscar, can this be true? Theft? Obtaining honours by bribery and deception? Conspiring with others to withhold evidence from the police?'

Sir Oscar nodded. 'The writer claims to have proof of all these charges in the form of letters, diary entries, even statements from fellow pupils. There certainly *was* a cover-up in the death of Andrew Trent last summer. It was instigated in good faith by those who wished to spare his family further hurt. Do you recall the case?'

'I do indeed,' Sir Giles nodded. 'Hanged himself with a riding whip, I believe. Some kind of bizarre accident, if my memory serves me accurately.'

'It was no accident, my friend. The boy was indecently involved with a fellow student and hanged himself when the relationship ended. It was a particularly distasteful affair ... disgusting practices ... quite disgusting. Now it seems there were letters, even a written account ...'

'Indecently involved with a fellow student?' his friend echoed. 'A cheap homosexual affair? My dear Oscar, surely you're not suggesting ...'

'For God's sake read the letter,' Sir Oscar exploded. 'Read it for yourself.'

There was silence in the room for several minutes, then Sir Giles expelled his breath in a noisy sigh and sat down heavily. He stared into the fire, seeing his friend's career and good name scorched in the flames of public scandal. Even if the letter contained no more than a grain of truth, its implications spelled disaster to a man in Sir Oscar's position. It was signed: *Friends and Patrons of the Brighton Academy* but was otherwise anonymous.

'Perhaps this is Sir Henry Mortimer's doing,' he offered. 'If the man has discovered that Horace is having an affair with his wife ...?'

'If he believed that,' Sir Oscar said, bitterly, 'he would not have troubled to write to me. Mortimer would as soon see me ruined as put pen to paper on my behalf. No, Giles, whoever sent that message intended it as a warning, an opportunity to save us all from the worst of this mess.'

Sir Giles scanned the letter again, then read aloud:

'... *that the said Horace Cavendish be removed, immediately and permanently, from the Academy itself and from all fashionable society in Brighton and London. Failure to do so will result in the full facts being made public property.* It gives you three days in which to act. What will you do, Oscar?'

Sir Oscar shook his head miserably and fell silent. Then he heaved himself to his feet and strode across the room. Once again he flung the door wide and bellowed for his housekeeper in a voice that echoed through the whole house.

'Get hold of Jack Rogers and Tom Tyler,' he told the startled woman. 'Have them prepare horses for the journey to Brighton. My son must be brought here without delay, even if it means riding through the night. I'll meet them in the coach house in half an hour.'

He closed the door, scowling and tight-lipped as he attempted to gather his thoughts together into a clear plan of action.

'You believe the accusations, then?' Sir Giles asked.

'Should I not? You know him well, Giles. Has he ever been better than a drunken bully, a debaucher and a wastrel? He has a warped sense of honour and his reasoning is, to put it mildly, oblique. Yes, Giles, I *do* believe him capable of cuckolding my most powerful enemy and then boasting of the conquest, and to the devil with any risks to his father's career or his own reputation.'

Sir Oscar lowered himself into a chair and once again rubbed at his face with both hands. He looked drawn. Shock and anxiety were etched upon his handsome face.

'I sometimes wonder if the very fabric of the Cavendish family is not somehow flawed,' he observed, wearily. 'There is a dark thread running through it, Giles, and who knows where next the evil of it will appear.'

'But is your son capable of the specific charges laid against him?' Sir Giles demanded. 'As you know, I have no particular liking for the boy, but I wonder if he is capable of all this.'

Sir Oscar spoke softly. 'By God, Giles, I do believe he is. Have we not already protected him from one charge of rape and two of theft, all of which he vehemently denied? How long can we go on judging him innocent and his accusers wicked liars?'

'But this other charge ... this unfortunate boy who hanged himself last year ... surely Horace is not guilty of such perversions?'

Sir Oscar groaned and nipped the bridge of his nose with finger and thumb. 'Oh, God forbid that it be so, but the writer of that letter claims to have proof ... love letters, statements, an explicit personal diary belonging to young Trent. Damning proof, Giles. Damning.'

'But this whole thing could just as easily be a pack of lies.'

'So what must I do?' There was anguish in his eyes as he asked the question. 'Am I to ignore the warning and perhaps precipitate a sordid public inquiry?'

Sir Giles shook his head. 'Of course not. Even if the story is a pack of lies, the dirt would stick and the unsavoury stink of it would ruin you.' He waved the letter in the air between them. 'Fact or fiction, if this is made public you will be forced to resign your seat in the House.'

'And if the story is true? Can you imagine what this will do to his mother? Lady Alyce has always adored him in spite of his shortcomings, but although he is her favourite, her religious beliefs would never allow her to ...' He stopped suddenly and his face became a grey mask.

'What is it ...?'

'We are forgetting the law,' Sir Oscar said, his voice hoarse with emotion as he slumped forward in his chair, lowered his head against his clenched fists and issued a loud groan. 'My God, Giles, if proof really *does* exist that Horace was the unnatural lover of Andrew Trent, then he is guilty of gross sexual perversions, and for that he will hang. My son will *hang*.'

V

Even if Leonora had been in full possession of the facts, she could not have orchestrated that meeting between father and son with greater skill or better timing. Two weeks earlier Lady Georgette Mortimer, already tiring of her moody and often disagreeable young lover, had discovered that one of her diamond and ruby pendants, valued at over three thousand pounds, had vanished from her jewel casket. Suspecting Horace immediately, she had the presence of mind to trace the whereabouts of the pendant and recover the bill of sale before confronting him in the presence of two footmen and a maid.

'You are a thief, sir,' she had accused, brandishing the bill of sale. 'I found this in the pocket of your coat, and there is a goldsmith in Banyan Square ready to identify you as the man who sold the pendant for five hundred pounds. *Five hundred pounds*! Hell's teeth, sir, it was worth five times that amount.'

'You are hardly likely to be impoverished by the loss, my dear.'

'You are a *thief*, sir, a common thief.'

'Come come, woman. Pull yourself together and stop making a silly fuss about nothing.' Horace had helped himself to a sugared nut and now lounged elegantly on a sofa, totally unconcerned by her indignation. 'The trinket was merely borrowed to set against a pressing gambling debt. I had every intention of returning it to you.'

'Then you are a liar as well as a thief,' she had screamed at him, her eyes alight with the pleasure of one who had gained the upper hand. 'You sold it. You stole my property and sold it for your own personal gain. I could have you arrested for this, Horace Cavendish.'

'Not without seeing our ... er ... *arrangement* made public, my dear Georgette.'

She had laughed at him then, thrown back her lovely golden head and cackled like an ill-bred woman of the streets.

She thrust the bill of sale into the bodice of her gown and stood with her hands on her hips, her breasts thrust forward, her smile challenging. There was venom in her voice when she said: 'It would be worth the scandal to see you hang, my *dear*. Footmen, show this *thief* the door.'

Horace had neither seen nor heard from Georgette since that day and now, two weeks later, he was taken from his rooms in the dead of night by two of his father's men, bundled into a coach and driven the fifty-eight miles to London in almost total darkness. They arrived shortly after dawn, and despite the comfort of a hipflask during the journey, Horace stepped down from the coach feeling chilled to the bone and slightly nauseated. Agatha Bonnar, his father's tight-lipped housekeeper, showed him into the morning room, where a fire burned in the grate and a breakfast of cold meats, game, broiled fish and new bread had been laid. He lifted the domed lid of a chafing-dish, stared at the kidneys, bacon and sausages keeping hot on the plate, replaced the lid with a grimace of distaste and reached for a bottle of port.

'Where is my father?' he asked when Agatha re-entered the room with a tray of tea and hot chocolate.

'His Lordship is shaving, sir. He says you are to wait on him here. He and Sir Giles were up the whole night.'

'Why was I sent for? What is this all about, Agatha?'

The woman pursed her lips, offended by the question. 'I'm sorry, Master Horace, I don't go speaking to *nobody* of His Lordship's private business.'

'All right, all right, just tell him I'm here, will you? And bring me a stomach powder and a glass of warm milk.'

'Yes, sir. Are you ill, sir?'

'Ill? Yes, I'm ill,' Horace snapped. 'I was dragged from my rooms after a *very* lively party, thrust into a coach and jolted and bounced for over five hours with only a flask of brandy to help contain my heaving stomach. Then I am expected to wait here like a naughty boy with the stink of an unwanted breakfast in my nostrils.'

'Yes, sir. I'll fetch the powder, sir.'

Horace closed the door behind her, then placed a hand to

his brow and closed his eyes. His head was throbbing. Long-distance journeys by road always left him horribly fatigued, while the lurching, sideways motion of the carriage made him feel sick and light-headed. Too many hours without sleep had added greatly to his discomfort. He was in no fit state to face his father, especially if the Earl and Sir Giles Powell had also spent a sleepless night. There was trouble in the house, of that he was certain, and it was almost a foregone conclusion that he, Horace, was the cause of it.

'His Lordship will see you now, sir.'

Horace started. He had not heard the door open and the elderly housekeeper come back into the room. He waved aside the tray on which she had placed a glass of warmed milk and an envelope containing a mixture of powdered chalk, arrowroot and ground ginger to settle the stomach. Instead he poured himself another port and drank it straight down. Then he took a deep breath, squared his shoulders and followed Agatha across the hall to his father's private study.

Sir Oscar was standing with his back to the fire, tall and impressive in a black velvet cut-away coat, tight trousers and high, well-polished boots. He did not look like a man who had been awake all night. His immaculate appearance made Horace uncomfortably aware of his own dishevelled state: his soiled shirt, crumpled coat and mud-spattered shoes. He should have shaved, washed, changed his clothes and combed his hair; anything rather than come into his father's presence looking hungover and unkempt. As the cold blue eyes flickered over him, he attempted to straighten his neck-linen and smooth some of the creases from his trousers.

'I hope you will pardon my appearance, Father,' he offered with a smile. 'I was virtually *kidnapped* by Rogers and Tyler. No time to wash or change, no time even to pack an overnight bag.'

Sir Oscar nodded grimly. 'They were acting on my orders.'

'So I understand. How is my dear Mama?' The question was a ploy, a timely reminder that he was his mother's favourite.

'The Countess is well.'

'Good, good.' Horace saw that his father was uncertain, perhaps even reluctant to proceed with the conversation. He began to hope that matters were less serious than he at first suspected. He grinned and glanced at the bottles of port and brandy standing on a side table. 'May I?'

'I think not,' the Earl said. 'You might wish to keep a clear head, since we have important matters to discuss.'

'In that case,' Horace smiled. 'I will take only a modest brandy to clear my head.'

Sir Oscar watched with distaste as his son poured himself a drink with trembling hands. What he saw was a brazen young man so lacking in respect that he came before his father half-drunk, unwashed and unshaven. He saw that his own hands shook a little as he held out the hand-written list of crimes to which Horace might or might not be answerable.

'You'd better read this. It arrived last evening.'

The younger man drew back, frowning. 'What is it?'

'It concerns *you*, boy,' the Earl growled. 'Go ahead, read it for yourself.'

'I'd rather not, if you don't mind, Father. The truth is, I don't feel very well ... in fact, not myself at all. If I might go upstairs and rest for an hour or two ...?'

'Damn it, Horace, there'll be no rest for *any* of us until this matter is settled. Here is the letter. Read it.'

Horace reluctantly took possession of the sheet of paper wafted in his face. It had become badly creased, with a jagged tear where the wax seal had been torn away. While Sir Oscar turned his back to stare into the fire, Horace slumped into a chair and attempted to focus his attention on the stylish, unfamiliar handwriting. His head swam and he was perspiring heavily. His mind was so filled with dread that he was barely able to make out the words. All he could think of was Lady Georgette Mortimer, an excessively passionate woman who bore her grudges badly. Fear began to claw at him as he realised that she was probably vindictive enough to try to destroy him for crossing swords with her.

'It would be worth the scandal to see you *hang*!'

With her impassioned declaration ringing in his ears, words

sprang from the page with no real sense of order. He recognised the name of Andrew Trent coupled with something about diaries and statements; saw accusations of fraud, lies, bribery, pilfering, deception. And then a sense of absolute terror settled upon him as his gaze fell on the name of Sir Henry Mortimer. She *had* betrayed him, after all. The stupid, malicious bitch had decided to carry out her threat to expose him as a thief and an adulterer.

'Well?' Sir Oscar demanded. 'What have you to say for yourself? Would these accusations stand up in a court of law?'

Horace screwed the letter into a tight ball and shook his head, his eyes tightly closed and his stomach churning with sick trepidation. He slumped against the back of his chair and began to mutter: 'Oh, God. Oh, dear God in heaven.'

'Would they? Pull yourself together, sir. Would they?'

'Yes.' The word came out in a whisper. 'Yes ... Yes ...'

'What? *What?*'

Without warning, Sir Oscar strode across the room, grabbed his son by the lapels and yanked him from the chair. He shook him violently, then slapped him hard across the face and shoved him back with such force that the chair slithered sideways under his weight. The Earl leaned over and snarled into Horace's face.

'Tell me it is not true,' he demanded, grinding the words between clenched teeth. 'For the love of God, tell me you are not guilty of this ... this ...' He could not bring himself to say the words that would brand his own son a sexual pervert whose lover had killed himself in despair. Instead he cleared his throat and finished: '... this *hanging* offence.'

Horace flinched before his father's rage. Georgette's pendant had been valued at three thousand pounds, enough to hang him several times over. And there was proof: the goldsmith, the incriminating bill of sale. He was trapped, ensnared in the web of his own folly. 'It's true, God help me, father, it's all true. I know I've been a fool, a stupid, self-indulgent fool, but love and passion can blind a man to all else except ...'

'Hold your tongue!' Sir Oscar struck his son a back-handed

186

blow across the mouth, a blow so savage that it drew blood and almost lifted the startled young man from his seat. 'How *dare* you refer to that ... that *perversion* as love? You disgust me.'

Horace lowered his hands from his face and stared at the sticky crimson stains on his fingers. He could feel a loose tooth and taste the blood in his mouth. His senses were reeling. He tried to stand, felt bile rise into his throat, fell back into the chair and prayed he would not be overcome by a sudden and very urgent need to vomit.

Sir Oscar rang the bell and moments later the door opened to admit a grim-faced Sir Giles Powell.

'I want you to hear this, Giles,' Sir Oscar said, smoothing the crumpled letter in his hands before confronting his son again. 'Horace Cavendish, have you read and understood the charges made against you by the authors of this letter?'

Horace hauled himself to his feet and nodded miserably. He had neither read nor understood the charges with any accuracy, but had seen enough to know that, along with his questionable behaviour at the academy, his affair with Georgette was now exposed. And the theft of her property, the 'hanging offence' his father had spoken of, was about to reshape his whole life. He had no alternative but to throw himself upon the Earl's mercy and pray that by doing so he would avoid prosecution.

'Answer me, boy.'

Horace flinched. 'Yes, sir.'

'And you admit to the charges?'

'Yes, sir.'

'To *all* the charges?'

'Yes, sir, but I beg you to give me leave to explain, to ...'

'Hold your tongue!'

Horace fell silent, defeated by his father's fury.

'It has been decided that you will leave for Europe immediately,' Sir Giles informed him after a lengthy silence. 'There will be no further discussion on the subject. A room has been prepared for you on the top floor of the house. You will be so good as to remain there, seeing no-one, until arrangements can be made for you to leave the country. We intend to spare Countess Alyce the details of your disgrace, and in this you will assist us by maintaining a discreet silence. Finally, your father expects your total co-operation in exchange for his protection. Do you agree to these terms?'

'Yes, sir.' In that warm, elegantly furnished room all reality seemed to have been suspended, leaving Horace to hang in the numbing vacuum of his own uncertainty.

'That will be all,' his father suddenly barked into the prolonged silence. 'There will be no further meetings between us. Rogers or Tyler will inform you of further arrangements as they are finalised.' Horace wiped the sleeve of his coat across his bleeding mouth. There was something too cold, too final in all this. He felt that he was being dispossessed of his parents' love and protection, cast adrift without forgiveness for his sins.

'That will be all. You may leave us.'

'... Father ...'

'That will be *all*, sir.'

'But sir ... I beg you to hear me out ...'

With a snort of disgust the Earl turned his broad back and stared into the flames in the fireplace. 'Agatha will show you to your room,' he growled. 'Now, be so kind as to remove yourself from my sight, sir.'

CHAPTER EIGHT

I

On the last day of March, 1823, the Honourable Horace Cavendish set sail for Calais aboard the cargo vessel *Ebony Lass*. The normally arrogant young man was now subdued, crushed by the wave of events that had overtaken him. His father, wounded and unapproachable, had refused him a second hearing. His beloved mother, knowing of his confession to crimes against the laws of man and God, had tossed his unopened letters into the fire and sent no word of comfort or forgiveness. When a son falls from grace he wounds the mother who bore him; when her precious darling, her favourite, proves undeserving of her devotion, it becomes not failure but betrayal. Finding herself thus betrayed, Lady Alyce closed her broken heart behind a stone-like exterior, retired to her private rooms and sought comfort in her Bible.

As the *Ebony Lass* put to sea on the afternoon tide, the bells of St Clement Dane were ringing out and the Thames was crammed with barges waiting to off-load their cargoes of lemons and oranges at landing places just below the churchyard. Hundreds of excited, squabbling children were gathering at the church to attend the special service and receive gifts of fruit. It was a time of celebration and thanksgiving, but the clear, familiar sound of the bells reached Horace's ears with a distinctly hollow ring.

He stood alone on that section of the ship's deck; a tall, muscular young man with features grimly set and blue eyes narrowed into bitter slits. A heavy black cloak added extra width to already broad shoulders, its collar high and dark against a pale face and wind-blown fair hair. With his hands thrust deep into his pockets he looked back toward that part of the river bank where Sir Giles Powell stood apart from the crowd. As that single witness to his departure became small and indistinct in the distance, he knew with absolute certainty that his comfortable life was at an end, destroyed by the power of the written word. Nothing remained of the security, the prestige and the pleasure-seeking that had marked his existence for so long. He had been stripped of everything that was of value to him. One moment he had been loved and pampered by friends and family, the next abandoned to his fate like a common criminal. Once he had been a gentleman of means, now he had just five hundred pounds in his pocket and a note of introduction to a wealthy wine merchant in Germany. This document he now took from his cloak and turned in his fingers. It was his passport to a new life, his ticket into the ranks of the working classes, and for this he was expected to be humbly grateful. With a resentful curl of his lip he ripped the letter of introduction into a dozen small pieces for the fitful afternoon breeze to carry away.

'I'll make my own way from now on, Oscar Cavendish,' he said into the cold, unfriendly waters of the Thames. 'And damn you to hell if you can disown a son for stealing a trinket and taking pleasure from another man's wife.'

II

The weather changed with the month, and by Palm Sunday London was blooming beneath blue skies and bright sunshine. The trees were in bud and the gardens and parks blossomed with spring flowers. It had been a long winter, followed by weeks of grey, dank weather that hung over the city in a depressing mantle. Typhus and dysentery had become so commonplace that in some areas the wealthier families had moved to the country to avoid infection. Fog and rain meant that the sewers stank and drains overflowed, and the streets in places became quagmires of mud and animal dung, market waste and sewage. But with April the weather rapidly improved, so that ladies ventured out in their colourful summer dresses and even the city slums took on a sunnier, more cheerful aspect.

Gilbert Cavendish was nineteen that year. Apart from his stunning blue eyes he was an unremarkable young man of modest manners who might easily pass unnoticed in more sparkling company. His hair was a light, rather mousy shade of brown and his features, while undoubtedly handsome, lacked the ruggedly aristocratic stamp so noticeable in his brothers and, indeed, in many of his cousins. In looks and build he favoured his mother, the Countess of Beresford, but in temperament he was very much his father's son. Sober and clean-living, he tended to judge others by his own high standards and was, as a consequence, very often disappointed.

Throughout April he took to riding every day in Green Park. He had chosen to spend the long Easter recess at the Earl's London house rather than return to the gloomy atmosphere of Beresford Hall. Malcolm was moody because the health of Lady Grace, now nearing the sixth month of her pregnancy after two early miscarriages, was once again giving cause for concern. The Countess herself had collapsed recently in her private chapel. A minor seizure, the doctor had said, too small and insignificant to give rise to undue alarm.

She was still grieving over the sudden loss of her favourite son, but sadness had done nothing to improve the capricious turns of her temper. There were times when she took a riding whip to her younger servants, and recently she had overturned a breakfast tray in anger, badly scalding the maid who carried it.

Gilbert reined his horse to one side and raised his hat politely as two young ladies of his acqaintance cantered by. He was recalling the way his mother had screamed at him to leave her alone when he tried to comfort her after that terrible business with Horace. She was not the sort of woman who could divide her love equally among her children. Horace had claimed the lion's share of her affection, and her youngest son could never hope to compensate for his loss.

'Ho, there! Good day to you, Gilbert! Must you and your animal claim the whole path while we lesser mortals take to the grass?'

'What?' He started from his dark thoughts, then his face lit with pleasure as he recognised his friend. 'Charles!'

'Make way, sir. Here's a fast chaise coming up behind you.'

Gilbert twisted the reins and the big horse side-stepped to allow the chaise to pass.

'Thank you, Charles,' he grinned. 'A timely warning, since my thoughts were heavily engaged elsewhere.'

'Sleeping in the saddle, I'll wager.' He stuck out his hand for Gilbert to grasp in a hearty handshake. 'It's good to see you again, Gilbert. Allow me to present my sister, Leonora.'

Gilbert raised his hat and bowed to the elegant young woman on the white-blazed bay. He felt he already knew her from Elizabeth's letters. He had also heard her described as one of the most stunning young women in London, yet still he found himself all but overwhelmed by what he saw. Here was a young woman of tremendous presence and physical beauty, who handled her mount like an expert and met Gilbert's gaze with a refreshingly candid stare. She was wearing a maroon riding habit that emphasised her curvaceous figure and tiny waist, and a neat black hat that complimented the lush auburn tones of her hair. She was fascinating. The most striking thing about her was her eyes. They were large and round, with ebony lashes and a colour reminiscent of fresh wild violets.

'Leonora, say hello to our cousin Gilbert,' Charles grinned.

Leonora smiled and inclined her head as her gaze appraised this youngest of the Earl's three sons. She barely remembered him from Malcolm's wedding, but she would have known him at once for a Cavendish by the strength of his jaw and the deep blue of his eyes. He was looking at her with an open and honest admiration that was neither impertinent nor embarrassing.

'Your servant, ma'am,' he said, reaching for her gloved hand. 'Having heard so much about you, it is my pleasure to meet you at last.' He raised the hand to his lips, still staring into her eyes as he breathed in the musky sweetness of her perfume.

'So, my brothers have spoken to you of me, cousin Gilbert?' she asked, glancing at Charles.

'Indeed they have, though their descriptions scarcely do justice to your beauty. I am enchanted, dear cousin ... quite enchanted.'

A smile curved Leonora's lips and danced in her eyes as he reluctantly released her hand. His statement had not been delivered with that ingratiating social skill designed to flatter its recipient. Here was that rarest of things, a true compliment, spontaneously offered and all the more disarming for its obvious sincerity. In his eyes she saw neither challenge nor mockery, and she suspected, to her pleasure, that everything she had ever heard about this likeable, unassuming young man was true.

The three rode together for some time before leaving the cinder path and trotting across the grass to dismount close to one of the park's milk-sellers. While Charles took charge of the horses, Leonora and Gilbert stood together at the makeshift stall, watching the young dairy maid prepare sillabubs by pouring thick, warm new milk over a measure of wine, adding honey and powdered spices.

'And how is your sister Elizabeth?' Leonora asked.

'Oh, she alters little. Her physical health remains good but

...' He smiled suddenly. 'She looks forward to receiving your letters. I am indebted to you for the pleasure your friendship has brought her. As you must realise, she is rather isolated and lonely, and few people bother to pay her even the smallest kindness. It was so good of you to befriend her.'

'Elizabeth is my dearest friend.' Leonora told him. 'I have a genuine affection for her.'

'Yes, I do believe you have.'

'And I'm happy that she feels able to confide in you. Until now I was not aware that *anyone* knew of our friendship. She insisted from the start that it remain our secret.'

Gilbert looked at her with a curious expression.

'The truth is, my sister can neither read nor write,' he said after a lengthy pause.

'Oh? But how ... who ...?'

He smiled rather sheepishly and handed her a dish of sillabub and a spoon.

'You?' she asked, and a warm flush rushed to her cheeks as she recalled the written endearments that had passed between herself and Elizabeth over the last year and a half. '*You* wrote them?'

He nodded his head and a tendril of fine, mousy hair fell across his forehead. He looked awkward, standing there with a dish of sillabub in each hand. He also looked relieved.

'Miss Shelley ... Leonora ... my sister is desperately fond of you. When your first letter arrived she carried it around in her pocket, unopened, for almost two weeks before I found it on the lawn where it had fallen. I took it upon myself to write back to you on her behalf and, quite frankly, I did not expect the friendship to develop as it did.'

'But all this time ... all those letters ...?'

'I confess they were all mine, although I hasten to add that Elizabeth approved every word.'

Leonora tasted the bitter-sweet cream on her tongue. Her letters had been very carefully worded; simple and newsy to amuse Elizabeth, innocuous so as to cause no offence if they fell into the wrong hands. Even so, it was rather disconcerting to discover that for all these months she had been corresponding on such friendly terms not with Elizabeth, as she had believed, but with Gilbert Cavendish.

'Hey there, you two! Am I to be left all afternoon with the horses while you enjoy the scenery?'

'Just coming, Charles,' Gilbert called out. Then he turned to Leonora and said: 'In my defence I can only plead that I deceived you with the very best of intentions, and with my sister's happiness uppermost in my mind. Will you forgive the deception, Leonora?'

'I will,' she laughed, 'but only if you promise to disregard the positive *wealth* of feminine frivolities my letters surely contained.'

'Not frivolous,' he replied. 'They were nicely written, kind and thoughtful, but never frivolous.'

'And now?' she asked, acknowledging his compliment with a smile. 'Is our correspondence to be discontinued now that I know your guilty secret?'

'Oh, I sincerely hope not, though it would help if you could address your letters to me at the main lodge. I suspect the Countess would not approve, and poor Elizabeth is inclined to be a little clumsy at times.'

'For heaven's sake, you two!'

They hurried up the slope to where Charles waited with the horses. As the two friends fell into easy conversation on the subject of steamships and iron bridges, Leonora sipped at her sillabub and allowed her thoughts to race ahead of the moment. She liked Gilbert. He was a Cavendish, the son of an earl and a likeable, warm-hearted man who obviously returned her interest in no small measure. It should not be difficult to insinuate her way into his affections.

As if to add weight and substance to the scheme forming itself in her mind, the perspiring, roly-poly figure of Christopher Fairfax came waddling across the grass in their direction. She noticed that his shiny black coach and four, no doubt containing that wizened old vulture, Nigel Fairfax, was waiting outside the nearest gate.

'Here comes your adoring spaniel, Leonora,' her brother said, dusting the rim of his hat with his gloves. 'Will you allow

195

him a few minutes of your time, just to demonstrate to Gilbert how he fawns and grovels in your presence?'

'I most certainly will not,' Leonora retorted. She took the reins of her own mount, placed one foot in the stirrup and said to Gilbert: 'Your arm, sir, if you please.'

A moment later she was in the saddle and galloping away across the park, the loose section of her hair flying in the sun-kissed breeze. Seeing that his objective was once again denied him, Christopher Fairfax brought his great bulk to a shuddering halt and stood gasping, handkerchief in hand, while horse and rider raced off into the distance. Then he raised his hat and bowed to the two young men, turned on his heels and waddled back the way he had come.

'The man follows her around like a besotted lap dog,' Charles explained with some distaste. 'I suspect that Father has even begun to encourage him. The family is very wealthy.'

'And a thorn in my father's side,' Gilbert added, swinging himself lightly into the saddle. 'His lordship hates those neighbours of ours with a passion. Oh no, Charles, your lovely sister must never, *never* marry a Fairfax.'

Charles mounted and turned his horse to follow that of his friend, who was already urging his mount in the direction in which Leonora had galloped away.

'Ah, but I would have my sister wed to a wealthy man, one who will cherish and indulge her and ensure her future.'

'Then give her the best,' Gilbert said, and turned in the saddle to tap Charles's arm with his riding whip. He grinned and winked, but there was a serious glint in his eye when he added: 'Give her the *very* best. Let her marry a *Cavendish*.'

'What? Are you serious?'

'The day is too pretty to be serious, my friend. Come on, I'll race you to the far side of the park.'

With a flurry of hooves and several loud whoops of exuberance, the two friends spurred their mounts into a gallop and raced off in pursuit of the subject of their conversation.

Leonora did not allow herself to be caught. She rode recklessly through the park, scattering walkers and riders alike, and eventually urged her perspiring horse homeward through the busy streets of St James's. In her mother's bedroom some time later she paced to and fro across the richly patterned carpet, her cheeks flushed to a rosy glow and her eyes sparkling with some inner excitement. Anabel disliked the wildness of her mood and was tempted to scold her into a calmer and more ladylike frame of mind, but Francine signalled that her daughter was to be left alone. She had never seen Leonora so animated, so aroused. There was a passion in her so potent that it seemed to alter the very atmosphere of the room.

Leonora still wore her wide velvet riding skirt and laced leather boots, but her jacket and bonnet lay discarded on the seat of a chair. She had pulled the pins from her hair and shaken it loose so that it cascaded from her crown to her hips like a lustrous veil. Each time she turned to retrace her steps across the sunny room, her hair swung about her face and shoulders dancing with auburn highlights. At last she turned to confront her mother and lifted her chin proudly, her hands on her hips and her eyes defiant as she made her announcement.

'I have decided to marry Gilbert Cavendish.'

Anabel's mouth fell open. She would have made some comment but for the restraining hand placed upon her forearm. Francine muttered a warning under her breath. She was propped against high pillows, her hair faded beneath a lace cap and her skin ashen against the snowy white linen. After a lengthy silence she cleared her throat behind a small handkerchief before asking:

'And when did you arrive at this momentous decision?'

'Today, Mama ... this very afternoon. Charles and I met Gilbert in the park while we were out riding, and I do believe he is quite taken with me.' She tossed her head, causing her hair to shimmer. 'It occurred to me almost at once that I, not my father, should be the one to determine *my* future.'

'And what of Gilbert?' Francine asked. 'What does *he* have to say on the matter?'

'As yet he knows nothing about it,' Leonora replied with a wickedly radiant smile. 'But I have a plan, and very soon he will fall so helplessly under my spell that he will be able to think of nothing else.'

Anabel could contain herself no longer. 'A plan, you say? It sounds more like a dream to me, my girl, a foolish fancy. Sir Oscar will never agree to such a match.'

'Oh yes he will,' Leonora responded. 'Once Gilbert makes his feelings known, and once it is discovered that my holdings are now worth almost three thousand pounds a year, I think the Earl will be persuaded to waive his objections.'

'But how can you be so certain, Leonora? On the strength of a single meeting, how can you possibly know that this young man will ...'

'Will *want* to marry me?' Leonara anticipated. 'Oh but he will, Mama. I saw as much in his eyes today. And besides, my instincts are never in error, and I know in my heart that soon he will *adore* me.'

'And what of your own feelings, my dear? Is it love? Do you think ...?'

'Love?' Leonora asked, seating herself on the bed and frowning a little at her mother's anxious face. '*Love*? What on earth has *love* to do with it? In August I will be eighteen and Papa will throw me on the marriage market like so much horse-flesh to be bartered for and eventually purchased by the highest bidder. Am I to go placidly into the unknown, trusting to the uncertain judgement of a man quite likely to wager my future upon the turn of a faro card?'

'Now, Leonora, I'm sure your Papa has only your best interests at heart.'

'*My* interests? Oh no, Mama, if that were so he would never have given Christopher Fairfax leave to call upon me. You both know how I feel about that man. Would you have me wait for Papa to arrange a match between us, or would you rather I chose my own husband ... a *young* man ... a *handsome* man, a *Cavendish*?'

'But you say nothing of love ...'

Leonora rose to her feet, suddenly exasperated.

'Love!' she snorted. 'If love is some silly romantic notion that devalues a woman in the eyes of her husband then I will have none of it. If this love you speak of is what turns women into mere subservients, dependent on a man's whims and degraded by his lusts ...'

'Leonora! How *dare* you speak to your Mama in that way!'

'I speak only as I find, and I will make no apologies for my opinions. Believe me, Mama, I would as soon remain a maid as surrender my all to the vagaries of *love*.'

Francine smiled and said: 'My dear Leonora, if you only knew the joy of being loved ... *truly* loved, and giving your heart in return.'

'Joy?' Leonora shook her head and her eyes flashed darkly beneath their ebony lashes. 'There is no joy in love, Mama. There is only *power*. And believe me, no man will ever gain absolute power over *me* in the name of love. No man will ever be *my* lord and master. And while we are discussing the subject of marriage, let me state once and for all that I will not, under *any* circumstances, reduce myself to lying in wifely obedience beneath that quivering lump of sweating flesh, Christopher Fairfax.'

'Leonora! That's *enough*!' Anabel jumped to her feet, appalled by the outburst.

'All right, Anabel, but you must mark my words. You too, Mama. I know what I want from life, and by hook or by crook I *will* have Gilbert Cavendish for my husband.' With a toss of her head she strode toward the door, turning as she reached for the handle. 'And you may both rest assured that *love*, on my part at least, will have absolutely no hand in it.'

'Leonora! Don't you dare leave this room until ... come back here at once ... oh, you wicked little madam ...'

'Leave her, Anabel,' Francine interceded. 'Let her be. She knows her own mind.'

'Aye, and a mite too well, if you ask me. Marry a Cavendish, indeed. Oh, I never heard anything so fanciful in all my life. And she can be so outspoken!'

Francine lay back against the pillows with a deep sigh, her face troubled and her fingers picking abstractedly at the trimmed edge of the coverlet.

'My daughter has her heart set upon a future at Beresford,' she said.

'And who is to blame for that, eh? Who has been filling her head with such high-born notions from the day she learned to speak?'

'Do not forget that she is a Cavendish, Anabel.'

'Aye, but a *small* one with dreams beyond her grasping.'

'Oh, Anabel, if only she could marry Gilbert Cavendish. You and I both know how stubborn she can be, how single-minded. I believe she will have her own way at any cost.' She closed her eyes briefly, then took Anabel's hand and added: 'Perhaps it is a blessing that she has no real inkling of the intensity, the sheer driving force of passionate love. She is so headstrong, so determined to have her way, that if once it touches her, I doubt she will deny herself the having of it.'

'Then we must hope it never does touch her,' Anabel said gently, seating herself on the bed and stroking her mistress's cool, delicately pale hands. 'At least until she's safely wed to a man who'll keep a tight and steady rein on the wild streak that's in her.'

'Ah, but can we be sure there *is* such a man, Anabel?'

'Maybe yes and maybe no, but if our haughty young madam *does* manage to get herself wed to a Cavendish, there'll be none strong enough to curb her conceits. Power, she says ... *power*, indeed. If the master ever heard her talking like that ... oh, sometimes I despair of that girl.'

'Yes, my dear,' Francine said with a tired smile. 'But has she not succeeded in convincing us both, these last few years, that she is destined for much greater things than you or I would ever aspire to?'

'Tell that to the master, if you dare.'

'Oh no, not I, but we can rely on Leonora to *show* him,' Francine said with quiet confidence. 'Though not, I think, until after her plot is hatched and the unsuspecting Gilbert is helplessly in love with her.'

In the privacy of her own room Leonora paced to and fro in a rustle of skirts, her eyes still bright and her cheeks flushed.

'Oh yes, I will have him,' she vowed. 'If I am to be denied the handsome heir of Beresford then I must be content to settle for the youngest son.' She lifted her head and struck a regal pose before the ornate oval mirror. 'Leonora Cavendish,' she announced to her reflection. 'Lady Leonora ... of Beresford Hall.'

III

Four men were hanged at Newgate on the first Wednesday in May. Two were highwaymen apprehended following a string of armed robberies along the notorious London to Gloucester road. Another was their confessed accomplice, a banker's clerk found guilty of alerting the robbers whenever valuables or large sums of money were to be carried on the Royal Mail coaches. The clerk was also a petty thief whose employers had long suspected him of embezzling small but regular sums from customers' accounts. A surreptitious watch was placed upon his activities and eventually he was caught in the very act of transferring two pounds and four shillings from the weekly deposit of a local goldsmith to the account of his own wife, Mabel. Thrown into a panic by the confrontation, he attempted to save himself by incriminating his wife and informing upon his friends. The two highwaymen were subsequently arrested at the Almstead Turnpike after shooting dead a passenger, Mr Cedric Podmoor of Gloucester, and seriously wounding the driver of the coach. On the morning of the executions the crowd began to gather long before dawn. This was free entertainment for the masses, who pressed in noisy flocks around the debtors' door like so many scavengers drawn by the promise of death. They came to hear the last cries of anguish, to taste the fear, to witness the convulsions separating life and death at the end of a stout rope.

'The woman got twelve years' transportation, more's the pity,' one of the spectators complained in a voice thickened by drink.

'Aye, more's the pity,' another slurred. 'I likes to see a pretty skirt dangling alongside the men.'

'Specially when she fights the rope and shows a nice bit of thigh afore she goes, eh?'

'Aye, a few high kicks while it's still warm,' another man guffawed. 'It'll all be dead meat by the time the surgeons get their share.'

'Not this time it won't,' a woman yelled in bawdy response. 'I reckon there'll be plenty of sex-starved sailors warming *them* thighs for a ha'penny a time between now and Australia.'

Herbert Shelley used his elbows and his considerable bulk to ease himself sideways by several feet so as to avoid the more unsavoury elements of the crowd. From there he had a splendid view of the Old Bailey scaffold, a large, movable platform hung all around with black cloth and containing a number of trap-doors on which the criminals would presently be directed to stand. At the appropriate moment the traps would fall away by means of a lever and rollers and briefly, grotesquely, the condemned men would dance like comic marionettes to their deaths.

Herbert shared the crowd's morbid fascination for the hangings. Here the savagery of human nature levelled all distinctions, making the aristocrat no better than the filthy bone-grubber, the high-born lady no more respectable than the cheapest whore. All were inflamed by the time-honoured desire to be in at the kill. Each succumbed to the compelling sensuality of lengthy foreplay leading up to the executions, followed by the sudden release of potent mob-energy with the snapping of a prisoner's neck. The yells of derision were crudely sexual, and many a casual carnal encounter took place in the heated shadow of the Old Bailey scaffold.

It was almost time. The cries of the mob became more urgent as the tolling bell rang out its doleful chime. In the press yard the prisoners' leg-irons had been hammered free, the clergyman in attendance had withdrawn with his cold comfort to a carefully measured distance, the Sheriffs were all in attendance and the Yeoman of the Halter was ready to place his ropes around the waiting necks. Soon the debtors' door swung open and the sad little procession passed through to a roar of enthusiasm so deafening that it momentarily obscured the mournful tolling of the bell.

Herbert Shelley felt the thrill of the moment tugging at his scalp. It dried his mouth and set molten fires burning in his belly. His gaze was fixed on the fourth man, a thin, anonymous figure in ragged clothes and a dirty, shapeless hat. This was the gentleman forger, who had drawn a thousand guineas upon his partner's signature in order to make up a fourth at whist. By morning he had won twice the amount, but by then his crime was discovered and neither his banker nor his business partner could be persuaded to accept the cash and overlook the offence. It better served their interests to have him charged with forgery and dispatched to Newgate. Now the young man was to hang, and for Herbert Shelley there was a macabre fascination in watching somebody die for but a fraction of his own undiscovered crimes.

'Hang the bastards! Swing 'em high! Throttle 'em all!'

The crowd shrieked for action. The prisoners were now in position on the gallows, each one blinded by a hood beneath which he was either drunk or drugged or limp with terror.

'Hang 'em! Throttle 'em, good an' proper!'

The yelling and jeering rose to a crescendo as the traps sprang open, the bodies dropped and the ropes jerked. There was a sudden sharp intake of breath followed by silence, then the spectators, as of one voice, emitted a loud 'aaaahhhh' of satisfaction. It was all over. The law had avenged itself in the name of justice and now its loyal patrons could disperse to sleep off their intoxications or eat a delayed breakfast or beat their wives or lift the skirts of a maidservant.

Herbert left with the main body of the crowd, leaving the more boisterous elements to hang about the gallows until there was nothing more to see. He broke his fast in a chop-house on Duckworth Row and arrived at the premises of Fairfax, Reece & Tilbury shortly after eight-thirty. He was shown into a darkly panelled office containing a large oak desk, several shabby chairs and a long wooden cupboard littered with legal books and papers. The dusty, uneven floorboards were graced by a single rug of uncertain pattern, and the ancient velvet drapes at the window stank of soot and tobacco smoke. Having been shown into this unwelcoming room by one of the lesser clerks, he was given a glass of rather mediocre claret and informed, in a manner none too civil, that Mr Fairfax senior would be down to see him in due course. He was not slow to grasp the implications of all this. A few short months ago he would have been *invited*, rather than *summoned*, to a meeting with his bankers. He would have been shown into the cluttered but comfortable drawing room on the first floor and offered the best port, a chair by the fire and a little tray of Turkish delight dusted with fine ground sugar. Only a few months ago he would have come here as a guest of this establishment's senior partners but now, with his cash flow virtually at a standstill and his loans due for renewal, he came on demand, humbled by uncertainty.

'Damn them for the pompous buffoons they are,' he muttered under his breath, contemptuous of those who were compelled by circumstances to toil for a living like common men. Wealthy bankers they might well be, but in truth they were little better than labourers.

Comforted by this sound reasoning, he adjusted his black stock and tugged at the lower edges of his silk waistcoat. Then he carefully measured the show of white lace protruding from each sleeve of his coat. His appearance was, as always, immaculate. He would allow no outward sign of the difficulties by which he was presently plagued. He touched a monogrammed handkerchief to his nostrils and sniffed delicately. Outside a tradesman's cart rumbled along the street, its iron wheels sparking on the cobbles and its tall, bulky load lurching drunkenly from side to side. Somewhere nearby a woman protested the quality of her oranges into the dusty atmosphere. It was a hot day when many stoves and fires would remain unlit, yet still the air of the city seemed hardly fit for a decent man to breathe.

The door of the room suddenly burst open to admit Nigel Fairfax, a skinny, black-clad figure with sunken features and a dusty wig atop his queerly domed head.

'Ah, there you are, Shelley,' he muttered. 'Haven't kept you waiting long, I hope?'

'Not at all,' Shelley responded rather stiffly. He was somewhat alarmed by the untidy collection of documents dumped on the desk to be fingered and squinted at by the old man. 'I trust the day finds you in decent health, Mr Fairfax.'

'Oh, well enough, well enough. Sit down, man, sit down. No reason to stand on ceremony. Enjoy the hangings, eh?'

'Quite, though I did not see you at Newgate.'

'Nor I you, dear boy. Didn't attend. Couldn't spare the time. Sent one of my nephews along instead.' A pale hand with knotty fingers scratched at the surface of the top document, drawing Shelley's attention to the deeds of transfer placing Jonathan's Manchester properties under the bank's control. The old man shook his head and added thoughtfully: 'Knew him well, you know. Foolish boy ... knew him well.'

Shelley swallowed the lump that had risen to his throat. 'To whom do you refer, sir?'

'Why, Townsend of course.'

'Townsend?'

'The forger, man. Signed his partner's name and took Grafton's bank for a thousand guineas. God damn it, Shelley, you watched him hang little more than an hour ago.'

'Ah yes, the young forger. His name was not familiar to me until now. Harsh justice, I believe, in that particular case.'

Fairfax's face jerked sideways and his beady black eyes fixed Shelley with an investigative stare. It was the quick, sharp movement of a bird of prey.

'Harsh justice? Why? How so?'

'Well, did he not offer to make good the loss, with interest?'

'So he did, but how should that fact influence the outcome of the case?'

'Well ...' Shelley shifted in his seat, crossed his legs at the ankles and used his handkerchief to dust a few specks of soot from his breeches. 'I believe there was no real fraud intended. His partner was out of town and the young man was rather desperately in need of ready cash. He clearly meant to return

205

the money as soon as it was in his power to do so. It was the merest mischance that his partner returned unexpectedly and chose to be so high-handed on the matter.'

'High-handed?' Fairfax echoed. 'But we are talking about a thousand guineas fraudulently obtained for the purpose of playing a game of whist! Suppose the money had been lost?'

'Then a charge of forgery might have been ... *would* have been quite reasonable,' Shelley offered. 'But the money was not lost. To my knowledge Townsend emerged from the game two thousand guineas the richer. Sufficient, would you not agree, to more than justify his impertinence?'

'I most certainly would *not* agree,' Fairfax exclaimed with some measure of indignation. He sucked air through his sparsely placed teeth and shrugged his thin shoulders inside his coat, a shabby black bird ruffling its feathers against a chilly wind. His fingers tapped at the pile of papers on the desk, once more drawing Shelley's attention to the deeds of transfer with which he had obtained substantial loans over past months.

'Forgery is a damnably serious business,' the old man reminded his visitor. 'Damn it, man, a bank must never condone behaviour of that kind, whatever the outcome. We handle money entrusted to us by respectable and honourable men and women. In return they expect nothing less than scrupulous honesty. We cannot allow ourselves to be duped, to be pillaged of that money by every impudent deceiver who intends to make good if – and only if – he has not already squandered every penny of it at the gaming tables. Was this unprincipled young man to be permitted to ruin his partner and bring a bank into disrepute simply because he *meant* well? Come now, Shelley. Anyone who commits forgery is a criminal, and the cost of his crime is the rope. Would you call that "harsh justice"?'

Shelley cleared his throat. 'On second consideration, perhaps not,' he conceded. 'When the argument is heard from that point of view ...'

'Come now, Shelley, the man was guilty of forgery from any point of view.'

'Quite. Quite. Though a thousand guineas is meagre value to place upon a man's life.'

'Ah, but the law judged otherwise.'

'Indeed.'

'The law *always* judges otherwise. Forgery, like theft and murder, is a hanging matter and quite rightly so.'

Shelley nodded, fingering his stock. By now he was halfway convinced that Nigel Fairfax suspected him of similar offences against his own bank. All this talk of forgery and hanging, and those claw-like fingers tap-tapping at the deeds of transfer as if to imply unspoken threats. Shelley had to do something to throw that sly old man off the scent, and he must act swiftly, before specific inquiries were made in certain very delicate areas. His mind groped for a solution. If he mishandled this interview, the full weight of Fairfax, Reece & Tilbury would come down upon him and he would be undone. The idea came to him in a sudden flash of inspiration. Ever the bare-faced gambler, he relaxed in the big chair and offered Fairfax the easy, open smile of an innocent man with nothing at all to hide. He was about to risk all on a bluff, and if by chance he overplayed his hand, he could only pray that Francine would claim those signatures as her own rather than see her husband hang for forgery.

'It occurs to me that this Townsend business has made you somewhat jittery, sir,' Shelley observed, raising his hands to forestall any response to the contrary. 'And might I add that I am, unlike so many persons of our mutual acquaintance, totally sympathetic toward your predicament. A case of this nature reminds one that gentlemen of your esteemed position may not always depend upon another man's integrity. So, my dear Fairfax, since I well appreciate that forgers come in many guises, let me assure you of my fullest co-operation.'

The old man's beady black eyes narrowed and he pursed his lips so tightly that the entire lower half of his face seemed to collapse inward below the bony overhang of his nose.

'Meaning what, exactly? Be specific, Shelley.'

'Well, my dear wife is still very ill, as you know, but if you or a member of your staff wishes to call upon her, by appointment, of course, then I'm sure she will be most happy to receive you.'

'For what purpose, exactly?'

'Why, to verify her signature, my dear Fairfax ... to ease your agitated mind ... to allay your sudden fears of being had by a forger!'

The old man returned his smile with a cold stare and said: 'I do believe you mock me, sir.'

'Not at all,' Shelley protested. 'If the bank is nervous ...'

'Nervous? A hasty assumption on your part, sir.'

'But your manner implied ...'

'*Hasty*, sir,' Fairfax repeated.

'Then I happily withdraw my offer,' Shelley said, grinning and slapping both palms on his plump thighs. 'However, in these troubled times, should the need arise for the signature of my poor, dear Francine to be further authenticated, you will have our fullest co-operation.'

Fairfax nodded and continued to stare at the immaculately dressed man whose fleshy buttocks were barely accommodated by the large chair in which he sprawled. Despite Fairfax's seventy-odd years his wits were razor-sharp and he had been too long in his chosen profession to be taken in by such a slick performance. Shelley had just proved himself either a transparent innocent or a guilty man gambling on a bluff. Since he who makes the loudest denials often has most to hide, the latter seemed more likely. And since the subject had now been raised, a closer scrutiny of Mrs Shelley's letters of consent would certainly not go amiss.

'Right, shall we get down to business?' he said briskly, tapping and coaxing the papers before him into a neat stack. 'It seems your credit has already been stretched to its very limits, Shelley.' He glanced up, saw the other man's face tighten and the bland smile become fixed, and was well satisfied with the situation. 'However, after much deliberation on the subject, we are prepared to extend the loans until August. Three more months, Shelley. Will that suit?'

Shelley expelled air from his lungs in a long, almost silent sigh of relief. It entered his mind that he had been given an eleventh-hour stay of execution, and with the thought came images of young Townsend twitching on the end of the hangman's rope.

'I am much obliged, sir,' he said. 'And you may rest assured that your forbearance will be well rewarded. By August I expect to have certain matters of finance turned to my advantage.'

'Oh?' Fairfax inquired sharply. 'Am I to understand that you have other investments? Perhaps you have found a source of income that we, your bankers and ... er ... *benefactors*, have yet to be appraised of?'

'Oh no, indeed no. Nothing so underhand, I assure you, my dear sir. I refer only to an anticipated windfall, a possible inheritance of sorts.'

'Quite, quite.' The keen old banker's eyes were bright with suspicion. He scowled at Shelley, disliking him intensely. The man was lying through his teeth in order to maintain appearances and preserve his credibility. The only windfall he had hopes of was a better run of luck at the gaming tables. 'And what of your daughter, sir, the very striking gel with those uncommon interesting eyes. Leonora, that's the name. Well, how is she?'

'In extremely good health,' Shelley replied, hardly taken aback by the abrupt change of subject. 'As your son will no doubt bear witness. We had the pleasure of Christopher's company at dinner only last week.'

As he spoke he rose to his feet and reached for his hat, which he had left perched on a pile of papers on the cupboard. Once again Fairfax fixed his visitor with his inquisitive, birdlike stare.

'She'll be eighteen, I believe.'

'Not until August,' Shelley corrected.

'August, eh? Well then, perhaps your plans for her future are something else to be discussed in detail when next you visit the bank. I take it you will raise no objection to my son's presence at the meeting?'

'None at all, my dear Fairfax,' Shelley agreed, certain that when the time came he would be offered no choice in the matter.

209

'And if this inheritance you speak of is not forthcoming?'

'Then I must hope that we are able to agree upon an alternative settlement,' Shelley said, still smiling as he drew on his pale kid gloves. 'A settlement that is to our mutual benefit.'

Fairfax nodded, his small black eyes giving nothing away. 'Until August, then,' he said. 'Shall we say Monday the seventeenth, promptly at nine?'

'I look forward to it, sir,' Shelley said with a stiff bow. 'And I bid you good day.'

Moments later he stepped out through the same side door by which he had entered the building. A short, pock-faced man was about to enter, and as he shoved past Shelley he emitted a disagreeable aroma of sweat and cooking smells. The man muttered a gruff apology and hurried inside, leaving Shelley to touch his nostrils contemptuously with a scented handkerchief. It seemed to him that any man wealthy enough to carry a gold-topped cane, and with the good taste to wear such a handsomely embroidered waistcoat, ought not to go about the city offending the nostrils of other men with his stink.

He hailed a chaise at Bott's Corner and rode as far as the daily congestion choking almost the whole of Fleet Street and Ludgate Circus. From there he walked, watchful of beggars and pick-pockets, to the dingy alleyway that would bring him out in White Horse Yard. Here he covered his nose and mouth with a larger handkerchief impregnated with strong perfume and aromatic herbs as a protection against fever and pestilence. The area was teeming with poor people, many of whom slept outdoors with the garbage and accompanying vermin. It was a place where sewage ran in the gutters and men pissed in the street, where children too young to work, steal or beg idled their dull lives away. A group of ragged women carrying covered, handled baskets swaggered by in the opposite direction, forcing Herbert to step from the pavement to the gutter in order to avoid making contact with their stained skirts.

'Dirty bitches,' he hissed, shuddering with distaste. He had recognised the women as pure-finders. They roamed the streets and alleyways in search of dog-dung, for which leather-dressers and tanners would pay up to a shilling a pail. Being an astringent as well as highly alkaline, the 'pure' was rubbed by hand into the roans and lambskins of the slop-leather trade, and into thinner leathers such as calf-skins, to dry and purify them. Not even the more superior class of book-binder, shoemaker or glover was above using such imperfectly dressed leathers for the less conspicuous requirements of his business. A man of good taste, therefore, must always be on his guard against such indelicate practices being thrust upon him by the miserable working classes, hence the common habit of selecting leather goods by nose, as well as by eye and hand.

Clegg was in the long bar of the White Horse tavern along with a number of rough-looking men all smoking and drinking and sharing lewd conversation. At his side were two small bulldogs and a short-legged English terrier, all of which bore the scars of many battles. Tonight a pit would be built up in the back room and scores of men would flock there to bet heavily on the outcome of the matches or simply to test the quality of their sporting dogs by pitting them against dozens of big brown sewer rats. The rats were provided by men like Clegg, who robbed the rodents' breeding grounds in the sewers of Whitechapel, Newgate and Smithfield, where they grew bold and fat on slaughterhouse waste.

'Evening, Mr Shelley, sir. If yer've come fer the rat-matches yer too early. Won't be startin' 'em afore nine o'clock tonight.'

The men at the bar turned to study the newcomer, taking in at a glance his expensive coat, rich waistcoat and black silk stock. One was a thin-faced street seller with a cage of goldfinches and larks at his feet and a consumptive hollowness in his eyes and cheeks. Another was tall and thick-set, with hands like muscular shovels and the vacant, slack-mouthed stare of an imbecile. The others were much alike: unpleasant, low-bred individuals in clothes no decent man would allow to be brought across his threshold.

'The dogs do not interest me,' Herbert said through his handkerchief. 'I am here on another matter.'

Clegg stepped forward, peering through his one good eye

and smiling to show twin rows of rotten teeth.

'It'll be a private matter, then ... personal, like?'

Someone at the bar laughed into his ale. Several elbows jerked sideways in a knowing nudge.

'A *very* private matter,' Herbert confirmed. 'If you would be so kind, Mr Clegg.' He drew the man aside, beyond the hearing of the grinning men around the bar, and producing two half-crowns said: 'Bring the mudlark to my room above the gin-house at three o'clock this afternoon.'

Clegg rubbed the stubble on his chin, eyeing the coins.

'Can't do that, Mr Shelley, sir.'

'What? Are you telling me she's already hired out for the whole day? I don't believe it, Clegg, but I'm in no humour to quibble over prices. Here's another half-crown, that's seven shillings for yourself and sixpence for the mudlark. What do you say?'

'Still can't do it, Mr Shelley. Joan's gone. She ain't here any more, but I can likely find you another.'

'I don't *want* another,' Shelley snapped. 'Where is she?'

Clegg clicked his tongue and said: 'She's dead, sir.'

'What?'

'Aye, she's dead all right. Bunch of young military gents took 'er last week after an all-day drinking party. They wouldn't take one of the others to help share the work and they used 'er bad, Mr Shelley, *really* bad. Left 'er bleedin' over in Holburn's yard, next to the wheelwright's shed. Died in my arms, she did, poor little thing, an' not so much as an extra *penny* by way of fair an' proper compensation. I told 'em no rough stuff ... I *told* 'em. 'tain't right, Mr Shelley, fer them high-born gents to come along an' take away a poor man's livelihood like that.'

'Damn,' Herbert spat. '*Damn!*'

'Trust me, Mr Shelley,' Clegg smiled, winking his single eye and scraping a dirty palm across his facial stubble. 'I can have one at the gin-house by three o'clock this afternoon ... er ... shall we say seven an' six fer meself an' whatever you think she's worth as extra, like?'

'Mm, will she be young?'

'I'll do me best, sir, knowing yer tastes.'

'And find me a plump one. I want no more skinny brats.'

'Aye, sir, I'll do me best.'

So the bargain was struck and Shelley hurried from the inn with its unsavoury smells clinging to his clothes. From there he went directly to the cleaner air of St James's, where a glass or two of good port and a wedge of sticky gingerbread would help revive his senses before luncheon.

IV

At three o'clock that afternoon Jonathan Shelley opened the door of his friend's house in Regent's Court to admit the Honourable Louisa Fenwick, only daughter of the late Lord Fenwick of Tewkesbury. He was wearing light buckskin breeches and a shirt with lavender lace at the throat. His thick blond hair was brushed off his face and caught in a black silk ribbon at the nape of his neck. He performed a sweeping bow, and as he reached for the hand of his visitor his handsome face broke into a brilliant smile and his blue eyes twinkled with delight.

'Your servant, Lady Louisa,' he said, bending over her hand. 'And may I say how glad I am to see you again.'

'It is a pleasure to be here, Mr Shelley,' she replied, returning his smile.

'I took the liberty of having refreshment laid out in one of the upper rooms. May I take your cloak?'

Louisa was eighteen, a tall, willowy young woman with soft blue eyes and a sprinkling of pale freckles across her nose and forearms. A natural redhead, she wore her hair flat on top with a host of thick curls gathered about her ears and a beaded coil twisted prettily at the crown. She was dressed in a bodice of mustard silk brocade over gold satin skirts, a large-rimmed hat with feathers and an unlined green cloak. As Jonathan lifted the cloak from her shoulders he stooped to brush her neck

213

with his lips, causing a deep flush to appear on her cheeks

'Mama believes I am taking tea with Jane and Harriet,' she said, shyly. 'I told her an entertainment of sorts has been arranged that will keep me there until seven-thirty. She has guests for whist, so she will not expect me home before supper.'

'Perfect. And we are alone in the house save for an elderly housekeeper and a kitchen maid, both of whom have orders to keep to their own quarters. As you can see, the place is virtually closed up while the Weston-Powells are in Europe. We will not be disturbed.'

He led her across the spacious hall to an angled stone staircase with slender wrought-iron balustrades. She moved ahead of him up the stairs, allowing him a tantalising glimpse of her ankles as she lifted her skirts above each tread. Most of the first floor rooms were closed off, but at the far end of the corridor was the sumptuous suite used by Georgie Weston-Powell whenever he needed somewhere to entertain his friends. Here an oval table had been laid with plates and dishes and covered with a white cloth, while candles flickered in every corner of the room. As if to remind her of the true purpose of their assignation, the door of the adjoining room stood open to reveal a carved mahogany bed with embroidered silk drapes and a cover of sculptured and fringed velvet.

Louisa removed her bonnet and patted her hair self-consciously with both hands, flushed and smiling as she contrived not to meet Jonathan's admiring gaze. There was still a measure of shyness in their meetings that left them awkward and tongue-tied at times when more experienced lovers would trust not to words or niceties but to natural instinct. Afterwards, when their joy of each other had been renewed once more and the passions of the moment exhausted, they would lie in each other's arms and savour that special closeness that demands no pretty speeches for its expression. But for now they were like loving strangers, new to each other.

Jonathan cleared his throat. 'Would you like to eat?'

She shook her head. 'Thank you, no ... I am not hungry.'

214

'A drink, perhaps? Wine? Brandy?'

Again she shook her head. Jonathan took both her hands in his, raised them to his lips and kissed each one in turn.

'I love you,' he said, and drew her gently into his arms.

'And I love you,' she replied. 'So perhaps we should save our refreshments until later?'

They laughed together, then walked hand in hand into the bedroom, closing the big door behind them. When Jonathan removed her clothes he did so slowly, like a man unwrapping a precious gift, and when they made love they did so with a tenderness that sprang from the great depth of feeling behind their mutual desire.

They were lying spent and sleepy in each other's arms when a watchman passed the house at four o'clock, and had barely stirred when he returned to call the hour at five. By then the fire had died to radiant embers in the grate and the lowering sun was casting long shadows across the room. Jonathan threw a robe about his shoulders and slipped out to fetch a tray of food and a bottle of madeira wine.

'Refreshment for madam,' he said, kissing the freckles that lay like golden dust across her shoulders. 'Are you hungry?'

She smiled into the pillow, trembling a little at his touch. 'I am *desperately* hungry,' she murmured.

'Then stir yourself and dine with me. Here's a warm shawl for your shoulders and a glass of madeira to spike your appetite.' He caught one end of the shawl as she went to cover herself, drew it back and stooped to caress her small, pink nipples with his tongue. Then he kissed her very lightly on the mouth before turning his attention to the cold fare on the tray.

'When will you speak to Mama?' she asked at last, her shyness now forgotten and her radiant face framed by a tangle of red-gold hair.

'Very soon, my love,' he told her between mouthfuls of cold meat and cheese. 'I have recently learned that the Manchester holdings held for me in Mama's name have more than tripled in value over the last five years. It seems I am to be quite prosperous, a man of substance and property, when my inheritance is realised later this year.'

'Then it is fortunate indeed that I am not entirely averse to finding myself wedded to so successful a gentleman.'

Jonathan smiled. 'I will speak to Lady Fenwick in about a month, when I hear what the Earl and Countess have to say concerning Gilbert's plans to marry my sister.'

'Are you so certain she will have him, then?'

'And make herself a lady? And assume the Cavendish name? Make no mistake on that score, my love. Leonora will have him.'

'I do believe Gilbert is quite besotted.'

'And that fact has not escaped my sister's attention,' Jonathan smiled. 'I believe my own suit will be all the stronger once they have consented to the match.'

'Oh yes, for then you would be even *better* connected,' Louisa said with a touch of bitterness. 'Related to the house of Cavendish by blood *and* by marriage. What more could Mama hope for in her search for a suitable husband for her only child?'

'And no doubt it will please the Countess Alyce to learn that her son's bride is so closely connected with the well-respected Lord Fenwick of Tewkesbury.'

'Who died leaving a string of grand titles, a run-down estate and barely a penny-piece remaining after his debts were paid. Oh, how I hate all the pretence, the dishonesty of the so-called marriage market. It makes people as disposable as cattle. Why can we not marry the person of our choice and dispense with these demands for fortune or title or influential affiliation?'

'Because, my love, such uncomplicated choices are the privilege of the lower classes,' he told her gravely. 'Only those with nothing to lose are at liberty to marry where they will and take romantic love for its own sake. You and I have a responsibility to what wealth or title our families have managed to maintain during their lifetime. We are simply not free to squander our heritage in the name of love.'

'Then I would rather be poor,' Louisa pouted.

Jonathan emptied his glass. 'Our trusty Anabel would say a careless remark of that kind is enough to tempt the devil.'

She smiled and held out her own glass for him to refill. 'A

silly superstition. Oh, Jonathan, I am so happy for Leonora. Gilbert obviously adores her, and she has always dreamed of living at Beresford. Do you think His Lordship will give his consent to the match?'

'Oh, I suspect so. As a younger son, Gilbert must marry money, and Leonora will soon come into lands and property of great value, all bringing in a substantial annual income. Our mother has always ensured that her children will fare well in the world. We have her to thank for our very adequate fortunes.'

'Is her health in any way improved?'

'A little. She is determined to come with us to Kingswood for the Midsummer Fair, if Sir Marcus agrees that she is well enough to undertake the journey.'

'I do believe Gilbert will receive the better part of the deal,' Louisa said, lowering her voice as if she feared her words might be overheard. 'They say his mother beats her servants for the smallest misdemeanour. I heard some time ago that she was once discovered horse-whipping her own daughter at the altar of her private chapel at Beresford Hall. I do not envy your sister gaining *that* woman for a mother-in-law.'

Jonathan laughed heartily. 'Even if these stories are true, you need have no fears on Leonora's account. It will take more than an ill-tempered Countess, with or without a horse-whip, to bring that young woman to heel. And now, my love, I will help you to dress and you must fix your hair so that we can order some of Mrs Wetherby's delicious honeyed tea.'

V

Two weeks later news reached London that Lady Grace Cavendish, bride of the heir of Beresford, had died in childbirth. A female child, born after a lengthy and difficult labour, outlived its mother by only a few short hours. Stricken by that temporary sense of guilt peculiar to men whose wives die bearing issue, Sir Malcolm retreated to his isolated lands on the Scottish border and refused to attend the funeral. The grand banquet planned for August had been cancelled. The funeral itself would be a family affair, with only a few specially invited friends expected to attend.

Gilbert wrote to Leonora that Beresford was a place of mourning and that poor Lady Alyce, robbed of a favourite son, a daughter-in-law and a grandchild all in the space of a few months, was quite inconsolable. Like all his letters, this one was long and charmingly frank. It pleased her immensely that his growing affection for her was so transparent. As yet he lacked the experience, and the guile, to conceal what was in his heart, and with every meeting, every exchange of letters, she was more convinced of the sincerity of his feelings towards her. This latest message closed with a plea that she and her parents attend the Midsummer Fair at Kingswood in late June, staying for two nights at a refurbished hunting lodge he hoped to place at their disposal. A single pink rose, dried and pressed and yet still retaining a delicate trace of its former perfume, had been slipped between the neatly folded sheets of paper.

'I have him,' Leonora whispered after reading his letter a second time. 'With barely an ounce of effort on my part, I already have this Cavendish by the heart-strings.'

For an instant she remembered Malcolm, with his deep blue eyes and hauntingly handsome face, and she was forced to remind herself that even now, as a widower, he was still beyond her reach.

CHAPTER NINE

I

They came to the Midsummer Fair in their thousands: well-off merchants and landowners looking to buy or sell at a handsome profit, foresters and peasants hoping to make a sizeable return on the season's labours, hungry men and women in search of employment. Here were farmers and horse breeders, peddlers, gypsies and travelling performers, men and women of every skill, trade and craft. And as many more came merely for the thrill of the show, the excitement to be had out of this heady mix of pagan rite and local tradition. Many travelled from as far away as London, Bath, Brighton, Oxford and Bristol, lying over with wealthy friends or at local inns until the morning of the twenty-fourth, when the great annual fair began. Others came for the age-old revelries preceding the fair, the rough-and-tumble carousing that marked a thousand years of Midsummer Eve festivities. A few miles away the faithful gathered at Stonehenge in preparation for the solstice celebrations that would begin when the sun, standing still in all its majesty at the very height of summer, would strike the sun stone at dawn on Midsummer's Day.

At the appointed hour and by long, unbroken tradition dating back to the days of the first Earl of Beresford, the fair was declared open, in grand and noble manner, by Sir Oscar Cavendish. His was the first goblet of mulled wine to be raised in the traditional Midsummer toast, though no-one doubted that many a casket of fine wine and good, strong ale had already been enjoyed long before the official opening.

For two nights the woods and forests of Beresford were lit by flickering campfires around which the travelling families gathered in eerie silhouette. At this time of year the area was a hive of lawless activity, fraught with dangers of every kind. In two thousand acres of forest already inhabited by woodsmen, gypsies, squatters and fugitives, the extra bailiffs employed by Sir Oscar Cavendish were hard pressed to protect the game from this yearly influx of thieves and petty adventurers. Deer-stalkers and poachers crept about during the dark hours, pitting their wits against the Chief Forester's bailiffs and sometimes losing a foot or a leg to the sudden snap of a spring-loaded man trap. Groups of tough, enterprising quarrymen roamed far from their tight little communities at night to shepherd the deer into carefully hung nets, kill and cut the beasts on the spot and bear them away at speed, a manageable portion of flesh to each man. Such spoils might be disposed of locally or carried as far as Stroud or Oxfordshire to be sold for a fine profit. It was a very lucrative business, and because the poachers faced death or transportation if taken alive by the bailiffs, they became ever more ruthless in their exploits. In a court of law no distinction was made between them and the wretched individual craving only a little meat for the family pot. Anyone apprehended whilst in possession of traps and snares, however makeshift, could claim no defence against a charge of poaching. Hence many a poor man had been hanged for a hare and many a bailiff silenced by a poacher's blade.

Oakwood Lodge was an old, ivy-clad house erected by an

ancestor of the present Earl on a natural hillock lying approximately midway between Kingswood village and Beresford Hall. Built on two floors above extensive cellars, it boasted twelve bedrooms, two water closets and impressive miniature gardens reclaimed from the surrounding forest. It had been stylishly modernised in 1761 with the addition of two mahogany staircases of Chinese design and four Jacobean-style bay windows looking out over vale and forest as far as the eye could see. In the westerly distance the country seat of the Earl of Beresford stood dark and splendid against the sky, its grounds and gardens laid out like sculptured skirts around its feet.

'This is the very house where I shall live,' Leonora declared as she watched the lowering sun leave gold and bronze stains across a deepening sky. 'If I may never live within the walls of Beresford Hall, then I will make my home here, at Oakwood Lodge, and live each day with the scents of pine and beech and oak in my nostrils.'

'Oh yes, the air here is wonderfully clean and fresh,' her mother agreed. 'So much kinder to the lungs than the dirt and grime of London.'

'And the forest! Sometimes it seems to me that the whole of Beresford is populated by trees. They frighten Joseph, but to me they are sombre and strange and secretive and ... and ... *exciting*. Oh, I love the forest, Mama. I really *love* it.'

'Yes, I know, my darling, and I believe you will find real happiness here,' Francine smiled.

'*We*,' Leonora quickly corrected. '*We* will be happy here, Mama. You know I will not even consider leaving Garden Square without you.'

Francine smiled and stirred her aching legs against the cool linen of her bed. Her own chance to make a home on the Earl's estate had been lost to her almost two decades ago. She would never live here now, but she would cherish with gratitude what little time she had been given as a visitor to this glorious place. In her girlhood Oakwood Lodge had been one of the favourite hunting lodges of Sir Oscar's father, Sir Edmund Cavendish, but the hunt had long since been disbanded, the kennels demolished and the stables converted into a fine coach house. Little by little the creeping forest had reclaimed every inch of unused soil until now it stood, watching and waiting, just beyond the stout walls.

The set of rooms prepared for Francine's own use was beautifully decorated in rose pink and palest green, with heavy damask hangings and tasteful furniture that might have come from the drawing room of one of the more stylish town houses. She was tired and glad of the suite's many comforts. The long journey from London had taken its toll, leaving her body weak with exhaustion and her chest and throat raw with inhaled dust. Sir Marcus had strongly disapproved of the visit, believing that the long journey by road would tax her failing health to the limit, but Francine had been quietly insistent upon it. There were matters of great importance to attend to on her family's behalf, and both she and Sir Marcus knew, without ever having discussed the subject openly, that her health was unlikely to improve. It was now or never. If she was to see her loved ones safely established she must do it now, while she still possessed the strength, the will and the influence to champion their cause.

'One trip,' she had promised Sir Marcus. 'One last trip to put my affairs in order. Then I will rest.'

'You may not survive the journey,' he had warned, 'but do as you must, since you will not listen to reason.'

And so she had made the journey, and was determined to do what was required of her before she was forced to succumb to the worst stages of her illness.

While Anabel dined with her mistress in the rose suite, a full dinner was served at six-thirty in the dining room on the ground floor. At the head of the table, Herbert Shelley presided over the meal with portly enthusiasm, elegant in his best crimson coat and white breeches. On his left sat Helen, by now a very plump thirteen-year-old whose pretty grey eyes had become all but swamped by her podgy cheeks. She favoured her father in build as well as temperament, and already the tiny bodices of her frocks, showing as they did so much of her chest and shoulders, seemed immodest on one so well developed. Her skirts, being of soft, semi-transparent gauze, caught beneath her full breasts, clung to her hips and thighs in a manner that was almost brazen. With the body of an overweight young woman, she still preferred to dress like a small child. In Herbert's eyes she could do no wrong, and she in turn adored him as much as she disliked her elder brothers and sister.

Next to Helen sat Joseph, as slender and as pale as his mother and similarly inclined to pick at the food on his plate. Sitting across from him in a gown of dusky pink, Leonora dominated the gathering with her quiet presence, her rich auburn hair and magnificent dark eyes. She ate well but sensibly, aware that her enviable figure and clear skin owed much to the quantity and quality of the food she ate. She prided herself on her natural discipline at the dinner table, and in the fact that she had never needed to unclip her bodice or unfasten her stays to accommodate the effects of overeating.

'Tomorrow His Lordship the Earl will be coming here to discuss important business matters with your mother and myself,' Herbert announced as the dishes of the fish course were being cleared away. He belched noisily into his handkerchief and rubbed the heel of his hand over the pocket of trapped wind lying just below his breastbone. 'Make sure you are present to pay your respects, Jonathan, and I expect you, Leonora, to receive His Lordship and then keep yourself available in case he wishes to speak with you again.'

'Yes, Father.' Leonora and Jonathan exchanged glances, both guessing the main reason for the meeting.

'But what about *me*, Papa?' Helen wailed, her cheeks bulging as she spoke through a mouthful of pickle and game pie. 'You said I could meet Sir Oscar ... you said I could ... you promised!'

'And so you shall, my sweet,' Herbert smiled. He leaned over to blow away the stray crumbs of pastry that lay across his daughter's half-clothed bosom, a gesture that caused her to squirm and giggle with delight. 'So you shall, so you shall.'

Leonora scowled her disapproval and said, more sharply

than she had intended: 'Use your napkin, Helen. There is a gravy stain on your chin.'

'Will you be coming with us to Kingswood after dinner this evening?' Jonathan asked his father.

Still smiling at Helen, Herbert licked goose-grease from his lips and said: 'I think not, my boy. Must get some rest, you know. Tomorrow will be a long day. You young people run along ... and take Leonora with you. I'm sure she'll be much amused by the local celebrations.'

'I intend to bathe and rest after dinner,' Leonora informed him stiffly.

'What? And miss all the fun? Oh Lia, *do* come with us,' Joseph pleaded. 'There will be such a lot to see.'

'But I believe the real celebrations do not begin until much later, Joseph. Why don't the three of you go ahead without me and return later, perhaps at ten o'clock, to escort me to the midnight entertainments?'

Her brothers nodded their agreement to her suggestion. Charles grinned mischievously.

'Your absence will give us an opportunity to flirt with the local girls and indulge in some riotous and quite unseemly behaviour,' he teased. 'Must we be sober when we come for you at ten o'clock?'

'Absolutely,' Leonora insisted.

'Dash it, and we were all hoping to be roaring drunk by nine-thirty.'

There was laughter around the table, to which Leonora responded with a tut-tutting of her tongue and a pout of feigned censure. She was still watching her father as he cast sidelong glances toward the rounded mounds of flesh rising out of Helen's bodice. The girl returned his attention with a half-smile and fluttered her eyelashes in a coquettish manner. While the others returned to their meals, Leonora stared down at the food on her plate, her appetite suddenly forgotten. She had seen a certain look pass between Herbert and his daughter: a knowing, teasing look that seemed charged with sexual implication. Even while she was attempting to dismiss it as part of some silly game played out between a precocious young girl and a doting parent, she witnessed the exchange for a second time. And now there was something else. Herbert's left hand had vanished from sight beneath the table, leaving him to spoon pudding into his mouth with his right hand. At the same time a flush rose to Helen's cheeks and she leaned forward as if perched on the very edge of her chair.

Suddenly chilled by an awful suspicion, Leonora allowed her napkin to fall from the table and quickly bent to retrieve it. By lifting the table-cloth she was able to see the folds of her sister's raised skirts, the dimpled thighs and the big, masculine hand that pinched and fondled at the plump young flesh. She recoiled from the sight as if struck in the face. Twin sensations of horror and disgust rose like bile in her throat, forming a painful obstruction. Too stunned to act, too sickened even to comment upon what she had seen, she remained motionless in her seat while fresh wine, cheese, ices, jellies and sillabubs were brought to the table. Then at last she recovered her senses sufficiently to mutter her excuses and leave the room.

'We'll return for you at ten,' Joseph called after her.

'And bring a warm cloak against the night chill,' Charles instructed. 'You will find it quite cold away from the bonfires.'

'Ten o'clock, then, and you will find me well prepared,' she called back over her shoulder, amazed that her voice sounded perfectly normal.

Confined to her suite on the first floor, Francine had eaten little and was now sleeping peacefully. All the dust of the journey had been sponged from her body and brushed from her hair by the devoted Anabel, who tip-toed across the room to stand beside Leonora at the window.

'You look troubled, my dear,' she whispered.

Leonora sighed heavily, unwilling to share her uneasy thoughts. The sky was now a deep, flawless blue fading into a pool of glowing gold on the western horizon. Against its warm colours lay the stark black silhouettes of nearby trees whose leaves dipped and turned like ebony dancers on the evening breeze. In the distance stood Beresford Hall with the lowering sun at its back; a proud, sombre outline edged with brilliant gold, and here and there a window bright and brassy with captured sunlight.

'I'm rather tired,' she replied.

'More than that, I suspect. Has something happened to distress you?'

'You fuss without cause. I am perfectly all right.'

Anabel took Leonora's arm and led her to a tiny curved sofa set in a curtained alcove. She looked into the dark, sapphire-like eyes and said gently:

'My dear Leonora. I have known and loved you since the moment you came into this world with your eyes wide open and your poor brother following like a lost lamb behind you. Only an hour ago you were happy just to be back on Beresford soil. Now a shadow darkens your mood. Will you not tell me what it is?'

On impulse Leonora put her arms around Anabel and hugged her warmly. The older woman rocked her to and fro, stroking her hair and whispering in that wordless but soothing way she had of giving comfort. Leonora spoke without freeing herself from the embrace.

'I feel that I am in limbo, Anabel, that I have come to a crossroads in my life and must decide on a new direction or lose my way forever.'

'Well, my dear, you have an instinct for these things.'

'But what am I do to? Should I go on towards my own ambition or should I look to my family? What of Mama? What of Helen?'

Anabel held Leonora away from her and studied her face in the half-light.

'My dear, I will always be close at hand to care for your Mama. As for Helen ...' She shrugged her shoulders, frowning. 'I fear she is her father's daughter. He will provide for her until the day comes when she must be found a suitable husband.'

'But she is still a child. She needs guidance ... advice.'

'And would she accept either from you, the sister whose beauty has always filled her with such jealousy? You must know she would not welcome your interference, my dear. She

226

would simply laugh in your face and continue to go her own way. Leave her to her father. They are two of a kind. They deserve each other.'

Leonora tried to read the other woman's face. Did she know? Was she already aware that the relationship between Helen and her father was not as it should be? She decided not to press the matter further.

'Then am I to care only for my own prospects?'

'Yes, Leonora, and *now*, while the time is so right for you. For Francine's sake, for your dear mother's peace of mind, you must marry Gilbert Cavendish and so secure your own future.'

'And Helen?'

'She is not your concern.'

At that moment a pretty, bright-eyed maid in a frilled apron entered the room and bobbed a polite curtsy in their direction.

'Your bath is ready, Miss Leonora,' she lisped in her soft Welsh accent. 'And I've warmed some fresh lavender water for your hair, just as you instructed.'

'Thank you, Catherine. I'll be along directly.'

'Yes, ma'am.'

As the door closed again Leonora rose to her feet and issued another deep sigh. From the window she could see the first of the night's stars twinkling above the forest.

'I will be happy to put this life behind me,' she confided in a whisper. 'Ever since I was a small child I have felt oppressed by the knowledge that our lives and fortunes are totally dependent on Papa's haphazard management. I believe it is something of a miracle that we have survived this far without coming to grief. I will feel far more secure with a worthier man as helmsman, and yet . . .'

'And yet?'

Leonora turned from the window. 'I would rather place myself at the helm,' she whispered passionately. 'I was born to lead, Anabel, not to trail meekly behind a parent or a husband like some inept and empty-headed thing. I have all the qualities my father lacks. Nobody will deny that I am more than a match for him in wit, intellect and strength of character, yet as a *mere woman* I am required only to follow in obedience. It is ludicrous that the wise should be led by the foolish.'

'Oh, Leonora, I do believe you would change the world, if it were possible, simply to thwart your own father.'

'Yes, if it meant that the reins of my life and my destiny could be taken into these hands ... *my* hands ... mine!'

Taken aback by the intensity of the declaration and the fiery flash of passion in the dark eyes, Anabel turned away to retrieve the scrap of fine needlework lying across the arm of the sofa. She did not look up when Leonora, clearly seething with frustration, tossed her head and swept from the room.

II

After her bath Leonora rested in the gathering darkness, listening to the night sounds beyond the open window. Too restless to sleep, she lay on her bed beneath a single thin cover, willing her body to relax. After a while she rose and dressed herself in a full velvet skirt the colour of rust on metal, with a tightly fitting boned bodice slashed at the front to reveal the lace on her stays. Over this she pulled a short matching jacket with a wide collar, narrow sleeves and neatly pinched waist. To her cheeks she added a touch of light powder, to her lips a glistening layer of rose-oil and cochineal, to her eyes a hint of saffron outlined in darkest charcoal.

She had not intended listening at doors or peeping into private rooms on her way down to the garden, but some perverse instinct drew her to the door of her father's suite of rooms on the ground floor. She was almost certain what she would discover there. Once before she had crept like a thief in the night into his bedroom, and the images of that other time were still etched in all their sordid detail upon her memory. She needed no proof of her father's infidelities and certainly wanted no confirmation of her latest suspicions, yet still she was drawn, almost against her will, to those rooms where Herbert entertained his youngest child in private. It was almost as if history had chosen to repeat itself, with Leonora once again its troubled witness. Driven by a compulsion to learn the truth at any cost, she moved silently into the unlocked drawing room, where a single neglected candle spluttered in its holder, then crossed to a small anteroom that smelled of camphor and imperial water. A few more cautious steps and she was lifting the latch and easing open the bedroom door to view at a glance that which she dreaded yet half expected to see.

Herbert Shelley was sitting in an armchair in a state of undress, his boots removed and his shirt and waistcoat discarded. Standing between his bent knees was a giggling Helen, naked to the waist and with her high, full young breasts given like pale fruits into the pawing hands and eager mouth of her own father.

The bedroom door closed with a soft click that went unnoticed by the room's occupants. Leonora retraced her steps like a swift shadow, gliding through the dimly lit rooms with no more than a soft rustle of movement. Her lovely face was ashen when she stepped into the corridor's brighter light. From there she went directly to the rear door and let herself into the garden. Desperate to escape, to breathe a cleaner air into her lungs, she hurried down the long pathway and out through the little wrought-iron gate separating the grounds from the forest beyond the walls. Here, on a rough pathway that twisted and turned into darkness, she stopped to place the palms of her hands against the hard bark of an elder tree, breathed the earthy forest scents and forced the painful images from her mind. She was familiar with the old country superstition that fairies and witches favoured the elder. It was said that on hot summer days when the tree was in full flower, a cut from a knife would cause the wood to bleed.

Although the wrought-iron gate and the high, ivy-clad wall of Oakwood Lodge were so close at hand, she could almost imagine herself alone in that secluded and leafy spot. She could see the pale, eerie trunks of ash, beech and oak lifting their black-leafed limbs to the dark sky and guarding like sentries the pathways winding about their feet. They seemed to beckon her with their timeless mystery, drawing her closer, pulling her into their dark, whispering company. It was Midsummer Eve, and a *magical* night, for there was a hazy, shimmering ring of light forming a bright halo around the moon. Somewhere an owl screeched and a nightjar answered with its mournful call. As her eyes became accustomed to the gloom she saw that weird shapes and shadows were everywhere, giving life and movement to what had, only moments before, been a solid darkness.

'It is so beautiful,' she breathed, her whole body tingling with excitement. 'So very beautiful.'

Against her better judgement she allowed her captivated senses to propel her deeper and deeper into the forest. As the pathway became narrower and less clearly defined the surrounding trees seemed to close in around her like inquisitive creatures come to investigate the stranger in their midst. When she looked back she could no longer see the ghostly white flowers of the elder tree or the comforting lights of the house. With every step she could feel the curious debris of the forest floor intruding upon her soft slippers and plucking at the hem of her skirt. She walked slowly, stepping with care on the rough ground and stopping each time some foraging animal, startled by her presence, darted away with a sudden flurry of activity. Something much larger, perhaps a deer, rustled and was still. A moment later she heard the sound again. It was closer now and more distinct, as if an animal stalked her in the darkness. It was just there, in the thick, dank undergrowth to her left, keeping pace. She stopped, her senses suddenly alert to danger. Her instincts told her that she was not alone. Something or someone was watching her.

Although never of a nervous disposition, Leonora felt the chilling hand of fear clutch at her. Her heart began to race, urging her to turn and run back the way she had come. She hesitated when a series of animal-like noises reached her ears from the blacker darkness up ahead. She stepped back in alarm, and that was when a powerful pair of hands reached out to grab her from behind. In an instant she was caught, her mouth covered, her arms pinned to her sides. She felt herself lifted several inches off the ground and borne backwards into the thicker shadows between the trees. Then she was held quite still, her heavy skirts somehow trapped and tightened to prevent all but the most feeble of movements. She knew at once that her attacker was a man: a tall, long-limbed individual with immensely strong arms and long fingers that gripped the lower half of her face like bands of steel.

'Be still! There is danger!'

Hot breath touched her skin as the warning was hissed against her ear. Her shoulders were pinned against a broad chest, her head pulled back so that her face was very close to that of her attacker. She could feel his steady heartbeat and hear the whispered rasp of his breathing. Then she held her breath as the series of sounds she had heard earlier suddenly increased in intensity. Her eyes grew wide above her captor's fingers as unearthly shapes, silvered by moonlight, began to materialise out of the trees. Dark-clad men with hooded lanterns tramped almost silently past the spot where she had stood alone only moments before, each following close on his companion's heels, each bent beneath a shapeless and weighty burden.

'Be still, my lady,' the voice close to her ear repeated in a husky whisper.

Unable to struggle, unable even to utter the smallest sound, Leonora watched the string of dimmed lanterns snake away and become swallowed up by the night, leaving the forest unmoved by their passing.

Only after a lengthy pause did she become aware that the powerful grip was being eased by degrees until her hands were free and her mouth uncovered. She suddenly felt quite weak, as if all the strength had been sucked from her body. Those men had been poachers, a band of some ten or eleven ruffians stealing through the dark forest with their ill-gotten gains, desperate to avoid capture. She tried not to speculate as to her fate if she had been discovered standing in their path when they broke through the trees. It was relief that caused her head to swim and a violent shudder to course through her body.

'Breathe deeply, my lady,' she heard him say as if from a far distance. 'The anxiety will soon pass. Breathe deeply and relax. Breathe and relax.'

His voice was unusually deep and rich in timbre, and it lacked the roughness of accent, the slurring of vowels that would have marked him as a common countryman. He sounded cultured, yet he was wearing a jerkin of wood-cured leather and his smell was the scent of the forest itself. She found herself wanting to surrender to his masculine strength and the almost hypnotic quality of his voice.

'Breathe and relax . . . breathe and relax.'

She allowed him to turn her body in his embrace until she was facing him and her breasts measured the steady rise and fall of his chest as he breathed. Unseen hands stroked her hair, exploring its length and texture, then came to rest on either side of her face, the fingers touching in the nape of her neck, the thumbs moving to and fro with sensuous slowness across her cheeks. Her skin tingled and grew warm with pleasure. She lifted her face in the darkness, but the Midsummer moon had slipped out of sight behind wisps of fine cloud, leaving her with nothing more than an impression of long, raven-black hair and strong, rugged features. He stooped to whisper something inaudible against her hair and she impulsively moved her head to meet his cheek with her own. The contact was electric. It flashed like a powerful current, charging the air between them. She heard him sigh as his lips brushed her mouth with a brief and tantalising lightness, and her response was immediate. She felt a shifting, an upheaval deep inside her. It was as if the essence of herself, the very rhythm of her being had been altered to beat time with this man's heart. And in the warm secrecy of her sex she experienced a potent and unmistakable sense of longing.

For all its intensity the encounter was brief. Within moments he was leading her away by the hand, striding ahead of her while she, hastening after him, clutched at her skirts to prevent them snagging on unseen obstacles. At the elder tree he stopped abruptly and lifted her hand to his lips. Now the moon was behind him so that its pale silver light fell upon her own face while leaving his in dark silhouette. Instead of brushing the back of her hand with his lips in the customary manner, he turned it over and pressed a long, lingering kiss into the very centre of her palm. Then he closed her fingers over it, the way a child might do in an attempt to capture and preserve something precious. And then he was gone. He simply turned and strode away, seeming to melt back into the shadows with the sure-footed skill of an animal blessed with night vision.

She stared after him, touched by an inexplicable sensation of loss. He had vanished as mysteriously as he had first materialised, leaving only her fist, still tightly clenched around his farewell kiss, to confirm their strange encounter, that and the cauldron of unfamiliar emotions simmering inside her.

Upstairs in her room she hurried across to the big bay window without pausing to take up a candle. In the dark glass her reflection startled her. She was pale and wild-looking, her hair gathered like an untidy cloak about her shoulders and her eyes bigger and more luminous than she had ever seen them. Beyond the window the moon's light touched the trees of the forest with a delicate glow that shimmered amongst the ebony leaves. She stared down at the spot beside the elder tree where he had slipped away like a dark and silent spectre. Then she lifted her hand to her lips, opened her fingers and greedily, hungrily, sucked the spot where he had left his kiss.

III

By ten-fifteen that evening Herbert Shelley was pacing his rooms in a state of acute agitation. He was impatient for his children to be gone. From time to time he hooked his gold watch from his pocket and scowled ferociously, comparing its

233

face with that of a large standing clock before returning it to his coat. Leonora had gone downstairs ten minutes ago. He could not imagine what was keeping her brothers. Their carriage was waiting outside the coach house, and horses stamping at the cobbles and rattling their harnesses at the delay. He could hear music coming from the rosewood piano on the ground floor and recognised his eldest daughter's flawless playing.

'Damn their infernal dawdling,' he swore aloud. 'They were expected to be gone by ten o'clock.'

He pulled out his watch again, then cleared his throat and spat into the fire, causing the coals to sizzle and a funnel of dark smoke to rise hissing into the chimney. It was high time he had the house to himself. He would suffer no trespass upon his privacy now that the long-overdue confrontation with Francine was finally to take place. Whether in good health or ill she was still his wife, and as such she bore certain obligations that could no longer be set aside. He expected the encounter to be over by the time the children returned in the early hours of the morning. He was also confident that his loyal and gullible wife could be manipulated into protecting him from censure, even if it came to defending him against her own children. With his whole life in crisis it was essential that he re-establish his position as lord and master of his own household.

They left in high spirits a little after ten-thirty, making as much noise as possible as they piled themselves into the waiting coach. Herbert stood on the landing until the sound of the coach faded into the distance, then finished his brandy and presented himself, unannounced and unexpected, at Francine's bedside.

'You may leave us, Anabel,' he said sharply.

'But sir, the doctor's instructions are that Miss Francine is not to be disturbed under any circumstance.'

'Damn the doctor. You may leave us.'

'But sir, the doctor was most insistent.'

'Out, I said!'

'But the mistress is ill,' Anabel protested.

'Get out!' he roared in sudden fury. 'Get *out*, woman.'

Anabel flinched and looked to her mistress, who waved her away with an anxious glance. She left the room reluctantly, leaving the door open. Herbert waited until the main door of the suite closed behind her before he shut the bedroom door and turned the key in the lock.

'Good evening, Herbert,' Francine said carefully, unable to keep the anxiety from her voice. 'I hope you will forgive my ... er ... indisposition.'

'Madam, you have been much indisposed these past months.'

'But my health, sir ...'

'Your health, madam, is surely not to be esteemed more highly than your duties as a wife.'

'But sir ...'

She watched him remove his jacket and lay it neatly across the back of a chair, then unfasten the buttons of his waistcoat one by one. This done, and with an almost dainty precision, he proceeded to undo the tiny pearl buttons securing the ruffles of lace at his cuffs. She drew up the covers and attempted to raise herself on her pillows. As she realised his intentions, her eyes grew wide and dark in her pale face. She could scarcely believe that even he, with his often savage appetites, would consider using her in her present state of ill-health. The prospect of being forced to gratify his lusts was never more abhorrent to her. She recoiled, protesting weakly:

'Herbert, surely you cannot mean to ...? But I am *ill*,' she reminded him. 'Herbert ... please ... you wouldn't ...?'

'Madam, you are in dereliction of your duty as a loving wife.'

'But you have no need of me,' she pleaded. 'I know there are others, so many others, surely any one of them ... please, Herbert, I implore you, spare me this, in the name of pity, spare me this ...'

'May I remind you that I have certain rights, madam. I am your husband. Your *husband*.'

He seated himself and began the ungainly struggle to remove his boots without assistance. His face and neck grew red with the effort.

'Tomorrow Sir Oscar is coming here to discuss our finances,' he informed her. 'He has agreed, in principle, to a large cash loan set against the Manchester shipping properties and the house and farmland in Kent. He quibbles only about the duration of the loan and a few minor legalities.'

'What? A loan ... a contract of *pawn*? But those warehouses belong to *Jonathan* ... and the house ... it ... it was left to Leonora by my own dear mother ... you cannot ... Herbert, you *cannot* ... may I remind you that I alone have control over those properties?'

'And it is my intention that you alone should have control over this deal, so you need worry yourself no more on that score, my dear,' he told her. He was just a touch contemptuous of her naïveté. Those properties had been hocked out of her control, and his own, many months ago. '*Your* signature will be on the contracts and your word will be sufficient to assuage the Earl's misgivings on the matter. I have asked for a year, but if he insists upon a limit of six months then so be it. The money will be repaid on time and the properties reclaimed.'

'And should it *not* be repaid?'

'Then the properties will be forfeit.'

'Oh, no. Oh, *no*! You cannot be permitted to take such a risk.' She shook her head, suddenly afraid for the future of her children. 'No, Herbert. You have no right ...'

'Do you dare to remind me of my rights, madam?'

He exhaled noisily as one of his boots hit the floor with a thud. He wiggled his toes, grimacing at the unsightly lumps and unsavoury stains caused by the sliced garlic he kept inside his stockings to ease the aches and pains of rheumatism.

'Herbert, will you *please* reconsider? The time is ill for such a gamble, while both Jonathan and Leonora are set to make excellent marriages. At the moment their prospects are far better than I had dared to hope. If those properties should be lost ... even to Sir Oscar ...'

'The papers are already drawn but require your signature,' he said, as if her protests had gone unheard. 'That cousin of yours infuriates me with his nit-picking and his overbearing superiority. He owns half the county, yet he still manages to behave like a penny-pincher in business. He also lacks the grace to take a gentleman at his word. Why, the man is demanding such proofs in excess of my word as would satisfy a whole *battalion* of lawyers.'

Another boot collapsed to the floor and the smell of garlic became evident in the room. Perspiring, he turned his attention to his voluminous neck-linen.

'I will not allow it,' Francine said in a small voice. 'I will never agree to these proposals, Herbert ... *never*!'

'Then you will starve, madam,' he said, in a manner that was almost cavalier, 'and your children with you.'

'Starve?' she gasped. 'Starve? My children *starve*?'

'Starve indeed, madam, and how may this poor health you speak of so readily serve you in a debtors' prison?'

'Debtors' prison?' She echoed the words in a horrified whisper, her pale hands coming to her face and her grey eyes bright with unshed tears. 'Oh, no ... no ...'

'Oh, *yes*! The harsh truth is that we face certain bankruptcy unless you can persuade Sir Oscar to part with his money, in *cash*, within the next few days. We are talking about a mere thirty-five thousand pounds in cash, Francine, for property valued at five or six times that amount. Of course, Sir Oscar is loath to pass over such an opportunity, yet at the same time he is cautious of the legalities involved. Only you can convince him that the property is yours by right, that the newly drawn documents are quite genuine and that the deal is legal and above board. He trusts you, my dear. Your word will move him to agreement; his desire for profit will do the rest.'

'But the children ... Jonathan's security ... Leonora's dowry?'

'They will all be forfeit under the laws of bankruptcy unless you are able to extract our salvation from the pocket of your cousin,' he told her bluntly. 'Cash or bankruptcy. It has come down to as simple a matter as that. I am not a greedy man, Francine. I ask for only sufficient cash to meet my most pressing needs, and so modest a sum will guarantee repayment within the stipulated time. The properties will be safe enough ... you have my word on that. So, if you succeed in this little venture, the money will be quickly repaid and they need never know of it. But make no mistake about it, madam, if you fail me you condemn your children to *poverty*.'

Having made his point perfectly clear, he removed his shirt and trousers and released the stays supporting his huge belly. The skin beneath was damp with perspiration, reddened and creased in places where the stays nipped or the bones pinched. He scratched at the soft flesh with both hands, causing it to quiver like jelly.

Tears coursed silently down Francine's cheeks.

'Is the wedding not to be discussed?' she asked. 'If Leonora's dowry is to be pawned ...'

'You must set aside all thoughts of a wedding, my dear. At least until we are out of the Earl's debt. Perhaps next year ...'

'But by next year it will be too late.'

'Madam, I would have done with this subject. There are other matters to be settled between us.'

He approached the bed, naked save for his stained stockings, and burped noisily before drawing back the covers. Francine shrank from him, her eyes staring and her face ashen beneath the damp tears. He lifted her pretty cotton night-shift and was amazed by what he saw. Illness had not dealt kindly with her. Always slender and delicately built, she seemed now to have lost what little weight and substance she had once possessed. Her limbs were thin, her once-perfect skin blotched in places and marked with a tracing of delicate blue veins. He could have counted the ribs that were clearly visible below her wasted breasts. Fire rushed to his loins.

'Oh, my dear,' he exclaimed, licking his lips as he hoisted himself clumsily on to the bed. 'Oh Francine, my dear, you look so different ... so ... so *young* ... almost like a child ... like a small child ... like a little mudlark.'

IV

Their carriage was reduced to a mere walking-pace on the
Drive of Oaks less than a mile from the village. Two slow-
moving farm wagons lumbered ahead of them, each drawn by
a matched pair of cart-horses whose metal shoes rang dully on
the road's surface. The first cart was decorated with willow
and hawthorn boughs entwined with summer flowers, and
from each bow hung a lantern that swung like a bright
pendulum to bathe the occupants in a shifting arc of soft light.
Packed inside on a bed of straw was a party of high-spirited
young people making their way to the Midsummer Eve
celebrations. These were some of the workers from Beresford
Hall, the fortunate ones whose duties ended in time for them
to participate in the annual fun and frolics. For a few hours
they would drink and dance and play like riotous children.
They would have their palms read by travelling gypsies, buy
good-luck charms and love-potions, eat roast potatoes and ribs
of beef, scorch their faces at the fires and explore each other's
bodies in the sheltered darkness well beyond the flames. Some
would stay until dawn, and as the fires died they would jump
over the ashes for good luck. And all the unmarried girls, the
young and not-so-young, pretty and plain, poor and
prosperous, would sleep tonight with a sprig of willow beneath
their pillows, that they may see their future husband in their
dreams. Tomorrow many of the revellers would rise at day-
break to carry coal, water, food and linen upstairs and
downstairs in the Great House, but tonight they were free to
enjoy themselves and on this, the most magical eve of the year,
life was sweet.

> *'Fairy's halo round the moon,*
> *Wish a wish and have it soon.'*

Their song was both a simple child's game and part of some
ancient yearly ritual.

'Fire's ash, midnight's dew,
Bring by day a lover true.'

In the eerie darkness beneath that canopy of oaks, with moonlight glinting between the leaves and the horses clip-clopping their slow, rhythmic pace, the chanting of the old song touched upon the senses like a prayer.

In the second, less decorative farm conveyance a group of about a dozen men were hunched together beneath a single lantern. Some were bound hand and foot while others sprawled or slumped as if barely conscious. All were dressed in dark, ragged clothes and all showed signs of having been involved in a violent brawl. They were accompanied by three footmen dressed in the Earl's distinctive livery, one of whom strode behind the wagon with a brace of pistols conspicuously placed in his belt.

The driver of the Shelley carriage held back, reluctant to draw too close to the lurching wagon. Impatient of the slow pace, Jonathan leaned from the window and hailed the nearest footman.

'You there! Where are you going?'

'Dursley, sir,' the man said, touching his cap and slowing his step. He held a hooded lantern in his left hand. He was a broad man with a lined, ravaged face, no longer young but tough and quick and stubbornly dedicated to his work.

'And who are these ragged-looking fellows?' Jonathan asked, leaning out so that his head and arm protruded from the window of the carriage.

'Them's prisoners, sir. We be taking 'em over to Dursley for gaoling, sir.'

'What, travelling all the way to Dursley in a farm cart at this time of night?'

'Aye, sir, 'er Ladyship says she'll not have 'em locked up at Beresford Hall an' 'is Lordship agrees with 'er. Too many of 'em, see, and some of 'em come from over yonder, Wychwood Forest way. Might get their pals comin' down 'ere making trouble, gypsies an' quarrymen an' such like.'

'And what crimes have they committed?'

'All poachers, sir. Caught near to St Eloy's Well with a deer and a hind all cut up for carrying off between 'em. Took three sheep an' all, they did. Clubbed a shepherd boy to death when he tried to raise th' alarm. 'Twas a nasty night's business an' no mistake, sir. It'll be the 'angman's rope fer 'em all, I reckon, soon as them magistrates hear what they been a-doin' of.'

Jonathan withdrew his arm, fumbled in his pocket for a guinea and leaned out again with his arm outstretched.

'Here's a guinea for your trouble. Tell the drivers to pull their carts over and allow us to pass.'

The man slowed his pace, frowning. 'Don't know as they can do that, sir. Road's too narrow in these parts and they wouldn't want to go trenchin' one o'the wheels, not wi' all this weight we're pullin'.'

'Now come on, man. We're in a hurry. Or would you rather make yourself responsible for delaying several members of His Lordship's family?'

The man shook his head and reached for the coin, then raised his lantern high above his head in order to stare at Jonathan in its dim yellow light.

'Why, 't ain't Mr Horace, is it? Nay, it can't be. He's gone abroad to them foreign parts an' ain't never comin' back.' He stepped a little closer and peered nervously into Jonathan's smiling face. 'Nay, 't ain't Mr Horace, is it, sir?'

'No, I am not he,' Jonathan laughed, 'but we are second cousins and bear a passing resemblance to each other.'

'Oh, strewth, sir, I could have sworn ...' The lantern flickered closer, lighting the young man's features for the other man's careful scrutiny. 'Well, as God is my judge ... if it weren't fer ye bein' that mild an' quiet-spoken ... oh, beggin' yer pardon, sir ... didn't mean no offence, like.'

Jonathan laughed again. 'And I take none,' he said. 'Now, sir, if you will be kind enough to allow us through.'

'Aye sir.' The man lowered his lantern, touched his cap politely and strode away, muttering loudly as he went: 'Strewth, as God is my judge I never did see the like. Same as twins, they be, same as two peas popped out o' the same pod.'

Leonora rested her head against Joseph's shoulder and

closed her eyes. She was suddenly touched by the memory of her mother and Sir Oscar Cavendish gazing with such obvious devotion into each other's eyes. Their love was a fact, yet she knew she might well be mistaken in her other suspicions. In many families a startling resemblance often occurs unexpectedly, with colouring or characteristics jumping a generation or two, while love, however enduring, is no proof of past infidelity. Leonora would never disclose what she suspected to anyone, least of all to Jonathan, yet she often wondered if he too had guessed the truth. How could he look at his own face in a mirror, or be reminded by strangers of his likeness to the Earl's own son, without doubting that Herbert Shelley was his father?

She leaned across Joseph to look out from the window as the carriage eased its way round the cumbersome wagons with only inches to spare on either side. She saw that the prisoners were all dark-clad and shabby, their coats and headgear encrusted with dried animal blood. A shudder went through her and her heart seemed to lurch toward a quicker pace. These were the very poachers who had passed her in the forest with their newly-slaughtered plunder. These were the killers of an innocent shepherd boy, the outlaws from whose path that tall, faceless stranger had so effortlessly conveyed her. With the memory her body warmed and her cheeks flushed hot and fiery. She could almost feel the gentle firmness of his hands and the erotic contact of his mouth as it touched so lightly on hers.

'Oh ...' The cry was little more than a sigh, a gasp of dismay at the unexpected intensity of her own feelings. Her brothers immediately misinterpreted her reaction.

'Not squeamish, are you, Leonora?' Charles asked.

'Well, this is hardly a pretty sight for a lady's eyes,' Jonathan said, wrinkling his nose. 'I believe I can smell their bloodied hands and clothes from here.'

Joseph placed his arm around his sister's shoulders and encouraged her to rest her cheek against his chest. He stroked her hair, careful not to dislodge the beaded net that held its thick waves in place.

'Do not waste your sympathy, Lia,' he told her. 'These are not penniless husbands and fathers desperate to have meat for a starving family. These are poachers, brutal thieves who would steal from our cousin and only sell to the needy folk at prices they can ill afford. We all heard what the footman told Jonathan. These men have set out to profit at the expense of others, then committed murder to avoid arrest. If they hang for this night's work it will be no harsher punishment than they deserve. Forget them, Lia. Save your sympathy for a more worthy cause.'

The carriage lurched past the halted wagons and, to the yells and whoops of the happy servants, gathered speed as the horses claimed the narrow road for themselves. After a few minutes they passed beneath the great arch of wrought iron bearing the Earl's insignia and hung with lamps to guide night travellers. Soon they slowed again in order to execute the steep, sloping turn that would take them down to the village. Now Leonora could see the bonfires and the lights, the lanterns slung between trees, the flaming torches held aloft by stout country men with mud-spattered boots and patient dogs trotting at their heels. Tomorrow the gentry would come with their thoroughbreds and their beautiful ladies, and in daylight the annual fair would be a bustling, almost respectable event, but tonight was Midsummer Eve, and this night's celebrations were for those who lived their lives much closer to the earth.

Once again Leonora experienced that feeling of familiarity, that odd sense of having known Kingswood for a lifetime. Light from many sources bathed the pale stone of village houses and cast flickering reflections on darkened windows. Beyond the farthest buildings, sheep huddled together in shadowed fields and strangers built their makeshift shelters against thorny hedges and walls of rough white limestone. Down on the river the ringed moon shimmered and rippled as if trapped beneath the bright water, overseen by a clearer, more dignified version of itself set low against a spangled sky.

'Just look at them all,' Charles laughed. 'They leap around like drunken heathens.'

He pointed out the group of figures cavorting around the

main bonfire, joyful men and women made to resemble dark, imp-like creatures in the bonfire's orange glow.

'I did not hear you complaining an hour ago, when you were one of them,' Jonathan grinned. 'You were not slow to join hands with the local miller's daughters and trip a few pretty steps of your own, as I recall.'

'Ah, but that was different.'

'How so? How was it different?'

Charles grinned sheepishly at Leonora sitting quite composed on the other side of the swaying carriage. He made a cup of his two hands and whispered directly into his brother's ear. Jonathan slapped his palms on his knees and roared with laughter.

'Forgive us, Leonora,' he said at last. 'This is man's talk.'

'Man's talk indeed!' Trying to feign disapproval, she smiled in spite of herself.

At the bottom of the winding slope their carriage was met by Gilbert Cavendish. He was elegantly dressed in top hat and tails, and his fair hair was drawn back and bound so that a short, straight tuft hung over the collar of his coat. As he handed Leonora down from the carriage his pleasant face lit with delight and his eyes shone. She was glad to see him again, for this young man held the key to her future happiness. He had also become a friend, someone to be encountered with genuine affection, yet his presence, agreeable though it was, left no real impression upon her. He lifted her fingers to his mouth in a loving gesture, but for Leonora, so recently awakened to passion, his kiss was without fire. It had no magic in it.

'My dear Leonora, I am truly delighted to see you again,' he said with feeling.

'And I am happy to be here, Gilbert. But where is Elizabeth? Did you not bring her along with you?'

'I'm afraid not. She was a little unwell earlier in the day. Nothing of a serious nature, I hasten to add, but Mama thought it best to keep her from the unpredictable night air. And she *is* inclined to wander off, you know, without regard for her own safety. We are rather afraid of losing her in the forest if we allow her outdoors at night. No doubt she will be here for the fair tomorrow, if the weather holds.'

'I cannot deny that I am disappointed. I was so looking forward to seeing her again.'

'Then I shall insist upon bringing her to you tomorrow, even if we can make only a brief visit to Oakwood Lodge, with your permission, of course.'

'Of course. One of the servants will fetch us if we are not at home when you call. Come early, then you can show me something of the forest.'

'I will count the hours,' he grinned.

A ragged child sidled from the crowds to offer him a sprig of willow: 'Fer th' leddy, sur. Onny a penny.'

Gilbert chose a sprig and handed it to Leonora with a shy smile. Then he took her by the elbow and led her away, making no effort to conceal his admiration or keep his gaze from straying back to her lovely face as they strolled toward the main activities on the north-east side of the village.

'Elizabeth charged me to pass on a remedy for your brother's poor eyesight,' he told her.

'Oh, really? And no doubt it is just one of the thousand and one natural cures she seems to have accumulated from heaven alone knows where?'

He grinned and nodded his head, still a little embarrassed by his sister's simplicity. Only that morning she had been discovered sitting at the feet of a visiting basket-seller, listening intently to the old woman's droning voice and struggling to recreate the fancy basketwork with her own clumsy fingers.

'You are to bathe Joseph's eyes with tonight's dew, gathered when the moon is high. And she begs you to watch for the Wild Hunt when you return to Oakwood Lodge.'

'The Wild Hunt? What on earth is that?'

'Oh, it's an old superstition in these parts,' he told her, leading her now towards the village green, where revellers still danced around the blazing bonfire in grotesque silhouette. 'They say tonight you will see men and women with hunting dogs and horns and fiery horses rushing through the forest or even flying through the air. And were you aware that by plucking fern seed at midnight you may make yourself invisible to human eyes?'

Leonora laughed, a pretty sound that drew a smile of pleasure from her companion. 'Well, well, and what delicious mischief I would employ if I were to be given *that* fine privilege,' she said.

Gilbert continued, warming to his theme: 'It is also thought that on Midsummer Night certain humans are given second sight.'

'Oh?' she smiled. 'But to what purpose?'

'Why, to enable them to gaze upon fairies and spirits and wandering wood-sprites, a rare gift for a common mortal.'

'Wood-sprites?' she echoed, and the memory of heady forest scents brought a sudden flush to her cheeks. 'Oh, a rare gift indeed.'

Gilbert stopped, raised her hand to his lips and dropped another kiss on to her gloved fingers. Although his blue eyes were twinkling, his face took on a more serious expression when he said: 'And, of course, there is the belief that the first man to kiss the hand of a beautiful woman by the light of a ringed moon on Midsummer Eve will claim her heart, and pledge his own, forever.'

Leonora stopped smiling and opened the fingers of her left hand very slowly, as if expecting to find something hidden there. She stared at her empty palm and felt that same tingle of excitement pass like an icy chill through her body; a strange coldness that left a trail of fire in its wake.

'Forever?'

'So they say,' Gilbert told her with a shy smile. He glanced back to see if the others were following, then took her hand and added softly: 'When I kissed your hand in greeting I hoped the story might be more than simple folklore. Do you see the moon in her frosty halo, Leonora?'

'Yes, I see it,' she whispered, turning her face to look at the shrouded silver orb set against a slate-blue background. Tonight the sun would hang too close below the horizon for the sky to become really dark, and the glow of flares and bonfires would preserve the gentler tones of evening until tomorrow's dawn. It was a night of enchantments, a night to dream.

> *'Fairy's halo round the moon,*
> *Wish a wish and have it soon.'*

The words of the old chant slipped unbidden into her mind. She looked back at Gilbert, who was watching her face intently, his eyes soft with affection. Until an hour ago she had known exactly what she wanted, but now her dream was clouded by uncertainty. Now there was something extra, some dark and secret thing stirring inside her. She could almost believe that her destiny had somehow been shaped and sealed by the kiss of an unknown man pressed like an indelible brand into the palm of her hand.

V

It was two in the morning when she and her brothers returned to Oakwood Lodge. Her body was weary, her eyes irritated by woodsmoke, when at last she slipped thankfully into bed wearing a light shift of embroidered cotton. It had been a fascinating and exhausting evening. She and Gilbert had danced with the common people, the servants, tradesmen, farmers and labourers, lowly folk whose annual quest for enjoyment had seemed tinged with an air of desperation. Even the very popular Scottish reel, so elegantly executed by the cream of London society, became a thing of earthy excitement when taken up and liberated by those who had no need of show and pretty manners. Their appetites sharpened by the night air, they had juggled with roast potatoes raked from the heart of a dying fire, singed their fingers on the blackened skins and scorched their tongues on the steaming white flesh. They had watched gypsies dance and seen leaping acrobats fly through the air as if jerked this way and that by invisible strings. Together they had tasted the hot, spiced ale brewed in

247

the cellar of the local inn, listened to the bawdy songs of travelling singers, watched a play performed in accents they could barely understand, seen the night come alive with simple, garish fireworks so appropriate to those pagan celebrations.

Now she lay between cool sheets and watched the shrunken moon, still bright at its heart and shrouded in a silver glow, riding ever higher in a sky already slipping into the new day. Gilbert had kissed her. In the kindly shadows beneath the old oak tree he had held her in his arms and kissed her with such tenderness that not for a moment had she thought to resist him. He was nineteen years old, mature and handsome and determined to make her his wife, yet his kiss had reached no deeper than her lips and the closeness of his urgent young body had lit no fires inside her. It was not enough. Gilbert would turn her into a fine lady, a wife and a mother, yet she knew she would never be a real *woman* in his arms. Some faceless man in the forest had already claimed that privilege by touching his spark to all her deepest and most secret passions. With a kiss that had barely brushed her lips he had breathed his forest scents into her, and with a touch as light as a sigh he had marked her as his own.

'A wood-sprite,' she murmured, touching her breasts, where the nipples had sprung to life, taut and full at the memory of that strange meeting. 'He was no living man but a forest sprite released by magic from some darker place.' She smiled sleepily, moving her hands over her breasts until her entire body was lit with delicious tremors. 'And if that be so then I am lost, for I would willingly follow him, and to the devil with Beresford Hall.'

> *'Fairy's halo round the moon,*
> *Wish a wish and have it soon.'*

The words of the old song slipped back into her mind like a childish taunt, reminding her that on this magical night no wish from the heart would be denied.

'I want both,' she breathed passionately. 'Beresford and the man. I want them both! I want them *both*!'

CHAPTER TEN

I

Following the shortest night of the year, the morning of Tuesday, June twenty-fourth dawned bright and sunny. By ten o'clock Kingswood was a bedlam of noisy activity as goods and livestock came under the hammer and men and women haggled over the price of farm implements and household goods. People converged on the village from every direction, some with goods to peddle, others seeking employment, many hoping to profit from a cut purse or a picked pocket. Following long-standing tradition the Earl and Countess had donated several cart-loads of bread, cheese and fruit, potatoes for roasting on the bonfires and dozens of barrels of strong, home-brewed ale. The afternoon would be for the fine ladies and their debonair escorts, the rich gentry here for a day of horse trading, side shows, races, wrestling matches, dog fights and other entertainments; but the morning hours were for the common man, and the air was thick with the sounds and smells of penned animals and sweating, yelling traders.

'Easy, old girl. Easy; now.'

Sir Oscar Cavendish urged his mount along the Drive of Oaks at an unhurried pace, acknowledging only briefly the respectful bows, curtsies and doffing of caps that greeted him along the way. He was a sombre man, rarely given to words of friendship and known as a hard, often unyielding taskmaster by those subordinate to him. Yet he was well esteemed for all that. The poor people of Beresford and its outlying districts had known hardship enough in the past to appreciate the fair and honest authority of their present master.

Instead of continuing on to Kingswood he took a right fork at the St Eloy turn-off and stooped low over his mount's neck as he entered a forest of soft sounds and filtered sunshine. He was riding the roan, a patient animal much favoured by Lady Alyce in the days when she could still be persuaded to take a little outdoor exercise. It picked its way carefully over the unfamiliar path, its ears twitching to identify every new sound but its step as certain as when it had walked the easier surface of the main drive. Here in the forest a layer of fine ground-dust deadened its footsteps so that only its close proximity disturbed the occupants of those leafy branches under which it passed. In the herbage there were soft rustlings and an occasional pattering of tiny unseen feet. Squirrels darted from tree to tree and a large hare, disturbed while enjoying a dust-bath among the thorn-stems, rose up on its hind legs to groom its face and ears before vanishing into the undergrowth with a toss of its furry white petticoats.

Tramping along some distance behind was a stocky black horse that shook its head and blew noisily down its nostrils from time to time to indicate a dislike of its uncertain surroundings. It carried the rough-tempered Ben Wheeler, the Earl's second groom, and its saddle was hung with bulging leather cases that slapped its flanks with every stride. The cases contained no less than thirty-five thousand pounds in paper and gold coin, a fortune in cash hastily raised to meet Herbert Shelley's latest demands upon the Beresford coffers.

Sir Oscar maintained his easy pace, lowering his head occasionally to avoid those branches that dipped low over the path. His strong, ruggedly attractive features were now grimly

250

set, his wide forehead creased into a thoughtful frown. He was not entirely happy with the proposed transaction. In the more than likely event of Herbert Shelley defaulting on the loan, Francine's personal properties would become forfeit, leaving her virtually penniless while he, Sir Oscar, might realise a massive profit at her expense. It was ludicrous that she should expose her fortune to such risk. For his own peace of mind he had decided to question her closely and privately on the matter. She had no head for business matters, no real understanding of the legalities involved in even the simplest contract, and she put too much trust in that scoundrel who was her husband. If he found that she was acting under duress, or if Shelley's persuasive arguments were based on nothing more than speculation, then the deal would have to be withdrawn and Shelley restrained from making a similar offer elsewhere.

'Not to be trusted,' he muttered under his breath, knitting his brows. 'A dishonourable man, not to be trusted.'

He broke through the trees to find Oakwood Lodge standing grandly in its neatly enclosed gardens, sunlight glinting on its windows and tall trees casting pleasant shadows across its frontage. The roses were perfect. Two gardeners in dark jackets crouched, round-backed among the blooms, their stained fingers sifting the earth for weeds and discarded petals, while all about them blossoms of every shade from ivory to crimson filled the warm air with perfume. Sir Oscar nosed his mount through the gate just as a maid appeared at the door of the lodge and curtsied, ready to receive him. At the same time a young stable lad in a faded red coat and patched breeches hurried from the side of the house and snatched off his cap to reveal an unruly thatch of dark hair. As their visitor approached along the smooth stone drive, Sir Oscar's groom turned in at the gate, whistling a cheerful song as he urged on his reluctant mount. After the muted sounds of the forest, the clip-clopping of the horse's shoes rang sharp and clear in the bright morning air.

'Good morning, Your Lordship,' the maid smiled, bobbing a polite curtsy.

'Good morning.'

Sir Oscar slid lightly from the saddle and handed the reins of his horse to the grinning stable lad. As a matter of habit he slapped his riding whip sharply against his thigh as he strode into the house. In the hall he could smell cider blossom and lilac flowers, and he noted with some satisfaction that the place was kept scrupulously clean, with not so much as a single cobweb left clinging to the brass lamps or the elegant plaster ceiling. Light streaming through the long windows fell in bright shafts upon the polished elm floor and linen-fold wall panelling. It lit upon the fine mahogany staircase with its delicate Chinese fret, adding a warm, rich glow to the wood. He saw that several vases had been placed on the tables, each one containing a selection of sweet-smelling blooms, beautifully matched and arranged. He was well pleased. In his absence the Lodge had lost neither its old appeal nor its very special associations with other, long-ago summers.

'Mrs Shelley will receive you in the pink room, Your Lordship,' the maid informed him. 'Will your man take some plum pie and port wine?'

'Thank you, I believe he will.'

'And for Your Lordship? Tea? Chocolate? Wine?'

He shook his head. 'No. My visit is to be a brief one, so I will not be needing refreshment.'

'Very well, sir. Will that be all, sir?'

'Yes, thank you. You may return to your duties.'

'As Your Lordship pleases.'

Blushing prettily, the girl curtsied and hurried away.

Several years earlier Sir Oscar had installed a rosewood piano of six octaves in one of the first floor rooms, a handsome piece of furniture designed by Thomas Tomkison and rarely played since the Earl's eldest daughter, Charlotte, had married Viscount Morley and moved with him to the family estates in Cornwall. As he was about to mount the stairs he found himself halted in mid-stride by the sound of someone playing the instrument. He turned his head sharply, his attention immediately held by the familiar purity of the music. He had heard the piece before, but never had he heard it

252

played with such feeling, such hauntingly delicate beauty. For a while he was content to stand and listen while the years slipped from him as if coaxed away by those gifted fingers moving delicately over the keys. How often he had heard that tune in the past, drifting from an open window to guide him here, to Oakwood Lodge and his dearest, sweetest love! And how often he heard it now, a quarter of a century later, sighing like a lost echo somewhere in the secret shadows of his mind. He could almost hear her clear voice singing those half-forgotten words:

> *'And I will heed thy call, my love,*
> *Though I be far from thee*
> *And oceans lie between.'*

At last, drawn by the bitter-sweet memories stirred by hearing the tune played again in this very house, he moved across the hall to the door of the music room and pushed it open, half expecting to find his lost love waiting there. Instead he saw a young woman sitting at the piano with her back to the door and her face lifted to the open window. Her magnificent hair alone was enough to tell him that this was Leonora Shelley, that very self-possessed young madam blessed with too little Cavendish blood to attain greatness and too much of it willingly to settle for less. She played with more than her mother's modest skill, plucking at his heart-strings with every note.

Beside her and sharing the same stool was his daughter, Lady Elizabeth, her own hair brushed to a rare glossiness and dressed with ribbons and tiny silk flowers. As the music came to a close she squealed with delight and slapped her hands on the keys in childish eagerness to reproduce what she had heard. Turning a beautiful profile, her companion chided her in the most loving tones.

'No, no, my dear Elizabeth. You must stroke the keys lightly, like so, as gently as you would touch the petals of a flower. Come, I will teach you. Just relax and allow me to guide your fingers. Lightly, gently, and see ... now you are playing our favourite tune.'

Unaware that she was being watched, the usually agitated young woman responded calmly to Leonora's words and allowed her hands to be guided over the keys. So skilful and patient was her teacher, and so untroubled the pupil, that a recognisable tune was produced at the very first attempt. At the end of it Lady Elizabeth laughed and leaned against Leonora, who placed her arm around Elizabeth's shoulders and held her, stroking her hair with her free hand, humming the tune she had recently played so beautifully on the piano. Feeling like an intruder, Sir Oscar closed the door and moved away. He had been astonished to see his daughter conducting herself with such grace and decorum, and it now occurred to him that no-one, not even her own mother, had ever offered her the tenderness and affection so evident in that touching little scene.

He had again reached the stairs when a door slammed with a loud crash at the farthest end of the hall and a man's voice rang out in greeting.

'Ah, good day to you, Sir Oscar. I trust you are well?'

Herbert Shelley appeared from one of the lower rooms and waddled along the hall, his shoulders broadened by a beautifully tailored coat of purple wool and his huge paunch buttoned into a fancy silk waistcoat. Sir Oscar clicked his heels and nodded stiffly, ignoring the man's outstretched hand.

'Good day, sir. I hope the accommodation is to your liking.'

'Indeed it is, sir. Indeed it is, and today we have the pleasure of receiving your children as our guests. At this very moment our sons are out riding together in the forest and, as you no doubt heard just now, our daughters are entertaining each other in the music room. Ah, may I present my youngest daughter, Helen?'

Sir Oscar bowed toward the young girl who had followed Shelley into the hall. Her cheeks bulged with unfinished food as she executed a somewhat lumbering curtsy in his direction. Like her father she was square of build, big-boned and already showing signs of growing from a podgy child into an overweight adult. Her mouth curved voluptuously when she smiled, which she did broadly, without thought of the bits of

254

meat and pie crust clinging to her teeth. She was inadequately clothed, dressed like a child in filmy gauze draped from a tiny bodice that left her neck and shoulders bare and her over-large breasts partially exposed. He recalled that she was no more than thirteen years of age, yet there was a look, a certain directness about her that belied the innocence of childhood. As unattractive as her sister was beautiful, Helen Shelley looked back at him with the bold and calculating stare of a mature woman.

'A pleasure, Miss Shelley,' he said without feeling. He scowled into her close-set eyes and wondered how two people could manage to produce daughters of such extreme dissimilarity.

'Ah, I observe that Your Lordship did not come unprepared,' Shelley said, grinning with unashamed satisfaction and rubbing his hands together across his very ample frontage. He was looking beyond his guest to where Ben Wheeler had placed the saddle cases on one of the tables by the door and was now standing guard over his master's property like a bewhiskered, red-faced general.

'You yourself have insisted that time is of the essence,' Sir Oscar reminded him, his tone irritable. 'In the event that we are able to reach an amicable agreement this morning, the deal can be finalised without delay, as you requested, and without the need for further meetings between us.'

'Quite, quite.' Still smiling, Herbert indicated the staircase with a sweep of his arm. 'Shall we go up?'

'We?' Sir Oscar's frown deepened. 'Sir, you have already presented your case more than adequately. It only remains for Mrs Shelley to confirm certain details, and for that your presence will not be required. My cousin and I will speak in private.'

'In private?' Herbert was crestfallen. 'But Sir Oscar, I do not think that at all wise, given the circumstances. Mrs Shelley has not been well. She is a little ... er ... vague, so I really must insist that I be present to avoid any ... er ... *misunderstandings* that might arise. After all, my wife and I have no secrets from each other.'

'In *private*,' Sir Oscar cut in, a note of finality in his voice. Then he clicked his heels and added curtly: 'With your permission, sir.'

On the point of further protest, Shelley hesitated, glanced toward the bulging cases on the hall table and conceded with a polite but rather grudging bow to the man who was to be his benefactor.

'But of course, Sir Oscar. If that is your wish, so be it.'

As Sir Oscar took his leave the girl offered another curtsy. She had fished something edible from her pocket and pushed it into her mouth so that her cheek bulged and her lips glistened with saliva. As she bent her upper body forward he had the distinct impression that she did so in the full knowledge that her bodice fell away to reveal more of her breasts than could be considered respectable in one so young and yet so well endowed.

On the first floor landing he found all the curtains drawn back and held with woven tapes to allow the maximum amount of sunlight to flood across the crimson and gold carpet. Here too an array of freshly-gathered roses filled the atmosphere with a sweet, warm scent that touched his senses as no other perfume could. At one of the long, gilt-framed mirrors he paused to adjust his stock and smooth the creases from his waistcoat. On the little finger of his left hand was a silver ring given to him over twenty years ago by the woman who had very nearly cost him his title and his family. He scowled down at its familiar peacock motif, and as he did so the same haunting music drifted up from the room downstairs, reminding him that some things might remain trapped within a man's heart forever.

He turned toward the so-called pink room, where a lifetime ago he had declared his intention to sacrifice everything for the sake of love. With an effort he shrugged the memory aside as the maid, Anabel, slipped discreetly from the room and bade him enter.

'How is she?' he asked in a whisper.

'Very weak, Your Lordship. The trip has exhausted her. She may fall asleep without warning, but only for a few minutes at a time. Be patient. I will be just along the hall in the alcove if she should need me.'

'Thank you, Anabel.'

He stepped inside and closed the door quietly behind him. Sunlight filtered through lightweight curtains to bathe the room in a soft, golden glow. There were roses everywhere, yet his nostrils detected that sad, underlying scent peculiar to the sick-room. He approached the bed with some reluctance, acutely aware of his size and height, faintly embarrassed to be alone with her in the very bedroom they had once shared as lovers.

Francine lay propped against a mound of pillows, her lovely hair faded and her face drawn and thin. Her eyes were closed, and there was a hollowness about her cheeks that shocked him. He had not expected to find her so reduced, so drained by her illness.

'Oh, my dear. My poor, poor dear.'

'Oscar?' She opened her eyes and extended her hand for his kiss. It was thin and deeply veined. 'Oh, Oscar, Oscar, it is so good to see you again.'

He sat down on the bed and pressed her hand to his cheek, his blue eyes clouded with concern. He reached out to touch her cheek but withdrew his fingers when they encountered the clammy warmth of her skin. It was a natural withdrawal, the reluctance of the healthy to make contact with the sick, yet it filled him with guilt. It was somehow a betrayal of everything they had once been to each other.

'My dear Francine, you look so ill, so thin. What is happening to you? What is it that eats away at your strength? Is the fever no better? Are your lungs infected?'

She nodded, avoiding his gaze. 'I fear so.'

'Then you must leave the stink and grime of London for a while. Stay here at Beresford, or better still travel abroad, to a warmer, cleaner climate.'

Francine offered him a small, tired smile.

'I plan to go abroad in the autumn, at the insistence of Sir Marcus. He would have me gone for the entire winter. I believe he favours Italy.'

'Good, good.' Uncomfortably aware of an awkwardness between them, Sir Oscar rose to his feet and pulled a folded document from his pocket. He waited for her to recover from a brief spasm of coughing, then said: 'Now, let us get this business over so that we can speak of more pleasant things. May I take it you are fully familiar with the terms of this agreement?'

'Yes ... er ... yes, of course.'

She closed her eyes and twisted a section of the bedspread in her fingers. She hated the lie. She had neither read nor signed the documents and knew only what Herbert had told her concerning them.

'My dear Francine, are you really prepared to place your entire fortune at risk for the sake of a mere thirty-five thousand pounds?'

'Needs must,' she said quietly.

'It is a paltry amount, Francine. Less than a tenth of its market value.'

'I am aware of that, but the smaller the loan, the more certain we are of making the repayments,' she murmured, quoting Herbert almost word for word.

'In only six months? Can you possibly expect to settle your present difficulties *and* raise the extra thirty-five thousand pounds within the half-year?'

'I believe it can be done,' she said, with a lack of conviction.

'And if he defaults?'

She coughed a little, then sighed deeply, her hands fluttering like pale flowers on the bedspread. She was frightened, appalled by the sheer scope of her husband's debts, but she must not lose hope. She must never lose hope. At last she cleared her throat and said: 'If Herbert defaults then I shall redeem the properties myself.'

'How? Just how do you intend doing that?' Sir Oscar enquired shortly. 'By cancelling your convalescence and wintering in London at the cost of your health, perhaps? By auctioning your furniture or selling off your mother's jewels?'

She raised herself on one elbow and said with passion: 'Yes,

Oscar. If needs be I will sacrifice my gowns, my horses, even my home.'

'For him?' he demanded, his eyes narrowed into slits of deep blue as he pointed at the door. 'For that pompous, strutting, useless ... my God, Francine, can you really love that man so much that you would risk *everything* on his account?'

'He's my husband ...'

'He's a wastrel, a spendthrift.'

'Oscar ... please ... you don't understand ...'

She fell back against the pillows, exhausted by the brief altercation. She wanted to protest in the strongest possible terms, to remind him that he had no right to question her motives. Instead she closed her eyes and lay still, defeated as much by his anger as by her own physical weakness.

For an instant Sir Oscar had started forward as if he might take her in his arms, only to check himself before striding angrily to the bay window, where he stood with his hands clasped behind his back and his features taut. There was an ache in his chest as he recalled those other times he had stood thus, deep in thought, while Francine rested. In the rear garden he could see Elizabeth and Leonora sitting close together on a stone bench, their fingers entwined as they shared an animated and earnest conversation. They made an incongruous pair, the stunningly lovely daughter of Francine Shelley and his own clumsy, sadly afflicted child.

At last he cleared his throat into a lengthly silence broken only by the sound of her laboured breathing.

'Francine, there are certain questions I must ask of you.'

'As you wish, my dear,' she whispered.

He turned to find her eyes bright with unshed tears.

'Are the signatures on these documents genuine?'

She hesitated, loath to mislead him with untruths. Her loyalties were torn between the husband who had needed to draw up legal documents in a hurry and could not wait for her signature, and the man with whom she had always, save for one heart-breaking lie, been meticulously honest.

'Francine?' he prompted.

'Yes. The signatures are genuine.' Even after it was spoken, the untruth seemed to form a painful obstruction in her throat.

'Obtained freely? Without duress?'

'Yes. Yes.'

'And these properties are still lawfully yours to pledge, having neither debt nor obligation elsewhere?'

'Of course they are,' she said, believing it to be so.

'Francine, are you *sure* this is what you want?'

'I am.' Another untruth, but more easily spoken now that the initial lie was out.

After a further pause Sir Oscar sighed heavily and pushed the documents back into his pocket. He saw that Francine's eyes were closed and her lips slightly parted, the fingers that had plucked nervously at the cover now still and limp. He guessed that she had fallen asleep, overcome by the stresses of the interview. He moved back to the bed and seated himself on its edge without disturbing her, watching her wasted face and marking the almost imperceptible rise and fall of her chest as she breathed. She had been so lovely once, so vital, so *alive*. It was difficult to believe that this frail creature had once filled him with a tender madness that made small value of his wife and two small children, his father's wrath, his family obligations. She had been his *grande passion*, but when he announced his plans to surrender the earldom so that they could make their lives together, she had without warning dealt him the most cruel blow imaginable. She had married Herbert Shelley.

'Why, my love?' he asked her now, recognising that the question was too long overdue for any answer to satisfy. 'Why did you desert me without a word, without so much as a farewell message? And is that why you still hold my heart, Francine, because although we parted we never said goodbye?'

While Francine slept on he reminded himself, just as he had been reminding himself for over twenty years, that she had left him for his own sake, before he could toss aside his family and his titles for love of her. She had sent him home to

Lady Alyce a broken man, humbled by grief but determined that the sacrifice should not be made in vain. She had saved him from himself, and for that he must be forever in her debt.

He stooped to kiss her lank, lack-lustre hair before leaving the room and closing the door very softly behind him. He did not see the tears that squeezed out from beneath her lashes, or the sobs that shook her body as she turned her face into the pillows and wept.

'Take care of her,' he said hoarsely to Anabel, who rose from her sofa in the alcove as he approached.

'Oh, I will, sir. Indeed I will.'

Anabel slipped into the room and locked the door behind her, then withdrew the key from the lock and dropped it into the pocket of her frock. It rang with a soft metallic sound against a pair of long, recently sharpened dressmaking scissors hidden there. She believed herself capable of stabbing Herbert Shelley to death rather than let him force himself upon Francine again.

Downstairs in the hall Sir Oscar was retrieving his hat and riding stick from the maid when Shelley appeared from behind the open door of the music room, where he had evidently awaited his moment to show himself.

'Ah, Shelley. There is an excellent doctor staying at the inn at Kingswood for the next few days. His name is Daniel Peterson. A good man with plenty of experience. I suggest you send for him without delay. I am far from happy with Francine's state of health.'

'But of course, anything you say, Sir Oscar.' Herbert rubbed his hands together and moistened his lips with his tongue. 'And the ... er ... other matter?'

'Settled upon my cousin's word.'

'Good. Good.'

'Not so hasty, Shelley.'

Sir Oscar raised his riding whip and brought it down on the money cases with such force that Shelley started back with a squeak of alarm and Ben Wheeler snickered behind pursed lips.

'Let me offer you a few words of warning, Herbert Shelley.'

'What? But you said the deal was agreed.'

Sir Oscar scowled down at the fat man through narrowed eyes.

'You have exactly six months to settle your debts and put your house in reasonable order,' he said. 'Six months. And if you ever attempt to pledge Francine's property again, to anyone, I will personally see to it that she and her children are adequately protected at *your* expense. Do I make myself clear?'

'Well, really, Your Lordship, if you think for one moment that ...'

'Six months, Shelley. Six months.'

Blustering with indignation, Herbert watched his benefactor stride from the house, swing effortlessly into the saddle and ride away. He shrugged off his irritation. Now that he had the money, the threats meant nothing to him. He could even scorn the offer of six months in which to straighten up his affairs. With a pack of creditors already snapping at his heels and Nigel Fairfax preparing to foreclose on his loans, Herbert knew he would be lucky to survive for *six weeks*.

II

Accompanied by a dashingly attired Joseph, Leonora arrived at the fair in mid-afternoon, when the crowds of fashionable visitors were at their thickest and most colourful. She was confident that her own appearance was perfect, having risen late and prepared herself with extra care and attention to detail. She had come to enjoy, even to expect as her due, those stares of envy and admiration that paid homage to her striking beauty, yet today she sensed in herself a new thing, an extra quality that set her above the realms of mere physical attractiveness. Today she was changed, different, somehow more alive than she had ever been before. A peculiar inner excitement touched her cheeks with a flush of delicate pink, added a special sparkle to her eyes and caused the promise of a smile to hover at the corners of her mouth. On Joseph's arm she strolled past cluttered stands, tables filled to overflowing with merchandise, tents bursting at the seams with people and alive with the bedlam of their combined voices. Poised and outwardly relaxed, she was secretly alert, her nerves as taut as the strings of an instrument waiting to be played. She almost believed that something magical was about to happen to bring her face to face with her destiny.

'Lucky heather. Who'll buy me lucky heather? Only a ha'penny a sprig. Lucky heather. Who'll buy me lucky heather?'

The voice belonged to a small, raggedly dressed boy who possessed no more than a half-dozen discoloured teeth, all of which he displayed in a wide grin. Bare-footed and burdened by a precariously balanced armful of flowers, he marked Leonora as a likely customer and so planted himself confidently before her, a dirty, impudent urchin determined to make a sale. Leonora found it impossible not to return his smile.

'Oh, look, Joseph. Fresh heather. I must buy a sprig for Mama.'

'What? Pay this fellow for something that grows in abundance for miles around?'

'For his time and labour, dear. And for his initiative. While we were lying abed this morning he was probably climbing the hills at the crack of dawn in order to earn his daily bread.'

She reached into her pretty silk reticule and withdrew a coin, which she flicked into the air for the child to catch in his grubby hand. In exchange she selected a spray of deeply toned heather and, removing one of the smaller pins from her hat, secured the blossom to the lapel of Joseph's neat brown coat. Then she slid her arm through his and led him toward a rough wooden stand bedecked with samples of fine local lace of every design and colour. From the clamour of noise surrounding them, her ears soon picked out an accented voice that called with a penetrating softness:

'Herbs a-plenty. Hyssop for the complexion. Fennel and

263

anise for poisons of the body.' The voice had a deep, sing-song quality. 'Dill and caraway to comfort the stomach. Borage for the melancholy. St John's wart for wounds.'

A prickling sensation at the nape of her neck told Leonora that she was being watched. Curious, she turned her head to find herself looking into the dark, impertinent eyes of a middle-aged gypsy woman.

'Herbs a-plenty,' the woman repeated in her sing-song chant. She was tall and swarthy and moved her hands in a shiny clatter of jewellery as she shifted the weight of her basket from one arm to the other. Against her untidy black hair her earrings glittered like purest gold and her teeth flashed like tarnished pearls. Her gaze was oddly penetrating, as if she might read with her dark stare the secrets of another's soul.

'Will you take red sage, my lady, or rosemary to preserve the natural ruby sheen of your hair?'

Leonora shook her head.

'Then I shall read your palm and tell you what the future holds,' she said, grasping Leonora's hand and peering into her palm.

Leonora felt her hand rest against skin worn to a wrinkled dryness by the harsh outdoors. The fingers closed like a sprung trap when she attempted to withdraw her hand.

'You will have no less than you desire,' the husky voice intoned. 'And no more than you deserve. Losses and gains, joys and pains .... and love .... ah, such love ...'

'Be off with you, woman. Leave my sister alone.'

Joseph was angry. He disliked gypsies.

'No, Joseph, wait.'

'Cross my palm with silver, lady, and I'll show you what lies in the future.' Her black eyes glintedd as if with secret malice and she smiled as she added: 'In the *future*.'

Joseph pushed himself between them, forcing the woman to release Leonora's hand.

'Be off, I say. Away with you. We want no gypsies here.'

'Another time, lady,' the woman said, still holding Leonora with her penetrating stare. Then she turned and with a small, mysterious smile vanished into the crowd.

'She meant no harm, Joseph.'

'Gypsies! Witches and heathens, all of them. Pedlars of spells and potions.'

'Nonsense, my dear, but since you feel so strongly about it ...'

'I certainly do. Come now, I would like to sample the spiced wine and strawberries while there is still some to be had.'

When she glanced back the herb-seller was gone, leaving behind that persuasive, rather sinister invitation to purchase a glimpse through the veil of the present into the dark mysteries of the future.

Also present at the fair on that glorious June day was Mr Frank Lacey and his stiff, doll-faced wife. Amelia Lacey was dressed in cream lace with a fine woollen shawl about her shoulders. At her throat was the large ruby brooch with which she had sought to purchase Leonora's silence. It glittered like a beacon between them as they exchanged polite greetings, an uncomfortable reminder of the unhappy circumstances of their last meeting.

In the main marquee Lady Georgette Mortimer made clandestine arrangements with a handsome young man dressed in the uniform of the 16th Lancers, while Sir Henry, her husband, argued the merits of steam locomotion with two men from a local iron foundry. In a corner of the same crowded marquee Nigel Fairfax discussed with his son his forthcoming marriage to Leonora Shelley.

'Here are the necessary papers, carefully drawn up,' he said. 'Shelley will have no choice but to sign them when I inform him that Fairfax, Reece & Tilbury foreclosed on his loans seven days ago.'

'W-what? W-without t-t-telling him? The b-b-bank foreclosed seven d-d-days ago and he was n-n-not t-t-told? Is that l-l-legal?'

'But of course he was told, my boy,' Nigel chuckled, a movement that caused his Adam's apple to bob against his over-large collar. 'Reece and two or three clerks will bear witness that Shelley was officially informed of the foreclosure seven days ago. It would be his word against ours if he chose to make public protest.'

'And a-a-are you sure he c-c-can't m-m-meet the s-s-sum involved, Father? He's a c-c-cunning man, c-c-cunning.'

'And penniless,' Nigel assured him, his beady black eyes twinkling and his toothless mouth twisting into a grin. 'At last we have him cornered like the tricky little weasel he is. He's hardly likely to make a scene right here in public, but if he does so we are in a position to have him arrested on the spot. You see, my boy, I also took the precaution of inviting certain of his major creditors to be here today. They can but hope for something on account, since he is raising ready cash by selling off his stables in the afternoon auction.' He chuckled again and rubbed his hands together in delight. 'We have him, my boy. We *have* him.'

Some distance away the object of their discussion elbowed his way from the auctioneer's stand where much of his own property had just come under the hammer. The four matched bays had done rather better than he had expected, fetching two hundred and fifteen guineas a pair, and the riding ponies had all gone, at eighty guineas apiece, to an Oxford cloth trader for his three young daughters. The large carriage and smaller, lighter chaise had gone for much less than he had hoped, but he had made a tidy profit on the saddles and harnesses, most of which he had bought cheaply as bankrupt stock only a year ago. After paying off the two men hired to bring the stock and certain other items from his home in Garden Square, he found that he had made a clear profit of nine hundred and forty-two guineas on the sale.

The Oxford to London Mail Coach was due to leave Harper's Yard at six-thirty that evening. Shelley had booked four seats, two for himself and two outside seats for the men who had already been of such assistance to him. They would be armed, of course, to help protect the passengers and cargo from bands of highwaymen haunting the busy turnpike roads. Locked in the heavily guarded mail boxes would be the money taken from Sir Oscar Cavendish that morning, while

Herbert, also armed with a brace of loaded pistols, would be travelling inside the coach with his daughter Helen. He had spotted certain of his more hungry creditors among the crowds at Kingswood, and he had no intention of waiting around for them to close in and pick him clean of everything he had. If some were paid off the others would catch the scent and begin demanding their share. Thirty-five thousand pounds was not sufficient to clear his debts in their entirety, and it seemed to him a pointless exercise to appease the few only to inflame the many. Now that he had a fortune at his disposal he had no desire to leave himself with an empty purse and the threat of debtors' prison still hanging over him. He had chosen his path and he would stick to it. The prospect of permanent exile was more than acceptable with thirty-five thousand pounds in his pocket and Helen his only commitment.

As he left the auction area Shelley collided with a youngish man who stepped nimbly aside, bowed and said, rather irritably: 'Oh, I do beg your pardon, sir.'

'My fault, damn it. My fault entirely,' Shelley blustered. Well aware that so crowded a place was a virtual paradise for thieves and cut-purses, he touched his coat conspicuously in several places to reassure himself that his money remained undisturbed. The younger man smiled at this and shook his head.

'Let me assure you I am no pick-pocket, sir.' He bowed stiffly. 'The name's Peterson. Doctor Daniel Peterson, at your service.'

'Quite. Quite.' Shelley returned the bow and scowled into a tired-looking face with hooded dark eyes over a long nose and full, almost feminine mouth. He had recognised the name immediately. This was the very doctor so recently recommended to him by Sir Oscar. He was expected to engage this awkward, shabbily dressed person to visit Francine at Oakwood Lodge. Well, he would do no such thing. He disliked the man on sight, and if Francine chose to fall into a relapse following the resumption of her marital duties, then so be it. She would have sufficient opportunities to recover her bruised sensibilities during her husband's absence.

'Sir?' Dr Peterson enquired, arching one brow toward a prematurely receding hair-line. The movement caused his mouth to curve up at one corner, giving him a slightly sneering expression.

Shelley wondered if the hostility of his thoughts had transferred itself to his face as he stared at the man. Little caring, he bowed curtly and touched the rim of his hat with his forefinger.

'My apologies, Dr Peterson, and I bid you good day, sir.'

He strode through the crowds preceded by his great paunch, huffing with self-importance now that he was once again a man of wealth and prospects. Every patch of grass seemed to have been claimed by some enterprising person offering coconut shies, shooting galleries, bob-apple, throw-the-disc and that most ancient of foolish entertainments, the Aunt Sally game. There was wrestling on the village green and dancing where the grass was flatter and shorter. Here lads from the nearby hamlets and villages strutted like grimy peacocks before the daughters of gentlemen, while common country wenches pranced and preened before young men of quality. Herbert heartily disapproved of this careless mis-match of the classes. At the same time he considered that very disapproval a clear mark of his superior breeding. No gentleman worth his salt would ever feel entirely comfortable while breathing the same air as the common rabble.

Over by the archery range Leonora seated herself at a table above which had been fixed a large fancy parasol to keep off the sun. She was quite captivated by the carnival atmosphere of the village and the easy way in which the country people welcomed their city visitors. She sighed and lifted her face to a warm breeze scented with woodsmoke. Images rushed unbidden into her mind, prompting memories of a long-bodied man with hard hands and a touch that lit fires inside her.

'A penny for your thoughts, Lia.'

She felt a flush rush to her cheeks as hidden nerves and muscles twitched into life, awakened by her thoughts. Joseph was watching her from across the small table, his eyes half-closed against the glare of the sun as he peered over the tops of his spectacles.

'I am simply enjoying the day,' she told him.

'You look beautiful today,' he smiled. 'You are somehow different, Lia, the way you always seem when you visit Beresford. Are you happy?'

'Wonderfully happy,' she laughed.

'And the crowds do not trouble you?'

'Not at all, so long as you continue to protect me from the would-be advances of Mr Christopher Fairfax.'

Joseph chuckled and screwed up his face in a grimace. Fairfax had accosted them earlier on the village green. He had clearly hoped, in spite of his ungainly mounds of perspiring flesh, to draw Leonora into the dance. She had rejected him quite coldly, yet he had tagged along behind them for some considerable time before they were able to give him the slip at one of the more crowded beer tents.

'Bulls-eye!'

A young man gave a triumphant whoop as his arrow thudded into the centre rim of the target. For a few moments the area was noisy with protests and friendly argument until a show of hands decided that the shot should be discounted. Leonora found her attention wandering to where a herd of seven white ponies was penned on the far side of a nearby field. They were spirited animals, all tall and long-maned, with thick, sturdy legs and broad backs. These were the gypsy ponies, bred for their looks and stamina, difficult to train yet expensive and much sought after by those who valued their special qualities. Now they were restless, pacing and prancing as if they would break from the confines of the pen and race away, back into the wild. Quite suddenly a man who had been crouching in their midst rose to his feet and turned his head sharply in Leonora's direction. Long black hair glistened in the sun and the blackest of eyes met hers across the distance, drawing from her an involuntary gasp. It was as if she had called his name out loud, or as if by magic he had been guided to meet her gaze on the instant. There was something so forceful, so compelling in the confrontation that a rash of gooseflesh raised itself over her forearms and an icy shiver raced along her spine. Then Joseph moved in his seat, breaking the spell, and a moment later the man had melted back amongst the restless horses like a shadow, leaving her with no more than an impression of his dark features.

'Well, hello there at last, my dear cousin. Leonora, may I present my elder brother Malcolm, Viscount Bixby and heir to all the titles, honours and estates of Oscar, Sixth Earl of Beresford.'

Leonora turned at the sound of Gilbert's voice and lifted her face to look into the deep blue eyes of Sir Malcolm Cavendish, who seemed to tower over the chair in which she sat. As he stooped over her raised hand she felt him tremble a little, as if her touch disturbed him.

'Leonora bears a striking resemblance to our exalted ancestor Joshua, do you not think?' Gilbert was saying.

'And to others,' Malcolm agreed, still holding her hand. 'I am reminded of the Countess Abigail and the Countess Ursula. The likeness is in the colouring, the hair, the eyes.'

'Cobalt blue,' Gilbert announced, almost proudly.

'Violet,' Malcolm corrected.

'Too much a Cavendish to remain a mere second cousin, eh?'

'Too much indeed. Perhaps ...' He appeared to gather his senses with a small jolt before saying: 'I am delighted to see you again, Miss Shelley.'

'Again?' Leonora echoed, doubting if he would recall that brief moment when their eyes met as he was leaving the church with his new bride almost two years ago.

'St Michael's Church,' he said. 'You were wearing a dress of white and mauve, and a bonnet with purple flowers.'

'That you should recall the occasion so clearly is a compliment indeed, Sir Malcolm,' she smiled, gracefully inclining her head in a movement designed to accentuate her lovely eyes. There was a touch of triumph in her smile as she held his gaze with her own, unwilling to relinquish the subtle hold she had unexpectedly gained on his attention.

A horse whinnied loudly as she at last withdrew her hand from his. The herd of white ponies were being released from the small pen to run free in the big field. A great cheer went up amongst the bystanders as the animals pranced and leaped from their confined pen, the leader straddled by a tall, dark figure with raven-black hair. She shivered and glanced at Gilbert, with his boyish grin and cheery, pleasant nature. Then her gaze was drawn back to Malcolm, who still surveyed her with his sad smile and troubled, dark-lashed eyes. In that instant of unpremeditated comparison she knew she could never allow herself to settle for second best. It was not Gilbert she wanted, not the immature youngest son who stood to inherit no part of his family's wealth. She would have Malcolm, the heir, the future Earl of Beresford.

III

Lady Louisa sighed with relief when she spotted Leonora coming toward her. She was tired of promenading around the fair with her stiff-backed Mama, the Dowager Duchess of Tewkesbury, who avoided any association with the commonplace as one might avoid physical contact with victims of the plague, and whose bright brown eyes were constantly on the look-out for a titled face amongst the crowds. The Duchess was dressed from head to toe in black and peered out from behind the same short veil that had concealed her face at the funeral of her noble but impoverished husband.

Louisa was bored with smiling and curtsying to people she barely knew, and by now the carefully worded phrases of polite conversation, deemed so vital to the social graces, had lost what small ring of sincerity they might once have possessed. She had but two things on her mind, neither of which included the company of the stern and unbending woman at her side. If she could not be with her beloved

Jonathan, then she would dearly love to slip away to the nearby gypsy encampments where, for the price of a single silver coin, she might learn what the future held in store for her. Her spirits brightened at sight of the distinguished group approaching from the archery field. There were enough titles among them to keep Her Grace diverted for some time.

'Your servant, Lady Fenwick.'

With a smooth and practised grace Sir Malcolm presented Lord and Lady Mornington and their house-guests Sir Reginald and Lady Lennard with their two eldest daughters, Lady Winifred and Lady Claire. Her Grace was also asked to welcome Georgie and Jane, children of the extremely wealthy George Weston-Powell, along with that most accomplished of gossips, Lady Caroline Rainer. She recognised Sir Ralph Marr and Sir James Trotter, and several younger people whose names escaped her but whose dress and manner expressed an acceptable level of breeding. She included amongst them Miss Leonora Shelley, who had cleverly contrived to place herself between the two sons of Sir Oscar Cavendish. Her Grace surveyed them with a condescending dignity. As one who out-ranked them all despite her reduced circumstances, she wasted no time in procuring the arm of Lord Mornington and leading the fashionable group at a dignified pace toward the main marquee.

In that lively, busy place it was inevitable that the group would become divided, with the elderly members in front and the young people bringing up the rear and allowing an increasing distance to develop between the two. Gradually the men became involved in various arguments about cards and racehorses, leaving the girls to form intimate little groups where the latest snippets of social gossip could be exchanged without censor. Leonora found herself in the company of Louisa and the two Lennard sisters.

'Oh, I wouldn't dare,' Winifred exclaimed in response to a suggestion made by Louisa. 'I simply wouldn't *dare*.'

'Of course you would,' Louisa insisted. 'What harm can possibly befall us, so long as we stay together and keep within sight of the fair?'

'But *gypsies*,' Claire exclaimed with distaste. 'Don't they carry horrid diseases?'

Louisa shook her head. 'That is nonsense, Claire.'

'But they steal,' Claire persisted. 'Mama says a gypsy will steal anything, from a purse of money to a lock of hair. Why, I do believe they even steal children.'

'What nonsense!' Louisa said. She glanced at the others, by now some considerable distance ahead of them, then turned to Leonora and gripped her by the arm, her freckled face alight with excitement. 'What do *you* say, Leonora? Do you think we should go? Claire! Winifred! Shall we let Leonora decide? Shall we do whatever she suggests?'

The sisters exchanged glances, then agreed with a show of reluctance that became their upbringing but belied their true feelings. The prospect of having their palms read by dangerous gypsies was exciting to them all.

'Well? What is it to be, Leonora? Shall we rejoin the others or slip away to the wagons over there? Look, there are already plenty of perfectly respectable-looking people eyeing the baskets and pots for sale and perhaps having their fortunes read. Oh, *do* make up your mind, Leonora.'

Leonora looked toward the gaily painted wagons parked close to the trees on the northern side of the village. Pale woodsmoke curled upwards from several small fires, sheltered from the light breeze by the nearby woodland. She was recalling the gypsy woman who had offered to read her palm earlier in the day. How tempting the offer had been then, and how doubly so now that she had discovered a new sense of personal ambition within herself. Some distance away Joseph was engrossed in conversation with Gilbert, who raised his hand in a wave as she looked in his direction. She smiled and squeezed Louisa's hand.

'Why not?' she said. 'Come along, if we go quickly we can be back before the others are even aware of our intentions.'

Laughing, they ran together across the grass, passed between two tents and hurried up the slope to where the gypsy wagons were parked. Two elegant young women were already sitting on a bench with their palms outstretched while their

273

escort stood awkwardly behind them.

'Oh, it was so exciting,' one of them said as she moved away on her escort's arm. 'She told me I shall marry a rich and dashing man, have three healthy children and live to a happy old age.'

'A frivolous reading for an empty-headed customer,' Leonora commented in a whisper.

Winifred was the first to sit down the moment the bench became free. She thrust her hand into the gypsy's lap, her earlier reluctance quite forgotten. At twenty-five she was the eldest and plainest of the four Lennard sisters and, therefore, desperately in need of a ray of hope to guide her into the future. She was told, predictably, that she would soon meet the man of her dreams and marry after a whirlwind romance.

Leonora looked about her at the shabby, colourful surroundings. She saw women with bright jewellery and skirts that revealed their ankles, old men with gnarled faces and quick, suspicious glances, young girls with pinched-in waists and flashing glances for the young male visitors. She was fascinated, but when her turn came to sit down at the fortune-teller's bench she shook her head and pushed Louise forward in her stead.

'So, you do not run with the pack, lady.'

Leonora turned and recognised the woman who had spoken to her earlier. She turned a silver coin in her fingers. She had known the woman would come.

'I have a mind of my own, if that is what you mean,' she replied.

'So you have. So you have.' The woman set down her basket and seated herself on a makeshift bench, patting the wood beside her. 'Come, sit down beside me and give me your hand.'

Leonora looked into the woman's weather-beaten face, then seated herself and extended her hand, palm uppermost.

The woman studied it carefully, back and front, stroking the fingers and testing the flexibility of the thumb. Then she pocketed the silver coin and stared very closely into Leonora's eyes.

274

'You are stubborn,' she began. 'What you really want you will have, but you must never forget that there is a price to pay for everything. You must always guard against wanting too much. Take care what you set your heart on, for it will surely be yours.'

'But only mine at a price, it would seem,' Leonora said.

'Aye, lady, and never you forget it.'

'But what about the future? What do you see in my hand?'

The woman touched her palm with a stained fingernail.

'I see love ... deep, powerful, destructive. I see two men. Both will love you.'

'And which of them will I chose?'

'Both! One you will love with your heart, the other with your soul.'

Leonora laughed prettily to disguise a sudden sense of unease. 'Why, is there a difference?'

The woman looked at her sharply. 'You are young. You will learn, and to your cost. There *is* a difference.'

'And will I be rich?' Leonora asked, laughing again.

'You will have your heart's desire.'

'Will I?' She was thinking of Malcolm. 'Will I?'

'Oh yes, but beware the cost, my lady.'

Leonora rose to her feet and dropped another coin into the woman's lap.

'Wait, my lady.'

'What, can there be more? I shall be rich and have the love of two men. What more can there be?'

'A warning. You will destroy them both.'

'What?' A strangely unpleasant sensation crawled along Leonora's spine.

'Your heart's love and your soul's love,' the woman persisted. 'In time you will destroy them both.'

Leonora stared down into the gypsy's glinting dark eyes, disturbed by her words and the sudden harshness of her tone.

'I did not pay to hear such words,' she said coldly.

'Did my lady want only good, only pretty words, then?'

'Is that not what your customers expect?'

'Well, if it's party games you want, go on and join your

friends at the campfire. But if it's the truth you seek ...'

'Truth?' Leonora said with a haughty toss of her head. 'I am told that you gypsies know nothing about truth.'

'Now you are angry, my lady. But mark my words, mark them well.'

As Leonora turned away the woman caught her by the arm, a light grip yet with the power to stop her in her tracks. The woman's face was suddenly close to hers, sun-browned and lined, with its glinting dark eyes.

'An old life for a new life. You will lose much to gain much, and you will fall low before you can rise again. Remember that in the weeks that are to come.'

'What ... what do you mean?'

'*Remember.*'

At that point they were joined by Louisa and Winifred, with a giggling Claire lagging behind in coy response to the comments of a good-looking gypsy boy. In the brief ripple of excitement that followed, the gypsy woman retrieved her basket of herbs and strode with a swish of her colourful skirts back into the increasing mêlée of the fair.

On the village green Big Jack McCallister sat with his knees wide apart and one elbow placed on the table before him, the great muscular forearm raised and the palm open, ready to receive the next challenge. Many had already tested their forearm against his. All had been defeated. When interest began to wane due to the predictability of the bouts, Jonathan threw down his penny and straddled the stool, rolled up his sleeve and set his right elbow firmly upon the table. With a wink the big Scot locked fists with him and the contest began. It went first one way and then the other, with the seemingly weary Scot now struggling to better the younger, fresher man. The crowd roared its encouragement as Jonathan pressed the great forearm down toward the table, their cheers growing louder as he strained to master those last few inches. At last their fists hit the table with a shuddering thud and Jonathan threw up his arms in a resounding yell of victory. The onlookers went wild with delight. Jack McCallister grinned broadly and winked again as Jonathan, claiming his modest winnings, swaggered away from the table. As he did so he received many a hearty slap on the back from local men now eager to risk a coin in order to follow his example.

'But you cheated,' Louisa said as they moved across the green. 'He let you win. He's the champion arm-wrestler and the strongest man in the county, so how could you possibly have beaten him in a fair contest?'

'Oh ye of little faith,' Jonathan said, grinning. Behind them the wrestling table was beset by would-be challengers. 'My dear Louisa, by the strength of my arm I have generated fresh interest in the game and added the princely sum of tuppence to our joint fortunes. How then can you mock my success?'

'Because you *cheated*,' Louisa laughed, slipping her arm through his.

'I did not cheat, my lovely, though I confess the Scot and I bent the rules a little to suit the occasion. And it was all in a good cause, since the takings are to provide improvements to the local schoolroom here in Kingswood. Look, Louisa, over there is Sir Malcolm's grey and white stallion, favourite for the big race this afternoon.'

'Oh, Jonathan, what a beautiful animal, but so big and wild-looking. Who will ride him?'

'I believe the jockey is to be Danny Pearse, a good man but a mite too handy with the whip for my tastes.'

'And will you bet on the outcome?'

'What, with a newly won fortune of tuppence scorching the lining of my pocket? I most certainly will!'

They stood together, arm in arm, watching the magnificent horse make its way toward the pens some distance away, led on a short rein by a young man who seemed hard-pressed to keep the high-stepping animal under control. On the other side of the village green Leonora watched it approach, her attention caught by the tossing head and flowing white mane, the hint of restrained power in every movement of its muscular body. Here was a thoroughbred of high spirits that would present a fair challenge to even the most accomplished rider. How she would love to test her riding skills against that restless beast, to race it across the open fields until it came to heel, exhausted, mastered.

Unobserved by Leonora, a small boy standing nearby struggled to contain in his arms a fat, wriggling piglet equally determined to be free of its new owner. After a few minutes the boy lost his battle and the piglet fell to the grass, whereupon it leaped to its feet and raced away in the direction of the advancing horse. As the little animal traced a zig-zag path across the grass, the stallion side-stepped to avoid it, causing the groom to leap back or risk being struck by a flying hoof. The piglet screamed in panic and the stallion rose up on its hind legs with a snort of alarm, dragging the short rein from the groom's grip. Finding itself unexpectedly free, it then began to rear and prance with its hooves flailing, scattering groom and bystanders alike and raising a noisy furore amongst the crowds.

'Oh, my God! Get back! Leonora! Get back!'

Standing only a few feet from the danger, Leonora heard her brother's warning but stood her ground, not out of bravado but from sheer fascination as the magnificent animal reared up against the bright sky. Then a swift, agile figure appeared from nowhere to lift her off her feet and propel her to the safety of a low wall where several other people had already taken refuge.

'You court danger, my lady.'

She recognised the voice, too rich, too hypnotically deep to belong to any other man. He did not release her. His big, hard hands gripped her upper arms and his long body pressed itself close to hers. He was wearing buckskins and a vivid white shirt left open at the front to expose his tanned chest, the sleeves rolled back over powerful brown forearms. His sleeveless leather jerkin was of reddish brown and smelled of woodsmoke and freshly turned earth. She knew this man. Her body and all its senses remembered him. She knew him by his clean, open-air scent, by the muscular hardness of him and the icy, needle-sharp chills that were her own response to his touch.

'You!' she exclaimed in a whisper.

'Aye, my lady, and well met, once again.'

Tall though she was he topped her height by a full head and shoulders. His face was startlingly handsome, big-boned and gypsy-dark, with a long, proud nose and teeth that were white and even in a wide mouth. His mane of jet-black hair was loosely caught by a leather thong so that its length hung down between his shoulder blades. What entrapped Leonora was the compelling blackness of his eyes. They were large and widely spaced, set above prominent cheekbones and heavily fringed by lashes as long and glossy as were her own. The smile slowly faded from his lips and those incredible black eyes stared down into hers.

'I am Lukan,' he said in a husky growl. 'Lukan de Ville.'

'And I am Leonora,' she responded in a whisper.

'I know. You are Lia.' He drew her closer so that her breasts were against his bare chest and his hips leaned hard and flat against her skirts. 'Lia, Lia.'

His powerful, animal-like masculinity was an assault on her senses. She was unable to resist him. With a moistening, a sudden loosening of her vaginal lips she felt her body offer itself to this man, and in that instant they both acknowledged the forbidden flame ignited between them. Right there in that public place, in full view of hundreds of people, they exchanged a silent carnal promise as binding as any spoken vow.

He released her then, to the brief flurry of concerned excitement as Jonathan and Joseph, along with several anxious bystanders, arrived to take charge of their sister. The two Cavendish brothers helped subdue the agitated stallion before joining the group as it made its way to the main marquee, from which dozens of people were now pouring in response to the commotion. When they were part-way across the green Leonora looked back to where her rescuer still stood, her eyes for a moment seeming as blue as the wildflowers growing in the hedgerow, then as purple as the bright choker at her throat, then a tantalising combination of the two. The impact of her gaze was no less potent for the distance now placed between them. As if moved by forces beyond his control de Ville inclined his dark head in recognition of the strange contract conjured between them, and his gypsy instincts prompted him to suspect that he had made his pact with Satan himself.

'You are a fool, Lukan de Ville. No man will ever tame that one. I have touched her. I have read the signs. She will destroy you.'

His half-sister set down her herb-basket and fixed him with a withering look from her dark Romany eyes. Even as she spoke she knew that forces of a sinister nature were already at work, forces that would bind the free spirit of this man to a woman who would never truly belong to him. Rebecca Adams had indeed read the signs. Lukan, she knew, was already lost.

'Lia,' he said quietly, and again: 'Lia.'

His half-sister gave a small snort of contempt. 'That one is as cunning and as wickedly selfish as she is beautiful. Be warned, Lukan, she will destroy you.'

The dark, aristocratic-looking gypsy continued to stare after Leonora and her increasingly large group of curious followers. His eyes resembled narrow ebony slits against the brightness of the afternoon sun.

'I know that, Rebecca,' he murmured. 'In my heart I knew it when I encountered her in the forest. And yet I must have her. Whatever the consequences, whatever the cost, I must have her.'

IV

Herbert Shelley paid no attention to the disturbance on the village green and showed no interest in the big grey and white stallion, since he would not be present to wager upon its performance in the four-thirty race. At the precise moment Leonora was hoisted to safety by the gypsy, her father was stooped over a small table in one of the crowded gin tents, putting his signature to a document prepared by his bankers,

Fairfax, Reece & Tilbury. That they sought to ensnare him by underhand practices was also of little consequence to him. In exchange for his signature he received an extension of his credit and a cash settlement of one thousand pounds, a handsome sum for one penned flourish on a single legal document. He held the money under his coat as he left the tent and, flanked by his two paid helpers, made his way to that area on the edge of the village where horses and carriages waited to be put back into service. The magpie-like Nigel Fairfax chuckled wickedly and sucked a generous pinch of fine snuff into each nostril in turn.

'And there we have it, Christopher my boy, all signed, sealed and irrefutable. You shall have your pretty little filly and the Fairfax name will have its links with the house of Cavendish.'

'Th-thank you, F-father,' Christopher stammered. His fat face reddened and his eyes glinted with delight. 'And n-now it is s-settled we m-must waste n-no more t-time. Leon-n-nora and I m-must m-marry w-within the m-m-month.'

CHAPTER ELEVEN

I

Leonora and her family stayed another full day at Beresford, intending to begin their journey home at dawn on Thursday morning, taking the Burford Road and staying overnight at the house of friends on the banks of the Cherwell at Oxford. On Wednesday morning they carried two large picnic hampers into nearby St Eloy's Wood, to a small coppice where several great oaks had been felled and carted away by the keepers. It was a pleasant place, sheltered beneath a rich and shady canopy and laid with a soft carpet of moss dotted here and there with pretty forest flowers. On one side a bridle path snaked upwards over the high bank before dropping down again to join the wider path to Oakwood Lodge. On its other side a number of smaller pathways led off into the denser parts of the forest. These ancient, poorly defined footways were best avoided by strangers to the area who might become lost in that shadowy world of a thousand hidden dangers.

Set into the steep bank below the bridle path was an old, half-buried trough made from local ironstone to withstand the extremes of heat and cold, and into this ran the sweet, fresh waters of St Eloy's Well. Leonora seated herself on the stump of a tree and sipped the cold spring water from a wineglass. She had never tasted its like before. It was crystal-clear and so deliciously pure that she disciplined herself as to how much passed her lips. She had been warned by Anabel that too much of St Eloy's elixir would fog her senses and render her light-headed. Only after much coaxing and pleading had she managed to persuade Anabel to join them on the picnic, leaving Francine in the capable hands of one of Sir Oscar's senior housemaids. She would have been shocked to learn of the special instructions that Francine's rooms be kept locked at all times and that Herbert Shelley, should he return to the Lodge in their absence, be denied entry unless accompanied by a doctor.

Over a private breakfast that morning, Leonora had spoken to Jonathan about her feelings for Gilbert Cavendish. She needed more time, she had told him, for in spite of her earlier certainty she was now beset with doubts about their future together. Jonathan had offered to speak to Gilbert on her behalf before the eager young man could take matters into his own hands. At all costs she wanted to avoid wounding him with a rejection, a thing she must surely do if he were to ask her to marry him in her present frame of mind.

'Take whatever time you need, my dear,' Jonathan had told her, covering her hand with his own. Then he had smiled and added: 'Only yesterday I had to warn him against shortening your name to Lia. That is still a privilege reserved for Joseph alone, I believe, even though he is no longer a lisping babe?'

'Yes, it is,' Leonora had said, feeling the colour rush to her cheeks as she recalled the velvet-voiced stranger who had so spontaneously called her by that special name.

'Gilbert cares very deeply for you, Leonora.'

'I believe he does,' she agreed, 'and that is precisely why I wish to spare him the pain of my refusal.'

In the end they had decided upon a delay of at least a

283

month before the subject of marriage was again mentioned between them, and Leonora had privately resolved to place as much distance between herself and Gilbert as was possible during that time.

Now she smiled across the coppice at Jonathan, whose blond hair had been bleached by the sun to an even lighter shade. Not once during their conversation had he made any reference to the fact that his own marriage plans were heavily dependent upon her decision. He needed all the support he could get if he was to steal Louisa Fenwick out of the clutches of her society-conscious mother.

Charles and Joseph were sitting together beneath an oak tree, their backs against the rough bark and their legs stretched out across a thick rug. They were discussing the merits of steam power, and the very articulate Charles, being passionately interested in all aspects of engineering, was giving little ground to his brother's less persuasive arguments.

After a while the small party was swelled in numbers by the arrival of Louisa and her personal maid, accompanied by Gilbert Cavendish and his sister. Elizabeth ran immediately to Leonora and hugged her warmly. She had brought a gift of misty-hued bluebells picked along the way, and a small silk handkerchief dampened with dew to ease the recurring discomfort in Joseph's eyes. She seemed not to notice that many of the blossoms had been crushed in her unladylike grip, or that the precious midsummer dew had evaporated overnight, leaving the handkerchief perfectly dry. She was clearly relieved that Helen, who had been unkind to her on their first meeting, would not be joining them on the picnic.

It was a cheerful group that later gathered around the picnic baskets to enjoy their meal. An apron and two extra towels were needed to protect Elizabeth's pretty yellow dress from food stains and to clean the spills from her hands and face. Her table manners left a great deal to be desired but this, like her clumsiness, was easily overlooked. It was clear to everyone that this childlike woman lacked certain skills simply because nobody had taken the trouble to teach them to her.

While Leonora was leaning over the ironstone trough to

284

rinse her hands beneath the icy flow of water, two riders broke through the trees on the far side of the coppice. They were met by a noisy chorus of greetings.

'Good day to you all, my friends.'

Smiling broadly, Sir Malcolm Cavendish dismounted and strode into the company. His companion slid from his own mount and held back, his eyes narrowed in his sun-browned face as he stared across the coppice at Leonora. Something shifted inside her with a sudden lurch as she met his gaze.

'Here is brandy to help your little party along,' Malcolm announced, producing three bottles from his saddlebags. 'And sugared almonds and raisins for the ladies. I regret I am unable to stay with you all, but duty calls me to Burford, where the killers of one of our shepherd lads are to be brought before the magistrate.' He approached Leonora, took her hand and raised it to his lips. 'My compliments on your gown, dear cousin. Blue suits you, though I swear your eyes have the most damnably elusive colouring.'

Leonora smiled, concentrating her attention on his handsome face with some difficulty while a taller, darker figure moved just on the periphery of her vision. He was here. The man with the strange manner and fascinating black eyes was right here at their picnic. The initial pleasure of Malcolm's unexpected arrival was stirred into a hidden tumult of emotions by that other's presence. As if sensing the interest she attempted to conceal, Malcolm released her hand, half turned and said with a grin: 'Leonora, allow me to present my very good friend and Beresford's senior forest ranger, Lukan de Ville. But have you two not met already? It seems you were almost trampled to death yesterday when Starlight Warrior bolted. Did he save your life, or has the story been wildly exaggerated in the telling?'

She shivered as Lukan de Ville pressed her hand to his mouth and, parting his lips, touched the backs of her fingers with the tip of his tongue. Once again she felt that melting sensation in her secret parts as his hot tongue made sensuous movements across her skin. Then as he lowered her hand he caused it to rest very briefly against his chest, reminding her of the powerful heartbeat behind the hard muscle.

'... and then he simply lifted her out of the stallion's path with only seconds to spare,' a voice was saying. 'It was the most terrifying scene I ever witnessed.'

'Lia.'

The husky whisper was as potent as a caress. She stared into his brooding dark face. She had tossed and turned in her bed until the early hours of the morning because of this man, and then her dreams had been filled with such longings and yearnings as she had never thought to experience. Now she saw the tiny scar on his upper lip, the slight cleft in his chin, the small chip that was the only flaw in his even white teeth, and those small imperfections only marked him as more handsome, more dangerously desirable than any man she had met before.

'... so he surely deserves a reward of some kind.'

'And what of Starlight Warrior?' someone asked. 'Did he win the race?'

'Indeed he did,' another voice confirmed. 'He won by a neck, leaving Lord Grafton practically foaming at the mouth because he was pipped at the post, yet again, by a horse out of the Earl's stable.'

'Lia.'

His breath was warm on her face as he whispered her name. It smelled of parsley and fresh garden mint.

'Lia.'

Then Malcolm's voice seemed to slice like a scythe between them. 'So, what say you, cousin? Shall your rescuer have his reward?'

'What?' She gathered her senses with a start as Lukan turned abruptly and stooped to drink from the spring. Cheeks burning, she took Malcolm's hand and offered him her most brilliant smile. 'Yes, yes indeed. There can be no doubt that your friend saved my life yesterday, and for that he must certainly be rewarded.' She walked with him to the spot where he had left his horse, then asked in a whisper: 'Should I offer money?'

'Good heavens no!' Malcolm exclaimed, then lowered his

voice and smiled into her eyes. 'Lukan is fiercely proud. To offer him a purse of money would offend him deeply, and I doubt if he would ever be persuaded to accept payment from a lady for services rendered. No, my dear, if anyone is to reward him it shall be me, and not with anything so base as a gift of money. I have a mind to offer him the stallion.'

'Starlight Warrior? But isn't he the pride of your stables?'

'That is so, but he is still half-wild, and with a peppery temper that makes him less than trustworthy. Lukan understands him, just as he understands those peculiar dogs of his, so the two are of a kind, you might say. Yes, I have a mind to offer him the stallion.'

From across the clearing Anabel looked on with mounting anxiety as the lean and angular gypsy strode from the well with a casual grace, grabbed a handful of hair from his horse's mane and swung himself on to its back with all the ease of a trained acrobat. She had felt the undercurrents created by his presence and noticed the challenging exchange between him and Leonora. And now there was something more. While the others behaved as if nothing of any importance had taken place, young Gilbert Cavendish looked on with a troubled expression on his young face. He too had watched Sir Malcolm show more than a mannerly interest in his cousin and receive much more than courtesy in return. Anabel was furious. What new game was the vixen playing to set brother against brother in this subtle way, and what wickedness had passed between her and the half-breed in those moments when they stood together at St Eloy's Well? As the visitors walked their mounts into the nearby trees Lukan de Ville, bringing up the rear on his huge black mount, turned in the saddle and lowered his head to peer back into the clearing from beneath darkly furrowed brows. Anabel glanced at Leonora and felt for herself the sheer potency of that illicit glance.

'Oh, you wicked girl,' she muttered under her breath, stunned that the so imperious Leonora would stoop to even a casual flirtation with such a person. 'You foolish, wicked girl.'

As the group settled down again to sample the brandy and

discuss in detail the capture of the band of poachers on Midsummer Eve, Leonora returned to the spring to cool her wrists beneath the ice-cold water. She was well aware of Anabel's angry stare, and of the sudden dampening of Gilbert's happy mood, but she was much too exhilarated beneath her composure to give either of them the benefit of her concern. Just as she had done in her restlessness the previous night, so now she tested the man's unusual name on her tongue, hearing the sound of it like a whispered chant from her own lips:

'Lukan. Lukan de Ville. Lukan. Lukan. Lukan.'

At that moment it seemed to her that she had embarked upon a hazardous obstacle course of emotions that left her breathless and intoxicated. She had rushed from a bland, safe friendship with Gilbert to the unexpected excitement of capturing Sir Malcolm's affection, and from there to the more dangerous ground on to which this Lukan de Ville sought to entice her. Two men, the gypsy woman had said, one to love with her heart and the other with her soul, and Leonora had doubted the existence of such a distinction. But now the small cascade of spring water splashed over her wrists to chill her skin while leaving the secret fires within her untouched, uncooled, and already she was beginning to suspect that there truly *was* a difference.

She stepped back at the sound of a footfall close by. It was Gilbert, come to be reassured that his attentions were still welcome.

'May I speak to you privately, Leonora?'

'Oh, Gilbert, if it concerns your conversation with Jonathan this morning, I really do not think ...'

'What conversation? I have barely spoken to your brother since yesterday. It is to you I must speak, Leonora, on matters of a very personal nature.'

She turned from the well and accepted the handkerchief he offered on which to dry her hands. She did so slowly and deliberately, all the while seeking to catch her brother's attention from across the coppice. He was sitting over by the picnic baskets, his blond head bent to catch something Louisa

288

was saying. It was the watchful Anabel who guessed what was happening and touched Jonathan's arm to make him aware of the situation. The young man excused himself and rose to his feet, calling out to his friend as he strode across the clearing.

'Ah, there you are, Gilbert. I have been meaning to talk to you on a rather serious matter. A few minutes of your time, sir, if you please.'

'But I was about to ...'

'Oh, I feel sure my sister will forgive me for dragging you away. Leonora?'

'Of course I forgive you, Jonathan,' and smiling at Gilbert she added: 'please excuse me.'

As a perplexed Gilbert was led away to hear his friend's advice, Leonora's company was claimed by a very excited Elizabeth, who had gone into the forest to relieve herself and returned some minutes later with a beautiful sprig of pure while lilac, which she immediately offered to her friend.

'But this is lovely. Wherever did you find it? Surely it does not grow here in the forest?'

'It's for you,' Elizabeth beamed.

'But where did it come from?'

'I found it. It's for you.'

Seeing uncertainty cloud her friend's expression, Leonora smiled and sniffed the delicately scented blossoms.

'And I will treasure your lovely gift,' she said. 'Thank you, Elizabeth. Why don't you help yourself to some of those delicious sugared raisins?'

As Elizabeth dropped into a crouch to rummage among the dishes, Anabel approached Leonora and said in a testy whisper: 'Either throw it away or leave it outside the Lodge. It must not be taken indoors. White lilac is terribly unlucky. It foretells death.'

'Nonsense, Anabel. That is just silly superstition. And besides, Mama *adores* lilac.'

'Not *white* lilac. She must not even hear of it. If she learns that you have so much as *touched* it ...'

'Very well,' Leonora conceded, carefully slipping the flower into the silk purse hanging from the waistband of her skirt.

'Mama will know nothing of it. And do stop looking so cross, Anabel.'

'I saw you,' the servant hissed. 'I saw you.'

'Anabel, I have no idea what you are talking about.'

'Wicked, you are. I saw you fluttering your eye-lashes at Sir Malcolm and flirting with that fearsome gypsy fellow.'

'Nonsense, Anabel. You are imagining things.'

'Oh no I am not. I don't know what you are up to, Miss High-and-mighty Shelley, but don't you come running to me for sympathy when you get hurt, because those who deliberately play with fire *deserve* to get their fingers burned.'

They were packing up their baskets with the intention of walking a little way along the bridle path before returning to Oakwood Lodge, when a young man came running along the main path, snatched off his cap and approached Jonathan with a breathless urgency. This was Sam Cooper, a thick-set, very likeable West ountry man recently hired as second groom to the Shelley household. Anabel blanched at the sight of his worried face, instantly fearing the worst. He hastened to assure them all that Francine had not suffered a relapse.

'The mistress be well enough and still sleeping. Nay, 'tis not the mistress I'm about.'

'Then why are you here?' Jonathan asked, drawing the man to one side.

Cooper twisted his cap against his chest.

'Beggin' yer pardon, sir, but I reckon as maybe it's a private matter, like.' He glanced at the unfamiliar faces gathered in the coppice and coloured with sudden embarrassment on finding himself the centre of attention in such grand company. Despite his awkwardness he was determined to maintain the family's privacy, so he dared to step closer to Jonathan and lower his voice before adding: 'It concerns the master, sir, and Miss Helen.'

Jonathan drew him back towards the pathway where they were joined by Charles and Joseph, and by a very anxious Leonora, who feared that an awful secret was about to be revealed which would bring shame upon her family.

'They be gone, sir,' Cooper told them. 'Last night Miss

Helen supped in her room and left word that she was not to be disturbed with breakfast, but her drapes were still undrawn at twelve o'clock, so one of the maids was sent in to see what was amiss. The bed hadn't been slept in nor the supper tray touched, and Miss Helen was gone with all her belongings. Same thing when Mrs Morgan let herself into the master's room after hearing no reply to her knocking. Gone, they are, sir. Both of 'em together. Gone since yesterday afternoon, we reckon.'

Jonathan's face had tightened until a pulse throbbed visibly in his left cheek. While the others held back discreetly, Anabel inched forward until she could overhear what was being said. She slid her hand into Leonora's and found it clammy with apprehension.

'There be more to tell 'ee sir,' Cooper said, still addressing himself directly to Jonathan. 'But maybe it's best telled back at the Lodge?'

'Tell us *now*,' Leonora cut in. Something crawled along her spine, touching an instinct, a premonition of impending disaster.

Cooper cleared his throat. 'Well ma'am, when I found Griffiths gone and all, I took the liberty of riding over to Kingswood village to see what I could find out. Squire Bailey's groom told me as how Mr Shelley had sold his coach and all his horses yesterday, even sold the riding ponies, he did, including your mare, miss, the brown one with the white blaze.'

'Go on,' Charles urged.

'Sold 'em all at the auctions he did, along with stable trappings and silver plate and candlesticks and the like. He had trunks of stuff brought up from London and sold the lot and now he's gone, and Griffiths and Miss Helen with him. They took the Mail Coach, Squire Bailey's groom reckons, with two armed guards travelling with 'em.'

'Men paid to protect the Earl's money,' Charles growled. 'Good Lord, he must be carrying upwards of forty thousand pounds ... by coach!'

'Aye, an' there be somethin' else, sir.'

291

'What?' Jonathan demanded. 'What else?'

Cooper cleared this throat again. 'They be headin' for Plymouth, sir.'

'*Plymouth*?'

'Aye, sir. They be booked right through to Plymouth and set to make a sea voyage.'

Jonathan's voice was suddenly reduced to a strained whisper.

'Absconded? *Absconded*?'

'Oh no,' Leonora gasped.

She gripped Anabel's hand for support and closed her eyes, seeing the family fortunes frittered away and all her personal dreams crumbling in the wake of her father's folly. Suddenly the words of the herb-seller, promising wealth, love and her heart's desire, rang with cruel mockery in her ears. This was the beginning of the end, for there could be no future for any of them if Herbert Shelley had fled the country with the Earl's fortune, leaving his family penniless and his debts increased two-fold.

II

London was ugly. It seethed with noisy activity beneath a noxious cloud of oil fumes and coal smoke, its sewers rank in the summer heat, its thoroughfares awash with human and animal filth. Pigs rummaged in the mud in fashionable Westminster, sharing their territory with stray dogs and hungry rats. It was a time of poverty and plenty, when children starved and old men died in the gutters while the prosperous openly despised them for their suffering.

'The poor are with you always,' Leonora quoted with an involuntary shudder.

'Close the window, for heaven's sake,' Anabel pleaded. 'The smell of the streets is disgusting and the dust is harmful to your Mama's lungs.'

Leonora fastened the window, shutting out much of the clamour.

'The poor are with you always,' she repeated, then forced herself to smile as Joseph reached for her hand. She leaned against him and closed her eyes as the coach moved at snail's pace along Fleet Street, its progress hampered by the inevitable congestion of traffic. She could smell urine and rotting cabbage and hear the squeal of foraging pigs above the general din of the streets. She was reminded of Daisy Kimble, and it suddenly seemed that she and that unfortunate, ill-used young woman were separated by no more than the upholstered walls of a borrowed coach and four.

The journey from Beresford had taken an exhausting four and a half days. Jonathan and Charles had ridden for home on borrowed mounts within an hour of receiving news of their father's defection, leaving Sam Cooper and Joseph to accompany the ladies home by coach. Added to the strain of their hasty departure had been the unexpected arrival at Oakwood Lodge of that most avid gatherer of social scandal, the sharp-eyed, keen-eared Lady Caroline Rainer. She was there, she insisted, solely to pay her respects to Francine, who had been conspicuous by her absence at the Great Fair, but could it possibly be true that the family had fallen upon hard times and been forced to raise money by auction to satisfy their more persistent creditors?

'My dear, there are rumours,' she had insisted against all Leonora's protestations. 'They say Herbert has absconded owing thousands of pounds to a whole army of money-lenders and traders, not to mention an absolute fortune owed to his bankers. Oh *do* tell me it is not so. I would simply *die* if my dearest friend was forced to retire completely from society, or if she ...' And here she had placed a hand delicately to her forehead and rolled her eyes as if she were about to fall down in a faint. 'Oh, my dear, the very thought of a debtors' prison makes the blood run cold in one's veins.'

She had left with not a scrap of fresh information with which to fuel the fires of malicious gossip, but her performance had ruined the family's hopes of keeping the worst of the news from Francine. Well satisfied with the dramatic effect of her visit, Lady Caroline had returned to the city by fast coach on Thursday morning. Leonora was certain that details of her father's desertion, no doubt exaggerated out of all proportion to add colour and spice to the telling, were already the main topic of conversation in London's more fashionable drawing rooms.

Despite the many stop-overs that had lengthened their journey to four long days, Francine was in a state of collapse when she was at last carried into the house and taken immediately upstairs to her own room. Sam Cooper had ridden on ahead from the busy inn at Aldersgate Street, so a fire had been set and the bed warmed ready for the mistress's return. A tearful Mrs Norris, brought almost to distraction by the events of the last few days, deemed it a blessing indeed that poor Mrs Shelley was too unwell to appreciate the shameful attack that had been made upon her once-lovely home. The invalid was given warm chocolate and laudanum to help her sleep and, after Anabel had rubbed her feet to improve the circulation, was left to rest in her quiet, darkened room. The seemingly tireless Sam Cooper was then dispatched to the home of Sir Marcus Shaw with a request that the physician visit them at his earliest convenience.

'I will not forget what you have done for us, Sam Cooper,' Leonora told him at the door. 'I will remember all the help you have given, the many little kindnesses you have shown during this terrible time.'

The ruddy-faced young man shrugged his shoulders and pulled the cap from his head to reveal a thatch of coarse brown hair that seemed to grow without order and in all directions at once. He was taller than Leonora by no more than two inches and perhaps a year older; a stocky, pleasant-looking man concerned with very little beyond his loyalty to his new employers.

'It be nothin' miss,' he said gruffly, staring at his boots.

'It has meant a lot to me,' she said. 'And also to my brothers. We want you to know that your loyalty is very much appreciated.'

'Thank'ee, miss.' He glanced at her and smiled awkwardly,

then shrugged again, shuffled out through the front door and broke into a sprint along the gravelled path. He had not been paid since Herbert Shelley gave him seven shillings and sixpence and a pair of partly worn boots five weeks ago, but so long as there was food on his plate and ale in the jar he would make no complaint about that. To be valued by his employers meant more to him than the jangle of coins in his pocket, so those few kind words from a grateful young mistress were as good as a whole month's wages.

The Shelley brothers were grim-faced when Leonora, washed and refreshed after the interminable journey, joined them in the dining room, where a meal had been laid out on the big table. She was wearing a dress of deep maroon velvet, one of the few dresses left to her after Herbert Shelley's purge of the house in search of anything that might be turned into ready cash. She took her place at the table without speaking, and for a while the unhappy family sat together in silence, picking with little appetite at the food prepared by Mrs Norris and her single remaining kitchen maid. Because Anabel had been a trusted member of the household since before any of them were born, she was asked to join them and perhaps add her voice to theirs in determining what steps were to be taken to best secure their futures. Also in the room was the faithful old Lancer, who sat beneath the table with his head in Joseph's lap and whined softly from time to time, unsettled by the anxiety he sensed in them all. It was Jonathan, now acting as head of the family, who eventually broke the prolonged silence.

'There is certain evidence that Father and Helen travelled to Plymouth last Wednesday, but as yet we cannot allow ourselves to assume they actually sailed from there,' he explained. 'We have just as much reason to suppose they sailed from Southend or even Bristol.'

'But surely they were seen,' Leonora protested. 'They must have purchased tickets, spoken to people, taken refreshment.'

Here Charles leaned forward over the table, his fists clenched and his eyes cold with anger.

'Father knew he would be followed, if not by his creditors

then by his sons, but in this he has displayed the cunning of a common criminal. He has left so many conflicting stories and false trails that he and Helen may be half a world away before anyone knows which direction they took.'

'And Mama's money?'

Jonathan pushed his plate aside and sat back in his seat.

'Every penny of it is gone. There is no easy way to tell you this, Leonora, so forgive my bluntness. As you have already seen, he has stripped the house of everything of value. Mama's dresses and jewellery are all gone, the staff have been without pay for months and not a single local tradesman is prepared to allow us so much as a pennyworth of further credit. Those who were prepared to wait for payment while Father fell deeper and deeper into debt are now shouting for their money and refusing to wait another day for settlement. No fewer than four banks are threatening foreclosure on loans we cannot hope to cover. As you have seen, tradesmen are beginning to gather outside the house and Mrs Norris is no longer able to keep the cupboards stocked. The situation is very grave, Leonora. Nothing remains against which capital might be raised, yet Father's debts run into tens of thousands of pounds and every hour the figure increases as more and more creditors seek settlement of their accounts.'

'And what of our friends?' Leonora asked. 'Have you spoken to Lord Mornington? What about Sir Reginald Lennard or Jeffrey Thettersly?'

Jonathan's laugh was no more than a bitter snort. 'They are hard-nosed businessmen who fear that any assistance they offer will prove but a drop in the ocean of Father's debts. They fear that ours is a lost cause, so they have closed ranks against us. Poverty is like a disease, Leonora. Even friends begin to panic if they suspect you might be infected.'

'Oh, yes. It's known as the "poor plague",' Charles cut in bitterly. 'One hint of it and a man suddenly finds himself as popular in society as a leper.'

Leonora sighed deeply. 'Then we must all dispose of a large enough portion of our personal fortunes to raise what cash is needed to put matters to rights.'

The brothers exchanged glances, then Jonathan shook his head and said: 'I am afraid that won't be possible, Leonora.'

'But we *must*,' she protested. 'Even if it means confronting Mama with all the sordid details in order to obtain her consent to the sale.'

Again Jonathan shook his head. 'No, Leonora. The truth is, there is nothing left to sell. Father took it all!'

'What? But that's impossible!' She looked at each brother in turn, unwilling to accept the awful truth of Jonathan's words. 'What of our lands, our properties and my ...' She paused to swallow the lump that had risen in her throat, then added in a smaller voice: '... my dowry?'

'He took it all!' Jonathan repeated bitterly. 'My dear, for years he has been stealing and gambling away our incomes, hence his constant refusal to release our inheritances into our own control. Now even the properties are gone, either pledged against loans he could not hope to repay, or simply handed over in settlement of some gambling debt. There is nothing left, Leonora. Nothing. We are penniless.'

'But how? How could he dispose of so much that did not belong to him?'

'By forging Mama's consent.'

'*Forgery*!' she almost choked upon the word. 'Oh, Jonathan, could he really be so stupid? Surely he was aware that forgery is a hanging offence.'

He nodded. 'Which explains his hasty departure to safer shores. Unfortunately, he robbed us of everything first, then used the Earl's money to finance his trip. Needless to say, the property pledged against the loan has already been heavily mortgaged elsewhere. It seems our Father has been systematically robbing his family for *years*.'

There was a lengthy silence during which Anabel dabbed at her eyes with a handkerchief and stared down at the untouched food on her plate. Lancer whined and buried his face beneath Joseph's hands, his tail thumping the carpet from force of habit rather than an expression of pleasure. Leonora felt stifled, as if the burden of her Father's debts pressed in upon her from the walls and ceiling of the room. At last she cleared her throat softly and declared: 'Very well, it seems we have no alternative but to sell our home, much as it will hurt Mama and ...' She broke off, chilled by the expression on her brother's face. 'No! Oh, Jonathan, no! Not the house, he didn't mortgage Mama's lovely house?'

Jonathan nodded. 'I'm sorry ...'

'I could *kill* him,' Charles suddenly exclaimed, bringing his fist down on the table with such force that wine slopped from his glass and Anabel flinched and uttered a startled cry. 'If I could only lay my hands on Herbert Shelley I would personally drag him to Newgate and place the noose around his worthless neck.'

'But our home,' Leonora whispered. 'How could we have lost even our home?'

Jonathan took her hand in his. Tears glistened in her eyes but he knew she would not weep. Perhaps later, in the privacy of her own room, she would allow herself a few moments of weakness, but not here, not where others could see. Leonora's pride was her strength. He doubted if anything, even poverty, would ever be allowed to defeat her.

'The house now belongs to a Mr Boris Mawsley of Hampstead,' he told her as gently as he could. 'We have spoken with his lawyers and ours, and it seems he holds the title deeds quite legally. Despite our efforts, we were unable to persuade Mr Mawsley to wait any longer than thirty days before taking possession. I fear we are obliged to leave by the end of next month.'

Leonora looked down at their clasped hands and fell silent. Several minutes were to pass before she lifted her head with that defiant little tilt of the chin her brothers knew so well.

'Then we must find modest rooms somewhere and set to work to salvage something from this mess,' she told them. 'And we must do it together, as a family.'

Jonathan smiled and reached out to hug her. She had risen to the occasion just as he had known she would. Here was one member of the Shelley family who would not go down without a fight, however dire the circumstances.

*

Leonora was pacing this way and that, prowling the room like a caged animal, restless and distracted, when Anabel appeared looking drawn and anxious. The woman's face was grey, her eyes red and swollen from weeping. The collar of her dress was grubby, as if she had not bothered to remove and launder it after the long journey from Beresford. A large linen handkerchief, tucked into the waistband of her frock, had become limp and damp with tears. It was a joyless time for them all.

'What is it, Anabel?'

'Your Mama is asking for you ... urgently.'

Leonora stopped in mid-stride and looked up sharply, her eyes widening with concern.

'What is it? Is she worse?'

'No.'

'You didn't tell her ...?'

'No, I did not, although she must be told, Leonora, and soon. She must be allowed the privilege of sharing even these sad times if they are all ... if they are ...' She paused, cleared her throat and repeated: 'No, I did not add to what she already knows about these awful circumstances.'

'Then what is it?'

Anabel reached out to take both Leonora's hands in her own, then led her to a small sofa and urged her to be seated. She could feel the tension in her young mistress, and that stubborn strength of character which had helped her bear the burdens of the last few hours with a quiet dignity.

'You must prepare yourself for the worst, Leonora,' she said.

'The worst?'

'I fear so.'

Leonora nodded.

'You are so brave,' Anabel sighed, and bright tears sprang to her eyes. 'Your Mama has something to tell you, child, and I fear her news may tax that courage of yours to its limits.'

Leonora nodded again, her eyes dark as she looked back at Anabel without blinking. She was prepared for this. In her heart of hearts she already knew the truth. She had nursed that dear lady too closely not to have guessed the true nature of her illness.

'Is it ... does she have ...?'

'Hush, child. She wishes to tell you herself. I simply wanted to warn you, to prepare you.'

A lengthly silence fell between them, during which Leonora sat like a beautiful statue at Anabel's side, still and silent. After a while she uttered in an anguished whisper:

'He has killed her! He has murdered her with his indiscriminate infidelities!'

'I fear so.'

'How can any woman deserve such a fate? How can a man be free to forage in filth like some stinking pig and then carry the consequences of his activities home to a clean and innocent wife?'

'It is the way of the world, child.'

'Then the world should be changed. God also created *women*, Anabel.'

'Aye, out of Adam's rib, to be subservient to him.'

'Nonsense! Utter nonsense! If the Bible is to be believed, God gave Adam dominion over the fish of the sea, the fowl of the air, the cattle and every creeping thing upon the earth. Only later did he create Eve, so that a man should leave his parents and cleave unto his wife, so that they may be of one flesh. Nowhere is it written that a man should *own* a woman. It is man's law, not God's, that forces a woman to endure grievous hurts and indignities before giving up her life for a man who lowers himself to the level of the beast.'

'But we cannot change it,' Anabel said quietly. 'We will *never* change it. And for your Mama it is already too late.'

'And what comfort can I give her? Oh Anabel, what comfort can I give her?'

'Your strength, Leonora. She needs to know that you will survive while she will not.'

'Will it be soon?'

'Quite soon,' Anabel confirmed.

'When? How long?'

'Weeks. Mere weeks.'

300

Leonora swallowed and held herself very erect. Slowly the colour drained from her cheeks, leaving her skin ashen.

'Are the others to know?'

'No. She is counting on you to see them through the final stages. She has little inkling of the true weight of the burdens you already carry. She needs your strength. She relies on you.'

'Then I must not disappoint her.'

'Can you bear it, child?'

'I must. For her sake.'

Leonora rose to her feet, smoothed down her skirts and lifted her head proudly. She allowed Anabel to pinch and prod her cheeks until the colour returned in a pretty pink flush, then smiled and strode towards the door with all the composure of a secure young woman with barely a care in the world.

'God help you, my dear,' Anabel whispered after her. 'God help us all.'

On Tuesday morning Leonora dressed with special care in a fawn silk gown and dark satin jacket. She was very calm as she walked the gauntlet of sharp-tongued creditors lounging in a group beyond the gates of the house, took a cab to Westminster and arrived at the town house of Sir Oscar Cavendish shortly after eleven o'clock. She was shown into a small, very elegant reception room by an elderly woman wearing a crisp white apron over a dark dress.

Leonora waited by a long window looking on to a paved courtyard where ivy crept over the walls and a group of hungry starlings quarrelled over a handful of food scraps. She was thinking about the inequality between the sexes, the long traditions that automatically made a man lord and master in his own house, regardless of his competence. The law decreed that any greedy, self-seeking fool such as Herbert Shelley was entitled to hang the well-being of his family on the outcome of a horse race, or to wager their safety on the turn of a playing card. It was ludicrous. The lives of decent people were subject to the whims of a scoundrel so long as that scoundrel happened to be a husband, father or other male relative. A man was at liberty to exploit his dependants as he saw fit, even if his children went hungry and his wife, who might well have come to him with a private fortune, ended her days in the poorhouse. While he took full advantage of the many privileges of his sex, the family he casually abused were no more free to question his authority than were the common menials who cleaned the mud from his boots.

She rested her forehead momentarily against the cool glass, recalling her last meeting with Sir Marcus Shaw and his crushing diagnosis of Francine's illness. She had not yet dared to disclose to her brothers the final measure of guilt that was to be laid at their father's door.

'His Lordship will see you now, miss.'

'Thank you.'

With a rustle of skirts she followed the housekeeper across the wide hall to the heavily panelled and rather lavishly furnished study. She was dismayed to find Gilbert and Malcolm also present in the room. Both young men acknowledged her solemnly, clearly taking their cue from Sir Oscar, who greeted her with a chilly civility. The rumours concerning Herbert Shelley had brought him from Beresford to his London house in some haste, and what he had learned from his bankers during the last few days had left him simmering with rage.

'You wish to speak with me, Miss Shelley?'

'I had hoped our discussion would take place in private, Your Lordship,' she replied.

'Hardly necessary, I'm sure.' His hair looked very white against the high black collar of his coat. He seemed taller, more substantial as he stood with his feet apart and his hands clasped behind his back. He looked like an older, sterner version of Jonathan. The grace with which he received her was underscored with hostility.

'You may speak freely in the presence of my sons, Miss Shelley. Would you care to be seated?'

'Thank you, no. I prefer to stand.'

'Then what may I do for you?'

'I believe you know the purpose of my visit,' she said. 'Mr

302

Jarvis has informed me of your meeting with him at his offices yesterday.'

'Miss Shelley, if you are here to confirm that your father has fled the country with my money, leaving me with worthless papers and no means of recouping my losses, then you are wasting my time and your own.'

'No, Sir Oscar,' Leonora cut in, refusing to be intimidated by his tone. 'I am here to remind you that we, his family, have been left to suffer the full consequences of his dishonesty. He has stripped the house of everything of value and left us with nothing. We are scorned by friends and virtually besieged by creditors, and yet we, his family, are innocent of any crime.'

'Ah, so it is sympathy you seek?'

'Sir, I seek only to acquaint you with the facts.'

'Indeed?'

'My mother is dying. Must she end her days in the poorhouse, or in a foul debtors' prison?'

She saw that her words had hit home. He stared back at her, his face blanching and his eyes narrowing with suspicion.

'Dying?' he echoed. '*Dying*? What nonsense is this? She has a weakness of the lungs, nothing more.'

'My mother is dying,' Leonora repeated. 'And by the end of July she will also be homeless, because the deeds of her home were lost to a stranger in a game of cards. You, Sir Oscar, have lost a great deal of money, but we have lost *everything*, even the roof over our heads.'

At this Malcolm, who had been watching Leonora closely, stepped forward to speak to his father on her behalf.

'Sir, perhaps under these extraordinary circumstances we should allow our cousins the benefit of our assistance.'

'I'll thank you to stay out of this, Malcolm,' Sir Oscar growled. Then his eyes narrowed again and his mouth pulled itself into a smile so contrived that it was little more than a sneer.

'So, Miss Leonora Shelley, you have been sent here to beg of my charity?'

'No, sir. I have not,' she said evenly. 'I am here of my own accord and I ask only that you consider the true position of

303

your cousin and her family, who have been brought to ruin through no fault of their own.'

'And just what would you have me do, young woman? Would you have me bring cash by the cart-load to place at your disposal? Should I stand in the street and dole out money willy-nilly to that half of the city to which your villainous father is in debt?'

Leonora did not shrink from his sarcasm.

'Bring her here,' she said instead, lifting her chin proudly and meeting his gaze not with defiance but with a quiet resolve. 'Let my mother live out what little time remains to her under your protection.'

The Earl's laugh was short and bitter. It rang like the crack of a whip in the silence following her words. Her arrogance was tantamount to disrespect, yet in spite of himself he admired both her style and her courage. She had come to plead for help, yet she did so without once lowering her gaze from his. She came to him as a poor relation seeking to save herself from the indignities of poverty, yet she had the effrontery to face him as an equal. In his present frame of mind he would take a certain pleasure in turning her away empty-handed and with her vanity bruised. He withdrew a folded document from his pocket and passed it to her, then eyed her closely while she scanned its formally written paragraphs.

'This is the contract giving your father thirty-five thousand pounds over six months in exchange for certain properties,' he explained. 'As you will no doubt be aware, it is not worth the paper on which it is written, since those properties have not been in your mother's possession for well over a year. Even so, she went to great lengths to convince me otherwise. She gave me her solemn word that the papers were legal and the signatures genuine.'

'In good faith, sir,' Leonora protested. 'She was not to know that the properties were already beyond her control.'

'Nonsense! She *must* have known. Jarvis and Steele are in possession of deeds of transfer.'

'Deeds my mother never signed.'

'Like these?' he asked, indicating the document she had been reading.

'Yes, Sir Oscar. All forgeries.'

'And the names of those who signed as witness to her signature?'

'Forgeries too, unless my father paid them to put their names to a lie.'

'Oh, how wonderfully convenient, Miss Shelley,' the Earl said, his voice once again heavy with sarcasm. 'And yet your mother readily confirmed that these were, in fact, her signatures. She was a willing accomplice to the fraud. She deliberately misled me. She cheated me.'

'Sir Oscar, you cannot possibly believe that.'

He snatched the worthless contract from her hands. 'She knew, I tell you. Small wonder she was unable to look me in the eye when all the time she was aiding and abetting that thief to rob me of thirty-five thousand pounds. His plan could not have succeeded without her assistance. She betrayed me on his behalf.'

'How can you believe that of her?' Leonora protested.

'I believe it,' he growled. 'I do not ignore what stares me in the face.'

Suddenly Leonora glimpsed in his eyes the pain of a man deeply wounded by what he saw as Francine's betrayal of the trust between them. He still cared for her, and so he allowed himself to be blinded to all but the harsh facts set out before him in black and white. As if suspecting that he had given himself away, he turned abruptly to stare into the empty fireplace, his hands tightly clenched beneath the tails of his coat. Gilbert had moved to one of the big windows to avoid meeting her eyes, a younger son cowed by the authority of his father. It was Malcolm who dared to approach the glowering Earl, but his restraining hand and whispered comments were roughly brushed aside. He turned to Leonora with a pained expression on his handsome face, and with a slight lowering of her head she managed to convey her thanks for his attempts to placate the Earl on her behalf. Then she returned her attention to the man who sought to dismiss her from his

305

presence by showing her the back of his head.

'My mother did not betray you,' she insisted.

'She lied.'

'As any woman would to save the father of her children from the gallows.'

'Or to profit a feckless husband.'

'That is not true, sir. She did only what she *had* to do.'

'Yes, but at my expense. At *my* expense.'

'Sir Oscar, my mother is dying.'

He rounded on her, his face tight with suppressed rage and his blue eyes flashing. There was contempt in his voice when he said: 'And you, young woman, are clearly blessed with your father's flair for the lie, the colourful untruth tossed into the conversation with perfect timing. How dramatically you Shelleys present your case when personal profit is the cause!'

She held his gaze, stung by his words but determined to stand her ground to the bitter end. She felt that she was fighting for her mother's life.

'Do you think me a liar, sir?'

'You are your father's daughter,' he reminded her bitterly.

'Then you also doubt the serious nature of your cousin's illness?'

'Exaggerated,' he declared. 'You merely seek to capitalise on her poor health.'

'At your expense, I suppose?'

'Yes, madam. Yes!' He lifted his head in that lofty manner so characteristic of his family. 'I am a proud man. I will not be used. Nor will I ever again be played for a gullible fool by these ... these *Shelleys*!'

'And so my mother, your own cousin, will be allowed to suffer a miserable decline so that your manly pride might be preserved?'

He looked at her through narrowed eyes, matching her steady gaze. Leonora stared back at him, outwardly calm while her emotions became a turmoil of anger, fear, exasperation and compassion.

'Sir Oscar Cavendish,' she said at last, 'I am asking, no, I am *begging* you to reconsider, to remember an honourable, loyal lady in her hour of need. Isn't there some comfort you can give her, some little hope?'

There was no reply to her question. In the quiet room a clock rapped at the silence with every swing of its long brass pendulum. Sir Oscar reached for a bell-rope hanging beside the fireplace and presently the door opened to admit the housekeeper. Knowing the interview was at an end, Leonora dropped into a dignfied curtsy.

'I bid you good day, Your Lordship,' she said, then turned and headed for the door, her eyes smarting with unshed tears and her cheeks hot with humiliation.

'Wait!'

She stopped but did not turn, and after a moment Sir Oscar strode across the room, wrenching a large, tight-fitting silver ring from the little finger of his left hand.

'I believe this trinket belongs to your mother,' he said gruffly. 'Let her do with it what she will.'

She was shown into the street by the housekeeper, and as the door of the house closed behind her, she turned the ring over in her fingers. It was large and bulky, with chips of fine turquoise set into an intricate peacock design on its upper side. On its inside she could just make out the faded letters of two names: Oscar and Francine.

When Francine's trembling fingers closed around it less than an hour later, she clutched it to her breast like a precious thing and fell back against her pillows, weeping softly. From that moment her failing health seemed to rush into its final decline. It was as if her inner candle, so fragile and storm-tossed of late, had finally succumbed beneath its burden of hurts and bitter disappointments. If such a thing were possible, Leonora might have believed that Francine's heart was broken by the gift.

III

At noon Sir Marcus Shaw was shown into the Earl's study and offered brandy, which he refused, and tea, which he readily accepted. The two old friends made small talk while the tea was brought in and served, but once they were alone in the room Sir Marcus wasted no time in speaking his mind.

'As you know, Beresford,' he said in his brusque, almost off-hand manner, 'I am reluctant to make common gossip of my clients' private health matters. It is not my habit to bandy such details between one patient and another.'

'Indeed, indeed,' Sir Oscar nodded.

'Not even between friends.'

'Your discretion is most admirable.'

'Thank you, Oscar. However ...' He paused to sip his tea, stinging his tongue on the hot liquid. '... I believe you mentioned certain special circumstances?'

'Quite so. The lady in question is a close relative.'

'I see. You refer, I take it, to the Shelley case?'

Sir Oscar nodded. For a few moments Sir Marcus returned his attention to his tea.

'An unpleasant business,' he said at last. 'Damnably unpleasant. Left the entire family penniless, I believe. Abandoned them without a bean.'

Sir Oscar nodded grimly. 'And heavily in debt.'

'Ah, and you wish to know how well your cousin's health will bear the strain, especially if she is reduced to the hardship of a debtors' prison, eh?'

Sir Oscar winced. The man was unnecessarily blunt.

'You are well aware of my position, Marcus,' he said. 'I merely wish to hear the truth of it. I am told she is dying.'

'That is so.'

Sir Oscar gaped. 'What?'

'You have been correctly informed. The lady is dying,' Sir Marcus said, stirring a spoonful of honey into his teacup.

'But that cannot possibly be so.'

'I can do no more for her. She may survive for another month or two, but I doubt it.'

'A ... a *month* or two?' The words sliced into Sir Oscar like a knife. That disturbing copper-haired girl had spoken the truth, after all. His beloved Francine was dying. She was *dying*. He swallowed in an effort to clear the lump that had appeared in his throat, but despite repeating the process a number of times he was still unable to speak. He was thinking about the ring. He had allowed anger and bitterness to cloud his judgement and now it was too late to undo the cruel thing he had done. Francine was dying, and instead of rushing to her bedside or sending some message of comfort he had returned the ring she gave him all those years ago as a token of the love between them. Now he stared at the white band on his finger where the ring had protected the skin from sun and wind for over two decades, and the silence in the room became almost unbearable.

'Her lungs were never strong,' he managed to say at last. 'She looked so ill when I saw her last, so frail, as if her poor body was being devoured by that terrible disease. And yet I had no idea that she ...' He slapped one fist into the palm of his other hand. 'Damn it, why did she not listen to my advice and travel abroad these last few winters?'

'Well, I suppose a kinder climate would have made the end a little more pleasant,' Sir Marcus offered.

'More than that, surely? Sufficient sunshine and clean air would have cleared her lungs and perhaps even saved her life.'

'No, Beresford, they would not.'

'But surely in cases of consumption ...?'

'My dear Beresford, the consumption will not kill your cousin. Certainly her lungs are slowly collapsing under the onslaught of infection, but no more than are the rest of her vital organs. No, I am afraid weak lungs are the very least of that unfortunate lady's problems.'

'Then what is it, Marcus? What *is* destroying her?'

'Syphilis, sir. Mrs Shelley is dying of syphilis.'

The brief statement, so bluntly spoken, struck Sir Oscar like a blow. He slumped back in his armchair as if suddenly robbed of his physical substance, a stricken expression on his face.

'Syphilis,' he echoed in a small voice.

Sir Marcus nodded. 'A common enough affliction, my dear Oscar.'

'But Francine ... syphilis ... oh, my God, does she know?'

'She knows,' Sir Marcus nodded again. He looked sideways at his friend, then rose from his seat to pour a large measure of brandy into a glass. 'Here, drink this. Good grief, man, you look as if I've just handed *you* a death sentence.'

Sir Oscar took the brandy and looked at the older man through anguished eyes.

'Perhaps you have.'

'You don't mean ...? You and Francine haven't ...?'

'No, not that. At least, not since her marriage to Shelley.'

'What then?'

Sir Oscar shook his head sadly, then tipped his glass and swallowed the brandy in one gulp. This time he had really lost her. She was dying. He had lost his Francine forever. How would he ever forgive her now, when she had willingly betrayed him in favour of the very man who had destroyed her?

IV

Within the next fortnight the house in Garden Square came under daily siege as angry tradesmen and women clamoured for payment of their accounts, some carrying written evidence of monies owing, others hoping for profit without proof, all gathered like noisy vultures, ready to pick what remained of the family's assets down to the barest bones. Nineteen days had passed since the morning of the picnic; nineteen nightmare days and nights in which Leonora felt herself plummeting from hope and promise to near-despair. She had written letters to all Francine's friends, all those who had once clamoured to dine at her table and share the spotlight of her social success, and as yet she had received not a single reply. As a last resort she had sent Anabel to the Lacey home with a note pleading for the sympathy of Amelia Lacey. All she asked was shelter for Francine, a single room in which a well-loved lady might end her life in dignity and comfort. Anabel returned, tearful, within the hour.

'She sent me away, Leonora. She kept me waiting in the hall and then sent me away. No message, that was all she said, and opened the door herself to show me out. No message. And after all you tried to do for Estelle. I'm so sorry, Leonora.'

'Thank you, Anabel. I know you did your best.'

Leonora plumped up her mother's pillows and cooled her brow with a cloth dampened with iced aromatic herbs. In a matter of weeks they had become social lepers, marooned in their ransacked home, despised by friends and creditors alike, and all the while dreading the day when they were left with only two alternatives, prison or the poorhouse. The so-called 'poor plague' had struck them down with a vengeance.

'I have brought you to this,' Francine muttered fretfully, her lungs labouring under the strain of every word. 'Oh my poor, beautiful darling, your own mother has brought you to poverty.'

'No, Mama. You must not blame yourself.'

'If only I had spoken out when I first suspected your father's dishonesty. If only I had dared confide in Oscar. He might have stopped Herbert before ...' She broke off, silenced by a fit of painful coughing.

Leonora waited for the spasm to subside, then wiped her mother's face and smoothed back her thinning hair.

'You are blameless,' she said. 'You could not have prevented any of this, Mama. Now rest a while. Try to sleep and think of tomorrow. Things may be easier tomorrow.'

She was dozing in a chair beside the bed when Anabel came to fetch her.

'There are visitors in the drawing room, Leonora,' she said. 'I don't know who they are because I was helping Mrs Norris in the kitchen when they arrived, but they've been in there

311

with the boys for about an hour, and now Jonathan says we must join them at once to hear what has been proposed. Perhaps it is good news, Leonora. Perhaps it is good news for us all at last.'

'Oh, Anabel, I do hope so. How do I look? Is my hair still in place?'

'Your hair is perfect. Take your shawl against the draughts. There, now, nobody would ever guess how bad things really are.'

'Hush,' Leonora hissed, glancing toward the bed. 'Oh, I hate to leave her alone, even when she's sleeping. Will you ask Mary to come up and sit with her for a while?'

'I'll do it now,' Anabel said, and hurried from the room.

A few minutes later Leonora, with Anabel close on her heels, entered the drawing room to find her brothers entertaining two visitors. One was the wizened and bird-like Nigel Fairfax, dressed from head to toe in black so that he resembled a thin and very elderly crow. The other was his son Christopher, whose yellow coat and lavender stock did little to compliment the rolls of soft pink flesh by which the features of his face were very nearly swamped. There were papers on the table and someone had brought a quill and ink-well from the desk. With a small whine Lancer got to his feet and lurched across the room with his tail flapping, to nuzzle his rust-coloured snout against Leonora's hand.

'M-Miss Shelley ... er ... good d-d-day to you.' Christopher Fairfax made as if to rise from his chair only to fall back rather heavily, his face deepening in colour as he grinned shyly at the object of his adoration. Having risen from the chair beside his son, Nigel Fairfax bowed and rubbed his hands together to produce a dry, rasping sound between his fleshless palms.

'Joseph?' Leonora said, ignoring the guests. She was concerned by his pale face and the bleak expression in his eyes.

'I am all right, Lia,' he said without looking at her.

The elderly Fairfax stepped forward, still rubbing his hands like a satisfied moneylender.

'Good day to you, Miss Shelley,' he said, grinning grotesquely. 'Please be seated. There are matters we wish to discuss with you.'

'Oh?' She allowed him to seat her at the table while Charles and Jonathan looked on, their faces giving nothing away. Her eyes went to one of the documents placed on the table before her. She picked it up and read it carefully.

'A marriage contract,' she said at last, her voice even despite the sudden pounding of her heart. 'So, as a parting gift my father sought to sell me like a prize milking cow in exchange for hard cash?'

'An unfortunate comparison,' Fairfax said. 'But might I point out that the money specified in the contract has already been paid over to your father.'

'*His* debt, not mine,' she said defensively. 'I will not be held responsible for this.'

'Miss Shelley, I believe you are not unaware of the esteem in which my son has held you for some time now?'

Leonora glanced at Christopher Fairfax. Nervousness had brought him out in a cold sweat that shone like grease on his face and neck and caused him to rub his palms on his thighs, staining the pale cloth with dampness. He was a roly-poly character, a flabby, toad-like creature teased by children and secretly ridiculed by his employees. In her mind's eye she saw the wild, fiercely masculine Lukan de Ville and felt her blood run hot at the memory of his touch. She shuddered and wondered if Fate was making sport of her.

'I have no desire to marry,' she said guardedly. 'I will not be forced into this.'

'Not *forced*, Miss Shelley,' the old man hastened to assure her. 'Persuaded, perhaps, but never forced. Be so kind as to read the other papers, which I am sure you will find more to your taste. Your brothers have already agreed in principle to the terms stated.'

Leonora looked up sharply.

'Charles? Jonathan?'

'It is a way out for all of us,' Charles said. 'The only way, Leonora. The only way.'

313

'Stop it, Charles,' Jonathan cut in angrily. 'Leonora must look at the facts and decide for herself what is to be done. We have no right to put pressure on her, no right at all.'

She glanced at Joseph. He was staring at the carpet, hunched forward in his seat with his head bowed. He looked vulnerable and desperately unhappy.

The document was clearly written and came directly to the point. Christopher Fairfax proposed to disregard his losses and marry Leonora without dowry. He would provide a home and medical care for Francine and make himself responsible for the future of Joseph, who was to be offered a position as junior clerk in the offices of Fairfax, Reece & Tilbury. Jonathan and Charles would be expected to sign papers accepting full responsibility for their father's affairs so that the burden of his debts did not fall upon the Fairfax name. As Mrs Christopher Fairfax, Leonora would reside at Fairfax Manor on the boundary of the Beresford estates, within sight of the Great Hall and the splendid Oakwood Lodge which might have been her home.

She sat perfectly still in her seat, her hands clenched on the table before her, her lovely face pale but composed.

'Mr Fairfax is one of Father's major creditors,' Charles said. 'He could have us thrown into debtors' prison if he chose to exercise his legal rights, but instead he has offered to see Jonathan and myself safely out of the country by tomorrow's tide, only steps ahead of our other creditors, I might add.'

Leonora nodded.

'And Mama will live near Beresford, where the fresh air will mend her lungs. She will have Anabel to care for her and you will be châtelaine of Fairfax Manor. How can you possibly turn aside such an offer?'

'*Enough!*' Jonathan exploded. 'Be silent, Charles.'

'No, I will not be silent, big brother,' Charles flared. 'You know the situation as well as I do. You know we could be taken at any moment and thrown into a stinking prison without hope of reprieve. A ship is our only chance and this marriage is the only simple solution to all our problems. We can hardly spare our sister the plain truth of that, Jonathan.'

Leonora lifted a hand for silence. 'Please do not quarrel on my account,' she said softly. She felt chilled to the bone, numbed by the enormity of the day's events.

'You can surely see that this is the perfect solution, my dear,' Nigel Fairfax chuckled, sucking air through his tombstone teeth as he stooped over her. 'You will be mistress of one of the finest houses in the country, and you will find my son a generous and affectionate husband. Well, what do you say, Miss Shelley? May we set a date for the marriage?'

Leonora looked at each of her brothers in turn: at Jonathan, with his own dreams of a love-match shattered, at the hot-tempered Charles, also thwarted in his future plans, and at Joseph, gentle, perplexed and poorly equipped to make his own way in the world. Upstairs her mother lay dying. Closer to hand stood the faithful Anabel, weeping because the family she loved was being torn apart. They were all depending on Leonora to make the right decision. She represented their last chance to salvage something decent out of Herbert Shelley's folly.

'Well, Miss Shelley?'

'Damn you, Fairfax,' Jonathan intervened. 'You might at least give my sister time to gather her senses.'

Leonora felt the trap closing around her. Beneath her calm exterior she endured a nauseating turmoil of distress. To become a Fairfax was to become an enemy of her own wealthy cousins at Beresford Hall. Ever since that first unscrupulous clerk had tricked away four hundred acres of prime Cavendish land on which to build his grandiose manor house, the two families had been locked in bitter conflict. The clerk's descendants demanded full social acceptance while their noble neighbours would accept nothing but the return of their land at a fair price and the prompt demolition of Fairfax Manor. So the feud continued from one generation to the next, and now Leonora Shelley, herself a Cavendish with shattered dreams of greatness, was finding herself driven by circumstances into the wrong camp, with a despised name and not the smallest hope of ever recrossing that crucial barrier.

She became aware of the toad-like Christopher bending over her, his flesh quivering with excitement as he held the contract in readiness for her signature. They all knew that she was trapped, that she would marry a man who sickened her rather than see her mother made homeless and her brothers arrested. She pushed back her chair and drew herself erect, lifting her chin with a haughty arrogance as she made the announcement that was to seal her future as Mrs Christopher Fairfax.

'You may set the date for whenever you wish, although I will sign nothing, of course, until the actual ceremony takes place.'

'But you do agree?' the elderly Fairfax pressed. 'You agree, in full, to the terms of the contract?'

'Yes, Mr Fairfax. I agree to marry your son on these terms.'

'Oh L-Leono-ora ... m-my d-d-dear ... my d-dear ...'

She felt her hands swallowed into two damp palms and a wet mouth pressed to her cheek as Christopher sought to express his pleasure at the outcome of more than a whole year's scheming to make her his wife. She drew back with a cold shiver, repelled by his touch. In a cold voice she addressed her future father-in-law.

'My brothers must be paid and dispatched to safety without delay,' she instructed.

'As you wish, my dear,' he grinned.

'And I want that unruly rabble removed from outside the house.'

'It shall be done.'

'And I must also insist that Anabel Corey and Sam Cooper remain in my employ until such time as I, and I alone, decide otherwise.'

'Anyth-thing you s-s-say ... a-anyth-thing,' Christopher stammered, beaming with delight.

She looked at Jonathan, meeting the sad expression in his deep blue eyes and finding the gratitude and relief she saw there painful to acknowledge. Once again she lifted her chin defiantly.

'And now, gentlemen, if you will excuse me, I believe I am needed in the sick-room.'

316

She swept from the room with her head high and strode along the wide corridor to her own room. Once inside she turned the key in the lock and leaned her head against the hard wood of the door frame. Not even Anabel was allowed to witness the collapse of her brave façade as all her courage drained away and she sank to her knees, weeping as if her heart would break.

CHAPTER TWELVE

I

Lukan de Ville raised the heavy woodman's axe high above his head and brought it down with sufficient force to split the log asunder with a single blow. He was working in a beechwood coppice in the heart of Beresford Forest, clearing away the old wood to make way for new growth. His palms were calloused after days spent working with a felling and splitting saw, yet he seemed oblivious to any discomfort as he grasped the axe shaft in a double-handed grip and swung it, marking the rhythm of his task with a steady thwack, thwack, thwack that echoed through the quiet woodland. He was naked to the waist. His legs were clad in rough brown trousers that fitted him like a second skin, tucked into high black boots and secured around the waist with a broad leather belt. The hairs on his chest glistened like strands of polished jet as every swing of the axe caused hard muscle to tense and ripple under his dark skin. Lukan de Ville was a solitary, brooding individual of twenty-eight who seemed to prefer the company of dogs and horses to that of other young men. He was also something of a mystery, too refined and well-spoken for a gypsy, too swarthy and untamed for a nobleman, yet as much at ease in a fancy drawing room dressed in top hat and tails as stripped half-naked in the forest, sweating like a beast of burden.

'A genteel barbarian' was how his close friend Malcolm Cavendish was wont to describe him. 'Educated, intelligent, yet never more than a wink away from the barbarian.'

Now Lukan bent his broad back to his work, stacking lesser logs upon the stump of a felled tree, swinging the great axe, reaching for another log, swinging the axe, all with the easy grace of a man in perfect harmony with his own body. He did not break his rhythm when Rebecca the herb-seller emerged through the trees and seated herself on a mossy slope with her back against a flowering beech tree. She had been to the nearby river to rinse her freshly gathered herb-roots, stepping where the ferns were thickest and the water ran deep and slow as it curved back in a lazy arc to join the main flow of the river. Her skirt was saturated from hem to hip, causing the fine green fabric to cling to her legs and accentuate the heaviness of her thighs and calves. She dried her hands on the front of her blouse and studied the tall, grim-faced man who toiled as one possessed over his twin mounds of logs. Damp tendrils of hair had loosened themselves to fall across his forehead and stick to his neck. The remainder hung down his back like a tail of coarse black horse-hair.

'So, the bird has flown,' Rebecca mocked. 'Your fine lady has packed her bags and gone back to the city, Lukan. Perhaps she will never return to Beresford.'

He glanced sideways, his long eyes glinting with reflected sunlight. The steady rise and fall of his axe was in no way impaired by the movement.

'They say she's penniless,' she persisted. 'Ruined by a wastrel father.'

'Aye, so they say.' His voice was a deep rumble from the very depths of his chest, a mellow voice, rich and cultured.

'And swindled out of her dowry, so I hear.'

'Then she'll not be wed to a Cavendish, after all.'

'Well, Lukan, according to the signs . . .'

The axe fell with a loud crack, briefly disturbing the rhythm. 'Read me no signs, woman,' he growled. 'I know what I know.'

'You know nothing,' Rebecca hissed. 'And you see only what you *want* to see.'

'I see enough. She will be back.'

'Aye, she'll be back, all right, but not to you, Lukan de Ville, not to *you*.'

He lowered the axe slowly and turned to face her, his chest heaving after his exertions, his handsome face glistening with perspiration.

'You lie,' he said quietly. 'You know as well as I that she belongs to me, Rebecca. She is my destiny, as I am hers.'

'But some destinies may be altered, Lukan, or avoided.'

'Not ours,' he breathed. 'One day she will return to Beresford, and when she comes I will be waiting.'

'Oh? And for how long? A month? A year? A lifetime?'

'Until she comes.'

Rebecca snorted angrily. 'And if she comes to wed herself to another man?'

The black eyes narrowed and the dark, rugged features took on a firmness that was almost cruel. A badger lumbered into the clearing, sniffed the air briefly and waddled away towards the river. Riding the summer thermals, a pair of crows circled the blue sky on motionless wings, drifting aimlessly in the hazy distance.

'She will come,' he said at last, his voice little more than a whisper.

Rebecca sighed and looked away from the chilling certainty of his gaze. Already he had changed, just as she had known he must. The violet-eyed woman had left her mark on him and now nothing between them could ever be the same again. Although they did not share the same name, she and Lukan had been sired by the same man. Their father was Daniel Adams, a handsome, reckless young gypsy who fell in love with a high-born lady and persuaded her to run away with him. After several months the lovers were traced to a small gypsy encampment just over the Welsh border and the young woman, by now heavy with her lover's child, was forcibly returned to the home of her illustrious family. When she died there in childbirth her unwanted infant was given into the care of Marcus de Ville, chief forester to the Earl of Beresford, to be raised by his childless wife, leaving Daniel Adams half-crazed with grief. He accused the family of murdering his lady-love and stealing his child, and the battle he fought to gain custody of his son was eventually to cost him his life. Condemned by his own claims to be the boy's father, he was charged with rape and abduction and beaten to death before the due process of the law could unfold at the expense of the lady's reputation. Then only thirteen years old, Rebecca had watched helplessly as he died, her herbal remedies useless against his terrible injuries, her childish love little comfort to him in his last pain-wracked hours. She had vowed to watch over the baby brother so cruelly handed over to strangers, but had she once suspected the heartache that was to come, she would never have claimed him as her own flesh and blood.

'The woman will divide us,' she said, more peevishly than she had intended. 'She will turn you against me.'

'Nonsense, Rebecca. You are my sister and she is my love. What rivalry can there be between the two of you?'

His words stung her, but she gave no sign of it.

'She will bring you harm,' she insisted.

'Nonsense.'

'But the signs, Lukan . . .'

'Enough! I will hear no more of signs and warnings.'

His work at the chopping block done, he set down his axe, unbuckled his belt, then seated himself on the tree stump to remove his boots. This done, he peeled off and stepped out of his pants, leaving them in a neat figure of eight upon the ground. He stretched his arms above his head, arching his body backwards, tightening his buttocks and thrusting out his hips so that his heavy penis protruded from its bed of glistening black hair. Then he relaxed and strode across the clearing to vanish into the foliage on its farthest side. Moments later there was a loud splash followed by the lesser sounds of a powerful body cutting its way through the water with slow, controlled stokes.

Rebecca sighed again and heaved herself to her feet. She picked up the discarded trousers, held them against her body and smoothed one leg against the other to remove the creases. On impulse she pressed the garment to her face to breathe in the strong, masculine scent of him. That he could so casually strip off his clothes and display himself naked in her presence was for her like salt rubbed into an ever deepening wound. She was thirteen years his senior, a rough-tongued, unattractive spinster of forty-one with poor teeth and a body that had never, to her certain knowledge, aroused the passions of any man. Why then should it ever occur to Lukan that, like so many other women who were captivated by his elegance and his gypsy good looks, his own half-sister secretly ached with desire for him?

In the icy waters of the river, Lukan propelled himself with steady stokes from one bank to the other and back again, his body a dark, sleek mass skimming just below the sun-kissed surface of the water.

'She will come,' he told himself with every breath of air that filled his lungs. 'She is mine, and someday, somehow, my Lia will come to me.'

II

The chapel at Beresford Hall was set in an arched niche directly below the historic west wing. Some believed that its cold stone floor sealed off the stairs leading down into the original crypt, and that the altar concealed the remains of those monks and nuns slaughtered by King Henry's rabble soldiers. The chapel was tiny, with inadequate windows and several pillars of Cotswold stone looming like sentinels in the gloom, robbing the place of much of its meagre supply of daylight. Even on a brilliant summer day this cold, dimly lit place was as dank and unwelcoming as a disused cellar.

'None but a heathen seeks the Lord in comfort,' Lady Beresford liked to remind the chapel's numerous critics. 'The truly devout have no need of coals in the grate or cushions at their backs.'

She considered the little chapel a hallowed spot where the faithful Christian heart might meet its maker in prayer, yet many who stepped into its claustrophobic chill were confronted not by a sense of holy sanctuary but by the odour of mould and dry rot and the imagined ghosts of a hundred butchered innocents.

While a handsome, dark-skinned gypsy swam naked in the river less than a mile away, Alyce, Lady Beresford, placed two lighted candles on the altar and lowered herself to her knees in an attitude of prayer. For several minutes her face was contorted with concentration, brows twisted into a deep scowl, teeth clenched so tightly that her lips compressed themselves into a thin, bitter line. The hands clasped before her in prayer showed white at the knuckles and trembled visibly under the strain of her fierce grip. Lady Beresford was distraught. She had endured the rejection of her beloved son with fortitude, praying only that he be restored to her in deepest penitence, bowed and broken by his humiliation, grovelling on his knees for his mother's forgiveness. Her recent bereavements she had also accepted with the quiet dignity of one who acknowledges God's will in all things. Her terrible disappointment was salved by the conviction that Grace was incapable of producing the healthy son expected of her. Better a daughter-in-law buried with her sickly offspring than a string of unwanted girl-babies and no male heir to the Beresford titles. The Good Lord had seen fit to visit intolerable suffering upon the Countess over recent months. Surely she had not borne those sorrows with a stout heart only to fall by the wayside now, defeated by an old, familiar antagonist?

'Whore! Whore!'

She cried the word out loud, her voice filled with anguish.

The altar candles spluttered, their flames restless in the damp atmosphere, their ribbons of dark smoke spiralling upward into the gloom.

'Oh dear God, why do you torment me this way? Why must my life be plagued by that harlot, that loathsome whore?'

A brass effigy of the crucified Christ stared with empty eyes at the spot where the candle-smoke vanished from sight into the beamed darkness of the roof. Impassive, remote, His gaze was fixed beyond the petty realms of human suffering while His ears were firmly stoppered by the limitations of the human craftsman who had given Him form.

Lady Beresford reached out to grip the wooden cross on which the effigy was nailed, issued a loud sob and fell back to her knees as if mortally wounded. The sole cause of her distress was Francine Shelley, that pale, delicately beautiful conniving hussy who had robbed her of her peace of mind for almost a quarter of a century. Like a common thief that woman had ensnared Sir Oscar and stolen for herself such love and affection as rightfully belonged to none but his wife and family.

'Right here!' she cried. 'That whore was right here on my land with her ill-gotten brood. Dear God in Heaven, had I but known of it, I would have burned Oakwood Lodge to the ground rather than allow her to remain there, to be visited in her bed by my husband ... by *my* husband.'

Now Francine Shelley had returned to the city, to be followed within days by Sir Oscar. How often did he visit her in Garden Square when Westminster supposedly kept him from his estates? How many times had that soft-eyed whore left her own house and travelled to Curzon Street to slip naked into the Earl's bed? How often did they satiate their ungodly lusts and thumb their noses in contempt at the Countess who had claim upon his name, home and titles, but not his heart, never his heart?

'Whore!' she cried again, beating her clenched fists against the altar. 'Whore who steals his love and bears his bastard son! Whore who even now, so many years on, kicks up her pretty heels and bids him follow her to London! Dear God, will you not pity me and rid me of this evil woman?'

The door of the chapel opened and closed noisily, admitting from the corridor a brief flood of light that was instantly devoured by the shadows within. Elizabeth shuddered and blinked her eyes rapidly in the dimness. That special coldness only found in this room seemed to strike through her bare feet and reach to her very bones. Already she was shivering and bitterly cold. As was customary on these occasions, she had stripped off her clothes and covered herself with a coarse woollen blanket which she now pulled more tightly about her body. Tears were pricking at her eyes as she moved quietly toward the altar where her mother knelt in prayer on the bare stone floor. She waited there without a sound, shifting her weight from one foot to the other in a futile effort to avoid the worst of the cold. It was some time before Lady Beresford rose to her feet and bowed solemnly before the brass Christ prior to facing her daughter. In her hands she now gripped a short leather riding whip. Its silver handle and weighted metal tip glittered momentarily in the uncertain glow from the candles.

'Come here, Elizabeth Cavendish.'

'Yes, Mama.'

The young woman approached the altar, head lowered obediently, untidy hair falling forward to all but obscure her face. She heard the soft slap, slap of the whip as it fell against her mother's palm.

'What ails you, Elizabeth Cavendish?'

The ritual had begun. She swallowed against a lump in her throat and whispered: 'I am touched, Mama.'

'Touched where?'

'In the head, Mama.'

'Touched by whom?'

'By the Devil, Mama.'

'And how may you be cleansed of this affliction?'

'By the whip, Mama.'

'And who has been entrusted to wield the Lord's blessed instrument of cleansing?'

Elizabeth sniffed back her tears, her eyes fixed on the steady rise and fall of the riding whip.

'Yourself, Mama.'

The Countess squared her shoulders and looked down with contempt at her daughter. The girl's addled wits were just one more cross for her to bear, one more evil to be driven from her life by prayer and faith, and by the strength of her own will.

'So, you wretched girl. Tell me again. How may you be cleansed of this evil affliction?'

'By the whip, Mama.'

The sudden slap of leather against the altar was the signal for Elizabeth to discard her blanket and present herself, naked and unclean, before the figure of Christ. After a short prayer the two tall candlesticks were set aside and the girl made to bend forward over the altar with her arms outstretched. In the pale light the marks of previous rituals were clearly visible on her skin. Lady Beresford crossed herself with great reverence and raised the whip for the first blow.

'*This* for your wickedness.'

The whip fell. Elizabeth's body jerked and a sob escaped her lips. A livid slash appeared amongst the paler scars on her back.

'And this is for the *Devil*.'

Another sob, and a long crimson weal rose across her pale buttocks.

'This is for the *Whore* ... and for the *Bastard* ... and for my wicked, wicked *Horace* ... and for your father's *lusts* ... and for the *Devil* ... and for you ... evil ... *afflicted* ... touched by the *Devil* ... touched with *wickedness* ... *touched* ...'

Lady Beresford considered it her duty, both as a mother and as a Christian, to continue with the cleansing lashes until the unfortunate Elizabeth collapsed and the evil influence was forced to loosen, albeit temporarily, its grip on her senses.

III

Leonora lay sleepless in her bed, physically exhausted yet unable to still the confusion of thoughts in her head or becalm the tempest of her emotions. Her brothers were gone. For want of money to meet the family's obligations they were reduced to the level of common fugitives, creeping from the house by the rear entrance at nightfall, grasping at any chance to remain one step ahead of the vultures. Having signed the documents accepting full responsibility for their Father's debts, they were doubly anxious to acquire a safe breathing space in which to pick up the shattered pieces of their lives. They took leave of their mother tearfully but with hope in their hearts, unaware that her days were numbered. The truth would have put them at great personal risk, for neither would have been persuaded to leave the house knowing that she was dying.

'Be happy, Leonora,' Jonathan had said, hugging her close to him in the darkness already gathering about the kitchen door.

'Oh Jonathan, I fear I shall never be happy again.'

'You will, my dear, when Mama is better and Father is brought to his senses. Then we shall all be reunited and ...'

'And I shall be a Fairfax,' she had reminded him bitterly. 'A *Fairfax*.'

'But wealthy, Leonora, and safe.'

She had kissed and embraced them both in turn, the handsome, self-possessed Jonathan and his more volatile younger brother, and she had wondered when, if ever, the three of them would meet again.

'Goodbye,' she whispered, giving them each the bravest smile she could muster. 'God be with you.'

While Christopher hovered adoringly beside his bride-to-be, the crow-like Nigel Fairfax had flung wide one of the first floor windows and climbed on to a low chair in order to address the crowd of traders and opportunists gathered at the

327

front of the house. His thin, penetrating voice brought an instant hush.

'Those of you who are in possession of signed letters of credit, accounts sheets, promissory notes or other written evidence against the purse of Herbert Shelley are invited to present your claim to the offices of Fairfax, Reece & Tilbury within the next forty-eight hours. Those of you without such proof are entitled to nothing, though you are free, of course, to take your complaints to a recognised representative of the law. However . . .'

Here he paused while murmurs of satisfaction and grunts of protest divided the few who were to benefit from the many who would receive nothing.

'However! Any one of you found loitering on these premises or attempting to accost a member of the Shelley family in any way will be guilty of trespass and common assault, and will be prosecuted accordingly. Now go away from here, all of you! Go away! Be off! Shoo! Shoo!'

To Leonora's amazement the crowd had then quietly dispersed. Those same individuals who had stolen every flower and vegetable from the gardens, damaged fences and shrubbery, defecated on pathways and yelled abuse at the family now allowed themselves to be turned away by a frail old man who waved his arms to shoo them away like a gathering of unwanted pigeons. They obeyed so meekly because he was the one with coins in his pocket and a powerful city bank to lend authority to his words. Fairfax represented money, which in turn outweighed even the most genuine grievance. Money was the answer to everything. With sufficient wealth at his disposal a man could command a decent place in society and the respect of his fellows. Without it he was judged no man at all.

Now Leonora dozed, dipping in and out of sleep so that her dreams were brief images, fragmented and vague. At one time she imagined herself dressed in a gown of silver lace and dancing beneath glittering chandeliers, laughing with happiness as she turned in time to the music until everything around her became a brilliant, shimmering blur. For a moment her partner was Malcolm Cavendish, and in his dark blue eyes she saw a love that was for her alone. Next she found herself spinning in the arms of Christopher Fairfax, his hot palm against the small of her back, his great perspiring bulk pressing her closer with every turn until she was trapped, suffocating within his fleshy embrace. And just as suddenly she was transported into the arms of a handsome gypsy, so tall and powerfully built, with eyes as black and as deep as midnight and a smile that melted her senses with wicked pleasure.

'Lukan. Oh, Lukan,' she murmured, her whole being reaching out to clasp him to her. But then her beautiful silver gown fell away in shreds, leaving her clothed in the dirtiest rags, her hair lank and filthy and her body scented not with rose or amber but with the hateful stench of poverty. She awoke with a start to find Anabel bending over her.

'Wake up, child! It's just a bad dream! Wake up!'

'Oh, it was so *real*,' Leonora shuddered. 'What happened? Did I call out?'

'Aye, you cried out loud and clear, so you did.'

'What? What did I say?'

Anabel sniffed and tightened her lips into a thin line of disapproval.

'If it's all the same with you, Miss Leonora, I'll not repeat private things what's best left unsaid.'

'It was just a dream, Anabel.'

'Yes, miss.'

'Is Mama all right?'

Anabel shook her head. 'She will not sleep. She is asking for you. I told her you were resting but she refuses to be settled until she has spoken to you.'

'Did you give her laudanum?'

'I did, but to no avail. Even now her will is so much stronger than my own. She insists on speaking to you without delay.'

Leonora was already pulling on her pink satin robe and slipping her feet into a pair of soft slippers. She hurried through the adjoining dressing room and into her mother's bedroom. Francine was feverish again. Her face was hot and damp and her eyes unnaturally bright. She moved her head restlessly this way and that against the pillows while her fingers, thin and deeply veined, plucked at the bedcovers in a distracted fashion.

'Mama. You are ill. You must rest.'

'No ... no ... there is something I must do. The letters, Leonora. I must destroy the letters. They must not be discovered. I must find them ... destroy them ...'

'What letters, Mama?'

'Safe ... hidden away all these years because I could not bear to ... to ...'

She fell back on the pillows, her eyes closed and her lashes glistening with tears. Leonora held her restless hands and stooped to kiss her hot forehead.

'All right, my dear, if it will put your mind at rest. Tell me where they are and I will fetch them for you.'

'Hidden. Hidden in the recess behind the dresser.'

'Which dresser?'

'The big one in my dressing room. They are all there, but it was wrong of me to keep them. I should have burned them long ago. They must not be discovered.'

'Well, Mama, if I promise to find your letters will you take more laudanum and allow yourself to sleep?'

'They must be destroyed.'

'Yes, yes, I will see to it. Now sleep. Sleep.'

'All these years ... oh, such a terrible secret.' She suddenly opened her eyes and clutched at Leonora with both hands. 'Where are my sons? Where is Jonathan? And Charles and Joseph? Where are they? Where are my sons?'

'Hush, Mama,' Leonora soothed. 'Have you forgotten so soon? Joseph is asleep in his room and Charles has gone with Jonathan to visit friends in Hampstead.'

'Hampstead?'

'Yes, dear. They will be home again next week.'

Reassured, Francine relaxed and sighed deeply, still holding her daughter's hands but with a lighter, less agitated grip.

'Find the letters,' she whispered. 'Burn them ... burn them all.'

'Yes, Mama, but first you must sleep. Close your eyes for a while and I promise to stay right here beside you until you wake again.'

An hour later Anabel and Leonora struggled together to shift the huge Chinese dresser that had stood against a wall in the dressing room since the house was first furnished. Its many cupboards and drawers had once housed all Francine's treasures, her best jewellery, her collection of gold and silver trinket boxes, cut glass jars, jewelled hat-pins, and rare mother-of-pearl collars. Now the drawers and cupboards were empty, their locks clumsily forced and their contents plundered.

'Just a little more,' Leonora gasped, throwing her whole weight against one side of the dresser.

'I can't. It won't move. It's too heavy ... oh!'

'There! I think that did it, Anabel. Yes, here's the recess Mama spoke of. If I can just stretch my arm a little further ... there, I have found a bundle of letters held together with ribbon. And here's a large book. It looks like a journal. And what's this? A box! A jewellery casket! Just look at all this dust. These things must have been hidden for *years.*'

Anabel stared at the dust-covered items rescued from the secret recess, and her heart was stirred by bitter-sweet memories from the past.

'Why, that's her little black jewel casket,' she exclaimed. 'And there's her private diary, and her precious letters. Oh, Francine, Francine, you should have burned them all twenty years ago.'

'What? Have these things been hidden away in this filthy hole in the wall for *twenty years?*'

Anabel nodded. 'I suppose I should have known she would not part with them. They were all she had, you see, all that was left to her after ... after ...'

She turned away, lost for words. Leonora stacked the items carefully, blew away a layer of fine dust that caused her to wrinkle her nose in distaste, then carried the things through into her own room, where she set them down on the stone ledge below the window. Early morning sunlight streamed through a gap in the curtains, and in its bright rays the dust became a thousand pretty sunbeams dancing and falling through the air. Her fingers tested the close-fitting lid of the little papier-mâché box. It was locked. Her fingers had left marks on the cover of the diary, clean marks that revealed the fine grain of expensive leather binding. The bundle of letters had yellowed with age and the ribbon's original colour had faded to a dingy grey.

'Perhaps I should not interfere with these things, Anabel. It seems such an intrusion.'

'I think you deserve to know the truth,' Anabel told her. 'And I suspect the box contains something of value that you can sell to raise the cost of ...' She paused and took a deep breath before concluding: '... your Mama's funeral.'

Leonora winced at the words. When she looked more closely at the woman's plain but very open face she saw that there were dark circles under her eyes and fresh lines that had not been visible before. Anabel was looking old and care-worn. The strain of recent weeks was etched into her face for all to see. She was about to lose the only true friend she had ever had, and that bleak expression in her eyes reminded Leonora that her life, too, had been broken apart by the cold-blooded cruelty of Herbert Shelley.

'Will you go back to the recess, Anabel, and look for a small key that will fit the box? Give me time. I need to be alone for a while.'

The older woman moved to the door but paused with her hand on the latch. Tears were glistening brightly in her eyes when she looked back at Leonora.

'You once scoffed at love,' she said. 'You scoffed, yet how little you know of it! How precious little you know!'

The door closed between them with a loud click and Leonora found herself alone with her mother's past. For a long time she remained sitting on the bed with the diary unopened in her lap, the letters undisturbed and the dusty jewel casket still holding its secrets behind its flimsy lock. She was tempted to toss them all into the big fireplace in the kitchen and watch them burn, yet at the same time she yearned to know what secrets Francine had concealed so closely for over two decades. It was with trembling fingers that she at last unfolded the letters and read them one by one. Most were written during the spring and summer of 1800 when Francine was seventeen, though some were dated as late as May 1801, only weeks before her marriage to Herbert Shelley. All but the very last were penned by her cousin Sir Oscar Cavendish, heir to the then Earl of Beresford and married with two small children. As she read each one there unfolded before Leonora a story of such love and devotion as she had never imagined possible. Francine and Oscar had been so much more than lovers. This had been their *grande passion*, a doomed affair filled with exquisite joy and destined, like all such entanglements, to end in heartbreak. When his father threatened to cut him off without a penny, Oscar had been prepared to forfeit everything for love of Francine but she, determined to protect him from himself, had made by far the greater sacrifice. She had married another man. Her last letter to Oscar had never been posted but was tucked away amongst this bundle of treasures, the paper faded and crisped with time but the words as poignant as the day they were written. It was dated May 19th 1801. It began:

My Dearest Oscar,
This obsession, this madness by which we two are bound must end with my marriage in two days' time. Let the cut be final, with no meetings, no recriminations to freshen the wound. There must be no contact between us, my love, lest Mr Shelley one day suspect that this child I bear is not his own.

Leonora paused to glance at the closed door behind which her mother lay dying. A child! There had been a child of that forbidden affair! Here at last was the reason for that haunted, almost lost expression so often to be seen in Francine's lovely grey eyes, for the sad smile and the quiet resignation with which she bore her lot. The letter was long and detailed, every word a measure of the grief she had taken upon herself for Oscar's sake.

333

. . . and so I pray for a son to comfort and strengthen me in the years ahead, and I bless you for leaving me with this, your unborn child to cherish. My dearest Oscar, you will always be close to me through him.

'Jonathan!'

Leonora whispered her brother's name as she re-folded the letters and bound them into a small bundle with the faded ribbon. What little they omitted the diary recorded in detail, charting their love affair from its tentative beginning to its tragic end, recording the joys, hopes and fears of a seventeen-year-old girl helplessly in love with a married man. Here was proof indeed of the burden of guilt Francine had carried all these years, for there could be no doubt that she was pregnant with her cousin's child when she entered into that hasty, unhappy marriage with Herbert Shelley.

It was mid-morning when Anabel returned to the room carrying a loaded breakfast tray. She set it down on a small table and began arranging cups and plates with a good deal of self-conscious clatter. The aroma of warm bread and pastry filled the room. Leonora was standing by the window wearing a plain velvet gown with a ruffle of emerald lace at the throat. She was brushing her hair with idle strokes as she stared into the distance beyond the glass, her thoughts clearly elsewhere.

'Here is food to break your fast, child. It's simple fare, I'm afraid, but I want to see you finish every scrap.'

'I'm not hungry,' Leonora said quietly. 'I have no appetite.'

'And since when did we eat simply to satisfy our appetites, young lady?' Anabel demanded. 'Food is strength, as well you know, so I'll thank you to come to the table and eat what has been prepared for you.'

Leonora turned from the window with a sigh and a smile.

'As I recall, you always were inclined to be bossy.'

'No more than was necessary to help raise a wilful child,' Anabel replied. 'Come and eat, child. It's a long time since supper.'

Leonora seated herself at the small table and helped herself to cold ham, cheese, toasted bread and thick, pale honey flavoured with clover. Once she began to eat she was surprised to discover that she was, after all, very hungry. Across the table Anabel poured tea into pretty porcelain cups and then sat without speaking, only occasionally reaching for a small portion of cheese or meat or a sweet biscuit, all of which she ate half-heartedly, as if she had lost her enthusiasm for food. It was Leonora who finally broke the rather lengthy silence between them.

'The letters came as no great surprise to me,' she said. 'I guessed they were deeply in love when I saw them together at Beresford following Malcolm's wedding. It just amazes me that their feelings for each other lasted so long. Twenty-two years is a long time for love to survive, especially when the lovers are unable to be together.'

'It never altered for them,' Anabel observed. 'It never lessened.'

'And yet he has turned his back on her now, when she is ill and needs him so badly. I find that difficult to understand.'

'Love is a strange thing, Leonora. Sometimes it runs so close to hatred that the two seem interchangeable. I believe he never really forgave her for leaving him all those years ago, and now he feels she has betrayed him, yet again, in favour of your father.'

'Then the man is a fool!'

'No, my dear. He is hurt, and people do foolish, even cruel things when they are hurting inside.'

Leonora nodded and spread honey in a thin layer across a slice of unbuttered bread. She ate thoughtfully for several minutes before saying: 'I have also long suspected that Sir Oscar was Jonathan's father.'

'A forgivable suspicion, under the circumstances, and an easy mistake to make, considering the almost uncanny family likeness they share.'

Leonora shook her head, smiling a little. 'There is no longer any need for you to protect her, Anabel, at least not from me. I know the truth, now. I read the diary and the letters and I know that Mama was pregnant with Jonathan when she

335

married Papa. Why are you shaking your head? How can you deny the truth when it is there for anyone to see, in Mama's own words?'

'No, child, the truth is not quite as straightforward as it would appear. She was pregnant, yes, but not with Jonathan. She miscarried Oscar's child within days of her marriage, no doubt because of your father's excessive demands on her. We concealed the miscarriage and managed to convince him that her courses were unusually severe that month, but even then he refused to leave her alone. He was always an animal, a dirty, lustful animal.' She checked herself with a firm tightening of her lips against bitter comments so long unexpressed.

'Go on,' Leonora gently prompted.

'Well, needless to say she caught with another child almost immediately, and all through her pregnancy that man ... he ... right up until the very last day ...' She paused, shuddering, and took a deep breath before continuing: 'She was barely into her seventh month when she went into labour. It was blessedly short, yet still it almost killed her. Jonathan was delivered with the help of a midwife virtually called in off the street, an old woman with warts and horribly gnarled hands who actually blew air into his little lungs to make him breathe. Poor Francine was at death's door for weeks, and even when she was back on her feet the doctor insisted she have no more babies for at least two years. As you know, your brother Charles was born only a year after Jonathan. She was pregnant again within weeks. Your father never cared a hoot for what the doctor said.'

'Poor Mama. She must have been desperately unhappy.'

'She was used, wickedly, selfishly used.'

'Did she never tell Sir Oscar the truth?'

'No, she refused to discuss it with him, but I have always known he suspected Jonathan to be his own son.'

'But there must have been gossip at the time.' Leonora said with a frown. 'When a child is born less than eight months after its parents' wedding, the birth must give rise to a certain amount of speculation.'

336

'In many cases, yes,' Anabel agreed. 'But Francine was a lady of delicate health married to a brute, and Jonathan was such a sickly, under-sized little thing that it was obvious to anyone he was no full-term babe. Besides, nobody except myself and Sir Edmund, Oscar's father, were aware of the affair. Francine and Oscar had been very, very discreet.'

Leonora recalled the hatred in the eyes of Lady Beresford as she watched her husband greet his cousin at the wedding breakfast, and she knew that Anabel was wrong. Someone else *had* known of the affair, and perhaps Lady Beresford also counted the months and was convinced that Jonathan, who so closely resembled her own favourite son, had been sired by the Earl.

'Oh, my poor, poor Mama,' Leonora sighed. 'How wretched life must have been for her all these years! And what a terrible sacrifice she made in the name of love! She could have had her heart's desire, yet she gave up everything for the sake of her lover and his family. I doubt if I could ever be so noble.'

'I doubt it too,' Anabel agreed. 'You have far too much self-interest. You are too strong, too determined. And why should you be expected to make sacrifices, child? Why should anyone be made to suffer in order to benefit others?'

'Why indeed, Anabel, why indeed? And yet history is about to repeat itself. Soon I must marry a man I despise so that my loved ones will be protected. I might have become the wife of Gilbert Cavendish, or even of Malcolm, the Earl's heir. I might have become Mistress of Beresford, but instead I must give myself in marriage to Christopher Fairfax, who I fear will prove as lascivious a husband as was Mama's choice.'

Anabel reached across the table to take Leonora's hand.

'Courage, child,' she said. 'You will survive. He is too fat and breathless to live to a ripe old age. Who knows, he might even drop dead of exertion on your wedding night, leaving you a very wealthy young widow.'

Leonora laughed bitterly.

'I wonder how often you tried, in the past, to comfort Mama with those same words,' she said. 'Oh Anabel, we must change the subject at once. It sickens me to my soul to contemplate the intimacies I will soon be forced to share with that man.' She pushed her plate aside, sat back in her chair and mustered a bright smile. 'Now, did you find the key to the jewel casket?'

'I did, and here it is.' Anabel fished the key from her pocket and dropped it into Leonora's palm.

Leonora left the table and crossed the room to where the box was placed on the window ledge. When dusted with a soft cloth its surface proved to be a glossy black decorated with dried marigolds, daisies and forget-me-nots still bright with colour beneath the glaze. She inserted the key in the lock, turned it carefully and lifted the lid. The box was lined with padded red satin and contained only a single item: a small draw-string purse of black velvet in which nestled a heavy, solid object about the size of a large walnut. She unfastened the strings and tipped the contents of the bag into the palm of her hand.

'Good heavens!'

Nestling against her pale skin was the largest, darkest, most wonderful sapphire she had even seen. It was set into a fancy casing of solid gold fitted with a stout pin and safety chain, a huge, glittering, priceless gem of rich cobalt blue almost the exact shade of her own eyes.

'The Cavendish Sapphire,' she exclaimed. 'This is *it*. This is the missing Cavendish Sapphire.'

She had seen the stone before, pinned at the throat of all but one of the Cavendish Countesses whose portraits hung in the Long Gallery of Beresford Hall. First owned by Sir Joshua in 1542, it was part of the legendary Cavendish Collection and had become the formal bridal gift from each successive earl to his lady. It was lost in 1800, supposedly stolen from the rooms of Countess Alyce during a Twelfth Night ball to which seven hundred and fifty guests had been invited. And she, the sixth and present Countess, was the only Lady of Beresford to be painted without the sapphire in two hundred and fifty years. Now Leonora held the gem so that sunlight glinted on its facets of lush blue, and she was as deeply stirred by its beauty

338

as was that first cobalt-eyed Cavendish.

'It belonged to Joshua himself,' she breathed. 'And oh, how he must have treasured it! I have never seen anything so beautiful. It positively glows with colour.'

'Sir Oscar had the original setting altered to open like a locket,' Anabel told her. 'If you press your fingernail into that tiny groove on the side, it will spring open.'

Leonora followed her instructions and found herself staring at the mirror-like inner surface on which was engraved a date and the words:

For my beloved Francine, forever my true Countess, to commemorate our secret betrothal. Oscar.

'What a gift! What a truly splendid gift!'

'And probably worth a fortune,' Anabel said. 'It will help pay your father's debts.'

'Oh, no, Anabel. I couldn't possibly *sell* the sapphire. Why, this is the most magnificent piece of jewellery I have ever seen. And it has such a wonderfully colourful history. Some say it was found in the abbey ruins on which Beresford Hall is built, that it is part of the lost treasure concealed by the monks before the soldiers breached the walls and murdered them all. They even say it carries an ancient curse that brings ill-fortune upon any owner who is not of the Cavendish blood.'

'Then sell it back to the family. I'm sure Sir Oscar will be happy to have it returned to him. After all, he *stole* it for your Mama, and what a scandal there would be if it fell into the wrong hands.'

Leonora moved to the mirror and held the sapphire to her throat, then leaned forward to compare its colour with that of her eyes. It was a perfect match.

'Oh, if only it could be mine. If only I could keep the sapphire for myself.'

'Spoken like a true Cavendish,' Anabel exclaimed in exasperation. 'What a covetous lot you are! And what would you do with it? Would you lock it away in a dusty recess for the rest of your life, as your mother was forced to do?'

'Oh no. I couldn't do that, but I wonder if . . .'

'If what?'

'If this sapphire is capable of changing all our lives. Perhaps Sir Oscar Cavendish would be prepared to rescue my family from ruin, and myself from an unwanted marriage, rather than have his affair with Mama made public property.'

'What, attempt to blackmail the Earl? Are you mad, child?'

'Why not? We are desperate, Anabel, and here is damning proof of his indiscretions.'

'But you wouldn't ... you *couldn't*. Think of the scandal, of your poor Mama's reputation.'

Leonora began to pace to and fro across the room, her brows puckered and her lips pursed in concentration. She was suddenly more animated than Anabel had seen her in weeks. She was muttering to herself, half-angry, half-excited and, as Anabel already knew to her cost, wholly unpredictable.

'Leonora, I wish you would sit down and calm yourself,' she said firmly. 'You know how I disapprove of these sudden changes of mood.'

'And you also know that I would never do anything to hurt Mama. I simply believe we should use any means available to alleviate our present situation. *Any* means, Anabel, however outrageous.'

'And just what do you mean by that?'

Leonora continued to pace the floor, tossing her head with each change of direction so that her long auburn hair swung about her face and shimmered with reflected sunlight.

'It could be done,' she muttered to herself. 'It could be done.'

'What's that you say? *What* could be done? Leonora, if you are plotting some wicked little scheme to ...'

'Leave me alone now, Anabel,' she cut in sharply. 'I need time to think about this, to work out a plan.' She clutched the sapphire tightly in her palm, her eyes alive with the old brightness, the old defiance. It was as if that huge cobalt gem had somehow touched upon a secret to liberate her inner reserves of courage.

'Leonora, I will not allow you to ...'

'Be silent, woman!' she exclaimed. 'You do not understand how important this is. At last I feel I can do something. I do not have to sit around a ransacked house feeling crushed and beaten, while my brothers flee their home like common criminals and my dear mother dies of a broken heart. I do not have to submit like a meek and helpless woman, Anabel, with no control over my own destiny. Nor do I have to degrade myself by marrying Christopher Fairfax simply because he has the fancy, and the means, to purchase my body as he might that of a *common whore*!'

Anabel gaped, taken aback by the heated, quite unexpected outburst.

'Now then, Leonora Shelley, just what are you up to, eh? I don't like the way you are talking and I don't like that wild look in your eyes, young lady. It frightens me.'

Leonora laughed aloud and lifted her chin as if ready to oppose any who would question her new-found courage. Her voice was steady and cold when she said: 'I am no Daisy Kimble to be shunted around by fate and circumstance. I will not be so manipulated.'

'Oh, Leonora, that fierce pride of yours will change nothing.'

'Oh yes it will,' she retorted. 'As of this very moment I am *finished* with cowering in a corner while others ... while *men* dictate what is to become of me, my home and my loved ones.'

'But the die is cast,' Anabel reminded her gently. 'There are certain things in life you can not undo, my dear.'

'I can and I *will*, Anabel. As of this very moment, I refuse to play the part of a mere victim.'

'Leonora, please ...'

'Oh, do go away, Anabel. Go away and leave me to *think*.'

'But you are talking nonsense, child. You are beaten. What can you possibly do for your family that hasn't already been done?'

Leonora rounded on her with fire in her eyes and a challenge to the world in the arrogance of her stance.

'I can *fight*,' she retorted. 'I will never, never allow myself to beaten. I am as strong and as clever as any Cavendish before me, and I can *fight*!'

IV

Christopher Fairfax had his office on the first floor of the Fairfax, Reece & Tilbury building, with windows looking on to the Strand and double doors that faced the staircase and main entrance. It was a medium-sized room with heavy panelling and furniture selected for its practical rather than aesthetic value, a purely functional room with nothing pretty or frivolous to detract from matters of business. There was no comfortable seating, only a few tall stools and a set of stiff high-backed chairs set at intervals around the massive desk which all but filled one half of the room. It was not a tidy office. Books, papers and bundles of files lay upon every surface and were stacked in corners or balanced precariously atop high cupboards already bulging with similar material. In a corner by one of the windows a thin, hook-nosed clerk stood to his work before an upright desk. He was dressed all in black, and muttered into the pages of his ledger as he worked.

'Hopkinson, Percy, seventy-five pounds, eighteen shillings and fourpence ha'penny. Williams, James Cedric, one hundred and three pounds, seven shillings and sixpence. Simpson, Philip, twelve pounds, nine shillings.'

The hair on top of his head had long since vanished to expose the scalp, yet that which remained hung over his collar in a tail of lustrous brown, mocking his baldness. He stood with one leg resting on a stack of old ledgers, his neck elongated at an angle over his work, his fingers protruding from coatsleeves several inches too long for his arms. From time to time he shifted his weight to allow the foot on which he had been standing to take its turn at rest on the ledgers. The nib of his pen scratched its busy way across the papers on his desk, while the pendulum of an ancient clock thudded a rhythmic tattoo within its dusty wooden casing. The only other sound in the room was the laboured breathing of the fat man sitting behind the big desk.

Christopher Fairfax was aware of a tingling sensation

creeping up his right leg. The seat of his chair was too small. Its sides squeezed against his thighs and its front edge pressed uncomfortably against the back of his legs to impair the circulation of blood through the veins. If he sat too long in the same position his legs became numb. If he stood for long periods his ankles swelled. Only that morning his father had rebuked him for being unable to mount the main stairway of the bank without stopping halfway, wheezing and perspiring, to rest and regain his breath.

'You're too fat, my boy. You should lose some of that weight before it kills you,' the skinny old weasel had said, striding on ahead in spite of the rheumatism that stiffened his joints. 'Too fat. Can't be healthy in a man of your age. No self-control, that's your trouble. Too fat. Too fat.'

Christopher had agreed in a way that implied he was only humouring his father, but his casual manner concealed an inner misery the old man would never have suspected. In truth his obesity sickened him. Even while it marked him as a successful man who could afford to indulge his much larger than average appetite, it robbed him of his self-respect. He knew the servants who helped him dress and undress had begun to sneer at him behind his back. Children often taunted him in the streets, running after him to mimic his waddling gait and calling him hurtful, embarrassing names. Lately the professional women whose services were so vital to his well-being refused to accommodate his great bulk unless he sprawled on his back like a beached whale and submitted himself to the indignity of having a woman mount *him* for sex. Following his father's rebuke that morning he had called in to see his senior partner and fellow fat man, W. R. Reece, who also had his office on the first floor. There his confidence was restored over hot chocolate laced with honey, pink and white marshmallows and deliciously fresh Turkish delight that left a layer of fine sugar to be licked from his lips and fingers.

That afternoon Christopher had returned from a heavy lunch at his club feeling bloated and sleepy. His stomach was so distended that he knew he would suffer from terrible indigestion unless he could unfasten his clothes and lie down.

343

There were a few papers needing his signature and a letter to write to one of the other large banks, after which he would slip next door into his private rooms and sleep until dinner.

A small commotion on the stairs outside his door drew his attention. He heard a woman's voice, followed by that of one of the senior clerks, then the door burst open and Leonora Shelley swept into the office in a flurry of rustling silk and heady perfume. The clerk hovered in the doorway with his mouth agape and his hands clasped as if in prayer.

'My profoundest apologies, Mr Fairfax,' he whined, hunching his thin shoulders in the manner of a man whose life was spent stooped over ledgers or bowing before superiors. 'I did my utmost to explain to the lady that you were busy and not to be disturbed, but she insisted upon coming up.'

'It's all r-right, P-Peterson. You may g-go. You t-too, Oxley. L-L-Leave us, if you p-p-please.'

The man in the corner set down his pen, replaced the lid on his ink-well and bowed from the room, daring only the briefest glance at the visitor as he left. That glance was enough to tell him that the rumours circulating amongst the lesser staff of Fairfax, Reece & Tilbury were nothing more than outrageous fancy. Beautiful young women like this one did not give themselves in marriage to obese monsters like Christopher Fairfax.

Leonora watched Fairfax struggle to his feet and heave his bulk from behind the big desk. His eyes devoured her as he lumbered across the room with both hands outstretched as if to take her in his vast embrace. Despite the repugnance he inspired in her, the brilliance of her smile did not falter for an instant. She knew she looked stunning in her snug-fitting jacket of emerald green and full pink skirt, with ruffles of soft lace at her throat and a profusion of flowers and feathers decorating her hat. Her perfume of saffron and gillyflower seemed to fill the room as she offered her hand for Fairfax's kiss and bestowed upon him that special smile which men seemed to find so irresistible. She made no attempt to remove her hand from his grip as she smiled provocatively into his eyes from beneath the rim of her hat. The effect on him was

344

predictable. Her unexpected attentions rendered him virtually inarticulate.

'M-M-Miss Sh-Shelley,' he managed to stammer at last. 'Oh, this is a p-p-pleasure ... a p-p-pleasure in-indeed.'

'I was in the area and thought I might call on you for a few moments,' Leonora offered in reply, still captivating him with her lovely smile. 'I trust my visit is not too inconvenient?'

'N-not at all. N-not at all. M-may I offer you a d-d-drink? T-t-tea? C-c-coffee? Ch-ch-ch ... ch-ch ...' he paused, defeated by the clumsiness of his tongue, then bravely cleared his throat and tried again. 'Ch-ch-choc ... choc-*chocolate*!'

'Thank you, no. But perhaps a chair and a glass of water for my maid, Anabel. I fear she is feeling rather faint. The weather, I suppose, and London is so terribly dusty at this time of the year.'

While Leonora seated herself in a chair close to the desk, Fairfax waddled out to the first floor corridor, where he waylaid a passing clerk and ordered him to bring clean, cold water and two glasses for the ladies. After a protracted interval of confusion during which he slopped some of the water over the floor and a good deal more down his trousers in his efforts to play the helpful host, he propped his bulk against the edge of his desk and hoped that neither the gurgling sensation in his stomach nor the tingling sensation in his right leg were a hint of humiliations to come. He could barely keep his gaze from straying from Leonora's beautiful face to her full breasts, tiny waist, slender ankles.

'I have been trying to decide upon a date for the wedding,' she said, smoothing the fingers of her gloves and pretending not to notice the purple flush that suddenly rose to his cheeks. 'I am almost settled upon the thirtieth of this month, but I wonder if the ninth of next month might be better, or even the twelfth. Oh dear, which date would *you* consider the more suitable, Mr Fairfax?'

'M-m-me? Oh yes ... I m-mean ... th-this m-month ... th-this m-m-month would ... er ... w-would be f-f-fine.'

'But the thirtieth, now let me see, that will be a Wednesday, I believe. Oh, dear, now I wonder if Friday wouldn't be an altogether better day. The ceremony is to take place at the church of St George's, of course. I really could not even consider ... oh, but you must forgive me, Mr Fairfax. Perhaps you have other plans? A different church, perhaps?'

'Oh n-no ... n-no, M-Miss Sh-Shelley ... er ... Le-Leonora ...'

She smiled brilliantly and said, 'Oh dear, this really will not do at all. You and I simply must get together to discuss our arrangements in detail. Why don't you dine with us next week? Tuesday will be a good day.'

His cheeks quivered and his several chins performed a merry dance as he nodded vigorously.

'Good, good. That's settled then,' Leonora smiled. 'Now, there is one other small matter ...'

'Y-yes? S-something I c-can d-do for you?'

'Well, yes, I believe you could. It concerns the papers signed by my brothers, the documents making them responsible for my father's debts. I wondered if I might take a look at them?'

'B-but why? Is th-there some p-p-problem?'

'Not at all. It's just that ... oh dear, you will probably think me very foolish, but for my own peace of mind I really *would* like to see them for myself, if that is possible.'

'Well, I-I sup-suppose I c-could s-speak to f-father ...'

'Oh, no, you mustn't do that.' Leonora shook her head, frowning prettily. 'I had rather hoped this might be a private matter between the two of us. I have no wish to involve your father in my private worries. It is of no real consequence, so please forget I ever mentioned it. I am disappointed, of course, having hoped for a little peek at those papers, just to put my mind at rest.' She sighed heavily, lowered her head so that he could no longer see her face, sniffed and shook a delicate silk handkerchief from the sleeve of her jacket. 'Oh, dear, this is so distressing. I do hope you will forgive my foolishness.'

As she had anticipated, the helplessly besotted Christopher was quite taken in by her performance. Dismay turned the corners of his mouth downward so that he looked like a fat, overgrown child about to burst into tears.

'P-please, you m-must n-not upset your-yourself,' he stammered. 'You are q-q-quite r-right. F-f-father n-need know n-n-nothing ab-about it.'

He began to rummage among the litter of papers on his desk until, unable to find what he was looking for, he turned his attention to a stack of files and envelopes piled on top of a nearby dresser. At last he pulled free a file marked 'Shelley' and lifted out the top two sheets. Leonora read them quickly, noting the two familiar signatures, then handed the pages back to Fairfax. Although she adjusted her gloves with her head lowered, she watched carefully as the documents were swallowed back into their file and noted its position as it was returned to the untidy debris on the dresser. Only then did she rise to her feet with a beaming smile and extend her hand toward her host.

'How sweet of you to indulge my foolish whim,' she said. 'Believe me. I am *most* grateful to you. And now I fear I have kept you from your business far too long. Come, Anabel, we must leave Mr Fairfax to more important tasks.'

As she got to her feet she noticed the upright clerk's desk in the corner and shuddered at the prospect of Joseph ever taking up the position offered by Nigel Fairfax. Such tedious work would destroy his eyesight long before it curved his spine into the distinctive stoop of the dedicated scribe. She had almost reached the door when Anabel, following behind her, suddenly threw up her arms, issued a loud moan and sank to the floor in what appeared to be dead faint.

'Oh, good heavens,' Leonora cried. 'The poor woman has collapsed in a faint. You must help her. Lift her head. Fan her face. Moisten her lips. Oh, where on *earth* did I put that glass of water? Ah, yes, there it is on the dresser. Perhaps you could get Anabel to a chair, Mr Fairfax?'

Flushed with uncertainty, Fairfax began to lower his bulk very gingerly toward the floor. He was halfway down when his legs started to tremble violently and the great over-hang of his belly took up a rhythmic quivering in response. His several chins wobbled as he flailed his arms windmill fashion in an effort to maintain his balance, all to no avail. Finding himself thus suspended in a precarious half-squatting position, he issued a sigh of embarrassed resignation as torpid muscles failed to rally to his support and his mountain of flesh toppled slowly forward. His knees struck the floor with a resounding crash that rattled his teeth and left him winded. He was profoundly relieved to discover that he had avoided coming to rest upon the person of his beloved's maid-servant by a meagre one and a half inches.

'Oh, please do something, Mr Fairfax. *Do* something,' Leonora pleaded.

Not knowing what was expected of him, he located one of Anabel's limp hands and proceeded to pat and roll it between his perspiring palms. He was not accustomed to this sort of thing. There was, of course, no question of him actually lifting her from her prone position. Already his knees ached and his stomach protested against all this strenuous physical activity so soon after lunch. He burped vociferously. He was in no doubt that any attempt to hoist a dead weight from floor level would result in acute embarrassment for everyone concerned.

He was still massaging Anabel's hand when Leonora appeared at his shoulder to thrust a tiny bottle of smelling salts at him. He waved it to and fro beneath the woman's nostrils until, much to his relief, she began to show signs of returning life. When Leonora handed him a glass of water he entirely misconstrued her intentions. Instead of offering it to the patient he threw back his head, drained the glass in a single gulp and emitted another loud burp against the back of his hand. At this point Anabel made a seemingly miraculous recovery. With a cry she jumped nimbly to her feet, shook the dust from her skirts, adjusted her neat blue bonnet and made for the door. Christopher, on the other hand, was left huffing and puffing as he clutched at the nearest chair for leverage in an endeavour to regain his feet. He was purple-faced wheezing and perspiring profusely from every pore when at last he was able to show his visitors to the door.

Leonora beamed and offered him her hand.

'Goodbye, Mr Fairfax, and thank you *so* much. You have been most helpful. *Most* helpful.'

'M-my m-my p-pleasure,' he gasped. 'M-my p-pleasure. M-most k-k-kind of you t-to c-c-call.'

'I will let you know about dinner.'

'B-b-but you s-said T-T-Tuesday.'

'Did I? Did I really? Well, now, I wonder if Thursday would be more convenient?' She frowned prettily, pressing her forefinger against her puckered lips and ignoring the sharp warning jabs from Anabel's bent elbow. Then she lifted her head to surprise him with her beautiful smile, patted his hand boldly and said in a conspiratorial whisper: 'I will make the necessary arrangements and send you a little note. Then we can discuss the wedding arrangements at our leisure.'

'In-indeed. I w-will l-l-look forward t-to it.'

'Good day, then, Mr Fairfax.'

He stooped to kiss her hand again. She was thankful that she had worn gloves.

'C-C-Christopher, p-p-please c-call m-me C-C-Chris ...'

'*Christopher*,' she said sharply, unable to bear his infuriating stutter a moment longer. 'Goodbye, *Christopher*.'

He watched her until she was out of sight. At the bottom of the stairs the main door was opened for them by the same clerk who had stood at the desk in a corner of the upstairs office. He bowed his bald head with its incongruous tail of thick, healthy hair. He smelled of dusty cupboards and old, damp books.

Once outside the two women linked arms and hurried away, giggling together like naughty children. After the strain of recent weeks, laughter was a heady tonic to them both.

'You were wonderful, Anabel, truly wonderful,' Leonora enthused.

'Oh my, did you ever see anything so funny? There he was, huge as a bull and panting like a worn-out steam engine. And he drank all the water himself without saving so much as a *drop* for me. Can you believe that? And as for you, young lady, you behaved no better than a common strumpet. Why, you were actually *flirting* with that man.'

'Ah, but I fooled him, and that is the important thing,' Leonora chuckled.

'You fooled me too … well, *almost*. And now will you tell me what it was all about and why I had to fall senseless at his feet at the risk of being crushed to death when he knelt beside me?'

'It was all part of a much larger plan,' Leonora smiled.

'Like the way you told Mrs Norris and old Mrs Mapplebeck that your father has been traced to Yorkshire, where he has been left a fortune in the will of a wealthy relative? Such a lie! Such a wicked piece of make-believe!'

'Yes, and by morning it will be repeated all over London and the search for Father will be renewed. My motives should be obvious, even to you, Anabel. While his creditors search for him they have no quarrel with Charles and Jonathan.'

'Oh, I see. And today's little performance?'

'I needed the distraction,' Leonora told her.

'For what, exactly? Just what were you up to while I was convincing that sweaty buffoon that I was at death's door?'

'*This* is what I was up to, my dear Anabel.'

From beneath her jacket she pulled a roll of paper which she opened for Anabel's scrutiny. It was the very statement signed by her brothers in exchange for their freedom.

'Leonora! You didn't!'

'I most certainly did.'

'But this is *stealing*.'

'Oh? And who will accuse me? I doubt it will even be missed for the present.'

'But sooner or later it *will* be missed, and Christopher will know that you have it.'

'Then let him prove it,' she retorted. 'Let Fairfax, Reece & Tilbury try to prove *anything* now that these papers are in my possession.'

'Very clever, young lady, but it sounds to me like a temporary stay of execution, nothing more. Soon enough those people will tire of running around Yorkshire on a wild goose chase, and the boys will be right back where they started.'

'Ah, but this is only a small part of my plan, Anabel. The rest, as you will discover in due course, is even more daring than this afternoon's little episode. No more questions now. We have already been gone from the house much longer than I had intended. We must find a carriage to take us home as quickly as possible.'

As they travelled home she gently deflected all Anabel's attempts to draw a confession from her. Soon they would all learn what she had in mind, but first she must get word to Jonathan and Charles. Now that those incriminating papers were in her possession and news was out that Herbert Shelley was still accountable for his own follies, her brothers must return at once to help with the next stages of her plan. She was feeling good for the first time in weeks because at last she was strong again, back in control. She wore an air of quiet confidence as she was borne homeward along the crowded, dusty streets, blissfully unaware that her sense of elation was only a temporary respite.

They arrived at Garden Square just as Dr Harry Squires, a surly young man who was new to the area, was climbing into his own carriage with a servant at his heels. Joseph stood in the drive with his spectacles resting awkwardly on his face, his hands thrust deep into his pockets and his head hanging. Leonora hurried up the drive to meet him.

'What is it, Joseph? What's happened? Who sent for Dr Squires?'

'I did.'

'But why? For goodness' sake pull yourself together, Joseph. Look at me. That's better. Now, tell me why you sent for Dr Squires.'

'Because you were gone from the house and there was nobody to help us. Where were you, Lia? You had no right to leave me alone with Mama. Where *were* you?'

She stared at him, seeing now the ashen colour of his skin and the anguished expression in his eyes. He was no longer just a timid young man moping about the house during a time of crisis. This was serious. Her blood seemed to chill in her veins as the truth dawned on her.

'Oh no. Not Mama. Not now.'

Joseph grabbed her cruelly by the arms and held her back when she would have made a dash for the house. She had never seen him like this. He was looking at her as if he hated her.

'She needed you,' he said bitterly. 'You should have been here, Lia. You should never have left her. She was sick and frightened and there was nothing I could do to help her. She kept on calling for you and for Anabel but you didn't come ... you didn't come.'

'Let me go, Joseph.' She attempted to shake off his hands but his grip was too strong for her to dislodge. 'Please, Joseph, I must go to her.'

'It's too late, Lia. It's too late. Mama died an hour ago.'

CHAPTER THIRTEEN

I

Francine was buried following a brief ceremony at St Augustine's Church, Kensington, on the morning of Monday, the twenty-eighth of July, 1823. She was laid to rest according to her own wishes, in the family plot containing the remains of her own dear mother and four infant sisters. The funeral was a modest affair with few mourners, though the rumour concerning Herbert's unexpected legacy had instigated cautious messages of sympathy from several hitherto indifferent sources. These overtures, however, came too late to comfort Francine in her enforced exile. Until such times as her fortunes were actually seen to be restored not even she, once the darling of the London social scene, could hope to be forgiven her altered circumstances and reinstated to her former position in society. Only her twins, her devoted Anabel, her old housekeeper and her groom were present when the plain wooden coffin was lowered into the earth in a quiet corner of the grounds of St Augustine's church.

Two days earlier a note had been delivered by hand to the town house of Lord Beresford, informing him of his cousin's death and inviting him to attend her funeral to pay his last respects. He had not responded. At the end neither her lover nor her husband had found it in their hearts to be at her side. The two men who together had dictated the ebb and flow of her short life obviously felt themselves released from all obligation now that she was dead.

At the grave-side Joseph hung his head and wept without shame, his narrow shoulders stooped and shaking, his face wet with tears. He was unable to come to terms with the sense of loss that left him feeling hollow inside, with his anger toward Leonora for not being there when she was needed, or with the guilt that gnawed at him because of his own inadequacies. He had panicked. When the maid came running for him and he rushed into the sick-room to find his mother wracked with terrible spasms and coughing blood from her damaged lungs, he had turned on his heels and fled like a coward. He had no stomach for the ugly, undignified face of illness. Instead of trying to help her he had walked the streets in a daze, and by the time he recovered his senses sufficiently to fetch Dr Squires from his house on the far side of the park it had been too late. His poor, beautiful mother was dead. And she had died *alone*. He knew he would be forced to live with the pain of that for the rest of his life.

'He blames me,' Leonora had said as a sullen Joseph trudged to the church some distance behind the main party. 'He has not looked at me, touched me or spoken a single word to me since Mama died. We have always been so close, but now he blames me for his loss and I do believe he hates me.'

'Give him time,' Anabel had said. 'He is shocked and hurt. For the first time in his life he faced a crisis and was unable to rely on his twin sister to shield him from the pain of it. You cannot be his nursemaid forever, Leonora. It's a hard lesson, but perhaps it will make a man of him.'

Leonora recalled those words clearly as she stood beside the grave watching his pale, stricken face and wondering how such a chasm of ill-feeling could possibly have grown between them. Then her thoughts and her sorrows were for her mother alone as the coffin slid into its final resting place deep in the freshly dug soil. She felt numbed. It was impossible for her to imagine a world in which that gentle, caring woman had no place.

'Herbert Shelley *murdered* my mother,' she suddenly exclaimed, gripping Anabel's arm so tightly that the older woman winced. 'In giving her that terrible disease he murdered her as surely as if he had placed a gun to her head and pulled the trigger, except that a bullet would have been swifter and more merciful.'

Weeping, Anabel made no attempt to offer words of comfort. She envied Leonora her inner rage. She could muster no such emotion to dull the cutting edge of her own grief. The first spade-load of earth fell upon the coffin. It struck the brass plaque on which had been engraved the name of their loved one, the measure of her life and a brief message of Leonora's choosing.

'One day he will pay for this,' she hissed.

'Hush, child. Hush.'

'They will all pay. *All* of them.'

Disturbed by the outburst, Anabel shook Leonora by the arm but was unable to distract her attention from the open grave at which she stared with wide, tear-brightened eyes.

'What are you saying, child?'

'I will make them pay. All those who had a hand in Mama's destruction will one day answer to me for what they have done.'

'Stop it! Stop it!' Anabel gasped. 'How can you possibly talk of revenge? Now you just listen to me, Leonora. Your mother's life was difficult and sometimes disappointing, but she would be the first to argue that it also had its joys, its blessings. She had a lovely home, social success, five beautiful children and a host of happy memories, and she would not thank you for all this talk of making others pay for her suffering. There must be no blame. What's done is done. It is God's will, Leonora, all part of His Grand Design. We are born, we play our parts and then we die.'

'What utter *rubbish*!' The girl's eyes flashed darkly and she shoved Anabel's arm aside as if it were a hateful thing. 'My mother was only forty-one years old. She lived with sorrow and betrayal and she died of a horrible disease, yet she never knowingly hurt another human being in her life. It's wicked and it's unfair, so don't you dare preach to me about some "Grand Design" for which we should all bow our heads in gratitude.'

'Leonora, *please* ... this is a *church*!'

'No, Anabel. This is a cold, dirty hole in the ground where a lovely lady lies buried because those responsible for her health and happiness either used her or let her down when she desperately needed their help. Well, you may forgive them if you can, but as God is my judge *I* never shall.'

Nigel and Christopher Fairfax arrived at the house that afternoon, their minds fixed on an early marriage, their anticipated commitments already reduced by a third now that Francine Shelley had succumbed to her illness. No mention was made of the stolen papers when Leonora, still wearing her mourning gown and veiled hat, questioned them concerning her father's business affairs. She was gratified to learn that they, too, had heard the gathering rumours of Herbert's windfall.

'Perhaps we should postpone the wedding until my father has had an opportunity to settle with your bank in cash,' she offered, testing the ground.

Christopher turned a deep shade of purple and reached for his handkerchief. He stammered a few incoherent syllables before looking anxiously to his father for support. Rising instantly to the occasion, Nigel Fairfax drew himself up to his full but somewhat diminutive height and squinted at her through narrowed eyes, his cheeks sucked in and his fingertips rubbing against each other in agitated little circles. He cleared his throat and declared loudly: 'With respect, Miss Shelley, I would advise you to proceed with the wedding arrangements without delay. We have already wasted too much time since our earlier agreement.'

Leonora stood her ground, her features indistinct behind her mourning veil.

'May I remind you, Mr Fairfax, that I agreed to the marriage due to pressures of circumstance? However, since those circumstances may no longer apply, and since the agreement between us was only verbal, I might wish to reconsider my position.'

'Forgive my bluntness, but the matter is far more complex than you could possibly understand.'

'Oh? You underestimate my intelligence, Mr Fairfax.'

'Not at all, my dear. I simply recognise that young ladies like yourself have no head for business. These are men's matters. You must allow yourself to be guided by those who understand these things.'

'And my improved circumstances?'

'Damn it, Madam, your circumstances are *not* improved,' Fairfax countered in blunt tones. 'We had sought to spare you the more unsavoury details of your father's dealings with us, but if you now insist upon a full explanation ...'

'I insist upon it,' she replied, very much to his surprise.

'Very well. Apart from signing that marriage contract on your behalf in exchange for a large sum of money, your father had been borrowing regularly and heavily from us over a period of several years. In recent months he made certain pledges against substantial short-term loans, all of which were forfeit when he failed to meet his commitments.'

'What pledges?' Leonora demanded. 'What exactly did you claim from him when the loans fell due?'

'Land, houses, warehousing, shipping interests, all of which originally belonged to your late mother, I believe.'

'Including my dowry? Including the properties set aside by Mama for Jonathan and Charles?'

'Indeed so.'

'But he had no *right* to pledge those properties.'

'Ah yes, you are referring, I take it, to the small matter of forgery, something for which a man might hang.'

'Or a contract be proved null and void.'

'Ah, not so, my dear,' Fairfax smiled smugly. 'You see, our

lawyers have done a very thorough job in protecting us from liability. The original deeds of ownership were rather loosely drawn up and therefore subject to, er ... shall we say *interpretation*? Believe me, we are experts in our field, Miss Shelley. No court in England would question our rightful ownership of those properties. Finally, there is the matter of several thousand pounds still outstanding, making us his major creditors and *still* in a position to have him arrested, imprisoned, and his newly acquired fortunes confiscated.'

He pulled out a large handkerchief and dabbed at his nose and upper lip. He looked gleeful, self-satisfied.

'So you are the people who supplied my father with unlimited funds to finance his gambling at the expense of his children's legacies?' Leonora spoke calmly.

'We are bankers, my dear. Lending money is part of our business. It is hardly our concern if a man chooses to steal from his wife and impoverish his family in order to borrow money from us, only to squander that money at the first opportunity. After all, a bank can hardly be held accountable for the moral fibre, or rather the lack of it, of its customers.'

Lenora felt her hackles rise but forced herself to remain calm. Until now she had been unaware of the full extent of Fairfax involvement in the family's affairs. Now she suspected that her father had been cleverly and wickedly encouraged to sink himself deeper and deeper into debt. The bank of Fairfax, Reece & Tilbury must have profited handsomely from the arrangement, and as a bonus Christopher Fairfax would gain himself a wife with sufficient Cavendish blood in her veins to score a notable victory in that old feud.

'I believe you have dealt badly with my father, sir,' she said at last, calmly but firmly.

The old man spread his hands in an apologetic gesture, smiling grotesquely.

'Business is business, my dear. Come, now. Let us set a date for the wedding and have done with these silly objections. You must grab your security while you can, my dear. After all, in just forty-eight hours you will all be thrown on to the streets like paupers. Is that not so?'

Leonora peered at the grinning old man through the dark web of her veil and ventured no reply to his gloating question. Throughout their conversation her would-be husband had been leaning awkwardly against the door frame with a worried expression on his flabby face. He looked more comfortable now. He was staring at her breasts, his lips moist and his tongue protruding slightly between his teeth. She shuddered, then pulled herself together with a start and returned her attention to the old man. Concealing her hostility beneath a calm exterior she promised him her final decision by special messenger within the next twenty-four hours.

Before she could prevent him from touching her, Christopher grabbed her hand and pawed at it in the most unpleasant manner before pressing it hungrily to his mouth. As she felt his wet lips touch her skin she was reminded of her encounter with the gypsy at St Eloy's Well, of his deliciously hot tongue and insolent, possessive gaze. She stared at her obese suitor through narrowed eyes and her thoughts were savage:

'Enjoy it while you can, fat man, for you will never again put your sweaty hands on me.'

II

On the morning of Francine's funeral Sir Oscar Cavendish strode along a remote cliff-top four miles west of St Austell, his shoulders hunched against the wind and his face stung by an icy spray from the sea. It was his first visit to the area in the seven years since his daughter Charlotte married Rodney, Viscount Morley, and made her home in a magnificent old house set on a hill between the sea and the River Fowey. Each day he set time aside to brave the elements in a solitary walk along the edge of the cliffs. The hostile beauty of the unspoiled Cornish coastline appealed to his present state of mind, while the threatening force of the ocean as it drowned beach and bay to hurl itself against the cliffs provided a fitting back-cloth to his sombre moods. He needed to think. It was not enough to spend his day charting the mines or inspecting the fleet of ships that would no doubt make his son-in-law a millionaire before he reached the age of forty-five, or to spend his evenings in lavish entertainments arranged by this or that local dignitary. He needed to get away to somewhere harsh and uncompromising, where he could wrestle with his own tempestuous thoughts.

As he struggled to make headway against the wind a sudden gust of unexpected force stopped him short. It ripped the hair back from his face, snatched the breath from his lungs and caused his coat tails to flap like the tattered sails on a wrecked ship. He was dangerously close to the edge. Above him the clouds, heavy with unshed rain, rolled across the sky in great, dark waves, matching the movements of the sea. Below him the ocean was a massive black-backed animal, restless and angry. Ancient rocks that had been buffeted by the tides of a thousand years stood like lonely sentinels along the coastline, meeting the bigger waves head-on and hurling them upward in a cascade of white spray.

'Did you betray me, Francine?'

He asked his question into the howling wind.

'Did you? Did you?'

His reply was another strong squall that sent him staggering sideways on to safer ground. Neither the pounding surf nor the harsh Cornish elements were sufficient distractions to prevent that same unanswered question from slipping back, time after time, to torment his troubled mind.

During the Earl's absence from London Sir Giles Powell had undertaken to make discreet enquiries concerning the business dealings of Herbert Shelley and his wife over the last few years. He intended to speak to the senior partners of Jarvis and Steele, to inspect the land and property mortgages first-hand and track down the two people who had signed their own names as witness to the signature of Francine Shelley. If Francine had herself been cheated, if she was indeed the innocent party her daughter believed her to be, then Oscar

Cavendish would go to her on his knees, if necessary, to secure her forgiveness. He prayed it would be so, that he would soon be free to make her last months happy and comfortable. He would have her moved to Oakwood Lodge, where he could see her every day and be close at hand when the end came. She would have the best medical care that money could buy, good food, fresh air, security and peace of mind. Too much time had been lost to them already. He needed to talk to her, to hold her in his arms and try to erase all the hurts and misunderstandings that had sprung up between them. And he needed to know the truth about Jonathan. There was so little time, and she must not be allowed to take that secret with her to the grave.

'Stay with us, Papa. Stay here with us for another month, at least.'

Charlotte had risen from her seat at the dinner table to place her arms around her father's neck and press her cheek against his. She was a handsome woman, blonde and blue-eyed, with a neat waist that had thickened only slightly following the birth of her three children. She was poised without being aloof, warm but not ingratiating. He had almost forgotten what pleasant company she could be and how very fond he was of her. Even so, he pursed his lips and shook his head, frowning.

'A month is too long,' he told her. 'That would keep me away from London for six weeks altogether, and from Beresford nearer eight. I don't know ...'

'Oh *please*, Papa. You know we would love to have you stay longer. Rodney is just *dying* to introduce you to the Melchers and the Wallaces, not to mention Sir Belvedere Saunders and his adorable young wife, Clementine. And the children are so happy to have you here at last. Oh please, Papa. Do stay with us.'

'It would be nice, my dear, but a whole month ...'

He was thinking of Alyce, bitter and unapproachable since Horace had left in such disgrace, and of Francine, her condition poor but stable, and of his friend's enquiries, which would surely take several weeks to complete. Perhaps a month away from the demands of Beresford and the city would suit him. It would be a breathing space, a time to gather his senses and set his mind to the task of healing old scars. He found himself smiling as he turned his head to kiss his daughter's cheek.

'Very well, my dear, I'll stay. But only until the end of August, not a day longer.'

III

Leonora was furious. She paced the floor, flinging herself angrily from one side of the room to the other and back again as if by doing so she might out-pace the emotions seething inside her. She was like a caged animal that constantly measures the width and breadth of its confinement, its anger magnified by impotence.

'How could he? How could he *do* this to me?'

A warning glance from Anabel silenced Sam Cooper when he might have ventured a reply. He stood by the door clutching his cap to his chest with both hands. Always eager to please, he found himself instead the unwelcome bearer of bad news.

'Of all the foolish, irresponsible ... oh, I can hardly *believe* this of him.'

All at once Leonora ceased her restless pacing and glowered at Sam Cooper, her eyes dark and accusing. It was impossible for him to meet her gaze for longer than a few seconds. She had the power to wither him or elate him with a glance, and now the sheer force of her anger defeated him. He stared at his boots in silence, feeling guilty for not preventing this latest addition to the burden of his mistress's problems.

'Where's Lancer?' she demanded.

'Gone, miss. Master Joseph took him.'

'And what else did he take? A bag? A trunk? Come on, Cooper. Talk to me, for heaven's sake. Tell me what you know.'

'Oh, do leave the poor man alone, Leonora,' Anabel chided. 'It isn't Cooper's fault that Joseph has suddenly decided to run off.'

'If you please, Miss Leonora,' Cooper offered. 'Master Joseph took an overnight bag and the money he got from selling his pocket-watch. Said somethin' about goin' up north, he did, lookin' to find 'is father.'

'What? Up *north*? But where? Why?'

'Place called Yorkshire, he said, miss.'

'What?'

''S'right miss. Said he'd heard as how Mr Shelley has come rich again thanks to a relative droppin' dead and leavin' 'im everythin'. Said 'e was goin' up there to see for 'isself if it were all true, like.'

'I *knew* it!' Anabel exclaimed. 'Didn't I warn you a thousand times? Didn't I tell you those wicked lies of yours would come home to roost? And now look at what you've done. You've sent your little brother chasing off after a false rumour of your own making.'

'Shut up, Anabel,' Leonora retorted. 'Stop your whining and give me a chance to *think*.' She began pacing again, muttering to herself as she became more and more agitated by this unexpected turn of events. After a while she stopped abruptly and asked: 'How long has he been gone?'

'Since afore dawn, miss, or else I would have seen 'im go. I reckon as how 'e must have been gone about five or six hours, at least, maybe more'n that.'

'Well, Cooper, here's what little money we can spare. Take it and go after my brother at once. Find him and bring him home.'

Cooper shook his head and stepped back to avoid touching the small leather pouch in Leonora's outstretched hand. Squaring his shoulders, he cleared his throat and dared to raise his eyes to hers.

'Can't do that, miss, beggin' your pardon.'

'What? Are you refusing to do my bidding?'

'I wouldn't, Miss Leonora, not for no other reason. But I'll not be goin' after Master Joseph an' leavin' yourself an' Miss

Anabel all alone in the house. Beggin' your pardon, miss, but my place is here with you. There's none but the two of you now, so Master Joseph will have to fend for 'isself because I'll not be leavin' you without a man's protection ... er ... beggin' your pardon, miss.'

Leonora was taken aback. It was quite the longest speech she had ever heard him make. His face had reddened and he turned the rim of his hat round and round in his nervous fingers. She could fault neither his reasoning nor his loyalty as she watched acute embarrassment overcome the brief conviction in his candid blue eyes. For the moment her anger evaporated and she was deeply touched.

'Thank you, Sam Cooper. You are right, of course. You are needed here and my brother should be quite capable of taking care of himself. And yet ...'

'And yet you wonder how he'll cope without his big sister leading him by the hand?' Anabel offered. 'Let him go, child. It's time he learned to stand on his own two feet.'

'But he's so young,' Leonora protested.

Anabel shook her head. 'He's just three minutes younger than yourself, and if he's the weaker of the two it's because you never allowed him to be otherwise. Let him go, child. He's grieving. He needs something to do, instead of moping around the house feeling sorry for himself and blaming you for his mother's death.'

'He blames himself,' Leonora corrected.

'Well then, the trip to Yorkshire will do him good, help him set his thoughts outward instead of inward.'

'I suppose you're right, Anabel. Sam, is Mrs Norris ready to leave for her new employment?'

'Yes, miss, she's all packed up an' waiting downstairs to be sent for. She says there's food prepared in the kitchen, and Nellie what's-'er-name says she'll be stayin' on to see if the new mistress wants 'er.'

'And what about you, Sam? Will you be staying here to work for a new master, or will you come with me?'

'Don't want no new master, miss. An' I'll not be desertin' you now. I'm your man for as long as ever you need me.'

Leonora smiled, touched once again by his simple loyalty.

'Thank you, Sam. You do realise that we must leave here tomorrow?'

'Yes, miss. I'm all ready to go.'

'Good. How well do you drive, Sam?'

'Well enough, the master reckoned.' He grinned proudly, eager to be of use. 'Let me stand in for Griffiths a few times, he did. Said as 'ow I done a real tidy job of it, too.'

'Good, good,' Leonora repeated, and resumed her steady pacing of the room, her anger subdued but her brows puckered slightly as she pondered the weighty problems facing her. Her two loyal servants quietly left the room, leaving her to the burden of her private thoughts while they attended to the many tasks still needing to be done before the new owners arrived to take possession of her home.

At dawn the next day Leonora walked from room to room of the house where she and all the other Shelley children were born. Taking her leave of the old place did not come easy to her. Every corner seemed to hold some reminder, some precious memory of the years too quickly and too carelessly spent. Now her footsteps rang loud and hollow on the bare boards and the hem of her skirt dispersed little clouds of dust as she passed. In the drawing room on the first floor she paused to rest her hands on the great slate fireplace. Francine's favourite high-backed chair was gone, as were the rare glass lamps and crystal chandeliers, the heavy velvet hangings and colourful Chinese carpets. On the chimney wall above the mantel shelf was a clean oval patch where her mother's portrait had once hung in its ornately carved and gilded frame. It too was gone, carried away by Herbert Shelley for what it would fetch on the open market. The fabulous gown in the painting had escaped the ransacking of the house only because Anabel, charged with the delicate task of cleaning and repairing it, had kept it in her own room under a cotton dust-sheet. Not even Herbert Shelley would bother to search and rob the room of a simple servant.

From her velvet draw-string purse Leonora lifted her

collection of prized possessions and set them one by one on the slate shelf. Here was the sprig of faded white lilac plucked by Elizabeth on the day of the picnic and perhaps, as Anabel had feared, the harbinger of death. Next came the golden guinea paid to poor Daisy Kimble for her services to a lecherous master, followed by the tiny farthing that had eventually cost Horace Cavendish so dearly. And here was the Earl's heavy silver ring with its lovers' names and unique peacock design, prised from Francine's fingers after her death. And last came the legendary Cavendish sapphire, extravagant souvenir of a past love and now the only possible key to Leonora's own future. These things reminded her that it was a man's world, a world in which the health, wealth and happiness of any woman rested solely upon the whim of the man deemed to be her lord and master. And now she herself, already brought low by the dishonesty of her father, must extricate herself from the Fairfax snare and pit her wits against the powerful Earl of Beresford and his family. She had set herself a daunting task, and in the midst of loss she knew she must find the strength to put aside her grief and fix her sights firmly on the future.

In a moment of weakness she placed her forearms on the shelf, lowered her forehead upon them and sighed: 'Oh Joseph, Joseph, why did you desert me? Why leave me to face all this alone? I need you beside me. Without you I feel I have lost everything ... *everything*.'

It was a cry from the heart, but the sorrow that shaped it was soon spent. Adversity would not defeat her. She was on her way to Beresford Hall to offer the ring and the sapphire to their rightful owner at a high price. She had sold what few pieces of furniture and ornaments remained in the house, plus carpets and curtains, even bed linen and kitchen utensils, and had finally realised the princely sum of two hundred and nineteen pounds, four shillings and eleven pence. Her wardrobe was depleted but sufficient for her immediate needs, and she had Anabel and Sam Cooper to lend support to her resolve. All she needed now was the courage to demand a fair price for what she had to offer, so that she could live modestly as far away from Christopher Fairfax as she could possibly place herself.

'A fair price,' she said aloud, lifting her eyes to the sapphire which, now set in shade and deprived of the light that gave it fire, appeared blue-black instead of cobalt in colouring. 'All I am asking is a fair price.'

You will always have what you truly desire ... but at a price.

The gypsy woman's words suddenly came back to her as clearly as if they had been spoken afresh in that bare and gloomy room.

You will lose much to gain much. An old life for a new life. You will have your heart's desire, but remember there is a price to pay for everything, and you will fall low before you can rise again.

The fine hairs on the nape of Leonora's neck stood on end as she realised how closely the gypsy woman's prophecy echoed what was happening to her now. She took the sapphire to the window and allowed the pale light of dawn to lift its colour from black to a rich purple-blue. It was then, while standing in that empty room with her gaze fixed on the sapphire, that an invisible weight seemed to lift from her shoulders and float away, leaving her stronger, less heavily burdened. It was as if the shattered fragments of her life were ready to slip neatly into place. She had the power to survive the heartache and grasp for herself a better, safer future. All she needed was faith. All she had to do to make it happen was keep her sights firmly fixed on that higher objective and *believe* in herself.

'I will not be beaten,' she said aloud, scooping back into her draw-string bag those symbols of men's dominance over women and her own obstinate desire to turn that principle upon its ugly head. The will to succeed shone from her eyes and her chin lifted instinctively. 'I will *not* be beaten.'

She was reminded that Fortune favours the brave, and that even now, in the midst of sorrow, her dream was still within reach. Her spirits strengthened, she swept from the house without a backward glance and stepped into the first bright morning of her uncertain future.

'As I live and breathe,' she declared, 'I will not be beaten.'

IV

From some considerable distance he watched the hired carriage as it pulled up the winding dirt track from Kingswood village and turned, lurching drunkenly, into the Drive of Oaks. He could see a stocky young man at the reins and two women seated together beneath the open canopy. She had come.

'Lia!'

He spoke her name into the warm August breeze that toyed playfully with his hair and brought the scents of pine and tansy and corn marigold to his nostrils. His mount moved restlessly beneath him and his two huge wolfhounds sniffed the air for the source of their master's excitement. She had come at last, that proud, violet-eyed woman who had touched his heart and stolen away his soul.

'Lia,' he said again. 'Lia.'

Now his big white teeth showed themselves in a broad grin that caused his eyes to twinkle and brought to his swarthy features an almost boyish softness. With a whoop of triumph he reined his horse to the left, heeled its flanks savagely and sent it crashing into the foliage. Lukan de Ville knew this immense forest as any other man might know his own modest garden plot. Every tree and natural landmark, each twist and turn of path or bridle-way was by now so familiar to him that he knew he could intercept the carriage before it had made a full mile along the Drive of Oaks.

Leonora breathed a sigh of relief once they were off the cart track and on to the smooth, four-mile-long drive leading to Beresford Hall. Sam Cooper was doing his best to control the light open carriage and matched pair, but his inexperience left a great deal to be desired. Twice he had almost ditched the near-side wheels by pulling too close to the edge, and at the steep crossroads it had been all she and Anabel could do to remain seated while he wrestled to keep the carriage from turning right over. Now at last they were jogging along at a safe, leisurely pace between ranks of massive oaks resplendent in their full summer foliage.

The main part of their journey from London had been made by public coach in which Leonora had purchased all six interior seats, an extravagance that assured them maximum comfort as well as privacy. On the first night they slept at the Bluebell just outside Oxford, while on the second they enjoyed the hospitality of Stroud's famous Dancing Cockerel, with its fancy stoneware hip-baths and ultra-fashionable water closets. Travelling through the Cotswolds and the Severn Vale had allowed them a feast of spectacular scenery with every mile, from meadows and pastures dotted with wild blossoms to sprawling woodland and brooding, hump-backed hills. They had reached Kingswood in time to refresh themselves with a change of clothes and enjoy a delicious early lunch before setting out on the final, very picturesque leg of their journey.

Like the countryside itself Leonora was dressed in vivid green and gold, with touches of pink and crimson setting off the richer shades. The embroidered rose-buds on her green skirts mimicked the scarlet poppies dotted here and there amid the meadow-grass. Even the perfume she wore was reminiscent of a hot summer day when blossoms surrender their scents to the breeze.

'Are you sure you know what you are doing, child?' Anabel asked yet again.

'Trust me,' Leonora told her, smiling confidently. 'Our fortunes can hardly be worsened by any failure on my part, but if I succeed ... oh, Anabel, if I *succeed* ...'

She left the rest to hang in the air between them. Anabel fell silent. If she could not find it in her heart to trust her young mistress to snatch a secure future for them all, she could at least rely on the simple knowledge that they had nothing left to lose.

At the Royal Oak in Kingswood Leonora had picked up a few interesting snippets of information regarding the 'big house'. The Earl, she discovered, was away from home on a

369

visit to his daughter and her family in Cornwall. In his absence Lady Beresford was entertaining a host of glittering house guests to a week of hunting, fishing, dancing and dining. It was a company of titles, a gathering of gentry from as far afield as Norfolk, Northumberland, Sussex and Devon. A garden party in the fully enclosed inner courtyard this very afternoon would mark the end of their sojourn at Beresford Hall, and by four o'clock the Drive of Oaks would be lined with fancy coaches and carriages bearing their well-to-do occupants homeward. Leonora had welcomed the news with a sly satisfaction. It meant that her arrival at Beresford Hall was to be witnessed by a gathering of seventy or so distinguished men and women before whom she must contrive to make an unforgettable entrance. For a plan so audacious as hers it seemed appropriate that an audience of such unequivocal quality be provided.

Not all the local gossip had proved so agreeable, in particular the news that Lady Elizabeth Cavendish had recently been ill of toxic poisoning of the blood. Leonora had questioned the parlour maid at the inn, a gregarious young woman only too happy to impart what she knew in exchange for a few small coins and a length of satin ribbon.

'She's afflicted, you know,' the parlour maid had begun, tapping her temple and lowering her voice to a conspiratorial whisper. 'Touched in the head, they do say. Won't ever be normal like other folks.'

'Tell me how she became ill,' Leonora had pressed.

'Well, they say as how it's all on account of her being *possessed.*'

'Possessed? Oh really, I never heard such rubbish.'

'Beggin' your pardon, m'am, but 'taint no rubbish to that Lady Beresford. She reckons as how Miss Elizabeth is touched by evil, and the Devil will only be ousted by prayers and a regular thrashing.'

At this point Leonora had lowered her hand-mirror and stared aghast at the plump, spotty face of the parlour maid.

'Good heavens, girl. Are you telling me that Lady Beresford seeks to cure Elizabeth by *beating* her?'

'Oh yes, ma'am. Common knowledge, it is. Everyone knows as how madam whips that poor unfortunate gel something unmerciful when the mood takes 'er.'

'She *whips* her?'

'Yes, ma'am. In the holy chapel under the west wing, right there in front of the sacred altar after special prayers.'

Leonora recalled with horror the marks on Elizabeth's shoulder and her passionate dread of the old chapel.

'But that is *horrible*,' she breathed.

'Aye, an' they do say as how she's forced to strip pure naked and then whipped 'til she drops.'

'My God!' Leonora exclaimed. 'That is barbaric. Does the Earl know about it?'

'Reckon not, ma'am. I reckon as how Miss Elizabeth's too afeared to speak out, and everyone knows as how the Earl will hear no wrong of his Countess.'

'Nor would he allow his daughter to be harmed in that way. He would put a stop to it. He would make sure she was protected from such horrible treatment.'

'I wouldn't know about that, ma'am, but I do know as how poor Miss Elizabeth took a fierce infection in her shoulder after one of these religious whippings and afore you know it she's set to die in her bed of a terrible fever. I reckon some folk might say 'twas the Devil pulled her through, him looking after his own, like. As for me, I think maybe them same folk should be asking themselves which lady has the *real* madness, the young 'un or the old 'un.'

The parlour maid's story had sickened Leonora. That the gentle Elizabeth should be punished because of her affliction was a terrible injustice. That she should be so tormented in the name of religion and at the hands of her own mother was little short of despicable. She had resolved to put an end to the situation without delay. Elizabeth's future protection had now become part of her own Grand Plan.

Now, as the carriage jogged along at a pleasant pace through Beresford's summer paradise, Leonora found there were more immediate things to claim her attention. The hedgerows were alive with glowing colour, from deepest gold

371

to pale yellow, from orange and purple to palest mauve. Here
the holly berries were hard and green, and the mauvy-white
blooms of blackberry thickets promised a record late crop. She
breathed the potpourri of wonderful scents and felt the beauty
of Beresford touch gently upon her hidden feelings of sorrow
and loss. It was a sensation akin to laying fresh flowers on her
mother's grave, sweet and satisfying.

The tranquillity of her mood was shattered when a dark
clad man suddenly appeared from the dense undergrowth. He
stepped into the road with his arms raised, bringing the horses
to a nervous halt. Tall, lean and strikingly handsome, he
grasped the reins of the nearest horse and smiled as he feasted
his eyes on Leonora.

'Lukan!'

'Aye, my lady.'

He had appeared too suddenly for her to prepare herself, so
the heady surge of pleasure she experienced on seeing him
again was clearly evident, stamped like an unbidden
confession on her lovely face. For a long, joyous interval they
held each other with their eyes, savouring the moment,
enjoying afresh the powerful sexual force that sprang between
them. At last Sam Cooper stood up and waved his whip
threateningly in the direction of the intruder.

'Unhand that horse and step aside,' he ordered bravely
'Let us pass, you rogue, for you'll be getting no rich picking
from the likes of us.'

'Quiet, Sam,' Leonora interjected without turning her head
in his direction. 'This is no common highwayman. This is
Lukan de Ville, esquire, keeper of the Earl's woodlands and
forests. He means us no harm.'

'Huh! No harm indeed!' Anabel huffed under her breath.

Lukan clicked his heels and bowed briefly, still holding
Leonora with his gaze. His smile sent a flood of warmth
through her body to settle in a hot flush upon her cheeks and
other, less exposed places. When he stepped toward her she
took his hand without hesitation and, ignoring Anabel's
whispered protestations, allowed him to hand her down from
the carriage. Fires ignited inside her at the touch of his hand

372

on hers, fires that flared to a startling intensity when she found herself standing so close to him that she could almost hear the beating of his heart. With a great effort of will she turned and walked ahead of him to where the road passed over one of the many water courses criss-crossing the land. At the fence she paused to look down at the shimmering trout darting like living gems beneath the surface of the stream. She was aware of him standing at a short distance, watching her so intently that he might have been trying to commit every detail of her features to memory. Somewhere a blackbird warbled and insects hummed a soft accompaniment among sunlit blossoms. The shadow of her parasol fell upon the water and a shimmer of fish moved in its patch of shade.

'I knew you would come, Lia.'

'You could not possibly have known,' she said, but without conviction.

'Aye, and yet I knew, right enough. I knew you would come.'

He stared at her profile, tracing with his gaze the classically beautiful lines of her face, the unexpected brush of lustrous ebony eyelashes, the delicate hollow at the nape of her neck where a stray strand of hair had come to rest, nestling against her pale skin in a dark spiral. He had never seen the like of her. She was quite extraordinarily lovely. She had an untamed quality running in dangerous undercurrents just below the surface, a wild freedom of spirit that found its counterpart in his own hot-blooded gypsy nature. Yet she was undoubtedly a lady, regal and haughty in her bearing and possessing the unconscious, rather arrogant grace of the true thoroughbred. For Lukan de Ville, himself half gypsy and half aristocrat, she represented everything most desirable in a woman.

'You will be mine,' he whispered, covering her hand with his own. 'We both know it. You *will* be mine.'

Leonora thrilled to the sound of his voice, yet the words he used sent a chill coursing along her spine and the touch of his fingers filled her with conflicting emotions. She struggled to free herself from the trance-like state induced by the heat of the day, by the glittering waters of the stream and the

373

intoxicating closeness of this strangely irresistible man.

'Lukan, you must not say such things to me.'

He drew her into his arms and whispered huskily: 'And yet you know it to be so.'

'I am not for you, Lukan de Ville. You must choose elsewhere.'

'Elsewhere? Alas, I fear no woman will ever move me again. My soul has chosen you, my Lia.'

His breath was warm and anise-scented on her face, his closeness heady, intoxicating.

'No!' She drew back, shaking her head. 'No, Lukan. Please let me go at once.'

'Do not fight me, my Lia.' He pulled her roughly against him until her breasts were crushed against the hard muscle of his chest and his face came so close that only a breath of summer air seemed to separate their mouths.

'Kiss me,' he whispered, his lips barely brushing hers.

'Oh, Lukan!' His name was drawn from her on a sigh. She was trembling. She felt the tip of his tongue part her lips for his hot breath to pass through, yet still he kept his mouth from hers by that tantalising fraction of space, while she ached to have him smother it with kisses.

'Kiss me,' he murmured again. 'Kiss me, Lia. Tell me you will be mine. Confess it. You will. You will.'

'Oh, no ... no ...'

'My Lia. My own beautiful Lia.'

'Oh, Lukan, Lukan.'

Suddenly her hands reached up to draw his mouth down to her own, and the contact was like an exquisite explosion somewhere deep inside her. A sob caught in her throat. Her body arched itself against him, seeking the hardness of his sex, aching to draw him into its moist and hungry fires. With a small, triumphant moan he gathered her more closely, more possessively into his arms and returned her kiss with such passion that she felt herself devoured by the potency of it. His tongue sought hers, his hands gripped her hips and drew them forward to meet the bulging hardness of his loins. As his kisses became wilder his words, hoarse and ragged with

374

desire, seemed to drop like fiery nectar into the back of her throat.

'You will be mine, Lia ... mine alone ... *forever*.'

And in her passion she was barely aware that she answered: 'Oh, yes, yes ... forever, Lukan ... *forever*.'

An eternity of excitement later he cupped her face in his hands and looked down at her from eyes that were hooded with emotion. She could see herself reflected in their glittering black irises, a tiny figure looking out from the sensuous prison of his eyes. She felt herself swallowed up by the heady witches' brew produced by his sexual arousal and her own re-awakened desire. Only gradually did she become aware that Anabel was calling her name, as if from very far away, in a high-pitched voice made sharp with anxiety.

'Leonora! Leonora!'

With a small cry of alarm she freed herself from Lukan's embrace, her cheeks burning and her hands trembling. With quick, agitated gestures she smoothed her skirt and plumped up the flattened lace around her bodice. She was confused and humiliated. What had she done? How could she have allowed such a thing to happen? She had let herself be borne away on a tidal wave of passion. She, Leonora Shelley, had succumbed, like some over-heated village wench, to the coercive, compelling force of this gypsy's masculinity. For a brief eternity nothing had existed for her but him. He had drowned her reason with his kisses, playing upon her virgin senses as a master musician plucks the strings of a familiar instrument. He had made her a willing, hungry accomplice to his lusts, and for that she despised him.

'Lia?'

With a shudder of distaste she shook his hand free of her arm and moved away to retrieve her parasol from the hedge where it had fallen.

'Leonora! Leonora!' Anabel's voice reached her ears. The commonplace sound helped douse her inner fires.

'I must go back,' she said curtly.

Once again he reached out to touch her and once again she shrank from him, this time tossing her head and flashing her eyes in fury as she met his stare. He smiled, content in his belief that he had measured the weakness of her character in the strength of her passion.

'There can be no going back, my Lia,' he told her softly.

'There *must* be,' she hissed, pressing the backs of her fingertips to her burning cheeks. Once more she asked herself how she could possibly have allowed such a thing to happen. Had she snatched up the reins of her own life only to hand them over to the first man capable of putting heat in her belly? Had she come this far only to surrender her plans, her dreams, to a man who lived in the forest like a wild animal?

'Don't fight me, Lia,' he said softly, his voice a caress.

She tossed her head again, facing him with all the indignation of one whose innermost secrets had been exposed to the scrutiny of another.

'Oh, but I *will* fight you, Lukan de Ville,' she said angrily. 'I will fight you with every ounce of strength I possess.'

He smiled gently. 'Ah, but in the end you will be mine.'

'Never! *Never*!'

'You cannot avoid your destiny, Lia.'

'Leave me alone. Keep away from me.'

'Lia ...'

'I *hate* you.'

His eyes narrowed into glittering black slits and he stared back at her as if she had struck him a physical blow.

'You cannot mean that,' he said.

She lifted her skirts clear of the ground and glared into his handsome face.

'I mean it, Lukan de Ville,' she told him. 'You will never put your hands on me again. *Never*!'

As she strode away from him he grabbed her wrist in a vicious grip and thrust his face very close to hers. Fury smouldered in his eyes where only a moment ago his passion had shone like dark beacons.

'Do not torment me, woman,' he warned. 'I'll not be made party to your coy games when you know as surely as I do that the two of us were meant for each other. We belong together. One day you will come to me, Lia. You will come to me and I will take you, and from that moment you will be MINE!'

'Never!' she cried. 'Never!'

'Woman, it *will* be so.'

'Never! My God, I would rather *die* than become the bed-mate of a common gypsy!'

With that she twisted free of his grip and strode back along the drive to the waiting carriage. She climbed aboard with Anabel's help and ordered Sam Cooper to whip the horses into a gallop. As they drew level with Lukan de Ville she stared straight ahead, her face still as stone and her sights set on the sombre silhouette of Beresford Hall looming in the distance.

Lukan watched her go, glowering after her from beneath his heavy brows. He had tasted his destiny on her lips. For those endless, timeless moments she had belonged to him, body and soul, but then she had snatched away that brief glimpse of heaven with her cruel taunts.

'Damn you, woman,' he snarled at the diminishing carriage. 'Damn you. *Damn* you!'

V

The letter she had prepared for Lady Beresford was brief and came directly to the point:

> *Madam, if you would avoid a public and very unsavoury scandal you will receive me as friend and relative without delay. This done, your illustrious guests will leave Beresford Hall in complete ignorance of the true purpose of my visit.*

She had sealed the letter with the Earl's ring, pressing the design into the warm wax until a suitably clear impression was attained. Although the result fell short of perfection, Lady Beresford would not fail to recognise the distinctive peacock design taken from the very ring her husband had worn for over twenty years.

Leonora was shown into the main hall, where she was invited to wait while a very tall footman in orange and black livery delivered the note, now neatly placed upon a silver salver, to her ladyship the Countess. Anabel sighed and twisted a silk handkerchief between nervous fingers, awed as much by the grandeur of Beresford Hall as by the enormity of Leonora's intentions. This plan of hers was bold, cunning, dishonest, yet what a marvellous plan it was. She could not decide if poor Francine would have been proud or dismayed by her daughter's determination to use any means available to lift the remnants of her family out of the jaws of poverty.

'Swear it,' Leonora had insisted. 'Swear upon Mama's grave that you will never, *never* repeat what you know to any other living soul. Swear it.'

Anabel had sworn, and now the events had been set in motion that would change their lives and set this spirited, conniving young woman on the road to realising her dreams.

Leonora stared up at the vast, brilliantly lit windows of fifteenth-century stained glass, her face lifted as if in prayer. Then she turned abruptly to check her reflection in one of the great gilt mirrors set at intervals around the hall. Her appearance could not be faulted. She had pulled on a fitted, high-necked jacket of quilted gold satin that hugged her body and accentuated the full swell of her breasts. Over her perfumed gloves she had pushed the Earl's heavy peacock ring, and at her throat the Cavendish Sapphire, nestling darkly against the gold of her jacket, echoed the radiant blue of her eyes.

'Stop me who dares,' she said, smiling at her reflection. She was still glowing with sexual excitement. The encounter with Lukan de Ville had left a sultry brightness in her eyes, a flush of colour across her cheeks and fiery warmth in her blood. Feeling the way she did, vigorous, positive, exhilarated, she believed herself capable of achieving anything.

The lanky footman returned to the hall, his slippers making no more than a whisper of sound on the polished stone floor. He was wearing an old-fashioned powdered wig and white cotton gloves, and the ruffle of white lace at his throat was perfectly laundered and pressed.

'Her Ladyship requests your indulgence and says she will join you here in fifteen minutes,' he told her with a stiff bow.

Leonora watched him cross the hall and vanish through one of the other doors. So, Lady Beresford believed she could keep her guest waiting in the hall for fifteen minutes without so much as an offer of refreshment? She was playing one of her clever social games, designed to reduce the impact of this visit by keeping Leonora firmly in her place and separate from the other guests. This gentle snub was calculated to disarm the visitor by reminding her of her lack of status. It would not have occurred to Lady Beresford that on this occasion her tactic might be equal to wafting a crimson rag in the face of a wild bull.

'Stop me who dares,' she said again, lifting her head proudly. A moment later the big double doors were flung noisily back on their hinges and an imperious, gold-clad Leonora swept into the crowded courtyard.

Her entry was dramatic. Those ancient abbey cloisters were perhaps sixty yards long by thirty-five yards wide, and offered the perfect stage on which a desperate young woman might make her mark upon a world that sought to exclude her. The whole place was ablaze with colour and bright sunlight. Flowers and garlands were everywhere. The waters of the rectangular lily pond, fed by four elaborate Italian fountains, had been dyed a deep royal purple upon whose surface floated the huge lemon and ivory water lilies like lazy dancers in rich green petticoats. The effect was stunning. Tables, chairs and sofas had been placed along the covered walkways so that guests could gather in intimate little groups beneath canopies of hanging flowers. The glass doors of the lower rooms stood open, their foamy lace curtains billowing in the warm breeze. Every guest was like a jewel set against a background of unashamed opulence, each group a tableau representing the pomp and vanity of the privileged classes.

Into this select assembly strode the proud figure of Leonora

Shelley. A hush descended as conversation petered out and every eye turned in her direction. She fixed her own steady gaze on the figure in purple silk seated in the high-backed chair at the opposite end of the cloisters. Head lifted high, she made her way with a purposeful stride to where Lady Alyce, Countess of Beresford, presided over the garden party, the unsealed letter in her hand and an expression of rigid composure on her face. Without exception the guests stepped aside so that Leonora's progress along the paved walkway was unimpaired. She looked neither to left nor to right but kept her gaze fixed firmly on her objective. The merest trace of anxiety brought her gloved hand briefly to her throat. It was a movement completely without premeditation, yet it exerted upon her hostess a subtle blackmail. Lady Alyce half rose from her seat and her lined, oval-shaped face blanched visibly. Even at that distance she recognised first her husband's precious signet ring, then the fabulous Cavendish Sapphire shimmering at the throat of her uninvited guest. The family treasure to which those slender fingers had so slyly drawn attention was unmistakable in its flashing cobalt beauty.

Lady Alyce assessed this new situation and chose her strategy on the instant. This dramatic and very public invasion of her privacy displayed that supreme arrogance only achieved through the acquisition of power. Her instincts warned her that she was under threat. It was quite obvious to her that something had come to light following the death of her husband's mistress, something detrimental to her own well-being. All her deepest, darkest fears lay amongst the ghosts this exquisite creature might well intend to resurrect. She could not, *must* not allow herself to be disadvantaged on her own territory and within sight and hearing of her peers. At all costs, the past must be prevented from raising its dangerous head before seventy witnesses waiting in speculative silence to receive the latest society scandal. Her eyes were hostile and her heart cold, but with a practised smile of acceptance the elderly aristocrat drew herself erect and extended both hands in the warmest of welcomes.

'Leonora, my dear. How charming you look, and how nice

380

that you were able to join us, after all.' As she pressed her dry cheek to Leonora's in greeting she added in a harsh whisper: 'How *dare* you force yourself upon my privacy?'

'Have a care, lady,' Leonora warned, turning her other cheek with a beaming smile. 'Have a care, for I would not hesitate to expose your dirtiest and most intimate family linen to the scrutiny of this illustrious company.'

'You wouldn't dare.'

'Oh no? *Try me,*' Leonora challenged, touching the sapphire with the very finger on which was placed Sir Oscar's ring. She was already scanning the nearest group of people for a familiar face. 'Ah, Lord and Lady Thettersly, how gratifying to see you here. And good day to you, Sir Andrew, I trust Lady Caroline is well? Why, Mr and Mrs Belgrave-Mornay, what a pleasant surprise . . .'

'Leonora! You are most welcome.'

She turned to find herself looking into the grave blue eyes of Malcolm Cavendish. He smiled and took her hand, lifted it to his lips and held it there, watching her.

'Hello, Malcolm.' She held his gaze, sensing his pleasure at seeing her again.

'I was sorry to hear of your mother's death,' he said awkwardly. 'My father has yet to be informed of it, but after his callous treatment of you . . .'

Her smile did not falter, though the unexpected reminder of her recent loss stabbed at her heart. Instead she hooked her arm through his in a possessive gesture and smiled up into his handsome face.

'Please, Malcolm, this is neither the time nor the place to speak of unpleasant things. I bear Sir Oscar no grudge. In fact, I do believe we will become great friends in the near future. And now, my dear, I shall not be content until you have introduced me to all these *wonderful* people.'

Hers was a heady triumph. She found herself skilfully guided from one group to the next, presented and withdrawn by her dashing and attentive escort and, since Malcolm was head of the family in his father's absence, readily accepted by everyone she met. She heard the occasional whisper of

381

speculation: 'Heavily in debt ... father a bankrupt ... mother dead ... quite penniless ...' but for the most part the comments were complimentary.

'Just look at that young woman. She has youth, beauty, good connections and a certain fashionable notoriety.' A foppish young man with a florid face listed Leonora's attributes in a stage-whisper that carried for some distance beyond his immediate group. 'My dear George, what more could a man desire in a woman?'

'A little money?' his companion offered. 'Property? Income?'

'Only if one is looking to *marry* the girl, surely? Personally, I would give my eye teeth to have her as she stands, money or no, though on a purely temporary basis.'

'I should take care not to let such comments reach the ears of Sir Malcolm,' the other warned, mentally measuring the girth of Leonora's tiny waist. 'I'll wager he's in love with that girl.'

When the introductions were finally at an end Malcolm drew her to one of the long, marble-topped tables and handed her a glass of fruit punch containing a large scoop of crushed ice.

'I do believe I am envied by every man present,' he smiled.

'And I by every woman,' Leonora offered, returning the compliment.

'Indeed you are, when your beauty places them all so firmly in the shade,' he said.

She smiled. 'Oh, Malcolm, you are so gallant.'

Just then she caught sight of herself in an angled mirror set to reflect one of the more elaborate flower arrangements. Her cheeks were flushed and her eyes were larger and brighter than she had ever seen them. She had turned every head with her beauty and won every heart with her charm, and the light of her success shone like a beacon in her eyes. Suddenly the voice of Lady Alyce, cold and brittle as ice, cut into her happy thoughts.

'If you will excuse us, Malcolm, my dear, I would like a few words with Leonora in private.'

'Of course, Mother, but only if you promise not to keep her too long.'

He bowed politely, too intent upon his lovely guest to perceive the frosty expression brought to his mother's face by his comment.

Leonora slipped her arm through that of the Countess and led her away, seemingly oblivious to the woman's carefully controlled animosity.

'Lady Beresford,' she said, softly but firmly. 'You will please have rooms prepared for myself and my maid and decent accommodation found for my footman, Sam Cooper. You see, I have no intention of leaving here until Sir Oscar returns, and that, I am informed, will not be until the end of the month.'

'How dare you? How dare you demand my hospitality in that impertinent manner? You burst in here without invitation, monopolise the attentions of my son, ingratiate yourself with my guests ...'

'And more, much more,' Leonora smiled.

'What? What more? What on earth do you *want* with us?'

The two women moved slowly around the outside of the courtyard, arm-in-arm like loving friends, the sour expression of the Countess far outweighed by the laughing, eager face of her vivacious young relative.

'You will know soon enough what my intentions are,' Leonora hissed through her brilliant smile. 'But first let me offer you a few words of advice, Lady Beresford.'

The older woman stiffened.

'Advice? I will hear no advice from you, young woman.'

'Then you would be a very foolish woman, Lady Beresford. First of all you must never, *never* raise your hand to Elizabeth again. You may be assured, madam, that for every slap, every blow you offer her in future I will repay you ten-fold.'

'How dare you?' the older woman hissed, struggling to maintain her composure. 'How *dare* you threaten me?'

'Oh, dear Countess,' Leonora said sweetly, squeezing her arm tightly with both hands. 'You are about to discover that there is precious little I do *not* dare. I wonder if you have noticed that I am wearing your husband's ring *and* the missing

Cavendish Sapphire. Oh yes, it is quite, quite genuine. A family heirloom, I believe, lost over twenty years ago in a robbery here at Beresford.'

'Stolen,' the Countess said hoarsely. 'Taken by thieves. Stolen.'

'Not so, Lady Beresford, I have proof that it was not so. I also have in my possession certain diaries, letters and other documents that could well bring your husband to ruin, should the information they contain be made public.' Her grip on the arm of the Countess became tighter and her voice took on a steely edge. 'And believe me, madam, I am no respecter of this family's standing in society. I would gladly see you all ruined and this ugly mausoleum razed to the ground, so do not think for one moment that any threat of mine is idly voiced.'

The features of the Countess had become chalk-white and her breathing shallow and rapid.

'What is it you want from us?' she asked at last.

'Everything that should have gone to my mother years ago.'

'What? To that Shelley woman, that ... that ...'

'And to her son!'

Now Lady Beresford gasped and clutched at her bosom with trembling fingers. She felt the ghosts of the past begin to claw at her with savage fingers, reopening old wounds and restoring old resentments. She would not have Francine Shelley's bastard acknowledged as her husband's son. Never! All the hidden bitterness inside her rose like fresh bile in her throat, choking her with its foulness. With Leonora's help she lowered herself into her high-backed chair, her breathing laboured and her lips blue-tinged.

'Her son? *Her* son? And what of *my* son,' she demanded in a voice now broken with emotion. 'Will you destroy Malcolm with what you know of his father's past sins?'

Leonora gazed around the courtyard, her eyes at last lighting upon the handsome face of the Beresford heir. He smiled back at her with a special warmth, his expression confirming what she had long suspected.

'Destroy Malcolm?' she echoed, then touched the shimmering sapphire at her throat and stooped to whisper her next words into the ear of the Countess. 'Oh, no, my dear lady, I am not here to harm Malcolm. I intend to *marry* him.'

VI

Alone at last in one of the lavishly furnished guest-rooms on the first floor, Leonora pulled off her hat and tight-fitting jacket and cooled her skin in a scented breeze from the window. She was elated, intoxicated by this total reversal of her fortunes. She had walked into Beresford Hall without right or invitation, and that ancient fortress had once again gathered her into its magical web of mystery and intrigue. She had always known that she belonged within these walls. Now it had come to pass. Somehow she knew in her heart that she was here to stay, that she would never leave Beresford Hall again.

From a casement window set into a corner of the room she could see part of the gate-house and the enclosed main courtyard where many of the visitors' coaches were already being prepared for their homeward journeys. The sight of an open chaise with chestnut horses reminded her of that brief encounter with Lukan de Ville on the road to Beresford Hall. The blood was hot in her veins even before his dark image sprang in vivid detail to her mind. She could still taste that hot and hungry mouth, still feel the big hands on her body and the muscular hardness pushing between her thighs. She ran her hands over the smooth white skin of her neck and breasts and felt the nipples spring alive beneath the fine fabric of her gown. She was experiencing afresh the burning, moist responses of her virgin body and doubting if Malcolm Cavendish, handsome and charming though he was, would ever arouse such an intensity of desire within her. In her heart she yearned to be Malcolm's wife, yet it seemed to her that a man half gypsy and half Devil had already put his claim, his own dark brand, upon her soul.

'Miss Leonora! Miss Leonora!'

Malcolm's raised voice accompanied a frantic knocking at the door of her room. She hurried to open it and was immediately struck by the shocked expression on his face.

'What is it, Malcolm? What on earth has happened?'

'It's my mother. Oh, Leonora, we all thought she was dozing in her chair when all the while she was desperately ill. She must have suffered some kind of seizure about the time you left the courtyard. Can you help? Will you come?'

'Of course I'll come. Did you send for a doctor?' She reached for a shawl and pulled it across her shoulders, running in order to keep pace with him as he strode back along the corridor.

'I sent for Dr Charlesworth, but it's more than an hour's drive and he might not be free to come immediately. I'm not even sure if she should be moved or left in her chair.'

'What about the other guests?'

'Some have gone, the others are all preparing to leave. The cloisters are clear now except for a few servants. Oh, Leonora, she looks so ill.'

They arrived at the courtyard to find the Countess sitting in her chair exactly as Leonora had seen her last; eyes staring straight ahead, hands clutched to her heart, face ashen and slightly twisted as if in a grimace of pain. One side of her body appeared to be lifeless, the other stiff and rigid, and when she tried to speak the words became a meaningless gurgle in the back of her throat. Leonora immediately assumed full charge of the situation, giving her commands in authoritative tones that brooked no argument.

'The Countess is to be carried in her chair to her room immediately. Once there, soft pillows are to be placed at her feet and back. She must be covered with a warm quilt and kept quiet and comfortable until the doctor arrives. Give her nothing to eat or drink, not even water, and certainly no medicines or powders. Nothing must pass her lips until the doctor has examined her. If her throat is blocked she may choke to death on someone's good intentions. You, there! Help the others. Careful, now. Lift the chair very, very gently

Wait, let me cover her shoulders with my shawl.'

She turned to Malcolm with a reassuring smile and dared to lay her hand on his arm in a caring, very intimate gesture.

'Try not to worry, Malcolm,' she told him softly.

'Thank heaven you were here,' he said, raking his fingers through his hair in a distracted manner. 'I felt so helpless. I just didn't know what to do.'

'That's all right, Malcolm. I'm here now and I'll do everything I can to help her. I will sit with her day and night, if need be, until this crisis is safely over.'

'Bless you, Leonora.'

'I must go now, your mother needs me.'

She hurried from the courtyard on the heels of those servants who bore the Countess Alyce aloft like a granite statue on a carved wooden throne. It was a strange procession that made slow and cautious progress across the sunlit main hall to the east wing where the Countess had her rooms. For Leonora this seizure came as the perfect finish to a wonderfully rewarding day. She would benefit enormously from so timely a drama. By the time she had finished nursing, organising, sacrificing and giving orders, she would be so well established at Beresford Hall that nothing, not even the cast-iron will of that embittered old woman, would be capable of dislodging her.

CHAPTER FOURTEEN

I

For Lady Alyce those weeks following the dramatic arrival of Leonora Shelley were a nightmare. Unable to move, unable even to make herself understood, she could only watch helplessly from her sick-bed while the daughter of her husband's whore cunningly and systematically usurped her position as Mistress of Beresford. They were all in it together, all part of the same wicked conspiracy. She could hear them in the next room, whispering and scheming, their voices never more than a fuzzy, ominous blur on the periphery of her hearing. Those miserable servants who looked to her for the food in their bellies and the clothes on their backs, disobedient, untrustworthy creatures that they were, had always secretly reviled her. Not one of them would weep to see her deposed. Not one of them would care a jot if their rightful mistress was found poisoned or choked to death in her bed. Her own son Malcolm, still wounded by the ugliness of his wife's death, lacked the stomach to approach any closer than the sick-room door. It would never occur to him to question the Shelley woman's constant demonstrations of saintly devotion. And there was Elizabeth, that foolish girl, creeping into the room to peer like a round-eyed imbecile into her mother's frozen features. They were all part of it; all guilty of falling under the spell of that auburn haired, purple-eyed witch.

'You will pay dearly for this,' she tried to warn them through her fixed stare. 'God help me, you will pay the price for what you have done to me.'

Nobody heard her inner cries, not even Gilbert, who had dared to sit beside her couch and bare his soul in the most sickeningly unmanly fashion. He, too, had fallen beneath the intruder's spell, bewitched by her devil's eyes and strumpet's body, only to discover that she aspired to higher pickings than the youngest and poorest of the Earl's sons. She would have the heir. Damn her, she would have the heir, the Hall, the lands, the titles, *everything*. And while Gilbert slunk away to lick his wounds on a relative's isolated estate in Scotland, his father's absence, his mother's seizure and his brother's blindness gave the witch a free hand with which to gather in her ill-gotten gains.

While her body remained a petrified shell no longer subject to her control, the mind of Lady Beresford slowly emerged from a state of confusion to a new clarity. At first she had believed herself to be mortally stricken. The witch had assaulted her in some vile way, pricked her into a seizure right there in the presence of seventy guests and a host of watchful servants. Then she had swept haughtily on her way, leaving her victim pinned helplessly in a chair with her chest constricted by invisible steel bands and all the life-giving air snatched from her lungs. For a terrible eternity Lady Beresford had seemed to hover between life and death, until the crushing pressure had released itself in a wave of hot, white light that flooded from inside her head to cause her whole being to writhe and shrink inwards upon itself. There had been no pain, only a fading, a relinquishing of the power to control familiar nerves and limbs and senses.

She remembered that they had borne her aloft in her carved armchair toward the great cathedral windows, where the brilliance of light and colour had made her fear that she was being carried into the very presence of God Almighty. And since then she had lain motionless in her bed, a defenceless old woman struck down by witchcraft, ignored by her servants and abandoned by her family. But hers would be the final victory, for she would beat them all when Oscar came. Oscar would know what to do. He would place his ear close to her lips and so discover that her powers of speech had not been destroyed, only reduced to a laboured, barely audible whisper. Oh yes, she would expose them all when Oscar came. She would tell him the truth and have the witch expelled from Beresford along with her growing entourage of admirers. Trapped within her paralysed body, deprived of authority and robbed of all dignity, Lady Beresford forced her mind to focus upon one thing: *revenge*. It became her only comfort during those interminable hours of isolation, sustaining her, keeping her sane.

It was a hazy day, quiet and still but for the hum of busy insects among the flower beds and the occasional cry of a bird as it circled high above the gardens. Leonora sat with her shoulders resting against the ivy-clad wall of the upper terrace, her eyes closed, her face lifted into the faintest breath of a breeze. She was wearing a very feminine dress of delicate white muslin over pale grey silk. Her pretty bonnet was held in place by a wide band of embroidered muslin loosely knotted under her chin, its ends left hanging so that they moved in the breeze. Although her haughty manner and often bold stare marked her as strong of character there was also a softness about her, an elusive gentleness that declared her to be as fragile and vulnerable as a summer flower. She was a woman of shifting moods and subtle contradictions, and while her physical beauty first arrested the attention, it was this spectrum, this baffling, indefinable quality that held the beholder captive.

On the bench beside Leonora sat Elizabeth, her bonnet

askance and her head propped at an awkward angle as she dozed in the warm afternoon. Across from them, in a chair set squarely in the shade of an ornamental orange tree, sat Malcolm Cavendish, book in hand, long legs outstretched and elegantly crossed at the ankles. The hot sun had bleached several pale streaks into his brown hair, narrow bands of golden blond so neatly placed they might have been put there with an artist's brush. He had been reading for several minutes, but now he lowered his book so that it rested, forgotten, in his lap. His eyes fixed themselves on Leonora, their expression soft, adoring. There were times when, believing himself unobserved, he gazed at her with all the quiet longing of a man who loves deeply but with small hope of ever possessing the object of his desire. At these times the will of his father and the responsibility of his inheritance weighed heavily upon him.

'Already the minx has enchanted him,' Anabel thought with a sigh. 'I do believe she is halfway to realising that impossible dream of hers.'

Anabel had shifted her own chair to a discreet distance to allow an impression of intimacy between the two young people. She guessed that Leonora was not, as she pretended to be, unaware of Malcolm's scrutiny. In the two and a half weeks since that eventful garden party, Anabel had watched this solemn, very proper young man become increasingly ensnared in a subtle web of Leonora's weaving. Barely a smile or a word passed from her to him without contrivance. Each turn of her lovely head, every flash of her black-lashed eyes was carefully calculated to delight, to amuse, to captivate this unsuspecting heir of Beresford. Not even here, in this warm, idyllic setting, did she dare rest from her labours and simply enjoy the pleasures of the moment for their own sake. She was a true Cavendish, and with that special tenacity peculiar to her breed, she had set her heart upon the prize and become single-minded in the winning of it.

Anabel had a tremendous amount of admiration for her young mistress. Leonora was no more than a girl, yet she rose to every challenge and opportunity in spite of the many shocks and griefs that had lowered her spirits in recent weeks. She had somehow managed to infiltrate the very fabric of the household with her enormous reserves of charm. Just as all those people of quality and breeding had instinctively made way for her when she swept like royalty into the crowded garden party, so the residents of Beresford Hall had willingly deferred to her forceful personality. During the absence of the Earl and the incapacity of his Countess, Leonora had cleverly succeeded in her objective: to make herself indispensable to the scheme of things at Beresford Hall.

'I have them eating out of my hand like so many tame birds,' she had boasted, and Anabel, though cautious in her praise, had been forced to admit the truth in her conceit.

In complete contrast to this success, Leonora's efforts to reunite her family had so far met with nothing but disappointment. There was still no news of Joseph, despite the fact that he and his ungainly canine companion would present a conspicuous twosome wherever they travelled. Then word reached them from the city that in early August Lady Louisa, only daughter of the late Lord Fenwick of Tewkesbury, had secretly departed from her home to join her lover, Jonathan, in voluntary exile. Taking only her jewel casket and a few other personal belongings, she had crept away during the night and thence vanished without trace, obviously preferring an uncertain life with the man she loved to a secure future without him. The elopement dashed all hopes Leonora had entertained of establishing a link between herself and Jonathan once he made contact with Louisa. With the girl he loved now by his side, and possessing no other friend worthy of his trust, he might well travel half the world before allowing his whereabouts to become known. This observation left Leonora frustrated in her efforts and angry with herself for not having had the foresight to include Louisa Fenwick in her plans. It grieved her to be separated from those she loved. There were times when Anabel saw that grief in her eyes, or encountered a locked door and knew that her young mistress wept in the privacy of her room.

Tears, however, did nothing to dull the keen edge of

Leonora's ambition. Too shrewd to overlook even the smallest opportunity to capitalise on a set-back, she wrote immediately to Lady Fenwick expressing her regrets and promising every assistance in locating the runaways. In a letter deliberately worded so as to fuel the fires of society gossip, she supposed her brother's intentions toward Lady Louisa to be above reproach and hoped that the Dowager Duchess might visit Beresford Hall for tea on Monday, September first, at two-thirty in the afternoon:

> It is Lady Beresford's express desire that the tea-party already arranged for that date continue as planned [she had written]. And there is every reason to hope that Her Ladyship will be sufficiently recovered in health to receive and entertain her guests in person.

Such an invitation, signed by a penniless relative yet seemingly issued on behalf of the Countess and bearing her distinctive personal seal, could hardly be ignored by anyone wishing to remain on that lady's very exclusive guest-list. Burning curiosity and strict protocol made such an irresistible combination that Lady Fenwick's hasty acceptance was but the first of many to arrive at the Hall in the following weeks.

'A brilliant stratagem, though I say it myself,' Leonora had beamed at the time. 'And if Sir Oscar can be home in time, his presence will fully endorse my success. They are all simply *bursting* with curiosity and are obliged to accept my overtures or risk offending the Earl and Countess. I must add the name of Caroline Rainer to the guest-list, just to make absolutely certain that no detail worthy of attention is over-looked. Oh, Anabel, such a gathering will be the making of me. I will be the perfect hostess, in full charge of all the arrangements and escorted by the Earl of Beresford *and* his heir. I will conduct myself as nothing less than Mistress of Beresford, and *then* we shall see how tongues will wag in those fancy London clubs and drawing rooms.'

Now the tea-party was only twelve days away and a grateful Malcolm was content to sit back and leave his capable young guest in complete control. Leonora could already taste her triumph. For her it would be the jewel amongst a cluster of minor victories when it was assumed, by all those important, distinguished pillars of society, that she and Malcolm were secretly in love. It would take little more than a clever hint, a shy smile, a certain look, for the gossips to link their names in a flurry of rumour and speculation. After that there would be no stopping her.

Anabel glanced up, squinting at the others from beneath the rim of her bonnet. She saw that while Elizabeth was still sound asleep, Leonora's eyes were now open and she was staring up at the fire-blackened stones of the west wing's enormous tower. She sighed provocatively, her thoughts concealed behind a small, mysterious smile. Sir Malcolm leaned forward in his chair to brush away a wasp that hovered lazily in the air close to her forearm.

'Tell me your thoughts,' he said softly. 'What is it that can bring such an enigmatic smile to your lips?'

Anabel feigned sleep and listened closely for Leonora's artful reply.

'Oh, I couldn't possibly reveal my thoughts to you, Malcolm,' she breathed. 'This is but a little game I sometimes play for my own amusement. Foolish make-believe, nothing more.'

'I cannot imagine that your thoughts are ever foolish or frivolous,' he told her.

'You are very gracious,' she smiled, 'but in this particular case I must confess that they are both.'

'Even so, I would like to share them.'

'Well, I suppose I might,' she began brightly, drawing him on only to stop him short with a firm shake of her head. 'Oh, no, I can't, Malcolm. I really shouldn't speak such thoughts aloud, not to *you.*'

'Not even if I promise not to laugh at you or think you foolish?'

'Do you promise?' She leaned forward, her eyes wide and urgent, her voice lowered to a whisper. 'Do you truly promise?' She was inviting him to share her secrets, tempting him into her confidence. It was all part of the game, just one more tactic in her far-reaching design.

'You have my word,' he agreed with a grin, leaning toward her as he placed both hands over his heart. 'You have my solemn oath as a gentleman.'

'Very well, I will confess all,' she smiled. Then she sighed again and gazed about her with a wistful expression on her lovely face. 'I was merely thinking that if *I* were mistress here, I would move Lady Alyce's private apartments to this side of the house, to the west wing. I would have the gate-house converted especially for her use, with a patio leading out to the rose gardens and at least two of the existing windows enlarged so that she can enjoy the forest views and the spectacular autumn and winter sunsets.'

'Ah, but how would all this please my mother?'

'Oh, tremendously, Malcolm. And it would give me such pleasure to see that dear, dear lady have her heart's desire.'

'But she has always seemed content with things exactly as they are. Indeed, her present apartments are quite the most spacious and luxurious in the entire house. How could you be sure that she would welcome such drastic changes as you propose?' He asked the question doubtfully, still gazing into her happy, animated features.

'Why, because she spoke to me on that very subject while we were walking together in the courtyard only minutes before she was taken ill at the garden party,' Leonora lied with ease. 'Oh, Malcolm, if I were mistress here I would see to it that the poor, dear lady was housed just over there in the gate-house, close to her beloved little private chapel. And then I would ... oh dear, I do beg your pardon ...'

He was watching her intently, delighting in the excitement in her eyes and the brightness lighting her face as she spoke.

'No, don't stop now,' he urged. 'Please continue, Leonora. What other changes would you wish to make if you were ... if it were within your power to alter things?'

'Well, I would certainly re-open the tower,' she exclaimed. 'I would order the best local craftsmen to tear out or make good all the charred beams and supports, lay new floors, repair the old staircase and make the ancient turrets safe again. Then every Cavendish who wished to do so could stand at the very top and view the earldom in its entirety, just as our ancestor, Sir Joshua, first intended.'

'And?' he prompted, quite taken by her enthusiasm.

'And if I were mistress here I would extend the Cavendish stables to include the finest, rarest stock in the whole of Europe.'

'And?'

'And if I were mistress here I would have peacocks on the terraces, proud, glorious peacocks fit to grace the lawns of princes.'

'And?'

'And if I were mistress here I would ask you to ... to ...'

She halted abruptly, allowing her words to hang on the warm air like a challenge, reminding him that he, too, was part of her day-dream. Then she began to dust down her dress rather hurriedly with the backs of her fingertips, ostensibly to conceal a sudden rush of embarrassment. At this point Elizabeth awoke with a start and proceeded to make a great fuss over the two plump ants found investigating the toes of her satin slippers. As if welcoming the distraction, Leonora shyly lowered her head so that her face was completely hidden beneath the rim of her hat.

'Why, the clever little minx,' Anabel thought to herself, still feigning sleep in her shaded wicker chair. 'If she were mistress here, indeed! She's planting seeds, that's what she's doing deliberately and wilfully planting seeds in that young man's heart so that she can sit back and wait for them to grow. And if I'm not mistaken she'll have her way. She'll trap him with her guileful ways and she *will* be mistress here.'

A few minutes later Leonora excused herself, begging the others to continue to enjoy the sunshine while she returned to her duties at Lady Beresford's bedside. Malcolm took her hand and brought it to his lips.

'You have given me much food for thought,' he told her.

'Have I?' she answered sweetly.

'Indeed you have. There was something else, something

396

you would ask of me if your day-dreams became reality. What was it? What were you about to say?'

'It was nothing,' she answered, lowering her eyes.

'Then I will not press you on the matter. Will you ride with me tomorrow, in the early morning?'

She looked up with a vivid smile. 'Oh Malcolm, I would *love* to ride with you.' Her smile faded abruptly as a sobering thought occurred to her. 'But how can I ride with you, much as I would welcome the opportunity? I cannot possibly leave the Countess alone. She *needs* me.'

'You must allow Anabel or the nurse to sit with her for an hour or two. Think of yourself occasionally, Leonora. You cannot remain cooped up in that sick-room, day and night, for the duration of Mother's illness. You need time away from the bedside if you are to maintain your own good health.'

'Well,' she offered doubtfully, 'it would be wonderful to ride again after all these weeks, and if you are sure it will be all right ...?'

'I insist upon it,' he said, kissing her hand again.

She smiled happily. 'Then how could I possibly refuse?'

'How indeed, my dear Leonora? Until tomorrow, then?'

'Tomorrow,' she smiled into his eyes, certain of her conquest. 'Tomorrow.'

And then she was gone, hastening across the lush green turf of the upper lawn, her dress shimmering silvery-white and soft as gossamer in the breeze and the ends of her muslin scarf streaming out behind her. Her step was light as she hurried toward the far side of the house where Lady Alyce, having been given a double dose of laudanum to which a few extra drops of tincture of opium had been added, slept soundly under the less than watchful eye of a local woman hired as nurse. Leonora grinned wickedly to herself. She was sure now that Malcolm was in love with her. Like Joshua Cavendish before her she had angled for her heart's desire and soon the prize, that same earldom of Beresford, would be safely landed. It mattered not a jot that the Countess might survive her crippling seizure. Everyone was aware of how devotedly, how tirelessly she had nursed the old lady through her illness.

Should the patient recover only to slander her saviour with wicked lies, nobody would doubt but that the paralysis had addled her senses. The only remaining obstruction to her plans was the Earl himself. Having been informed by Malcolm that Lady Beresford was in no immediate danger, he was not due to return from Cornwall until the end of the month. Until then the field was hers. She had another twelve days in which to secure for herself a permanent position, both at Beresford Hall and in Malcolm's affections.

'He loves me, he loves me not,' she sang as she ran lightly across the grass. 'He loves me, he loves me not, he loves me ...'

She and Malcolm met at dawn, when a pale mist hung over the ground, hugging every dip and hollow so that the land appeared flat and the trees of the forest rose like dewy ghosts out of the vaporous breath of morning. They rode for over an hour, kicking their mounts into a gallop from time to time for the sheer exhilaration of riding fast and hard across the open countryside. At a small brook they rested to allow the horses to quench their thirst, but soon they were off again, cantering as far as the forest's edge and back via the primitive wooden bridge that spanned the tumbling, rock-strewn waters of Monk's Crossing. From there they could see the morning sun shrinking the mists over the Welsh peaks and lighting upon the shadowy, slate-grey outline of the Cotswold hills. Between the two ran the glittering River Wye, half-Welsh, half-English, drunkenly dissecting the land as it reeled away into the green distance.

'Magnificent,' Leonora breathed, quite intoxicated by the sight. 'Truly magnificent.'

And Malcolm, seeing little beyond the vital, vivacious beauty of his riding companion, echoed her words with a full heart.

It was then Leonora spotted the eerie figure of a lone rider moving toward them from the swirling ribbon of grey mist still clinging to the skirts of the forest. It was a tall, dark man riding a spirited grey and white stallion. He moved with an easy grace, at one with his half-tame mount as he bore down upon them from out of the mist. Leonora's heart gave a sickening lurch as she recognised the rider. It was Lukan de Ville.

She could feel his seductive power reach out across the meadow to caress her senses, and she realised with a jolt that she must avoid him at all costs. On the spur of the moment she reined her mount in the direction of Beresford and urged it into a full gallop, ignoring Malcolm's cry of surprise as she rode away from the intruder as if the devil himself were snapping at her heels. She rode recklessly, jumping fences and streams as if caring nothing at all for her own safety. When at last she reached the stables she jumped down unaided, handed her perspiring horse to one of the waiting grooms and hurried into the house. For the moment at least, she had managed to avoid a confrontation with the only man who posed any serious threat to her purpose. It she was to motivate Malcolm into proposing marriage, she must not allow him to see the devastating effect that gypsy had on her.

From that day on they rode each day at dawn. Sometimes they walked together across a meadow or a cornfield, their horses on the outside, their heads bent in conversation, their fingers making occasional shy contact. Often they sat beside the river in companionable silence to watch the sunrise, or else they raced their mounts impetuously along the Drive of Oaks in response to a childish wager. But always Leonora headed for home at the first glimpse of the gypsy ranger or the two loping, voiceless wolfhounds who rarely wandered far from his sight.

'Leonora, why are you so determined to avoid Lukan?'

Malcolm asked the question following one of her mad gallops back to the stables.

'Would you have the gypsy join us, then?' she countered.

'Gypsy he might be, but he saved your life at the fair, when Starlight Warrior might have trampled you to death.'

'Yes, and for that he was amply rewarded.'

Malcolm sighed. 'Lukan is also my closest friend, and as honourable a man as you are likely to find in the whole county. Sooner or later you will have to speak to him, Leonora.'

'Then let it be later, rather than sooner,' she smiled, 'because our times together are maddeningly short and I value them too highly to have them spoiled by *anyone*, even your friend Lukan.'

The instant the words were out she clamped a hand to her mouth and stared up at him as if stunned by her own outburst. When she made as if to walk away he caught her arm in a gentle but firm grip and smiled into her eyes.

'Is that the truth, Leonora? Have our morning rides become so important to you?'

'No ... that is ... oh, Malcolm, I am too outspoken. I should never have said such a thing to you.'

'But is it true?'

She nodded and coyly averted her gaze, then suddenly looked up at him with her eyes wide and bright, as if brimming with unshed tears.

'It is foolish of me to even entertain such feelings,' she cried. 'Soon enough your father will return and put an end to our simple pleasures. He will not take kindly to seeing his eldest son squander time and energy on a *poor relation*.'

She was far from surprised when he drew her into his arms and kissed her, pressing his mouth to hers with a gentle passion. She returned his kiss with genuine warmth, finding her heart stirred by his quiet strength, his tender sincerity.

'I love you,' he murmured against her lips. 'I love you more than I ever believed myself capable of loving anyone. I want to marry you, Leonora. I want you to be my wife.'

'Oh, my dear,' she whispered, feeling her body become warm and yielding as she enjoyed the unexpected pleasure of his kiss. 'Oh, Malcolm, if only it could be so simple. If only ...'

'My love, my dearest Leonora.' He cupped her face in his hands and kissed her cheeks, her eyes, her mouth. His fingers trembled against her skin. He held her as if she were fine porcelain to be handled with a delicate touch.

'My dear, we mustn't,' she whispered.

'Will you marry me, Leonora?'

'Oh, Malcolm, you forget that I am penniless.'

'I forget nothing,' he said, kissing her again. 'Will you? Will you marry me?'

'But how? What of your father? What of your family?' She spoke passionately, knowing that all her hopes and dreams may hang upon this single conversation. 'Oh, Malcolm, Malcolm, if only it could be so!'

'Just say the word and I will *make* it so.'

'Oh, my dear . . .'

'Do you love me, Leonora? Will you be my wife?'

'Yes, Malcolm. Oh, yes, *yes*!'

She sighed and drew his mouth down to her parted lips so that she could breathe a hotter, more urgent passion into him.

Later, in the privacy of her room, she pressed her fingers to her burning cheeks and laughed aloud at her reflection in the mirror. It was done. At last the heir of Beresford had openly declared his love for her. They were to be married! Leonora Shelley, penniless daughter of a wastrel and scoundrel, was to become the next Countess of Beresford. And not all her feelings were of a mercenary nature, for at that moment she happily acknowledged that, despite the handsome gypsy's strange hold over her senses, she was more than a little in love with her future husband.

II

At Leonora's suggestion the guests began to arrive on the thirty-first, so that she and Malcolm were firmly established as host and hostess by the time Sir Oscar reached Beresford on the morning of the first of September. Rumours were rife concerning the lovely young woman who had moved herself into the Hall to nurse the old Countess through her illness. Even in London, where the Earl had stayed over for two nights with his friend Sir Giles Powell, word was out that Leonora Shelley, already being tipped as the next season's leading lady of society, had won the heart of the widowed heir of Beresford.

The stories disturbed him, not least because the match was so popular that several high-ranking individuals had already delivered their compliments to his London home. There was much speculation in the better clubs and drawing rooms as to which names would appear on the forthcoming list of wedding invitations. It was a foregone conclusion, as far as London society was concerned, that the two would soon marry.

The idea of a love-match between one of his sons and the daughter of Herbert Shelley did not appeal to Sir Oscar in the slightest. He recalled his rage and indignation when Shelley had once dared to suggest that such a thing might be possible. The prospect of her now becoming the bride of his heir, the mother of Malcolm's children, filled him with misgivings. Not even for Francine's sake could he welcome the tainting of the noble Cavendish line with Shelley blood.

Oakwood Lodge had been made ready for the Earl's return, with flowers placed in every room and a splendid selection of food laid out beneath a crisp white cloth on the massive dining room table. Port and brandy had been brought from the cellar along with several bottles of his favourite wine. After bathing and changing into fresh clothes, he found himself drawn from room to room in search of the bitter-sweet ghosts of his past. Two days earlier he had been told of Francine's death. She had finally succumbed to the ravages of illness while he was nursing his own private hurts on the Cornish coast. The brief note informing him of the funeral arrangements had lain, still sealed inside its neat white envelope, at his London house for a whole month. She was dead, yet if he closed his eyes he fancied he could still hear her pretty laughter or catch the last echo of a tune from her piano. In her favourite upstairs bedroom he stood at the long window just as he had done on their last meeting, that warm summer day only a few short weeks ago yet already a memory, sinking with a million others into the past. Now the big bed was empty, its mattress covered by a yellow satin quilt with a shimmering fringe. It pained him to recall how frail she had seemed then, her body wasting away with disease while he, still loving her yet insanely, blindly jealous of her loyalty to the man she had married, had stood at a distance and offered her scant comfort. And now his precious Francine was gone, lost to him forever. The only woman he had ever loved had slipped quietly away, leaving him no time to learn the truth and come to her in shame and contrition, begging forgiveness. How had it come to this? That they had loved for a lifetime, only to be separated at the end by anger and suspicion, was enough to break a man's heart. The waste, the brutality of that would haunt him for the rest of his life.

'Sir Oscar?'

He turned to find Francine's eldest daughter standing in the doorway, surveying him with her dark, oddly tinted eyes. As always he was momentarily taken aback by the sheer magnetism of her presence. She was dressed in a riding habit of ruby-red velvet, and in that room of pastel shades and gentle memories she was a vibrant, colourful reminder that life continues with its own unstoppable forces. He was reminded that hers was a dangerous beauty. She had the power to move a man's heart, or his loins, on the instant, to touch upon his vulnerability with a flash of those dark Cavendish eyes. This daughter of his lost love had captivated his entire household and intoxicated his son with her special magnetism. For Francine's sake he wanted to believe her innocent, yet in his heart of hearts he wondered if such beauty could ever be without guile.

'Welcome home, My Lord.'

She held his gaze as she sank gracefully into a deep curtsy, from which she rose in a single smooth movement. Then his eye was drawn to the cobalt gem at her throat: the Cavendish Sapphire. *Francine's* sapphire. His scalp prickled with a brief sense of foreboding. He turned his gaze from hers with some effort, reached for a bottle and splashed brandy into a stemmed glass. He felt suddenly exposed.

'It seems I am in your debt, Miss Shelley,' he said at last. 'You have nursed my dear wife through the worst of her illness and seen to the running of my household during this unhappy period. Indeed, I believe Lady Beresford may have choked to death but for your timely intervention.'

Leonora smiled and said: 'I merely protected her from the good intentions of those who might seek to revive her with medicines or strong drink while her throat was in spasm. And, of course, I remained at her bedside while I feared she might choke for want of a regular clearing of the throat.'

'You are too modest, young lady. I have spoken to Dr Wainwright and to his assistant, Dr Grantham. Both speak very highly of your dedication. They tell me you attend my wife night and day, with little care for your own comforts.'

'I do what I can, Sir Oscar. After all, when I was all but destitute Lady Beresford received me into her heart and into her home. She gave me leave to make use of her clothes and jewellery, introduced me to her closest friends, accepted me into her family. I seek only to repay her many kindnesses.'

'Quite. Quite.'

Sir Oscar scowled as he sipped his brandy. The liquid was hot and sharp against the back of his throat. It burned its way into his stomach to remind him that he had not eaten for several hours. Looking back at Leonora, with her challenging stare and quietly determined manner, he could not begin to guess his wife's motives for welcoming her so readily into their home.

'About our last meeting . . .'

'You were harsh,' she cut in. 'But now you have discovered that my mother really *was* duped into signing those papers. Now you know she did not betray you.'

'You are very sure of yourself, Miss Shelley.'

'Yes I am, because I happen to know she loved you very deeply, and I believe you loved her in return. You must have made it your first concern to uncover the truth concerning my father's affairs.'

'I have,' he said softly.

'And are you now convinced that she was innocent of any conspiracy to defraud, especially against yourself?'

'I am.'

Leonora was tempted to remind him that the knowledge came too late to help Francine or ease her heartache. Instead she tilted her chin a little and said: 'My mother loved you to the end, Sir Oscar, even though you left her to die all alone.'

'Alone?'

'Yes, quite alone. She died clutching the ring that had been her gift to you on your secret betrothal, all those years ago.'

'Alone? Francine died alone?'

He repeated the words in a whisper, neither wanting nor expecting any reply, then seated himself wearily in the nearest chair. His face had drained of colour and his shoulders, still broad and well-muscled, had sagged visibly under the burden of his thoughts. Leonora stepped forward to place a small bundle of papers on the table before him. She saw that a few drops of brandy, spilled from the glass that hung forgotten from his fingers, had stained the velvet-covered foot-stool set close to his chair. Her words had struck him like a blow, but she had no regrets. She wanted him to suffer.

'There was something Mama wanted you to know,' she told him. 'Something she would have told you herself, had you come to her before she died.'

'I couldn't ... I thought ...'

There was anguish in his voice and a bleakness in his eyes that almost moved her to pity. He had loved her mother, of that she was certain.

'I will wait downstairs in the music room.' She moved to the door, hesitated, turned to see him reaching for the small bundle of letters. 'Sir Oscar?'

'Yes?'

'My mother sacrificed a great deal on your behalf.'

'I know, I know that.'

'You abandoned her, and yet she kept faith with you and preserved the secret you shared, right to the end. I am still the only person who knows what is in those letters.'

'Then I am once again indebted to you.'

'Oh yes, Sir Oscar, I do believe there is a debt outstanding. It is a debt of love, a great wrong that may yet be put right.'

She closed the door very quietly behind her and went downstairs to the sunlit music room where Francine's piano stood before the window. She lifted the lid, settled herself on the stool and began to play, and soon her thoughts wandered out to the little pathway just beyond the back gate, to the elder tree and the dark, whispering woodland beyond. As her fingers skimmed delicately over the keys she smelled again those wonderful forest scents and felt the presence of a strange man in the darkness, a man grasping her, lifting her from danger, holding her until she breathed his minted breath and felt herself become a part of him.

'Lukan. Lukan.'

Her hands stilled above the piano keys, then sank like pale, forgotten flowers into her lap. The smallest thoughts of him could fill her with a burning passion or a dull ache, a raging fire or a sense of longing so acute that only by saying his name out loud could she bear the weight of it.

'Lukan,' she whispered again. 'Lukan.'

Then she lowered the lid of the piano, rose to her feet and left the room.

Upstairs in the pink bedroom Sir Oscar allowed the last of Francine's letters to fall from his trembling fingers and lie with its scattered companions on the carpet. He had known. Long before the boy had grown to bear such a close resemblance to himself, long before he had assumed full financial responsibility for his education, he had known the unspoken truth. In his heart he had always suspected that Francine had been carrying his child when she rushed into that ill-fated marriage with Herbert Shelley. Yet despite this inner knowledge the stark reality of her written confession left him devastated. She had given him a son. Jonathan was his son. She had, after all, left something of herself for him to cherish, to hold on to, now that she was gone.

He did not hear Leonora enter the room, nor was he aware of the silky swish of her skirts or the scent of her perfume as she approached the chair in which he was now slumped. One moment he was alone, the next his head was cushioned upon her softness and his hot tears were darkening the bodice of her gown. Held thus to the bosom of this enigmatic young woman, this daughter of Francine and sister of his unacknowledged son, he allowed grief and regrets to overwhelm him and he wept without shame.

'No good will come of it,' Anabel said, after pressing Leonora for every detail of the meeting. 'You know his secrets. You have seen a proud and powerful man at his very lowest, his least manly.'

'Oh, do stop fussing, Anabel, and help me into this gown. I must be there to greet him, at Malcolm's side, when he arrives at the Hall. Is everyone ready? What about Lord Mornington and Sir Ralph Marr and their party? Are they back from their ride?'

Anabel nodded and pulled the buckle of Leonora's belt a notch tighter in order to emphasise her tiny waist.

'Everyone is here, just as you planned,' she said. 'And the Earl is due in twenty minutes. We can rely on him to be prompt, I do believe.'

'And Lady Beresford?'

'All spruced up and ready. Flowers everywhere, hair washed and dressed, shawl in place, face powdered. Don't worry, one look at her and he will be convinced that you are the finest nurse in all Christendom.'

'Then why are you wearing that disapproving frown, Anabel? Why are you not happy for me?'

'Because I don't like it, child.'

'But we *agreed*, Anabel. We agreed that this was the only way to secure the protection of the Cavendish name, for all of us, *permanently*.'

'Aye, but not atthe cost of the Earl's pride. He will make a dangerous enemy, Leonora.'

'Enemy?' Leonora laughed prettily, touching her hair into place with both hands. 'How can you even *think* such a thing? Why, Sir Oscar will become my ally, not my enemy, you just wait and see if he doesn't.'

'I wouldn't be too sure of that, if I were you, young madam. You have held that man in your arms while he wept like a helpless child, and I doubt he will ever find it in his heart to forgive you for that.'

Within the hour Lord Beresford arrived home after an absence of almost seven weeks to the warm applause of over fifty guests, many of the estate workers and every last member of the household staff. Tea had been served on the middle terrace, with seats and tables dotted across the lawns, fancy cushions piled here and there on the grass and the fringes of gaily coloured parasols blowing in the warm breeze. As he stepped down from the carriage his eldest son and Leonora descended the great stairs together and hurried, hand in hand, down the pathway. Their welcome was a joint affair which he acknowledged openly, but with a great deal of inner reserve. Leonora looked superb. There was a certain radiance about her, a glow that told the world she was in her natural element as mistress of the Great Hall. She was the centre of attention and the subject of much whispered speculation as she took Sir Oscar's arm and led him through the press of guests toward the main doors of the Hall. Once there she paused to take Malcolm's arm, a happy, very beautiful young woman respected and admired by everyone she met. In his son's adoring smile the future of the earldom was surely sealed. The boy was in love, enraptured by the lovely creature who had slipped so neatly and effortlessly into all their lives.

'I cannot like her,' Sir Oscar thought, his misgivings etched in the troubled scowl on his face. 'Nor can I forget for a moment that she is the daughter of that scoundrel Herbert Shelley. For the sake of my own son's happiness and my dear Francine's memory I must accept this situation, but despite her goodness, despite her apparent suitability, I neither care for nor trust this clever, conniving young woman.'

Leonora turned her dazzling smile upon him and Sir Oscar felt a sudden chill, as if a shadow had passed in front of the sun to rob him of its warmth. Once again it seemed that someone, somewhere, had stepped upon his grave.

III

During the next month Beresford Hall saw many visitors as friends and family flocked to see the stricken Countess for what might prove to be the last time. Sir Marcus Shaw was now in official attendance, having recently returned to his fine house and extensive medical practice in Chepstow. He held out little hope of recovery. In his measured opinion one stroke had followed upon another in rapid succession, leaving the lady permanently incapacitated. He was reluctant even to suppose that, beyond the anguished expression in her staring grey eyes, poor Lady Beresford was in any way conscious of her miserable predicament. Leonora was not so sure. The eyes were watchful, she thought, accusing, and on several occasions a yellowed hand, made claw-like by paralysis, had snatched at a passing skirt or a stiffly starched apron as if its owner would impart some close-held secret into a sympathetic ear. Fourteen-year-old Vivienne, brought protesting from her school in Cheltenham to witness her mother's decline, had refused to enter the sick-room after Lady Alyce had suddenly grabbed her by the hair and held on, despite her infirmity, until the girl was quite hysterical with pain and shock.

'She knows,' Leonora told Anabel. 'I can feel her watching me, hating me. She knows she is finished and I will soon be Countess of Beresford, and it stings her to realise that Francine Shelley has beaten her, after all.'

Anabel clicked her tongue and shook her head, deploring Leonora's harshness. Any grudge she herself might have borne the Countess on Francine's behalf had vanished with the onset of this terrible paralysis. The woman had suffered enough. It would be a kindness and a blessing if her mind had become like her body, crippled and useless, its functions totally without order. It would simply be too cruel for her to be aware of all that had befallen her, for this was a sorry end indeed for a woman of her intelligence and character to endure. While Leonora was credited with being a dedicated personal nurse, in truth she kept to her adjoining rooms and left the more distasteful work to hired strangers who cared little for an old woman's dignity. It said much about the life of this powerful Countess of Beresford that not even the lowest of her servants could be called upon to nurse her out of simple loyalty or compassion, regardless of extra wages.

It was with mixed feelings that Gilbert returned home in mid-September. He had been avoiding Leonora ever since that unpleasant meeting at the London house, when her reduced circumstances had so embarrassed him and the Earl's anger had prompted him to acknowledge her presence with a frosty civility. She had changed much in recent weeks. She was, if anything, even more beautiful than when he had seen her last, regal and at ease as she took the Countess's place at the dinner table. Watching her, he could scarcely believe that he, the shy and awkward younger son, had once dared hope that he might win her love for himself. She belonged to Malcolm now. They made a fine couple, and they were clearly very much in love. Not even the impending death of his mother would prevent Malcolm from planning an early wedding, now that his heart was won.

The season's most eligible widower and society's most talked about young beauty.

So the gossips and society columns described the lovers, and Gilbert, while secretly nursing a bruised heart, took pleasure in their happiness and generously wished them well.

For Elizabeth it was a time of growth and pleasure, of being shifted from her horrid little bedroom to one of sumptuous furnishings where the windows were lit each day with bright sunshine and the big four-poster bed was as pretty and as comfortable as any in the whole house. She was beginning to blossom like an opening flower under Leonora's care and attention. Her manner became less twitchy, altogether more confident as she learned to enjoy a life completely free of fear and stress. In the early days she would creep timidly into the sick-room to stare at the figure on the bed, perplexed that so huge and frightful a presence could have shrunk to such ineffectual proportions. Thus, prompted on the one hand by the joy of her new-found freedom, and on the other by the restrictions placed by nature upon her intellect, she soon came to accept that the woman who had been both parent and tyrant was now banished from her life forever.

While his wife lay dying and his son became increasingly besotted with Leonora, Sir Oscar Cavendish was a deeply troubled man. He travelled to London to stand in the modest graveyard of St Augustine's church, staring at the narrow mound of earth beneath which his poor, dead Francine had been laid to rest. In silence he begged her forgiveness, poured out his remorse, wept and made promises, and stole away, hours later, with his burden of grief and guilt uneased. He returned to Beresford Hall and made full confession to his wife, begging *her* forgiveness for past sins and finding no comfort in this quiet baring of his soul.

'I loved Francine,' he admitted, speaking softly into the room's flickering shadows, never once turning his gaze to the mask-like stare of the figure on the bed. 'I would have given up all this to be with her, sacrificed my title, home and children for her sake, but instead she saved me from myself by marrying another. You never really knew me at all, Alyce. In all those years I doubt you ever once suspected that you were short-changed, that another woman had claim on my love. And now I must find my son, *our* son, mine and Francine's. I must find him and bring him home to Beresford, where he belongs.'

As he spoke the veined hand that lay across the covers began to move with spasmodic little jerks. Its bent fingers picked and plucked like stiffened talons, leaving long scratch-marks in the deep velvet pile. A sound half-gurgle and half-sigh escaped into the silent room, and the invalid's chest began to rise and fall at a distressingly rapid rate. Sir Oscar rose from his chair, alarmed. Still avoiding his wife's terrible stare, he looked to her mouth and saw that saliva trickled from its corners in unsightly rivulets of dark foam. He drew back, reaching for the servants' bell, his nostrils offended by a particular smell now emanating from the sick-bed. It was the odour of human excrement. The proud and elegant Lady Alyce, ensconced like royalty in her splendid and beautifully kept apartments, had soiled herself like an untrained infant.

Sir Oscar did not visit his wife again. There seemed little point in it. She was clearly unaware of his visits and the ugliness of her illness loomed between them, threatening to destroy the ever-fragile fabric of their relationship. Instead he turned all his energies to running his estates, and all his passions to locating his missing son. In his determination to make amends, to compensate for all the lost years, he allowed the search to mushroom into an obsession.

'Jonathan will go to earth,' Leonora predicted, gloomily. 'He has eloped with a girl of eighteen after signing papers accepting responsibility for those enormous debts. What else can we expect him to do when he hears of a search party organised by no lesser personage than His Lordship, the Earl of Beresford, Papa's major creditor? He will go to earth, Anabel. He and Charles will go to earth like wily foxes running ahead of the hounds.'

'Perhaps so, but sooner or later they will hear of your marriage to Malcolm, and then they will all come home, or at least write to you, knowing that all is well.'

'I pray it will be so, but it is all so unsatisfactory. And still there is no news of Joseph. Oh, Anabel, I was so certain he would return for our birthday last month, but there was nothing, not a word. Oh, why doesn't he contact me? I miss him so. I should never have allowed him to go off alone like that.'

'Now don't go blaming yourself, child. As I recall, Joseph just packed a bag and ran away of his own accord. He gave you small choice in the matter,' Anabel reminded her.

'But I should have known what was on his mind,' she replied hotly. 'He is my twin, Anabel, my *twin*. I should have *known*!'

In that sultry late September, when the royal colours of August were reluctantly beginning to give way to the burnished tones of autumn, only one man in all England knew the precise whereabouts of the three Shelley brothers. Fairfax Manor stood but four miles from the Great Hall of Beresford, so closely situated to the boundaries of the western slopes that a man might stand upon Fairfax property, and, merely by stretching out his hand, pluck blossom from a tree whose roots were planted in Cavendish soil. The manor house itself could be seen from the Hall. Like a squat stone beacon it marked the four hundred acres of prime land sliced from a young man's inheritance for the benefit of a common and corrupt clerk. It marked the only part of the earldom ever to fall into the hands of an outsider, and there were those who would see a family ruined, if necessary, to bring that portion of land back to its rightful owners.

Christopher Fairfax had found London unbearable. The heat during the summer months had become oppressive. The dirt and the constant noise put such strain upon his nerves that his whole constitution had begun to suffer. A rash of painful boils plagued the back of his neck, and no amount of remedial powders would ease the periodic attacks of indigestion to which he had recently fallen prey. He had also returned to Fairfax Manor in order to be close to Leonora, though he had not yet seen her in spite of long hours spent sitting or standing in his garden, staring with love-lorn eyes across the slopes to Beresford Hall. They said she was to marry Malcolm Cavendish, but it was all gossip; cruel, ridiculous tittle-tattle to be dismissed out of hand. He refused even to entertain the possibility that he had lost her to another. He would not, *could* not relinquish the prize that had so nearly been his own.

The first letter had arrived at the bank during the second week in August: a short, urgent note asking Leonora Fairfax, formerly Shelley, to contact an accommodation address in Paris within the next few weeks. It was unsigned but bore the initials J and C, and was clearly a message from her elder brothers.

The second letter was long and wordy, written in a scrawled, rather immature hand and addressed to Mrs Christopher Fairfax at the Manor House. In it young Joseph

Shelley apologised most humbly for his behaviour, pleading grief as the main cause of his abrupt departure at a time when he was most needed by his beloved sister. He begged her to write to him care of a hospital in Dublin, where he was recovering from a serious illness. It was his fervent hope that he might return to take up the position as junior bank clerk recently offered by Mr Fairfax senior as part of the marriage contract. A fond word from his sister would restore his spirits and bring him home by the very next tide. It was signed: *Your ever loving and repentant brother, Joseph.*

From time to time Fairfax lifted the letters from the locked drawer of his bureau, smoothed them flat with his sausage-like fingers and re-read each word with a feeling of malicious satisfaction. This was his secret spite, his small compensation for the loss of that which, even now, he coveted almost to distraction. When bouts of gluttony failed to ease his sorrows, when pies and pastries left him stuffed but uncomforted, those letters convinced him that he still had some small hold over the perfidious Miss Shelley.

IV

Lukan de Ville stood in the gathering dusk while a lowering, copper-toned sun pulled elongated shadows across the land. His face was a brooding mask, his eyes two long, ebony slits between glowering brows and high, very pronounced cheekbones. Motionless save for the steady movements of his breathing, he stood with his shoulders resting against the trunk of an oak tree, his hands hanging by their thumbs from his belt, his eyes staring into the distance. Against the dark trees of the forest at his back he was but another shadow melting into deeper shadows. Tonight she would come. His message to her had been explicit. She would come, or he would ride to the big house and confront her there.

While he waited there the western sky became a cauldron of

bright liquid gold which seeped brilliant stains on to its backcloth of blue. Wisps of cloud were dyed from white to bronze, and one by one the windows of Beresford Hall were illuminated with a blaze of reflected sunlight. And against the gold the forest stood in dense black silhouette, robbed of its diverse greens and browns by the strange, other-worldly glow of twilight. In less than an hour the light would be gone, but she would come, he knew she would come.

In the beginning Lukan had deeply resented her decision to avoid him. He had seethed with frustration each time she rode away as he approached, simmered with inept rage whenever she left a room rather than remain in his company for a moment longer than protocol demanded. On one occasion he even lay in wait for her behind the stables and, finding her at last alone, crept from the shadows to take her in his arms. For an instant he had felt the passion flare in her, felt her heart race and her lips burn for his kiss, but then she tore herself free and struck him savagely across the cheek with her riding whip.

'Impudent devil!' she spat. 'How *dare* you lay your grubby hands on me.'

'Have a care, lady,' he warned, touching his fingers to the welt raised on his cheek by the whip.

'Never touch me again. Never!'

'Don't fight me, Lia. I know you too well. I *know* how you feel.'

'Leave me alone,' she cried, eyes blazing, cheeks hot, fists tightly clenched as she struggled to contain her emotions.

He shook his dark head, scowling.

'I'll *never* leave you alone, Lia.'

'Then I will have you turned off the estates.'

'No, my Lia, you will not so easily be rid of me.'

He spoke softly, holding her with his gaze, knowing that she too was a victim of the overwhelming forces at work between them. She had stared back at him, pale and trembling with rage, until a soft moan escaped her and suddenly she was in his arms, kissing his mouth, his face, his neck, murmuring his name as if nothing in the world existed for her but him. He could still hear that whisper, scorching his soul with its fierce,

415

despairing passion: 'Oh, Lukan ... Lukan ... Lukan.'

Since then she had doubled her efforts to keep a safe distance between them, while every glance, every determined toss of her head only served to reinforce the covenant they shared. Now Lukan had learned that Malcolm intended to make her his wife, and the news lay in his chest like a stone. That his Lia should return his love in full and yet pledge herself to another man was unthinkable. That she should be adored by two men of opposite temperament who had been friends since childhood and were as close as any brothers, was at once the most understandable and the least acceptable of dilemmas. The three had become bound by love in a situation that could only resolve itself in heartbreak and betrayal.

'I will not stand by and see you wedded to another man,' he had told her when the announcement was made, his face white with fury, his hands gripping her slender wrists.

And she, equally angry, had spat: 'Then look the other way, gypsy, for you'll not prevent it.'

'Damn you, woman. You think yourself so far above me, but you will belong to this gypsy, body and soul, before ever the Earl's son can take you to his marriage bed.'

And later, in the forest, he had thrown aside the meal prepared for him by his half-sister, too sick at heart to eat.

'I curse the day I ever laid eyes upon her,' he declared.

'You will,' Rebecca had muttered into the campfire, her knowing eyes half closed against the heat of the flames. 'Believe me, you will.'

All these things Lukan pondered afresh as he stood in the shadow of the trees with the late September sunset glinting in his eyes. For a long time he waited with his back against the oak tree, then his eyes narrowed slightly and a small pulse showed itself in one cheek as he brought his long body erect in one easy, fluid movement.

'Lia!'

She came alone, riding Midnight, the all-black mare presented to her by Malcolm as a belated birthday gift. For several minutes horse and rider became a silent spectre approaching from the abbey-like silhouette of Beresford Hall, now moving into some hollow shaped by the uneven ground, now rising upon a grassy knoll, coming on at a steady, cantering pace. Her skirts and the folds of her dark cloak flapped along the horse's flanks. She spotted the two wolfhounds as they loped towards her through the long grass, two graceful, blue-grey shadows sprinting at speed through the twilight.

'Come, Gillan! Come, Garvey!'

She called their names softly, then slowed her mount to a walk as the shape of a man unfastened itself from the forest's edge and seemed to glide in her direction. With the width of the long meadow between them, Leonora could almost believe that she was crossing an immeasurable chasm to meet him, an abyss from which she might find herself unable, or unwilling, to return. As he drew closer she dismounted and stood with the reins in her hand and the dogs at her heels, watching him approach. Then he too stopped, leaving a gap of several strides between them. He was wearing an open-necked shirt and the jerkin of supple leather that had become impregnated with wood-ash and a dozen forest scents. His rugged, angular features were softened by the weird light of a deepening dusk so that they appeared perfectly proportioned. He wore a solemn expression and was quite extraordinarily handsome. They faced each other across the short distance, each held by the same uncanny fascination.

'Come, lady. A few more steps, if you please.' His voice surprised her, as always, by its unusual depth and resonance.

Her eyes danced with mischief and a smile tugged at her lips.

'Impudent gypsy,' she responded.

Lukan extended his hand with a wide grin. His skin had a rich, tawny glow in the sunlight. His black eyes seemed to draw her towards him.

'Come to me, Lia,' he insisted.

Closing that last gap, stepping forward to place her hand into his big palm suddenly became the easiest, most natural thing she had ever been asked to do. He looked down at her, still smiling as he stared into her eyes before allowing his gaze

417

to travel, slowly and lovingly, over every inch of her face. Then he sighed quietly and, cupping her face in his hands as if it were a precious thing, kissed her mouth in such a way that the sweetness, the tender honesty of it, swelled her heart.

Leonora had been wrong. For weeks she had been telling herself that she was drawn to this man because of his compelling good looks and his powerful animal magnetism. She had almost convinced herself that it was so, that the strange hold he had over her was merely his ability to awaken those intense sexual hungers within her. Now she realised that this was but a fraction of the truth, just the tip of an iceberg whose true menace lay in its hidden, unfathomable depths. What she felt for Malcolm was an easy, comfortable fondness that fell short of sexual passion, but what she shared with Lukan de Ville went far beyond either physical or romantic love. While she had vainly set herself against the carnal forces he inspired in her, something deeper, something dangerously enduring, had been weaving its spell to bind them, inexorably, one to the other.

From a sheltered hollow beyond the meadow they watched the sun drop behind the western horizon, drawing its colours after it until the sky was left a deep, velvet blue. The moon rose big and misshapen in its final quarter, and the evening star, steady and unflickering, inched its way in pursuit of the vanished sun. Now the creatures of the night stirred and went about their busy nocturnal lives. The dogs rested, always watchful and silent, while the patient black mare stood with her head lowered and only moved to twitch an inquisitive night insect from her flanks. The lovers, cushioned by the grass and encouraged by the moon's light, kissed and touched and whispered, of things secret or profound or commonplace, throughout the long night hours. They spoke of the past, of his life and hers before their paths had crossed and their destinies became interwoven one with the other. They spoke of her love for Beresford Hall and of the deep bond of friendship between Lukan and Malcolm.

'I owe him much,' he told her in his deep, cultured voice. 'There has been a de Ville as senior ranger at Beresford's

418

Western Lodge for more than four centuries, and but for Malcolm the line would have been broken when Marcus de Ville was drowned in a storm at Monk's Crossing. He brought me back to claim my doubtful inheritance, knowing that in doing so he opposed the wishes of his own father.'

Leonora nodded. 'I know Sir Oscar never wanted you to return to Beresford,' she said. 'He has always disapproved of your close friendship with his son, especially since the two of you were quite inseparable as children.'

'And so he provided the means to have me raised as a gentleman, two hundred miles away.'

'Did he try to prevent your return when your foster father was drowned?'

'He did indeed, even though his own past evidence eventually secured my entitlement to the ancient rights and privileges of the de Ville heirs.' He paused and sighed deeply before adding, without bitterness: 'Twenty-eight years ago nobody anticipated that the bastard son of Daniel Adams would one day inherit for want of a legal heir.'

'Perhaps the Earl is jealous,' she suggested. 'Malcolm has always loved you as a brother.'

'And now he loves you, too. What is to be done?'

Leonora sighed and shivered a little.

'It seems we are both of us tied, in our different ways, to this place,' she whispered.

'Much more than you realise, my Lia.' He bent to kiss her cheek, his face dark against the starlit sky. 'We will die here, you and I. There can be no escape for us, my love, no escape.'

They did not make love. Neither did they attempt to shape their futures by plans and promises. As a new day lightened the sky in the east and the stars began to fade, one by one, against a paler canvas, they walked hand in hand through the dewy grass toward Beresford Hall. Only when they were about to part, when he had brought her hand to his lips and placed that special kiss in its palm and closed her fingers lovingly around it, did he ask again: 'Lia, my Lia, what is to be done?'

'Nothing,' she told him. 'The die is cast, Lukan, just as you

419

say your sister predicted. I am to marry Malcolm.'

'But we are one, you and I. How can I see you wedded to another man, to my only true friend ... to have you so close to me and yet so far, so far beyond my reach?'

He was still standing like some dark and brooding sentinel on the edge of the meadow when she reached the orchard and the bridle path leading to the stables. She twisted in the saddle and raised her arm high, but he did not respond to her wave. Instead he turned abruptly and strode for the forest, his dogs loping behind him and his long black hair swishing to and fro across his back like the tail of a horse. She watched until he was out of sight, then turned her horse and urged it along the narrow path. They had spent the whole night together, she and that strange man who was half nobleman and half gypsy. They had lain in each other's arms without a care for the world that separated them, and yet, alone and free for those precious hours, they had not consummated their love. He could have taken her to his own house less than two miles inside the forest, and there claimed her willing body in his own bed. They could have made love right there on the grassy hillside with only the moon and the animals as witness but instead, by some unspoken mutual consent, they had left that treasure untouched. She was returning to Malcolm intact, yet in the secret heart of her she knew that this night of tender and innocent love had bound her more tightly to Lukan de Ville than even the most passionate sexual encounter might have done.

'We are one, you and I,' he had told her, and the simple truth of it could no longer be denied.

She dismounted, closed her eyes and rested her cheek against the mare's neck, already yearning to be back in the man's arms. And in a soft whisper she echoed his words: 'We are one, you and I, my Lukan.'

V

In a modest but fashionable house on the outskirts of Paris, Horace Cavendish poured himself another measure of brandy and downed it in a single gulp. The letter from Gilbert lay crumpled in a corner by the fireplace, tossed there in a fit of drunken pique. Horace stooped to retrieve it, carried it to the table and smoothed out its pages with both hands. The writing was neat and angular, evenly spaced and as precisely written as one would expect from a man with a Harrow education. It brought news of Lady Alyce's seizure and the impending marriage between Malcolm and Leonora Shelley. Every word stabbed at Horace like a knife, reopening old wounds, renewing old grievances.

'Damn her,' he growled. 'Damn the Shelley woman for ingratiating herself into my family, for taking for herself what should be mine ... *mine.*'

The months of enforced exile and heavy drinking had not dealt kindly with Horace Cavendish. His health was not good, and the poor condition of his liver often reflected itself in fierce, quick-silver changes of mood. He suffered black depressions that laid him low for days at a time, followed by long periods of elation during which he was the toast of Paris society, then the slow plunge through discontent and remorse to the depths of melancholy. Now sporting a heavy beard and whiskers, and with a temper that sent grown menservants scuttling for cover at the sound of his voice, he lived mainly by his social wits and his skills at the gaming tables. Yet for all his faults he still possessed his share of the irresistible Cavendish charm, the twinkling blue eyes and the easy, lop-sided smile ever capable of melting even the chilliest female heart.

His latest conquest was Madeline Farrar, mistress of Sir Roger Trevanion, a close friend of Sir Arthur Wellesley, Duke of Wellington. Madeline was both wealthy and generous, and she was also blessed with such sexual appetites as Sir Roger Trevanion, single-handed, could never hope to satisfy.

Although she was almost totally dependent upon his patronage, she found little gratification in his bland and lustreless embraces. It was to Horace she turned for the excitement she craved, for the pain and tears, the fire, the uncertainty her affair with Trevanion lacked. And with a clever combination of cruelty, tenderness, brute force and blackmail, Horace kept the lady interested and profited handsomely from the arrangement.

'I will not have it,' he bellowed now, lifting his clenched fist above his head and bringing it down again with such force that his brandy glass lurched drunkenly from the table top to the floor, shattering into a shower of fragments. 'I will not have some cheap little outsider steal the plum from the pie while I am treated no better than a ... a ...'

'... a leper, my dear?'

Madeline had entered the room wearing a delicate muslin night-robe and carrying a fresh decanter of brandy. She was beautiful, plump and smooth-skinned, with a cascade of dark brown hair and the full, firm breasts of a Greek goddess. It was a stroke of uncommon good fortune that had brought into his precarious existence a woman of private means who possessed a lady's pedigree and a whore's lusts. There were times when Horace adored her and, because she knew him so well, times when he despised her.

'And what will you do to prevent the wedding?' she asked. 'How will you stop your elder brother taking for himself this auburn-haired woman whom you have coveted for so long?'

'She has angled for this,' Horace spat, snatching the decanter and swigging its contents without benefit of a glass. 'Since she was ten years old that vixen has schemed and plotted for this. She has tricked him. The scheming little witch has tricked them all.'

'And would any of them believe you if you tried to tell them as much?' Madeline enquired with a sympathetic smile. 'Who would listen to you, Horace? And who would give a fig for your opinions on the matter?'

'My mother would believe me,' he said petulantly. 'She has always loathed the Shelleys. Mother would believe me.'

422

'But your mother is beyond your reach, my dear,' Madeline reminded him. 'She believes you to be a thief, a lecher ... even a *sodomite*!'

'Lies! Filthy lies!' Horace flared, his face reddening with outrage.

'Quite so, my dear, but because of it she has severed her affections and kept herself from you for almost two years. Oh no, my dear, she would not lift a finger to help you, even if she were not paralysed by a seizure.'

'That Shelley woman has angled for his,' he spat, distracted by memories of the beautiful, strong-willed Leonora. 'I should have taken her while I had the chance – taken her and ruined her and put paid to her cunning plots against my family.'

'But for now you can do nothing,' Madeline said, unfastening the ribbons from her robe. 'If you set foot upon English soil you will be arrested and thrown into prison. Your letters will continue to be returned unopened. Your protests will fall upon deaf ears.'

Horace turned unsteadily, leaned back against the table and took another long swig from the brandy decanter. He watched the muslin robe slither from Madeline's shoulders to fall in a delicate heap around her ankles. He licked his lips. His head throbbed and the brandy tasted strangely stale on his tongue, but his loins stirred hotly at the sight of her nakedness.

'To hell with the Shelley woman,' he slurred, reaching roughly for Madeline's breasts. 'I wish my brother joy of her.'

Madeline smiled with satisfaction as she stroked the head nuzzling greedily at her breasts. She was a wise woman who had long since learned to protect herself against any eventuality. It would not be in her personal interests for Horace Cavendish to return to England at this time on some foolhardy campaign to put an end to his brother's marriage plans. She needed him in Paris, and between the brandy and the bed she was assured of keeping him there.

VI

The wedding was arranged for the afternoon of Friday, October 31st, the Eve of All Hallows. The ceremony itself was to take place in the tiny chapel under the west wing, which was to be specially renovated for the happy event. It would be a short, simple service conducted by the Reverend Mr Cedric Evans, the vicar of nearby Wortherton and its neighbouring village of Bishorne. It would be a family affair with barely a hundred and fifty specially invited guests and neither a Grand Ball nor the customary village fair to mark the occasion. It was agreed by all concerned that a long delay was pointless, since the Countess may linger for months in her present state, and that a large society wedding would be in poor taste, given the unhappy shadow hanging over them. The arrangements were, therefore, an acceptable compromise only arrived at after a good deal of very careful consideration. Even so, the wedding would be nothing short of magnificent and several cartloads of ale, cold meats and hot pies would find their way from the kitchens of Beresford Hall to the waiting campfires of Kingswood.

'It's a bad date,' Anabel said, shaking her head and frowning deeply. 'All Hallows' Eve. A bad date. Bound to be unlucky.' And later, as the day drew closer and the last glittering beads were added to the bridal gown, she became increasingly agitated by what she saw as Leonora's dangerous disregard for the old beliefs. She was still complaining when the first house-guests, Lord Morpeth and his unmarried daughter, with Sir Humphrey and Lady Allsop, arrived at the Hall on Monday afternoon.

'It is not too late to have it changed to another day,' she persisted.

'What? And change all my complicated arrangements for the sake of some foolish superstition?' Leonora demanded with a smile.

'Aye, because every superstition needs a grain or two of

truth to keep it alive. You shouldn't tempt Fate, my girl. It doesn't do to fly in the face of Fate.'

'Nonsense, Anabel. You are merely finding fault because you are still upset that I persuaded Malcolm to reopen the tower over the west wing. Really, all that silly talk of ghosts and ancient curses. I do believe you grow more gullible as the work progresses, you and your fears of shadows and ravens and whispers of the great Unknown.'

'Ah, you may mock, my girl, but there's truth enough in many of those old tales.'

'Truth, indeed,' Leonora smiled. 'And what about Lukan de Ville? They say he was born on a Friday and drew his first breath while the chapel bell was ringing the noon hour. According to local superstition this makes him a Chime-child, touched with witchcraft and destined to be either murdered or hanged. Surely you cannot hold with such superstitious nonsense?'

Anabel looked up sharply. She was ready to believe *anything* of that black-eyed devil.

'Nonsense, is it? Well, if you want *my* opinion he *will* be murdered, if ever his lordship discovers him in your rooms. Or else hanged in the forest as an adulterer, if you don't put a stop to this reckless affair of yours.'

Leonora smiled at that. There was no sordid affair for his lordship to uncover, no betrayal by adultery, only the frequent, furtive visits of his best friend to the orchards and the tiny walled garden at the rear of Lady Beresford's apartments. Every visit, every stolen moment was precious to them, a sweet torture they were unable to resist. On the eve of the wedding he paced to and fro across the garden like a caged animal brooding upon its captivity. He was like a man possessed, simmering with an inner rage he could barely contain .

'Put a stop to this, Lia. End it. End it *now*, while there is still time.'

'No, Lukan. I cannot.'

'Or will not?' he demanded, his dark eyes smouldering.

'The wedding must go ahead as planned, Lukan.'

'Then you cannot possibly love me as you say you do. You cannot!'

'Lukan, you know I love you. I will *always* love you.'

He fell silent, his fists so tightly clenched that the knuckles became bloodless and the nails pressed like claws into his palms. They had said all there was to say. Her eyes were filled with tears, his swarthy face pale and drawn as he struggled to accept the inevitable. Leonora was resolute. She would marry Malcolm Cavendish in less than twenty-four hours, and neither Lukan de Ville, nor Providence, nor the Devil himself must be allowed to interfere with that. Her dream came first. It must. For her there could be no other way.

When at last he took his leave of her it was in bitter silence. He strode across the garden, grabbed her roughly with both hands and clutched her against him in a desperate embrace. Then he climbed the high wall and dropped lightly to the ground on its other side. He had left with neither a backward glance nor a word of farewell.

'And good riddance to the man,' Anabel thought, though she feared what Leonora's decision might have been had she suspected for one moment that by marrying Malcolm she would actually lose her gypsy lover.

The ceremony was to take place at three o'clock in the afternoon and the guests would sit down to a splendid wedding breakfast in the Great Hall at four. After that everyone would rest for an hour while the Hall was cleared in preparation for the evening's dance. It was to be a fine wedding despite the circumstances, and none would be reminded of the life that hung by a thread in the first floor rooms of the east wing.

By two-fifteen Leonora was ready, dressed in a gown of ivory silk overlaid with rainbow gauze and glittering with crystal beads. Her hair was elaborately dressed with beaded net, strands of pearls, flowers and dyed ostrich feathers, its lustrous dark locks rinsed with rosemary to enhance their colour with a silky shine. She had surely never looked so lovely, with her huge, violet-blue eyes, superb complexion and full, rouged mouth. Her creamy shoulders were framed by a cascade of delicate flounces and her tiny waist enhanced by the stiffened petticoats that swelled the fullness of her skirts. Between her breasts and echoing the rare blue of her eyes, the great Cavendish Sapphire nestled in a bed of gauze, as priceless as it was magnificent.

It was not from sentiment alone that Anabel wept to see Leonora looking so wonderful. There was real pain in her heart for Francine, who had not lived to see the day her daughter realised her own stolen dream of becoming mistress of Beresford. And she wept, too, for those missing brothers, so loved and yet absent on this very special day in their sister's life.

She left Leonora standing like a vision before the mirror while she hurried into the next room to check the pale ivory orchid that was to be pinned to the bride's hair at the very last moment. Only then did she discover that something terrible had happened, something that would shatter Leonora's plans and hopes. The wedding would have to be postponed after all, the dream set aside, leaving the would-be bride at the mercy of a black-eyed devil who might steal her away to live the life of a common gypsy. It would be weeks, even months before another date could be fixed and that lovely, headstrong creature in the next room safely wedded to the Beresford heir.

'What is it, Anabel?' Leonora spoke into the mirror as Anabel returned to the room. Then, seeing the other woman's stricken expression, she whirled and demanded: 'What is it? What has happened?'

'It's the Countess, she's ... oh, Leonora, the wedding will have to be called off. The Countess has had another seizure. She's dead. Lady Beresford is *dead*.'

CHAPTER FIFTEEN

I

'**N**o! no!'

For Leonora this blow was too cruel to bear. How could she possibly accept, meekly and without protest, this eleventh-hour impediment to her future happiness? In that initial moment of shock she saw the announcement made, the wedding arrangements put aside in favour of a sombre burial, the period of mourning shaping itself into an impenetrable barrier between her and everything she had ever dreamed of possessing. As a consequence of this untimely event she foresaw her passion for Lukan de Ville rushing beyond her control to make them the subject of a humiliating scandal. She imagined the slow cooling of Malcolm's desire and the steady strengthening of the Earl's unspoken disapproval of the match. She could even see the return to Beresford Hall of Horace, her old enemy, a man who would surely stop at nothing to prevent her achieving her dream of becoming first mistress, then Countess of Beresford. Ever aware that she was standing on uncertain ground, she felt it shifting now beneath her feet as if some force, more powerful than her own will to succeed, were striving to topple her.

'I will not have it, do you hear?' she flared. 'I will not tolerate her interference. She must not be allowed to do this to me.'

'Leonora ... the woman is *dead*.'

'Yes, she's dead. And the wedding ceremony due to take place within the hour!' She flung herself to and fro across the room, her pacing hampered by the full skirts of her gown. 'The dream within my reach, right here within my reach, and she is dead ... dead!'

'Leonora ...'

'How could she?' she fumed. 'How could she *do* this to me?'

'Leonora, she didn't choose to die.'

'And just look at me, Anabel. Am I to be left standing here in all my finery, abandoned, forgotten, while the household sinks into mourning for that hateful old woman?'

'I'm sorry, child.'

'Sorry is not enough. I will not let her do this to me.'

'But the family must be told ...' Anabel began, only to break off with a look of horrified disbelief as she read the intention in those flashing dark eyes. 'Oh, no ... you wouldn't ... you *couldn't*.'

'I can and I will,' Leonora corrected in a tone of chilly malice. 'This is *my* day, not hers. Today is the single most important day of my whole life, and I will not allow Lady Beresford, living or dead, to rob me of it.'

'But how?' Anabel gasped. 'How on earth ...?'

'By keeping silent. By saying nothing of this to anyone. We can do it, Anabel. Nobody visits her because of the way she looks, so who is to know the difference if we remain silent?'

'But what about the servants? On your own instructions someone must be with her at all times. Surely you don't expect me to ...?'

'No, I need you for other duties. We must send for that timid little Welsh girl who fetches and carries for Mrs Wheeler. She so fears the evil eye that she cannot bear to look at the Countess's face. Nobody will suspect anything if she sits

429

outside the sick-room until the ceremony is over. And if the door is locked and only I have a key ...'

'Locked?' Anabel exclaimed, her expression incredulous. 'What, turn the key on the dead?'

'It must be done. The windows must be tightly closed and the fire made up to keep the room warm so that the body ...'

'Stop it, Leonora! Stop it! You cannot even think of doing such a thing. Lock the door on the dead? Close all the windows? Trap a departing soul within four walls? Nay, this time you go too far, madam. Flout the old superstitions as you will, but I'll take no part in this ... this ... *blasphemy*.'

'Then you are free to leave,' Leonora retorted.

'Leave?'

'Yes, go on your way, abandon me if you must, if you are too faint-hearted to help preserve everything I have worked so long and hard to achieve.'

'You would turn me out?' Anabel asked in a small, shocked voice.

'The choice is your own,' Leonora replied, acidly. 'If you cannot be wholly loyal to me, your services are no longer required. I will not be thwarted in this, Anabel. I will not be cheated, yet again, of everything that is dear to me. The wedding will go ahead as planned. I *will* be mistress of Beresford, with or without your blessing.'

Stunned, Anabel sat down heavily on a chair that was mercifully well padded in the seat. Standing there in her beautiful bridal gown, her fists clenched and her aristocratic chin raised defiantly, Leonora represented a force to be reckoned with, a force this simple and loyal woman was not prepared to set herself against. She had lost too much of late to risk parting from this wild, determined young woman who was all that remained of her beloved Francine. Without Leonora she had nothing. Everything she loved and cherished was right here in this room. She could stay or leave, it was as simple as that, to be part of the dream or defect for want of but a fraction of this girl's courage. When at last she found her voice it sounded flat and unfamiliar to her own ears.

'Very well, Leonora. I will do exactly as you say.'

*

The wedding ceremony went off without a hitch. Malcolm had on a cut-away coat in palest dove grey with toning trousers, grey top hat and gloves, white shirt and quilted, slate-grey waistcoat. His eyes were misted with emotion as he surveyed the beauty at his side. His smile said it all. He adored her.

For Leonora it was both an end and a beginning. Never again would she fear that all she loved might be snatched from her by forces beyond her control, that poverty would continue to stalk her footsteps or that some conniving, self-interested guardian would make mockery of her dreams. She was safe at last. She entered that tiny, candle-lit chapel beneath the great tower as Leonora Shelley, eighteen and penniless save for a huge sapphire from which she had sworn she would never be parted. She came out as the Viscountess Cavendish, bride of Sir Malcolm, heir to all the titles, honours and estates of Oscar, Sixth Earl of Beresford. Now at last she had wealth, position and a safe future that nobody could ever take away from her.

'I did it, Anabel,' she whispered, blinking back tears of triumph and happiness as she hugged the woman who had always been there to share her joys and sorrows. 'Oh, if only Mama could have known. If only she could have lived to see this day.'

Anabel's cheeks were dampened by tears but her eyes were bright as she smiled back at Leonora.

'You deserve your happiness, child,' she said.

'It will be a good life for us, now, Anabel. A secure life.'

'Yes, child. Now hurry off with you. Your fine guests are waiting.'

Despite the restrictions placed upon the celebrations by Lady Beresford's illness, the wedding breakfast was a truly impressive affair, with course after course of elaborate dishes served with all the pomp and splendour expected at the Earl's table. All the people who really mattered to Leonora's schemes were present: the nobles and noted politicians, the

431

imitators and prophets of fashion, the titled, the wealthy, the gifted and those who boasted royal connections. Here were people of whom she had read in the journals of Lady Beresford, that fascinating collection of leather-bound volumes now stacked away under lock and key in Leonora's own rooms. Here was Lord Dubray, whose sexual encounters had held such a morbid fascination for the Countess; Sir Walter Fellows, with barely an honest penny to his name; and the pompous Philip, Lord Marchieson, whose lands came into his possession by default and whose title was bought with cash and flattery from the mistress of the Prince Regent. And here were those others of the Cavendish family who had come from far afield to judge and scrutinise her, those stiff aristocrat whose china-blue eyes and Viking hair marked them as brothers, sisters or cousins of the present Earl. Thanks to those leather-bound journals she knew them all, their secrets and their weaknesses, and her stolen knowledge gave her a certain cool superiority over them. The doors of society, so recently closed against her, were once again thrown open as these illustrious personages sought to make her acquaintance. And Leonora, hungry for their acceptance, offered them her hand and her vivacious smile, while heartily despising them for their hypocrisy.

After the meal the guests began to disperse to bedrooms and drawing rooms where they would loosen tight clothing and refresh hot bodies and jaded appetites in readiness for the evening's entertainments. The sun was lowering behind gilt-edged clouds when Malcolm took her in his arms in the privacy of their bridal suite and smothered her face with kisses.

'At last. At last we are alone,' he breathed ecstatically drawing her down upon a long couch. 'My wife, my own darling wife.'

Their embrace was warm and loving, but when passion strengthened his grip and brought to his kisses a breathless urgency, she gently pushed him away and smiled into his clear blue eyes.

'We have but an hour or so in which to rest before the

ance begins,' she reminded him, 'and there are many things
must attend to during that short time. Elizabeth needs my
elp with her ball gown, and I would like to check that the
hampagne is properly chilled. But first I must visit the
Countess to make sure her maids are taking good care of her.'

'Always the caring Leonora,' he whispered, covering her
mouth with hot kisses. 'Very well, my dear, we will attend to
ll these tiresome little chores together ... but first ...'

Once again she pushed him from her, this time lifting his
ands from her breast and kissing the fingers one by one to
revent them returning to that softer place. She was gentle but
nsistent in her rejection of his amorous advances.

'Tonight is our wedding night, Malcolm,' she reminded
im. 'We shall have all the hours of darkness to ourselves,
ollowed by a lifetime of being together as man and wife. But
uty first, my dear husband. We must put duty first.'

'No, let it wait. You are so beautiful, Leonora, so desirable.'

'No, Malcolm, this is not the time.'

She broke away from him and rose from the couch, lifting
er hands to her hair and shaking imaginary creases from her
kirts. In a mocking, playful tone she added: 'Really, Sir
Malcolm, you do surprise me. Would you have me fail in my
uty within hours of becoming your bride? Would you have
ur guests make ribald jests at our expense because we could
ot wait until the appropriate time to ... to ...' She turned
way from him with a coy smile that seemed charged with
ntimate promise.

With a roar of laughter Malcolm jumped to his feet, clasped
er around the waist and spun her into a merry dance that
ad her squealing with playful protests.

'You are absolutely right, my darling,' he at last conceded.
see I must bridle my passion for a while and leave you to
our obligations. Shall we meet in the Great Hall in exactly
he hour?'

'No, better to meet outside the Long Gallery,' she
uggested. 'After all, if we are to make the proper impression
pon our guests, is it not better that we descend to the Great
all *together*?'

433

He stepped away from her and executed a sweeping, very
elegant bow, his eyes bright with happiness.

'Your servant, ma'am,' he conceded.

'Sir,' she acknowledged with a deep curtsy.

Anabel was waiting for her upstairs, where the Welsh maid,
nervous, freckled-faced girl of no more than fourteen, hovered
timorously on the threshold of the sick-room. Leonora went to
the next door along the corridor, entered her own well
furnished rooms and ordered the small fire to be tended. Then
she submitted to Anabel's insistence that her bridal gown be
scrutinised for wine stains and other possible damage. She
waited until the woman was on her knees before reaching out
to open a small drawer in the nearby dressing table. Then
while selecting a perfumed handkerchief with which to cool
her face and neck, she surreptitiously removed a small, dark
bottle from its hiding place amongst a dozen miscellaneous
items. This she quickly slipped between her breasts so that
lay concealed by the layers of snowy gauze above the body
hugging bodice of her gown. As she had intended, her action
went unnoticed by Anabel and the young maid.

'How is the Countess?'

Anabel looked up sharply. 'There has been no change in
her condition,' she replied, guardedly. She glanced at the
Welsh girl, who in turn eyed the adjoining door leading into
the sick-room, fearful of the stiff, withered figure lying like a
effigy on the Countess's bed.

'And is Her Ladyship quite comfortable?' Leonora asked
'Has she been given her medicine?'

'... er ... yes,' Anabel stammered. 'I ... er ... believe she
sleeping peacefully.'

'Good, then I'll not bother to disturb her for another hour
or so. Come, Anabel. Walk with me as far as the Long
Gallery.'

'But Leonora ... Your Ladyship ... have you forgotten ...

'I have forgotten *nothing*,' she answered sharply. 'And if Her
Ladyship the Countess is sleeping comfortably I see no reason
in the world why she should be disturbed. Another hour or s

434

will do no harm.' She turned to the maid, who was attempting to wipe smears of coal-dust from her fingers with the underside of her white apron.

'You, girl, will remain outside in the corridor, since you are so afraid to look upon the sick. You must send word to me in the Great Hall at once if you hear even the slightest sound from Her Ladyship's room. Miss Anabel will return presently to keep you company.'

'Yes, ma'am,' the girl said with a curtsy.

'Come, Anabel.'

She swept out, locking the door behind her and testing the main door of the sick-room as she passed to ensure that it, too, was firmly locked. Then she lifted her skirts and walked swiftly along the corridor with Anabel hurrying at her heels and protesting in a hoarse whisper that the dead should never be so abandoned, that a corpse should never be left alone behind locked doors with all the windows shuttered.

'Foolish superstition,' Leonora retorted.

'She'll be trapped here. Her soul will be made earthbound. You'll cause a haunting, Leonora, you just see if you don't. Her Ladyship will never rest easy in her grave after this.'

'Nonsense,' Leonora laughed. 'Her Ladyship is far beyond caring a fig, either for the company of others or for your simple-minded rituals. Now, Anabel, we must discuss more immediate matters. There is something I want you to do for me, something very, very important that requires ... oh ...'

She broke off and stood perfectly still. Her eyes widened as in sudden alarm before her features relaxed into that strange, covetous expression Anabel had come to know so well. They had stopped before one of the big, south-facing windows just as Lukan de Ville stepped down from his carriage and strode toward the main entrance. By that uncanny sixth sense they shared he felt her eyes upon him and looked up sharply, his progress toward the house arrested in mid-stride, his face grim and unsmiling, his black eyes smouldering with emotions too long held in check. He fixed Leonora with a lengthy, glowering stare before turning abruptly to stride indoors.

435

'Is *he* the reason for your delay in announcing Lad Beresford's death?' Anabel demanded. 'Oh, you wicke wicked girl. Have you arranged a tryst with that fearful man On this, of all days? On your *wedding* day?'

Leonora made no answer. On seeing him her heart ha seemed to stop, checked by the potency of his dark stare. Sh had wanted to run to him, to retract the vows she had s recently made, to undo the marriage contract binding her t another man. She had yearned to rest her face against tha wide, hard chest with its powerful, hidden heartbeat, to reje her dream and declare herself, instead, his for the taking. Th moment soon passed, but it left her deeply shaken. Sh recognised that such powerful forces, even when onl momentarily experienced, were a dangerous threat to he happiness.

She found Malcolm waiting for her near the orna balustrade outside the Long Gallery, a handsome, grey-cla figure looking down into the Great Hall where their gues were beginning to reassemble for the evening entertainments. He looked up as she approached, grinned an reached for her hands.

'Welcome. You have been too long away from me, m love.'

'A mere hour,' she smiled, touched by the adoration in h deep blue eyes.

'An hour is too long. Was that Anabel I saw rushing off i the other direction just now?'

'It was indeed,' Leonora said. 'She had hoped to watch th dancing from downstairs, with some of the other servants, b I judged it best that she return to sit with the Countess.'

'And is that why you were quarrelling?'

'Quarrelling? My dear Malcolm, Anabel and I nev quarrel.' She laughed up into his face, her merriment addin conviction to her words. 'I was simply a little firm reminding her that her services as chaperon are no long required. She has cared for me since birth, so there are tim when I find her a little too motherly, but she is a dear, kir woman and I can assure you we never quarrel.'

436

'And neither shall we,' he promised, kissing her hand.

She frowned and shook her head.

'But my dear, if we have no differences, will it not mean that one of us is subservient to the other and therefore afraid to speak out, freely and honestly?'

'If so then I shall be that one,' he laughed, hand on heart. 'I shall indulge you, forgive your extravagances, turn a blind eye to your misdemeanours and a deaf ear to your feminine tantrums. I shall be your slave, my dear, your willing, adoring slave.'

'Fool,' she smiled, knowing full well that he was no weakling to be so used by a woman. He was a proud man with strengths she had already sensed beneath his gentle exterior. Only love, carefully nurtured and freely offered, would keep him under her spell in the years ahead.

Arm in arm they descended the great marble staircase to that tumultuous applause which always greeted the happy couple following the wedding breakfast. By now Leonora had removed her long gloves and unpinned the froth of gauze from her bodice to reveal a wide, plunging neckline that showed the pale swell of her breasts to fullest advantage. A fringed shawl of shimmering peacock colours hung loosely about her shoulders, so skilfully woven that it appeared constantly to shift from palest green to deepest blue, touching upon all the varied shades between the two. From a velvet ribbon at her throat hung the Cavendish Sapphire, and on the third finger of her left hand shone the huge diamond ring given to her by her new husband. This was her dream blossoming into reality, her victorious, dramatic entrance into a wonderful new life. In triumph she was radiant, with every eye upon her as she stepped into that glittering company as Lady Leonora Cavendish, Mistress of Beresford. In her cleverly beaded gown and peacock shawl she sparkled and gleamed beneath crystal chandeliers, and with every movement echoed the colours of the Hall's magnificent stained glass windows. This was Leonora's moment, and for her and those who shared it, the moment was unforgettable.

*

437

Lukan de Ville watched her with a sickness in his heart as the music began to play and she glided around the hall in Malcolm's arms. He had come there only because to refuse would have offended Malcolm and perhaps given rise to speculative gossip, but he had come under sufferance, with the look of a man in pain. He was wearing a finely tailored cut-away coat of deep moss green, narrow fawn trousers, white shirt and cream-coloured waistcoat; a tall, slender, strong-looking man whose brooding good looks turned many heads and caused several young women to heave a quiet sigh. Above the fancy white ruffles of his shirt his face was rugged and tanned to a warm brown by the sun, his grave expression relieved from time to time by the appearance of a dazzling smile that lit his features but failed to reach his eyes. He conducted himself in that august society with the solemn dignity of a gentleman, but when at last he stooped to kiss her hand, Leonora felt the turbulence of his desire and the violence of his rage reach her with equal intensity.

'Damn you, woman, you have placed me in an intolerable position.'

He ground the words through clenched teeth as he swept her into the dance, his palm hot against the small of her back, his breath mint-scented on her cheek.

'Then why are you here?' she retorted. 'Certainly not at *my* invitation.'

'No, simply to please the man who is my friend and your husband, madam.'

She looked up to meet his angry stare and suddenly her heart lurched and a rush of colour stained her cheeks. They were moving around the Great Hall as one being, their bodies united, their movements perfectly matched and so sympathetic that they might have been dancing together for a lifetime.

'Oh, Lukan!'

His name was torn from her in an unexpected wave of passion. She saw him wince and close his eyes, wounded by the sound of it.

'I cannot bear this,' he groaned.

438

'You must, Lukan, for both our sakes.'

'I am in torment, Lia.'

'Forgive me. Oh, please, forgive me.'

'Never!' His eyes flashed their dark fires. 'Love you I must, and for all my life, but never, *never* will I forgive you for this.'

There was such agony in his voice that a sudden fear sliced across her heart like a knife.

'You wouldn't leave? Oh Lukan, you must not leave Beresford. I couldn't bear it if ...'

'*Damn you*, woman,' he cut in with a growl of rage. 'If you but cared enough I would never even *think* of leaving.'

'You know I care!' she protested. 'You are my soul's love, Lukan. I could not live if you were gone from here.'

He groaned again and closed his eyes. They had slowed their steps, yet still their bodies moved together in perfect time, as if swaying to the rhythm of a different melody, created for their ears only. Now other eyes were upon them, interested, curious. She thought of the locked sick-room, of her heated quarrel with Anabel and the small phial of opium now hidden in a locked cabinet in the bridal suite. With some effort she opened her fan and forced herself to smile into his dark face as she struggled to make their conversation appear innocent.

'Meet me at midnight,' she hissed. 'In the west wing ... the unfinished gate-house apartments.'

'What? You mock me with talk of a tryst? Have a care, woman. Make no false promises to rub salt into my wounds.'

'You once vowed that I would belong to you, body and soul, before ever Malcolm took me to his bed.'

'I did, but that was before ...'

'And would you not now have it so?'

'Oh, Lia, Lia, you know I would.'

'The gate-house, then, at midnight.'

He stared down at her, searching her violet eyes for the truth behind her words.

'I am quite serious, my love,' she assured him.

'My God,' he gasped. 'I do believe you are.'

'Until midnight, then,' and she felt his grip tighten.

'Lia ... my Lia ...'

'No! Do not touch me again, Lukan. Not here. Not now. People are watching, and here's Malcolm coming to join us. Well? Shall I come to the gate-house? Will you be there?'

'I will be there, my Lia,' he murmured, taking her outstretched hand and leading her off the floor. 'I will be there, though heaven itself say otherwise.'

From his place by the ornamental fountain, where his eldest daughter stood with her arm through that of her amiable Cornish husband, Sir Oscar Cavendish had observed the couple moving so effortlessly, so conspicuously amongst the other dancers. Something in their manner, so proper and yet so strangely *united*, had reminded him of those moments of exquisite torture when he and Francine had been thrown together in some painfully public place. The man was a handsome devil, with his high cheekbones and long black eyes. Too tall, too elegant, he could be recognised at a glance as the son of Daniel Adams, gypsy, and of that tragic, genteel young woman whose name the Earl could not bring himself to utter, even in the privacy of his own thoughts. And Malcolm's new bride, however innocent, was a temptress from whose charms no red-blooded man could possibly be immune. They made a striking pair, and unless his senses were sadly awry, there was something between them, something fierce and instinctive. With a stab of intuition he realised that they, too, were playing a part for the sake of appearances. His blue eyes narrowed, watchful and suspicious. Those two might have been mortal enemies feigning friendship for the benefit of protocol; or secret lovers masquerading as innocent partners in the dance.

II

The dance ended at ten-thirty when trays of cold meats, cheeses, frilled oysters, pastries and puddings were brought nto the Hall by a procession of liveried servants. A few trestle ables held tea, coffee, chocolate, fruit punch and wine. One y one the musicians packed up their instruments and crept way, while guests made hurried, last-minute assignations vith hot glances and whispered directions. By now the bride nd groom had retired to their own suite to enjoy an intimate upper by the fireside before sharing their first night as usband and wife. Their bed was warmed, the covers turned ack, the sheets perfumed with rose petals, the pillows ecorated with sprigs of aromatic herbs tied up with scraps of right yellow ribbon.

'A wonderful day,' Malcolm said, stretching luxuriously as .eonora refilled his glass. He was unaware that his speech had ecome slurred and his body so comfortable that it seemed to oat on a soft cloud. He watched Leonora through half-closed yes, smiling as her image drifted this way and that before his yes.

'Oh, yes, a truly memorable day.' Her voice came to him as from a great distance. 'Come, now, drink up your wine, my ear. It will help clear your head.'

Malcolm felt himself floating toward the bed, felt the erfumed softness of Leonora's hair falling across his face, the ool touch of silk against his skin. A moment later he was uite senseless, with his eyes tightly closed, his lips curved in a ontented smile and his body limp. Leonora removed his hoes and covered him with a quilt, then smiled and stooped) kiss his mouth.

'Goodnight, my dear. Sweet dreams,' she whispered.

She left a glass close at hand into which she had poured a neasure of wine and a few more drops of essence of opium. he covered the glass with a small cloth, then stooped to press nother kiss to his cheek.

'I will make you happy, Malcolm,' she vowed, running the ps of her fingers across his lips. 'You will find me a loyal and ffectionate wife, for I believe I will always love you with my eart. And if the fates are kind, and if he and I are careful, you ill never discover that Lukan has my soul.'

With that she kissed him for the last time, pulled on her

hooded velvet cloak, turned down the lamp and tip-toed soundlessly from the room.

She went the way Elizabeth had showed her, via the nursery and the school rooms, up through the old servants' wing and out through a narrow attic door to the roof above the Great Hall. The night air was sharp and cold, with a stiff breeze that tugged at her hair and whipped at her clothes. She lifted her hood and pulled her cloak more closely about her. Carefully, with her fingers gripping the waist-high stone barrier that stood between her and a sheer drop to the paved terrace below, she made her way along the narrow pathway traversing the very edge of the roof from east to west and leading to a door above the gate-house rooms. The tower of the west wing loomed before her, bleak and sinister in the blustery night. Her heart was pounding and her cheeks stung by the cold when at last she reached the other side, slipped through the door and groped her way down a flight of narrow, unlit steps. Now her heart took up a different rhythm and her blood grew warm with anticipation.

The gate-house was in darkness. Work had been postponed on the new apartments for the duration of the wedding festivities, leaving only two rooms near to completion. Leonora passed through into the bedroom, where the shutters were tightly closed and a log fire crackled in the grate. Two draped armchairs stood upon a thick rug, and between them a table was set with food and wine. Jugs of hot water stood in the hearth with folded towels warming nearby. The whole room dominated by its massive Jacobean four-poster bed, was scented with lilac and honeysuckle and illuminated only by flickering firelight. For all her pleading and her tearful protests, Anabel Corey had followed the instructions of her young mistress to the letter.

'I came, Lukan.'

He had been standing at the window, peering out at the dark night through a gap in the wooden shutters. Now he turned and came toward her, stopping short with a hissed intake of breath as she unclasped her cloak and let it fall to the floor at her feet. She was still wearing her ivory bridal gown with its shimmering overlay of beaded gauze, only now her hair was brushed loose, a cascade of soft, dark waves to which firelight added sparkling copper lights.

'Lia,' he breathed.

'You always knew you would be the first,' she said.

'Aye, Rebecca told me it would be so.'

'Your sister foresaw it all. She always knew how it would be.'

'And yet I doubted,' he confessed. 'At the end I doubted.'

'But here we are, as she predicted, and you *will* be the first, Lukan.'

A shadow crossed his dark face.

'And Malcolm? What of your new husband, my lady?'

'He is sleeping like a babe with hemlock and opium in his wine. He will not stir until the morning. I will not be missed.'

He smiled, his eyes reflecting glimmers of bright firelight.

'Well, then, my Lia,' he said at length.

'Well, then, Lukan.'

Solemnly he reached out his hand as once he had done when she went to him in the long meadow, compelling her to be the one to take those last few steps that would close forever the distance lying between them. She reached for his fingers, then moved with a sigh into his arms, her long battle at an end as she bowed, at last, to that which she had always known to be inevitable. Slowly and tenderly he gathered her into his arms and carried her to the bed, setting her down like a prize upon the soft velvet cover.

He removed her clothes unhurriedly, item by item, kissing every curve, every swell of pale skin and firm flesh that revealed itself to his searching fingers and eager mouth. When she was quite naked he caressed her beautiful body with his eyes, feasting upon the swell of breast and thigh and buttock, running his dark gaze into every hollow, every warm and secret place. Her own hands helped divest him of his clothes until he lay naked on the bed beside her, his tanned, muscular body hers to explore at leisure, and to quiver in response to the touch of her lips and fingers. Somewhere a clock chimed the witching hour of midnight and an owl screeched in the distant forest.

'It must be now,' he said, his voice husky with passion, his mouth hot and hungry on her swollen breasts. She lifted her hips to meet his, parted her lips and with her whole being whispered a single word: 'Yes.'

And with that word Leonora, Viscountess Cavendish and future Countess of Beresford betrayed her marriage bed and pledged herself, body and soul, to her gypsy lover.

III

Dawn streaked the sky with a wash of silver-gold and lit the forest with an eerie light that hung as a dewy shroud about its dark-clad trees. The river shone white and flat as tin, and here and there the shadowed contours of the countryside were filled to the brim with a mist that gathered in its deep places like so many fallen clouds. The wind of a new day blew light and cold, bringing with it the autumnal scents of the land. Even the sheep stood silent on the uplands as if in awe of the softly unfolding day.

They had come up from the gate-house via the Monk's Stair, that steep, narrow access of spiralling stone set deep in the massive walls of the tower and kept hidden for many long centuries. Now they stood at the very summit of the tower, the gypsy and his lady, surveying those rolling Beresford acres as i looking out upon their own private kingdom. She stood with the back of her head against his chest, his muscular arms encircling her body, his wide shoulders shielding her from the chilly core of the wind. In a little while they must part, she to rouse the household with news of the Countess's death and he, brooding upon his destiny and hers, to return to the fores from whence he came. For these remaining moments they were one, standing like a single shape atop the ruined tower.

'We are pledged, one to the other,' he had declared, his

long body brown and muscular against her own paleness. 'For good or ill, we two are bound.'

And she had whispered, knowing the truth of it: 'For ever, Lukan.'

While they were still naked she had solemnly fastened around his neck a golden chain on which hung an old, ornate key. It fitted the tiny arched door set by those long-dead monks into the base of the West Tower. Its twin was clutched in her hand, the same hand that carried on its third finger her dazzling diamond wedding ring. Henceforth the ancient tower would be their love-nest, their own secret meeting-place. In that silvery dawn she knew she had finally triumphed against all the odds. She had claimed it all. The dream, dropped like a fertile seed into a child's heart to grow and flourish with the passing years, was here and now. The new life had already begun.

'At last all this is mine,' she declared, breathing deeply, greedily of the new day. Then she glanced up at his dark profile and felt the wonderful hardness of his body pressing closely against her own. Malcolm's ring glittered on her finger, the key to the tower lay cool in her palm and the whole world, it seemed to her, was spreading itself as if in supplication at her feet. She sighed again and said:

'Mine. All of it mine. Mine!'

And like the furtive stirring of half-forgotten shadows somewhere in the farthest reaches of her mind came a warning that sent a chilly shiver racing along her spine:

'Take care what you set your heart on, for it will surely be yours.'

Warner now offers an exciting range of quality titles by both established and new authors. All of the books in this series are available from:
Little, Brown and Company (UK) Limited,
P.O. Box 11,
Falmouth,
Cornwall TR10 9EN.

Alternatively you may fax your order to the above address. Fax No. 0326 376423.

Payments can be made as follows: Cheque, postal order (payable to Little, Brown and Company) or by credit cards, Visa/Access. Do not send cash or currency. UK customers: and B.F.P.O.: please send a cheque or postal order (no currency) and allow £1.00 for postage and packing for the first book, plus 50p for the second book, plus 30p for each additional book up to a maximum charge of £3.00 (7 books plus).

Overseas customers including Ireland, please allow £2.00 for postage and packing for the first book, plus £1.00 for the second book, plus 50p for each additional book.

NAME (Block Letters) ....

ADDRESS..

....

☐ I enclose my remittance for _____

☐ I wish to pay by Access/Visa Card

Number ⬚⬚⬚⬚⬚⬚⬚⬚⬚⬚⬚⬚⬚⬚⬚⬚

Card Expiry Date ⬚⬚⬚⬚